Double Blind

Copyright © 2015 by Carrie Bedford

ISBN: 978-1515161882

DOUBLE BLIND

A Kate Benedict Paranormal Mystery

BY

CARRIE BEDFORD

For James, Charlotte and Madeleine, with love.

Acknowledgements

Firstly, thank you to my wonderful family for encouraging my writing endeavors.

Special thanks to Carl Ingber, M.D., pediatric doctor, and to Dr. Sophie Cayeux for your invaluable assistance with the medical aspects of this book. Any technical errors are entirely my own.

I couldn't have come this far without the assistance and encouragement of my writing group. To Diana Corbitt, Maryvonne Fent, Sue Garzon, and Gillian Hobbs, many thanks for reading, editing, commenting, and for your own amazing stories that inspire me to do better. Writing wouldn't be half the fun it is without you to share it with.

Thank you to J. Leonard DeCarlo, MD, who came up with the title, and to the talented Melissa DeCarlo for her encouragement. And I'm immensely grateful to Julie Smith for her guiding hand and incisive comments.

1

The morning was going so well until I saw the auras. A glimpse of that halo of trembling air over someone's head usually casts a dark cloud over my day. These particular auras, it turned out, were going to unleash a storm, much like the one rumbling across London's Hyde Park. A ceiling of dense grey clouds hung low over the city and thunder growled in the distance, keeping away the usual crowds of joggers and mothers with toddlers and strollers.

My friend Anita and I were enjoying our run, although I was starting to tire. My calf muscles burned, yet Anita didn't look the slightest bit fatigued. Her glossy black hair swung in a high ponytail and her golden skin was sweat-free. Even the kohl around her eyes had stayed perfectly intact. She was unusually quiet though. Normally, she'd talk the whole time we were running, but not today.

We settled into a slower pace, taking the path that ran alongside the Serpentine, the slate-colored water choppy in the strengthening wind. When several joggers came around a bend towards us, Anita and I moved into single file to let them pass. The first of them looked like a soldier, young, muscled, his broad chest encased in a tight green T-shirt. Behind him, two men ran together, both in their early fifties, I guessed, one tall and quite striking with fair hair, the other shorter and darker. As they loped past us, the fair-haired man raised a hand to thank us for moving out of their way.

I stopped running, turning my head to watch them go, sure I was wrong about what I'd seen. But I wasn't. The two older men each had a distinct aura swirling around his head and shoulders, like waves of air coming off hot asphalt.

"That was Simon Scott!" Anita had stopped too, watching the men disappear around a curve in the path.

"Who?" The name meant something, but my brain was preoccupied with processing the presence of that ominous swirly air.

"Really? You can't tell me you don't know who Scott is. He's the leader of the Labor party and there's an election in less than a month. He could be our new Prime Minister."

"Of course. I knew that. He's on the television all the time." I bent over to retie a shoelace. My heart rate was soaring and it wasn't because of the running. "But you know I don't do politics."

"You should. Don't you worry about the environment or education or health care?"

"Who was that with him?" I asked, changing the subject. Once Anita got started on talking about her causes, it would take a lightning strike to stop her. I stayed on one knee, waiting for my heart to slow down. An aura over a public figure. That was a first for me.

"Kevin Lewis," said Anita. "He's a City guy, a finance genius. If Scott's party wins the election, Lewis will be Chancellor of the Exchequer. I can't believe I saw them in the flesh like that. The third guy must have been a bodyguard. He was rather cute."

I straightened up. In the center of the lake, a rowboat bobbed up and down, its sole occupant a man who was looking through binoculars at the ducks and other water birds. Just watching the boat rock made me feel seasick. Or maybe it was the sight of the auras that was making me nauseous.

Anita grabbed my arm. "I have an idea. I've just started volunteering on Scott's campaign. You should do it with me. I usually go a few evenings a week to a campaign office in Shepherd's Bush. There's plenty to do, especially now, calling voters, handing out brochures, making banners, that kind of thing."

"How do you have time to do that?" Anita was a doctor in the pediatric department at London General hospital. She worked very long hours.

"It's easy to make space for the important things," she said, bending down to pull one of her socks straight. "But if you want to know the truth, it's also an evasion tactic. Every time my parents ask me home for dinner, I tell them I'm volunteering."

"How's that working out?" I hoped Anita would attribute the shake in my voice to exercise. I couldn't tell her about the auras, not yet anyway. "Is your dad still trying to find you the perfect husband?"

"Oh God, don't even ask. We had a massive fight about it last time I ran out of excuses and went over there to eat. He just doesn't get it. I don't want an arranged marriage." She sighed. So that was what was bothering her. Leaning over, she touched her toes, which she could do easily. She was a natural athlete, while I had to work a little harder at it.

"Anyway," she continued, straightening up. "What do you think? Will you come help out at the campaign office? I'm going tonight. The other volunteers are good people, very committed to what they're doing to support Scott. You'd like them."

Sitting in a political campaign office in Shepherd's Bush would normally be at the very bottom of my list of favorite-things-to-do-on-a-Monday-night, but auras had changed my priorities in the past. It seemed that they were about to do so again.

"Sounds like a lot of fun." I tried to inject enthusiasm into my words.

Anita rolled her eyes. "You'll be glad you came, you'll see. I have to go. Oh, I didn't think to ask. Josh isn't back is he? Is he still just coming home on weekends?"

"Yeah, just weekends." My boyfriend was often away on business nowadays. "We've got Saturday tickets for that new play with Kevin Spacey."

Anita gave me a hug. "See you tonight. I'll text you the address."

After watching her jog away, I walked to a nearby bench and sat down. The green wooden slats pressed cold and damp against my back as I looked out over the granite-grey lake. It was April, but England was still in the grip of winter. I rubbed a sore spot in my calf muscle and took a few deep breaths. The auras over Scott and Lewis had left me feeling rattled.

It had been almost a year since I saw my first aura. Since then, I'd become quite good at looking past them, the way we sometimes pretend we don't see a conspicuous birthmark or a missing limb. Often I could get through a week or two without acknowledging that I'd seen one.

But now this. Two of them, which meant that both men were in danger. That probably ruled out health issues, but left open a world of other possibilities: an accident in a car, a train or a plane, or perhaps a terrorist attack. That was what the auras meant. That the person would die very soon. Trying to calm down, I clenched my fists, digging my nails into the palms of my hands. It wasn't my responsibility to save everyone who faced a premature death. At least that was the argument I had with myself whenever I saw an aura. But I hadn't seen one over the head of a leading politician before.

The clouds opened, releasing fat drops of water that quickly coalesced into a downpour. Through the deluge, I saw that the birdwatcher was rowing his boat towards a dock on the other side of the lake. I knew I should go home, dry off and get warm, but I was so preoccupied with the auras that I didn't have the energy to stand up. So I just sat on the cold clammy bench, feeling the rain soak my running clothes.

Finally, drenched and shivering, I jogged back to my fourth-floor flat in an old Victorian house in Bayswater. After what had happened last year, I sometimes thought about moving. I still had nightmares about the front door being broken down, a man with a knife stalking through the hallway. But I loved my flat, with its soothing olive green walls and whitewashed pine floors, the evening light that poured through the dormer windows, and the views towards the park. Josh had fitted an extra high-tech lock on the front door and, when he wasn't traveling, he usually stayed over. We'd eat by candlelight at the kitchen window that overlooked the slate rooftops.

Josh knew all about my aura-sighting ability. We'd started dating around the time that I had seen my first aura. My strange behavior as I struggled to understand what was happening to me might have been enough to derail our nascent romance. But it didn't. Once he'd had time to think about it, Josh had come to terms with the auras, and the way they made me act. I wished he were here with me right now, but he was working on a project in Bristol for a few weeks, coming home to London most weekends. It wasn't easy, being apart, but we were managing. He'd recently been promoted at the architectural firm where we both worked. Where I *had* worked, I reminded myself. Following the tragic events of the previous year, when one of my bosses had been convicted of murder, the company was going through a rocky period. The loss of a major client had created a major financial shortfall, so I'd volunteered to take a few months off until things stabilized. I'm an architect, but I was doing something different for the moment — filling in time and making some money using my skills as a photographer and graphics designer on a variety of freelance projects.

After slipping off my soggy running shoes just inside the door, I walked slowly up the hallway towards the bathroom, pausing to straighten one of the framed black and white photos that I'd taken in Tuscany where my father lived. It reminded me that I should call him later to see how he was doing.

Poor Dad. Our phone calls were difficult for both of us, stilted and superficial. We'd chat about the weather or gardening, anything to avoid talking about what really mattered. My mother had been killed by a speeding car the previous spring, leaving him alone and bereft in the rambling eighteenth-century villa that they had restored together. And, at the time when he'd needed me the most, we'd had a falling out. The auras were to blame. While he was mourning my mother, I was telling him stories of swirling air that predicted death.

I think that my sudden ability to see auras was a way of dealing with my terrifying realization that we live in a world of risk and unpredictability. Seeing auras gave me a sense of control, however illusory. I could tell when someone was about to die. In theory, I could do something to stop it happening. In practice, of course, it didn't always work that way.

In the bathroom, I turned on the shower, savoring the heat of the water, which warmed my chilled skin and helped to clear my head, but I still had no idea what to do about the auras over Simon Scott and Kevin Lewis. The last time I'd tried to intervene, things hadn't turned out too well. I scrubbed my skin until it turned pink. I'd saved my nephew Aidan, I reminded myself, and a homeless man. Maybe I could save Scott and Lewis too. But I couldn't exactly call and tell them I knew they were going to die.

2

That evening, I took the Central Line from Lancaster Gate to Shepherd's Bush, just a few stops on the tube. Most days, I took the escalators down to the tracks without a second thought. Sometimes, and this was one of them, I found myself wondering what possessed us to descend so far underground, to hurtle through dark tunnels deep beneath the gas lines, electrical cables, and tarmac streets of the city above.

Despite my apprehensions, however, I reached my destination without incident, and emerged through the windblown concourse into cold rain that quickly soaked my woolen jacket. Avoiding puddles on the potholed pavement, I walked past rows of small shops, closed at this time in the evening. A hair salon stood next to a hardware store that displayed an ambitious pyramid of galvanized buckets in its darkened window. Further on, rap music spilled from an all-night convenience shop where the owner stood in the doorway, keeping an eye on the racks of exotic fruits and vegetables that sheltered under a green awning.

The campaign office next door to it had also been a shop at one time. Now its windows were plastered with poster-sized photos of a beaming Simon Scott and placards exhorting passersby to get out and vote.

When I pushed the door open, a bell chimed but was barely audible above the racket inside. The large space was warm, smelling of burned coffee and wet wool with an undertone of glue and permanent marker.

A dozen people talked on phones at long tables down one side, while a group of young men with stubbled chins huddled around a laptop, loudly debating with each other. They were probably political science students. At the back, bent over a trestle table, were Anita and four other women, all with paintbrushes in hand.

Anita looked up and waved me over. "You came! Here, let me introduce you." As she reeled off a list of names, the volunteers nodded, smiled or held out a hand to shake mine.

"Will you help us with this banner?" Anita asked. "You have a good eye for graphics."

"Okay." I dumped my bag under the table. The poster was horrible. Wrong colors, wrong everything. I made some tactful suggestions, which the volunteers seemed happy to implement, and my assistance earned me a cup of tea, freshly brewed by Anita. The mugs were thick and chipped, but the tea was good, and hot. I needed the heat. My skin was still chilled from my run in the rain that morning, but the cold went deeper than that. I had an icy feeling in my stomach, a sense of dread. I hadn't been able to put those auras out of my mind.

"Come and sit over here," Anita said, indicating a small formica table that leaned against the wall. I took a seat on a wobbly wooden stool.

"I wasn't sure that you'd come," Anita said. "Did I prick your conscience?"

"Something like that." I couldn't tell her I was there because of the auras over Scott and Lewis. She didn't know anything about my aura-seeing gift. The previous year, when I'd first started seeing auras, she'd been working at Massachusetts General Hospital in Boston. Although we'd promised to stay in touch, to talk on the phone every weekend, it hadn't happened. We'd ended up communicating through short texts. There'd never been a good opportunity to tell her about my newfound ability to see portents in moving air.

She'd been back in London for several months now, and I still hadn't told her. She was my best friend and I loved her dearly, but my bizarre ability would make no sense to her. It didn't follow the scientific rules she lived by. She wouldn't understand and I didn't want to risk ruining our friendship.

Taking tiny sips of the scalding hot tea, I looked at her over the rim of my mug. Her dark brown eyes usually sparkled with energy. Tonight, they were dull and flat, barely meeting mine as she twirled a lock of black hair around her finger.

"What's wrong, Anita?" I asked. "Did you fight with your dad again?"

She shook her head. "That's an ongoing problem. Nothing new."

"So what's upsetting you?"

She looked around as though to make sure no one else was paying attention. "I can't put my finger on it, but Dr. Reid has been behaving strangely. Distracted." She put her mug down on the table. "I caught him prescribing the wrong medication for a juvenile patient yesterday. I didn't say anything to anyone. I just amended the prescription before the child's mother could take it to the hospital pharmacy."

Dr. Reid was Anita's head of department, a doctor of god-like abilities by all accounts.

"Was it dangerous? The wrong prescription?"

She shrugged. "It could have been. What if I don't catch it next time?"

"Have you tried talking with him? Suggested he take a week off or something?"

She cocked her head to one side. "First-year residents don't suggest *anything* to head of department. They definitely don't suggest that he's losing his marbles and writing out bad prescriptions."

"Well, it seems as though you should do something."

The hair stood up on my arms. Here I was dishing out advice to Anita while I was achieving nothing to ensure the safety of Scott and Lewis. I'd read up everything I could find on the Internet about Simon Scott. Married, no children, popular, he'd become leader of the Opposition party the previous year, when his predecessor retired due to illness. Scott had been a doctor, then a Member of Parliament. Two years ago, he'd been appointed Shadow Under-Secretary of State for Health, and he served on a clutch of Committees on global health, women's health and veterans' health. From what I'd read, his party was ahead in the polls. But his distinct aura meant he was going to die, probably before the election.

Anita waved a hand in front of my face. "Hellooo? Where did you go?"

"I'm sorry. So, what will happen, do you think, with Dr. Reid?"

"Nothing, with any luck. I'm hoping he's just tired and will bounce back soon. I'll keep an eye open but I don't feel as though there's anything concrete I can do."

That's how I felt too. Useless, as I always did when I saw an aura in a situation where I had no chance of intervening. Once, I'd approached a young woman to strike up a conversation in an attempt to identify whatever it was that threatened her. She had been friendly at first and then quickly retreated, understandably wary of a complete stranger asking her personal questions on a station platform. I often wondered what had happened to her.

I looked around the room at the volunteers, who were all intent on their tasks. They were here because they believed in Scott and his political party. My motives were very different. I wanted to spend time with Anita. And I needed to find out more about Scott.

"I suppose Simon Scott never comes over here, does he?" I asked. "To meet the worker bees?"

Anita shook her head. "He's never been here as far as I know. I was hoping I'd meet him at the hospital some time. He's really into health issues, and he did his residency in Pediatric surgery." She raised her eyebrows. "Why do you want to meet him? Don't tell me you've suddenly got all excited about politics?"

"Well, maybe a little."

"Good. Then you should plan on coming here for the next couple of weeks. We'll have a lot to do with the run-up to the election. And you never know, maybe we'll get to speak to him if we go to some of the campaign rallies."

She sipped her tea. "I'm feeling quite proud of myself. I've made a convert. You're now a fully-functioning citizen, exercising your right to participate fully in the electoral process."

She was smiling so I knew she was teasing me. Still, I wanted to tell her the truth, that I didn't really care about politics at all, but that I did feel an obligation to try to stop something bad from happening before the election. Now was the right time to tell Anita about the auras. She was committed to ensuring the successful appointment of Scott as Prime Minister. If I didn't tell her now, when an aura was over someone she cared about, when would I? Besides, it felt wrong to me that I hadn't shared this intimate detail of my life with her. Keeping something so important from her skewed our friendship, threw it off balance.

"Anita, there's something—"

"Anita?" A middle-aged woman in a grey pantsuit interrupted me. "Sorry, love," she said. "Can you give us a hand with the script for the weekend phone bank?"

Draining the last of her tea, Anita stood up. "Come on, Kate. We're needed."

3

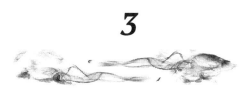

Once we'd finished the script, Anita said she needed to go back to the hospital. Her working hours were not only long, but also erratic. We walked to the tube station together, but the moment to tell her about the auras had gone. She was quiet and distracted. I couldn't tell whether she was more upset about the fight with her father or her boss's unusual behavior.

"Let's have lunch tomorrow," I suggested.

She shook her head. "I'm sorry. I'm going to be crammed with work for the next couple of days. But we'll talk. I'll text you when I'm free."

Accepting that as the best I'd get out of her in her current mood, I gave her a hug goodbye before hurrying to catch the tube back home. When I got off the train, my phone buzzed with three texts, all from my boyfriend, saying he was coming home for the night. He'd taken a late train from Bristol. Elated, I walked along Queensway, where ethnic restaurants were still busy with diners, and groups of locals and tourists strolled past the souvenir shops, enjoying a break in the rain. Above the brightly-lit buzz of commerce below, the silver moon hung low in the sky, garlanded with threads of ebony cloud. Perhaps there was a chance of clear weather tomorrow.

It was still cold this evening though, so I turned the heat on in the flat before opening a bottle of cabernet, one of Josh's favorites. When I heard the key turning in the lock, I hurried down the hallway to greet him, feeling a familiar tingle down my spine. Pulling the door open, I turned my face up for a kiss. He was eight inches taller than me, except when I wore heels. I pushed a lock of dark, glossy hair back from his face. "I missed you."

He stepped inside, dumped his briefcase and overnight bag on the floor, and gave me another long, deep kiss. "I missed you too. I always do," he said.

"I opened some wine. Do you want some?"

"Aye, but first I need to get out of this suit and tie." His Scottish accent grew a little stronger when he was tired. "And I may need some help with that." Taking my hand in his, he led me to the bedroom. When he held me, I felt the stress of my recent aura sighting melt away. Focusing only on him, I relaxed, savoring the touch of his skin against mine.

It was late when I went to the kitchen, where I poured two glasses of wine and carried them into the living room. Josh joined me, freshly showered and dressed in a white t-shirt and red tartan PJ pants. His mother gave him Stewart clan clothing for Christmas every year.

"Nearly forgot," he said, going out into the hallway. He came back with something wrapped in gift paper and tied with green ribbon. "I found a small bookshop tucked away in the Old City and spent a couple of hours rummaging around in there one evening. I thought you'd like this."

I untied the ribbon. The smell of old books wafted upwards, one of my favorite scents of all, a magical mix of paper, ink and dust. The cover of dark red leather had faded to brown in parts, and the title was tooled in gold across the front. *A Gathering of Flowers*. The pages were of thick creamy paper. Each one held a short description of a plant, accompanied by an illustration drawn in black ink and finished with fine washes of color. Every page was a small work of art.

"It's beautiful," I said. "Just what I need to inspire me for Dad's book." I was working on illustrating a gardening book that my father had written. The joint project was an attempt to put our relationship back on an even keel, and it gave us something to talk about that didn't concern auras or my career.

Josh smiled before his eyes shifted away from my face for a second. Then he squeezed my hand and kept hold of it. "It's good that you're working on your photography and illustrating," he said. "But I think you should come back to work now. We just signed a new client. We need you."

He hadn't agreed with my decision to take six months off work. Business had slumped, it was true, but Josh's view was that I would have been able to contribute to the company's faster recovery had I stayed. At the time, a temporary leave of absence had seemed like a good idea. I'd almost died in the office car park. Avoiding the office and the memories it held made sense to me then. Now I wasn't so sure. Even though my attacker was safely behind bars, I sometimes felt vulnerable and nervous, so what was the point of distancing myself from my work, the one thing that provided continuity and stability? And I knew that my career had been set back. Alan had promoted Josh, and promised to make him a partner in a year or two. I was happy for Josh, of course, but sometimes I wondered if I would have got that promotion if I'd been in the office every day, helping Alan put the company back together.

"Kate? What do you think? Why don't you come back now? There's no need to wait any longer."

"I'll think about it."

His aquamarine eyes clouded with disappointment. "You seem a little distracted," he said. "Is there anything wrong?"

"No, nothing."

"I know you much better than that," he said. "Out with it."

So I told him about the auras I had seen over Simon Scott and his colleague. When I'd finished, he held me tightly and kissed the top of my head, a gesture that I always found soothing and protective. He'd worked hard to overcome his skepticism about my ability to see auras. Now he talked about them as easily as other people discussed what to eat for dinner.

"How distinct were they?" he asked.

On the basis of several experiences, I'd learned that there was a connection between the strength of the aura and the amount of time before death occurred. "The air was moving fast," I said. "I think so anyway. I only got a short glimpse as the men ran past. I should try get another look, don't you think, so that I have a better idea of how much time they have?"

"It seems to me that there's nothing much you can do about this." Josh settled back into the sofa, stretching his long legs out in front of him. "Let's be honest, even if you tried to warn them, no one will believe you."

"I know. I can't just stand by, though, and do nothing."

"And both men had the auras? It wasn't just one?"

"No, I'm positive there were two. That implies something like a deliberate killing, don't you think? Like the time when the IRA tried to kill Thatcher by planting a bomb in the hotel in Brighton? Or maybe a shooting, although that's more of an American thing."

I stood up and went to the kitchen to start some coffee. Josh had bought me a fancy Italian espresso machine for my birthday. I'd become slightly — make that very — addicted to coffee ever since.

"I think it might be an accident." Back in the living room, I picked up where I'd left off. "They could both be in the same car. Or maybe a helicopter. Don't politicians fly to important meetings in helicopters?"

Josh took my hand in his and squeezed it. "Take a breath. Slow down. This isn't your problem to solve, Kate. I know you want to help, but nothing good can come of your going public about an aura."

"I don't have to talk about the aura. I could just try to convince someone that Scott's in danger."

"And how can you do that?" he asked.

"I don't know." I clasped my hands together, watching my knuckles turn white. I knew something I couldn't share because no one would believe me. Maybe losing a modern-day politician or two wasn't as earth-shattering as the destruction of Troy, but I felt just like Cassandra, who'd foreseen the war and the subsequent defeat. Her warnings were ignored and her family and friends thought she was insane. Frustrated, I slumped against the back of the sofa.

Josh pulled me into his arms. "I know it's hard for you," he said. "But you need to let this one go. I'm sure there's a slew of people looking after Scott, making sure he's safe. There's nothing you can do that they can't."

I fidgeted and wriggled out of his arms.

"Okay," I said. But I wasn't going to give up that easily.

4

The following day, Josh left at dawn to drive with Alan Bradley to a meeting in Southampton. Then he had to go back to Bristol for a few days. We'd stayed up late, talking, mostly avoiding the subject of Simon Scott and Kevin Lewis. But now, alone in the empty flat, thoughts of their auras scurried around in my head like mice.

A couple of weeks ago, I had won a freelance contract with a gardening magazine and my assignment was due, so I worked on the illustrations. But my heart wasn't in it. After an hour or so, I found myself clicking through television channels looking for any news of the election, but only found daytime soaps and a program about obesity.

I made some tea, sat at the coffee table with my laptop, and ran more searches on Simon Scott. I soon found what I was looking for. He was appearing in Kensington that evening, speaking to the public in a grammar school gymnasium. I wasn't totally sure what I expected to get out of seeing him again, but having a plan made me feel better. I went back to my art assignment.

At six o' clock, I dressed warmly against the arctic wind that had swept in to replace the rain. The biting cold was a stark warning to those foolish enough to think that spring was anywhere in our future. At the last minute, I grabbed a press pass given to me by Gardener's Monthly for an event at Kew Gardens. It had my photo on it and hung from a lanyard that I put round my neck.

The gym was packed when I got there, but was barely any warmer than it was outside. People sat on benches and beige foldout chairs, with their coats and scarves still tightly wrapped around them. Standing at the back, I could see that a stage had been set up at the far end, draped with banners and posters bearing the logo of the Labor Party. Spotting a table where several women were handing out cups of tea and slices of cake on paper plates, I pushed my way over. If I had to stand for the evening, I needed some sustenance. It seemed that everyone at the back had the same idea, however, and I queued for some time with little hope of achieving my goal before the speeches began.

A woman walked past me, eyeing my press pass. "You should be at the front, love," she said. "Press is up there and there are a few empty chairs."

I hesitated just for a second and then walked up an aisle to the front, taking a seat in the second row. A dark-haired man with glasses glanced over at me when I sat down, but he didn't speak. He had a notebook and a pencil ready. I retrieved my iPhone from my purse; I didn't really plan on taking any notes, but I should at least look as though I was. My neighbor eyed the phone before turning to talk to a middle-aged woman who sat on the other side of him.

Rather like a concert, there were some warm-up acts before the party leader took the stage, a series of speakers who varied in their delivery from hectoring to droning. I was sure Anita would have been enthralled, but I was perilously close to nodding off. Finally, a good-looking young man with gelled hair and a large red rosette pinned to his chest ran on to the stage and raised his arms to encourage the audience to applaud. "Ladies and Gentlemen," he shouted. "Please welcome your party leader, Simon Scott!"

As the gymnasium erupted into a storm of cheers and clapping, I realized that this was an event for the already-converted. The applause went on for some time, while the young man stood on stage absorbing it all as though it was meant for him. Finally he held up both hands, palms out, until the echoing hall began to fall quiet. "Thank you, thank you," he said, stepping to one side, throwing one arm out like a vaudeville performer to summon Scott to the stage. Simon Scott walked on to a renewed burst of applause. He waited patiently for silence. From where I sat, his aura was very pronounced, with the air rippling around his head and shoulders fast enough to blur the photograph of himself on the wall behind him.

Something about him reminded me of Josh. He was older, of course, but he had that same boyish look and floppy hair, light-colored eyes and lean figure. The similarity made the fact of his aura even harder to accept. I felt protective of him just as I would be of Josh. He was far too young to die.

Scott talked for some time, but I didn't listen to what he was saying; I was concentrating on the swirling air. It was only when the man next to me stood up that I realized Scott was taking questions from the press. The young man with the gelled hair assisted by selecting the journalists who would be allowed to ask a question. My neighbor sat down and wrote some notes while Scott responded.

Without thinking, I stuck my hand up. The young man pointed to me. "Yes? Just call out your name and publication, then your question."

Oh damn. I put my hand down and hoped he would move on, but he kept looking at me and repeated, "Your question?"

I stood up. My knees trembled and my voice felt as though it had caught in my throat. "Kate Benedict, freelancer."

The man next to me turned and glanced up at my press pass. "Gardener's Monthly," he called out. Those close enough to hear him began laughing. The assistant on stage smiled too and nodded at me.

"I wanted to ask Mr. Scott…" I stopped. My brain had frozen in place and I couldn't think of anything to ask. Berating myself for not being sufficiently up to date on politics to even know what the questions should be, I felt heat blazing in my cheeks.

"Ask him what he plans to do about funding for school lunches," my neighbor murmured quietly. I took a deep breath and repeated out loud what he'd said. As I sat down, Scott nodded as though he had expected the question and began talking about the difficulty of meeting nutritional standards with a budget of forty pence per student. I tried to listen, but my heart was still pounding so loudly that I couldn't concentrate on his words. He had a good speaking voice, which easily filled the gym and when he finished his answer, everyone applauded.

"Thank you," I whispered to my neighbor.

"No problem. I was a rookie once. Long time ago. Name's Colin Butler by the way, the *Messenger.*"

I passed the rest of the evening in a daze, getting over the shock of my unexpected moment in the spotlight. And I was sitting next to a real journalist from a serious newspaper, and he undoubtedly knew I wasn't even close to being a reporter. So I was relieved when Scott left the stage to thunderous clapping and cheering from the audience.

"Well, it wasn't exactly Cicero, but it wasn't too bad," Butler said. I assumed he was referring to Scott's speech. Personally, I'd found it rather boring. Scott's colleague, Kevin Lewis, hadn't made an appearance, so I couldn't check on his aura. I'd learned nothing about Scott that I didn't already know. The evening felt like a waste of time. I wanted to go home to the warmth of my centrally-heated flat.

"I hope he makes it," said Butler, watching Scott disappear behind a curtain at the back of the temporary stage.

The hair stood up on the back of my neck. "What do you mean, makes it?"

He dropped his notebook and pencils into a beige canvas bag. "I hope his party wins. It's going to be a close race."

"I thought they were leading in the polls?" Standing up, we waited for the crowd to empty out through the double doors at the far end of the building.

"It depends which polls you look at. Many voters are going to make a decision based on Scott as the party leader. He can't afford to lose even a fraction of a percent. Tonight he didn't say anything of substance. Nothing that would pull an unbeliever into the fold. Still, I'm holding out for a win. Just have to hope nothing crops up to cause any problems."

"What sort of thing?"

"Oh, you know, the usual crazies come out of the woodwork at about this time, often dug up by the competition."

"Anything specific?" My brain was functioning again, enough to wonder if there could be a link between the 'crazies' and the potential threat to Scott.

Butler took his glasses off and wiped them with a handkerchief. "Just rumors. Probably nothing to any of them." He folded the handkerchief before putting it back in his pocket, and then carefully settled the glasses back on his nose. The lenses were strong, making his brown eyes look huge behind them.

"Rumors? What kind of rumors?"

Ignoring my questions, Butler stuck out his hand out to shake mine, but I pretended not to notice, anxious to continue talking with him.

"What do these people, the crazy ones, do? Do they talk to the press?" I asked.

He headed towards the exit, so I stayed at his side. We wound our way through clusters of people who dawdled near the doors, unwilling to leave the chill of the hall for the frigid cold outside.

"They try to. The sensible press don't listen of course, but the tabloids and the talk shows often give them air time. Another broken wall in the crumbling edifice of professional media. People don't want facts, they want entertainment. Most papers don't report any more. They analyze, which is to say they opinionate. And their opinions are often wrong."

We'd reached the doors at the tail end of the crowd. The wind blew scraps of paper along the sidewalk, sending them flapping like white bats in the amber light of the street lamps. I wrapped my scarf more tightly around my neck.

"Sorry," he said. "Didn't mean to climb up on my hobby horse."

"That's okay. I agree with you, if that helps at all. So, are there any particular rumors? Anything that could damage Scott's reputation?"

"Nothing I'd give the time of day to." Butler peered out at the polar night, like a swimmer gathering courage to jump into a cold pool. "Well, I have to go. Maybe I'll see you at another of these shindigs," he said. "Although you might want to jot down a question or two before holding your hand up next time."

His mouth twitched with a faint smile, taking the sting out of his words. He turned and walked away, leaving me to ponder what he'd said about the crazy people.

5

The following morning, I got up early, cleaned the kitchen, and sat down at my computer with a cup of tea. The experience of the previous evening had left me confused and unsure of what to do next, if anything at all. I'd been ten feet away from Scott, but may as well have been on the other side of the moon in terms of being able to communicate. I just couldn't think how to get to him.

I did my best to ignore the whole issue and was working on a photo of *clematis terniflora* when my mobile buzzed. It was a text from Anita. "Hey, wanna have lunch. Hospital cafeteria at noon?"

I smiled. Typical Anita. We'd often met for lunch when I was working in the city close to St. Paul's Cathedral, but today I'd have to spend thirty minutes on the tube to reach the hospital. Still, I wanted to see her and there was nothing I was doing that wouldn't wait until later in the day, so I sent a "yes" back to her and got ready to go out.

Anita's department was on the fourth floor of the hospital, which had enjoyed a major overhaul about ten years earlier. The original external facade of red brick and black paintwork still evoked the Victorian era. It was easy to imagine gaslights, nurses in ankle-length uniforms with starched aprons, and wards full of iron beds stretching as far as the eye could see. Instead, the new interior was a testament to modern architecture and man-made materials. A two-story atrium filled with greenery, glass and marble was busy with visitors and reception staff.

I bypassed the reception area and made my way to a bank of lifts, waiting only for a few seconds before one arrived. Inside were two men, one of them dressed in a dark suit. He was in his forties, I guessed, with slicked-back dark hair. His skin had an oily sheen, exacerbated by the bright overhead lights. He faced another man, a doctor in a white coat.

"Later," the man in the suit said when I entered. It was obvious that they'd been talking. Now they both fell silent. The doctor had his back to me and I could only see that he was tall, with abundant grey hair that sprang out in unruly corkscrews. He also had an aura that trembled around his head and shoulders.

I pressed myself into the corner of the lift, staring up at the ceiling, trying not to look at the aura that danced just inches away from me. When I had first started seeing the auras, my body would react as though I'd been punched in the stomach. Now, I usually felt sad. Sad for the person with the aura and sad for myself for knowing it was there. It always made me deeply uncomfortable, to know something so intensely personal about perfect strangers. It felt as though I was spying on their private lives.

When we reached the fourth floor, the men stood aside to let me out and I turned right along the corridor that led to the area where Anita worked. At the reception desk, a young nurse told me that Anita was with a patient, but should be finished soon. She directed me to a small waiting room before hurrying away, her shoes squeaking on the shiny linoleum.

The waiting room was bright with yellow paint, a chalkboard, and colorful posters. Baskets of toys were stacked against one wall. Today there were no children, just a young couple who stared at the muted television screen, the woman threading a handkerchief through her fingers. I remembered the anguish I'd felt when my nephew, Aidan, was in surgery for a burst appendix and how awful the wait had been. I gave them a small smile of encouragement as I sat down.

Fifteen minutes later, Anita strode into the waiting room, giving me a quick nod of acknowledgement that I was there. She approached the couple, and put her hand on the woman's arm.

"The procedure went very well," she told them. "Joey is going to be just fine." While the father beamed, the mother burst into tears. Anita led them out of the room and was gone for about ten minutes. My stomach was growling by the time she came back.

"I'm so sorry," she said, giving me a quick hug. "The kid's spleen was damaged in a fall. He'll be all right now, though."

As so often before, I found myself overawed by Anita's ability to heal children. While I played around digitally enhancing photos and drawing pictures of plants, she dealt with the daily trauma and drama of sick and injured kids and their terrified parents. And she loved her work. I envied anyone who could combine career and passion as she did. Josh was the same. He looked forward to Mondays in the same way most people can't wait for Friday to arrive. "Life's too short not to love your job," he'd told me more than once.

"Lunch? I'm starving," Anita said.

The hospital cafeteria was busy, all the plastic-topped tables and chairs occupied by a mix of ambulatory patients in robes and slippers, doctors in white coats, and visitors dressed against the cold. The smell of boiled vegetables and frying oil transported me back to my school dining hall and lunches of overcooked food concealed under granite-colored gravy, with gelatinous dollops of tapioca or semolina for dessert. Surprisingly, the selection of food in the cafeteria looked quite appetizing. After gathering mugs of tea and plates of quiche and salad, we settled at an empty table where we chatted for a while about Josh, my project, and my dad.

"How are you doing?" I asked, watching her cut into her quiche with surgical precision.

She paused to swallow before answering. "The usual crap with my father. After I refused to marry that fellow from Mumbai, Dad seemed to give up on the arranged marriage thing, but now he's found someone else. The son of a business acquaintance. We had dinner last night and the poor sod doesn't want to marry me any more than I want to marry him. But his dad is threatening to cut him off from the family money if he doesn't accept a girl preapproved by his parents. At least my father can't pull the inheritance threat on me, as there isn't any money to withhold."

She gave a humorless laugh before taking another bite of the quiche.

"I'm sorry." I couldn't imagine being forced to marry someone I didn't love. "What does your mum say?"

Although Anita's mother was also Indian, she'd been born and raised in England. It seemed that for the most part, her English side was the dominant one, but, for some reason, she'd married a very traditional man from Chennai. I had seen for myself the fireworks that erupted when their views clashed, as they often had when Anita and I were students at University College in London. Her father had been angry about Anita living in a co-ed dorm, and had gone ballistic when Anita and I moved, in our second year, to a cramped studio in a dubious neighborhood. He thought she should live at home while she studied.

"Mum's doing her best to convince my father to drop it," Anita replied. "But even she sometimes caves under pressure from the rest of the family and gives me the dutiful daughter lecture. You'd think they'd be thrilled to have a doctor in the family, a mature woman who's independent, but no. I should marry Jamal and have babies. It's a load of cobblers, is what it is."

I patted her hand. "It'll be all right," I said. "Just stick to your guns and they'll come round eventually. They're extremely proud of you. I think your dad is a little scared of you, actually."

Anita grunted and finished the last few crumbs of her food.

"How's Dr. Reid doing?" I asked, to change the subject from Anita's family. She frowned, playing with one of her pearl earrings while looking around to make sure we were out of earshot of anyone else. "Not good. That's one reason I assisted with the operation on that kid this morning."

"What's going on?"

"Yesterday, Dr. Reid was doing a pulmonary lobectomy, but he was about to make the incision on the wrong side. As soon as I noticed, I pretended to drop some instruments so that the two nurses were distracted and came over to clean up. I just guided his hand to the right place and asked if he was all right. He said yes, and he got through the op without any more issues, but, bloody hell, Kate, can you imagine cutting a kid open in the wrong place? That could have been the end of Reid's career. Afterwards, I tried to ask him what happened. I wondered if he felt ill or if there were problems at home, but he kept saying he was fine, just a little tired. All I can do is keep an eye on him and hope he doesn't do anything reckless when I'm not there."

"You don't think you should report him?" I asked.

A look of anguish passed over Anita's face. "I don't know. He helped me so much when I first started here and he's incredibly supportive, which isn't very common among surgeons. Usually they think they're God's gift, and they treat first-year residents like dimwits. I dread to think what would happen to him if I make an official report."

"Then tell him you don't want to do that, but convince him to take some time off," I suggested.

Anita nodded, and we fell silent for a minute, sipping our tea.

"Anyway, that's enough about me and my problems," she said, pushing her empty plate away. "There's something I've been meaning to say. I wasn't a good friend to you last year and I want to apologize. You lost your mum, your friend was murdered, and you were attacked in your own apartment. I mean, that's a lot of bad stuff to happen to someone and I didn't know about most of it until after the fact. And even then, I didn't come running to help."

"You were busy and you were far away. There's not much you could have done." How would she feel if she knew that last year had also been the start of my aura sightings. "Don't worry about it."

"Really?"

I nodded.

"Can I buy you another cuppa?" she said with a grin, obviously relieved that I was letting her off lightly.

"Yes, you can, and some of the ginger cake too."

Just as she got back to the table with the refills, I saw the man in the dark suit from the lift heading in our direction. "Dr. Banerjee!" he called.

Anita muttered something under her breath, but shook his outstretched hand when he offered it. "Hi Eric." Although her tone was glacial, he didn't seem to notice.

"Do you have a few minutes?" he asked.

Anita waved a hand in my direction. "I'm busy, as you can see."

"How about later this week then?" he said. "Tomorrow or Thursday?"

"Please check my schedule with Mary," she said.

"I'll do that. See you soon then. Thanks, Dr. Banerjee."

"Snake oil salesman?" I asked Anita once he was out of earshot.

"Yeah. There's something about him that just rubs me the wrong way."

"Do you have to meet with him?"

"I'm the designated gatekeeper to keep the drug reps away from the senior doctors as much as possible. That way, the higher-ups don't waste time, but the reps can still tell their bosses that they are meeting with a doctor. It's a game, but everyone plays it."

"I saw him talking to a doctor in the lift," I said. "But maybe they were just passing the time of day." As I spoke, I realized I wasn't sure that was true. Eric had said "later" as though they'd planned to meet again.

Anita shrugged. "I'm sure Eric does everything he can to bypass the admin staff and me. If he can grab a minute in a lift, he'll make the most of it. Who was the doctor?"

"I didn't see his name tag," I said. "But he had a lot of wild hair. A bit like Albert Einstein."

"Oh, that's Dr. Reid," Anita said. "Odd. He'd usually walk up the stairs rather than get stuck in a lift with a sales rep."

There was an aura over Dr. Reid? I gasped loudly enough for Anita to notice.

"What's wrong?" she asked.

"Nothing. Air went down the wrong tube."

"Air doesn't usually do that," she replied drily. "Really, Kate. You look upset. Did I say something?"

This was it, I thought. Anita was my best friend. I had to tell her.

"It's complicated," I began.

She glanced at her watch. "I've got time, so why don't you tell me what's going on?"

I decided to plunge straight in. "Last year, about three months after my mother died, I saw her and talked to her. On a hill not far from Dad's house in Tuscany."

Anita's usually open and animated face tightened. Her eyes narrowed.

"I know," I said. "It sounds mad. But wait, it gets worse. After the bizarre encounter with my dead mother, I began seeing auras over people. Auras that predict death."

"Auras," Anita repeated.

I nodded. "And the stronger the aura, the sooner the person will die. But, I also worked out that it is possible to change the fate of the victim so that they don't die and then the aura disappears. I saved my nephew. His aura has gone now."

Anita tapped a manicured fingernail on the table. "But we are all going to die at some point, so surely we all have auras?"

"I only see them when death is imminent, anything from a few days to a few weeks in the future."

Anita leaned back in her chair, as though trying to put some distance between us.

"What does an aura look like?"

I hesitated before answering, thinking of the ways I'd tried to describe them before. No one really understood. "It's as though the air is rippling around the person's head and shoulders. You know how air is all wavy over hot asphalt? It looks like that."

Anita pursed her lips. "Does anyone else know?"

I kept the answer simple. "Leo, Dad, Josh." I didn't want to recall the painful details of those conversations, the confrontations with my brother Leo, and my father, who hadn't wanted to believe me. And poor Josh, torn between loving me and doubting the impossible stories I was telling him. There were other unbelievers too, like Clarke, the detective chief inspector who'd handled the investigation into the deaths of my friend and her neighbor. When I'd told him about the auras, he'd closed up like a sea anemone poked by a crab. Sometimes, during the trial, when we had to be in the courtroom at the same time, he'd looked at me warily, as though I was an unexploded bomb. He'd made me swear not to tell anyone about my strange gift, convinced it would demolish the prosecution's case if the jury thought that I, as a key witness, was mentally unstable.

"Okay." Anita drummed her fingers on the table. "How would you feel about going for some tests, Kate? MRI, CT scan?"

"I've done them all," I said. "Nothing shows up. I'm perfectly normal." I laughed, but Anita didn't.

"So what did I say that made you gasp earlier?" she asked. "Something to do with Dr. Reid?"

"He has an aura, Anita."

When she looked skeptical, not shocked, I felt a familiar sense of frustration.

"And you really believe that means he will die?" she asked.

"I'm sorry, but yes," I said. "His aura and his recent erratic behavior are probably connected. What do you think? Could he be ill? Ill enough to affect his ability to work?"

"Ill enough to die?"

"Maybe you can persuade him to get a check-up? Tell him you're worried about him and recommend he has an EKG and an MRI or something?"

Anita stared off across the cafeteria. I could almost see her brain ticking through the options. "I'd be taking a huge risk, talking to him like that. I have to admit that I don't feel comfortable about it."

"You don't believe me."

She looked at me. "Would you believe me if our roles were reversed?"

"Yes, actually I would, because it's you. But I don't blame you for doubting me. It's hard to accept."

"I'll try to persuade Dr. Reid to take some time off. The rest of it, I just don't know. I need time to think about it."

When her pager buzzed, she glared at it. "I'm sorry. I have to go. We'll talk later. I want to help you if I can."

I watched her stride away from the table, white coat flapping around her knees, dark hair wound in a neat bun. Her words echoed in my head. She wanted to help me, as though *I* were the victim. It was an understandable reaction. Sometimes I did think of myself as a victim, cursed with this extraordinary and unwanted ability. Wiping the table clean with a napkin, I let my mind wander, recalling the scrambled emotions of the previous year, the grief for my mother, the strange and unsettling encounter on the hill in Italy, followed by the terrifying realization that I could see auras that predicted imminent death.

It was so weird. How could I expect Anita to believe me? Still, I wished that she'd just trust me. Acceptance could come later. Once, when we were students, I was about to turn down a chance to work on a research project with a celebrated professor, sure I wasn't smart enough to keep up with him. Anita had talked me into saying yes. "Trust me," she'd said. I did and it had all worked out. That coveted research opportunity had given me a choice of premium jobs when I graduated. I was always grateful to Anita for her faith in me.

But now, I felt lonely, cast adrift. I'd have to find a better way to talk with her about it. Something that would make sense to a medical professional. I decided to walk part of the way home, to give myself time to think about how to broach the subject with her again. Turning out of the hospital, I took Newgate Street towards St. Paul's. I loved this part of the city, where ancient and modern buildings stood side by side in the shadows of Sir Christopher Wren's beautiful dome. Circling the cathedral, I weaved through the usual cosmopolitan mix of Londoners, interlaced with out-of-season tourists. Across the river, the spire-like structure of The Shard, currently the tallest building in Europe, soared upwards to the overcast sky. I dreamed of working on a project like that, something that would stand as an icon of contemporary architecture.

The thought was an unwelcome reminder of my current status as a freelancer. I should do something about that. Later, once I'd solved the current aura situations perhaps. Pulling my mind back to the problem at hand, I strolled along the Embankment, inhaling the musty cellar smell of the Thames. After thirty minutes, I still didn't know what to do about Anita. My hurt feelings seemed to be blocking my thought processes and I couldn't come up with a single idea on how to break down the barrier between us.

6

I decided to take the tube the rest of the way home, not because I was tired of walking, but because I was weary of wrestling with my thoughts. Anita's reaction had been understandable and I couldn't blame her for it. But, as always, when confronted by someone who didn't believe that I could see auras, I struggled. Should I just start ignoring the auras, pretend I didn't see them, let fate take its course? That approach would certainly smooth the path of my many tortuous relationships with friends and family.

I got off one stop before my own, remembering that I needed to visit Josh's flat to water his plants and collect his post. When his small mailbox in the lobby filled up, the postman started leaving the letters in a pile on the floor, which upset the landlady.

Today, among the usual bills and flyers was a postcard depicting red-tiled roofs and stone towers against a backdrop of snow-capped mountains. Turning the card over, I saw that it was from Munich. The handwriting, in green ink, crammed every spare centimeter of space. Although I was curious, I put it, unread, with the other letters on the kitchen counter. I'd take it all back to my flat.

Five minutes later, my watering duties complete, I picked up the post to put it in my bag. The image of brilliant blue sky and carmine rooftops again caught my attention. Unable to help myself, I flipped the card over and read it. The scrawled name at the bottom confirmed that it was from Helena, Josh's university girlfriend. All I knew about her was that she was half-English, half-German and that she'd gone back to

Germany right after they'd graduated.

Josh hadn't been dating at all for the several years that I knew him before we got together. I knew he'd had a college girlfriend he'd been serious about, and I'd asked myself if he was still in love with her. Mostly, it was his refusal to talk about her at all that had worried me.

After the first few lines of the hope you are well variety, Helena wrote that she had a new job and had just moved to Munich. She included an email address and told Josh to get in touch. The last line caught my attention. "I miss you."

Really? After nearly four years? Did Josh still miss her? For a fraction of a second, I considered throwing the card away. Josh wouldn't know anything about it. It seemed likely that Helena didn't have an email address for him, or she would have communicated that way. But I couldn't do that, so I put the card back in my bag. On my walk home under leaden clouds, I thought of that azure sky.

Leaving the letters on the hall table, I went to my desk in the spare bedroom, intent on finishing my magazine project. I tried not to think about Helena, but her message ate away at me, destroying my concentration. There was no way to settle down to work. After looking at the clock for the umpteenth time, I decided to go for a run. There was even a remote chance that I'd see Scott again. I could check on whether his aura was still there.

A strong wind shook the bare grey branches of the trees and there were few people in the park. I had the path to myself for the first half a mile or so and I ran hard, concentrating on my breathing and refusing to think about Helena or auras. A momentary break in the clouds allowed a solitary ray of sunshine to fall on the lake, illuminating a few rowboats and a couple of canoes. I thought I saw the same birdwatcher out there, with his binoculars in hand. He must be a dedicated ornithologist to sit out in the wind and damp to spot a few ducks.

Looking ahead, I saw the muscled security man coming towards me. Behind him ran Simon Scott, with Kevin Lewis trailing behind, their auras clearly defined. A spur of the moment impulse propelled me to the ground, where I sat, holding my leg and rubbing my calf. The security man ran past me, but then I heard Scott call out. "Whoa, Frank. Woman down. Let's see if we can help."

The three men stopped. With a wide, reassuring smile, Scott crouched down next to me. "What seems to be the problem?"

I was so stunned that my ploy had worked that I could barely summon any words. "I, er, my leg. It's a muscle cramp I think."

"Can I?" he asked, gesturing to my calf. Frank stood right behind Scott, eyeing me uncertainly. His whole body appeared tensed and ready to jump. A few yards away, Lewis bent over, trying to catch his breath. The auras over him and Scott were even more pronounced than they'd seemed from a distance. I realized with panic that there wasn't much time left. I had to say something.

Scott was pushing on my calf muscle, and I reacted to the pressure with what I hoped was a genuine-sounding 'ouch'. He moved my lower leg up and down a couple of times and asked me to point my toes. I'd forgotten that he'd been a doctor before becoming a Member of Parliament.

"The good news is that it's not a muscle tear," he said. "More likely just a strain from over-exercising or not warming up properly. I'd recommend a hot bath and some ibuprofen and rest."

Up close, he was good-looking in an understated way. His fair skin was smooth and finely freckled and he had unusual eyes, hazel irises ringed with gold. Even in his sweaty T-shirt, and hair flattened with perspiration, he exuded charm.

He held out his hand. "Let's see if you can stand on it," he said, helping me to my feet.

I nodded. "It's fine. I can walk on it easily enough."

"Are you sure?"

"I'm sure. Listen, Mr. Scott, sir, there's something important I need to tell you."

Frank took a step forward, his eyes fixed on me. Lewis straightened up.

You have an aura and you're going to die. The words ran through my head but I couldn't say them out loud. Frank would probably shoot me or grab me in a neck lock, and they'd call the police or the psychiatric unit. Scott looked at me, confusion clouding his eyes.

"I'm going to vote for you," I said.

Scott laughed. "I appreciate that." He held out his hand to shake mine. "What's your name?"

"Kate Benedict."

"I feel as though I've seen you or heard your name. Have we met before?"

"Well, I was there for your speech in Kensington earlier this week," I said.

"That's it. You're a journalist?"

Lewis stepped forward. "Time to go, Simon. I'm not sure what Miss Benedict's motives are but I'm beginning to doubt the pulled muscle story." He turned to look at me. "Can't you people leave him alone? There are plenty of press opportunities without hounding him when he's trying to relax. Jeez."

"I'm not that kind of journalist," I said. "I don't have any motive. I am a voter, though, and you might be glad of my vote when the election comes."

Scott grabbed my hand again, the politician in him taking over from the doctor. "Kate, we're delighted to have your support."

"We need to move, sir," Frank said. Scott held up a hand in a gesture that told him to wait. Frank frowned and, although he stood still, I could almost see his leg muscles twitching. It was some comfort, I supposed, that Scott was guarded so zealously. But the aura negated any sense of safety. Someone or something would kill him, and soon. Lewis glared at me from a few yards away, dark eyes under bushy eyebrows looking me up and down as though measuring the extent of the risk I posed. I didn't like him much, but I didn't want him to die either.

"Mr. Scott, I've heard rumors of threats against you. I just want you to be careful, okay?" I spoke very softly, but Frank's strength obviously extended to his ears. When he took a step forward, I felt the energy coming off him in waves.

Scott nodded. "There are all sorts out there who would like to have a go at me," he said. "Not me, personally, of course, just what I represent. My party, government, authority, call it what you will. It's a risk that comes with the job, but I appreciate your concern."

He gave my hand one last squeeze and turned away. I watched as the three of them jogged away under the first drops of rain. I'd lied about the rumors of threats, but there was a danger of some kind; I just didn't know what it was.

I jogged slowly to my flat. Halfway back, I had the idea of calling Colin Butler, the journalist I'd met at the campaign event. He was obviously a supporter of Scott and he'd said he was following him closely. Perhaps he might know something that would give me an idea of where to start. Suddenly energized by having something specific to do, I hurried home to look up Butler on the Web. There was no number listed for him, but I found an email address. I sent him a message, reminding him how we'd met and asking if I could talk with him about Scott. By the time I'd showered and dressed, Butler had replied, writing in the same shorthand style of speech I'd noticed when I met him. He gave me a phone number and said to call any time. He picked up on the sixth ring, just as I was about to give up.

"Kate, what can I do for you?"

"I'm researching Scott and his background. I hoped I could ask you some questions."

"Why the interest? I'm sure you're not writing an election piece for Gardener's Monthly."

"No, I'm not, but I'm working in Scott's campaign office and am curious to find out more. Just for my own interest, not to publish or anything."

While I had indeed been to the campaign office that one time, it was stretching the bounds of truth to say I was working there; ever since I'd started seeing auras, I'd fallen into an unhealthy pattern of telling lies. They were all told with the goal of protecting or helping to save people with auras, but they were lies, nonetheless.

There was a lengthy silence, so prolonged that I thought he'd put the phone down. "You said that the crazies would come out of the woodwork," I said, hoping to get him talking. "Are there any in particular? Anyone who could pose a real threat to his chances of winning?"

"Hang on." I heard papers being rustled before he came back on the line. "I can give you a lead. I'm too busy to follow up on it."

"Great! What is it?"

"It's a who. Her name is Eliza Chapman, and she went to college with Scott. She contacted me to tell me that she has information she thinks the voters should know about. Personally, I think she's more than a bit off her rocker, but I told her I'd look into it. Do you have a pen? I'll give you her phone number."

"You want me to talk to her?"

"Up to you. You said you were interested in finding out more about Scott. Maybe she really does have some information. Tell her I sent you. Let me know what you find out."

I scribbled down the number. "Why aren't you following up with her yourself?"

"There's some history there that I won't go into. Plus, I don't have time. But I'd be interested to know why she wants to talk. Natural curiosity, you might say. I have to go."

The line went dead. I stared at the screen on my phone for a few seconds, wondering what the history was that Butler wouldn't go into. It was all a bit strange, but I had nothing better to do and no other leads to follow. It was worth making the call to this Eliza Chapman, to see what she had to say.

7

I left a message for Eliza, with a request for her to get in touch. She didn't. Later that afternoon, I left a more detailed voicemail, explaining that Colin Butler had asked me to ring her. It seemed unlikely that she'd respond. Another dead end. My attempts to find a solution for saving Scott weren't getting me anywhere. Perhaps Josh was right, and I should let it go. Scott's bodyguard, Frank, was obviously capable and attentive. I had little chance of doing anything to make a difference.

My final project for the gardening magazine was due early the next day and I spent the evening polishing it. I was getting ready for an early night when Anita called. She sounded upset, her voice scratchy as though she'd been crying, and I feared that something had happened to Dr. Reid. The aura around him had been very distinct. I thought, with a stab of guilt, I'd done nothing to help him.

"Kate, do you recall seeing Dr. Reid with Eric Hill in the lift?" Anita asked.

I'd forgotten the name but I remembered the man with the bad complexion. "Yes, of course. He's the drug salesman, isn't he?"

"Yep, and remember I told you that Dr. Reid would rather climb the stairs than have to share a lift with him?"

"Uh huh," I said, pouring hot water over a chamomile teabag.

"Well, I just saw Dr. Reid and Hill together in Reid's office. The door was closed and I knocked but I didn't hear an answer so I pushed the door open."

"So? What's the problem?"

"It's so odd, that he would be meeting Hill at all, let alone at ten o
clock at night. That's way off normal working hours for a sales rep."

I sat on a stool at the kitchen counter and wrapped my hands
around my mug of tea. The heating had already gone off for the night
and it was growing chilly. I'd been planning to be curled up under my
duvet by now. "Is it normal for Reid to be there at that time?"

"Sometimes yes, if there's an emergency surgery. There were two
tonight and I wanted to ask him a question about the medication for
one of the patients, which is why I went to his office."

I thought back to hearing Hill mutter "later" to Dr. Reid. Could Hill
have something to do with Reid's aura? I realized that Anita had
stopped talking.

"Anita? Are you all right?"

"Yes. Well, not really. Reid was rude to me. He said he was busy
and he'd see me tomorrow. He's never spoken to me like that before.
He was so cold and distant."

"I think his behavior has something to do with his aura," I said, half
to myself.

Anita cut me off. "We don't have time for that right now."

I stood up, hoping I'd feel more authoritative than when I was
sitting down.

"Just listen. You're telling me that Dr. Reid is acting out of
character, meeting late at night with someone he'd normally go out of
his way to avoid. I'm telling you that Dr. Reid has an aura, which
predicts his death in some form or another, and possibly quite soon.
There has to be a connection. It's too much of a coincidence
otherwise."

For the first time in the eight years I'd known Anita, she didn't
answer back.

"Anita? Are you all right?"

"There's something else," she said, and her voice was shaky. "I'm
probably imagining it, but I felt sure I was being followed on my way
home just now."

My mouth went dry. Anita wasn't prone to vivid imaginings and had
never admitted to being scared of anything. When we'd shared the
studio in a seedy area of London, she'd always carried a switchblade
and a can of pepper spray in her purse. On at least two occasions she'd
frightened muggers away. She was everything I wasn't; calm, centered,
self-confident and fearless, while I carried my own insecurities and fears

around like a backpack full of rocks.

"Did you see who was following you?" I asked.

"No. I didn't notice anything unusual on the bus. It was when I was walking from the bus-stop to my flat that I realized there was someone behind me. It was dark and I couldn't see much. But I heard footsteps and they slowed when I did and sped up when I began walking more quickly. When I got to the house, I had my keys ready and ran inside and locked the door. I've been looking out of the windows but I can't see anyone."

"Maybe it was nothing," I said, wanting to calm her. "You're upset about Dr. Reid and perhaps a little shaken. It's easy to imagine the worst at a time like that."

"Yeah, I think you're right. I'm sorry. This whole thing at work has got me unsettled. And..." she paused. "The aura thing too. I can't get it out of my mind. Any of it. That you can see them and that Dr. Reid has one. It's crazy, but what if you're right?"

Sighing, I flipped the switch on the kettle to make a second cup of tea. Insisting that I was right was not going to make Anita feel any better, but if there were any chance of helping Dr. Reid, I needed her to believe me.

"I wish it weren't so, Anita, but Dr. Reid does have an aura and it's pronounced enough to mean that death is imminent. We need to work out what to do to help him."

"We?"

"Well, I'll need your help, as I don't know him at all."

"But why would you care? As you say, you don't even know him."

"But I care about you and you care about him." I poured water on to a fresh teabag and took a sip. It was scalding and burnt my tongue. "I've seen hundreds of auras in the last year," I continued. "Nearly all of them over strangers, people I couldn't help even if I wanted to. Others over people I've had some kind of connection with."

"You told me about Aidan," said Anita.

"Yes, and others too, people I knew. I did what I could but sometimes..." I trailed off, realizing that this wasn't what Anita needed to hear. Carrying the phone and tea to my room, I slipped into bed and pulled the comforter up around me. I'd often talked to Anita like this. We'd had long conversations late into the night when we'd first started working and didn't have time to see each other during the day.

"Let's assume for a minute that you were being followed," I

continued. "Why? Something to do with whatever is going on with Dr. Reid perhaps?"

Anita was silent for a few seconds. "I can't see any connection," she said finally.

"Do you want to come over and stay? We could talk it through."

"Thanks, but I'd rather stay home now I'm here. The doors are locked. I don't usually freak out, you know that, but…"

I'd run out of ideas, other than feeling that Eric Hill had something to do with Reid's aura. But I didn't have enough information to work out why or what to do about it.

"I'm knackered," Anita said. "I'm going to catch up on some sleep. My first patient appointment is scheduled for 8 a.m. Thanks for listening to me. Let's talk again tomorrow."

"As long as you're certain you'll be all right? Let me know if anything unusual happens at work, do you promise? I'll think about it some more."

I meant to keep my word and do some serious thinking but, after the late nights finishing up my projects, I was tired. Even so, when I turned off the lamp, Anita's fears of being followed brought back painful memories of the man who'd attacked me in my hallway and I switched the light back on. When I finally fell asleep, I had nightmares of killers in the dark, of doors that wouldn't lock, and of crimson blood pooling on white carpets.

8

My head ached when I woke the next morning. I felt as though I'd barely slept. My first thought was about Anita. I texted her and she responded at once to say she was all right and on her way to work. After a quick breakfast of tea and toast, I emailed my assignment to the editor of the gardening magazine, hitting the send button with a sense of relief that it was done on time. Now I could focus on my aura issues.

Waiting for the kettle to boil for more tea, I gazed out of the window. Rain streamed down the glass, obscuring the view beyond. It was like looking at an aura, everything behind it blurred and hazy.

I took my cup of tea to the den, thinking about Dr. Reid and Simon Scott. I felt like beating my head against the desk. I knew something bad was going to happen to both of them and I couldn't think of a single thing that might stop it. My eyes drifted to my mobile. Calling Eliza Chapman again was probably a waste of time but I did it anyway. To my surprise, she answered. I'd prepared what I was going to say and quickly introduced myself.

"Colin Butler suggested I get in touch with you," I finished.

"Ah, Colin," she said. "And why didn't the great journalist contact me himself?"

"He's tied up with something," I said. "He sends his apologies but said to let you know he trusts me to talk with you." I cringed as I embellished the facts, but now I had her on the phone I was anxious to make sure she'd see me.

"All right," she said. Her voice had the raspy timbre of a long-time smoker. She gave me an address in Cambridge and suggested I go up that afternoon. I hesitated very briefly. The trip would take several hours, but she was my best link to Simon Scott.

A couple of hours later, I was on the train, zipping through the northern London suburbs. Soon we were out in the countryside, passing through fields of dark soil and stands of bare-branched trees under ashen skies.

After buying a cup of tea from the refreshments cart, I used my mobile to do some preliminary research on the woman I was going to interview. Her name had been in the papers a couple of years previously for giving the wrong treatment to a child, which resulted in the suspension of her medical license. That was interesting. I couldn't wait to meet her. When we reached the station, I grabbed a taxi and soon stood at the door of her shabby semidetached house.

Eliza Chapman had to be in her late forties, about the same age as Simon Scott, but she looked ten years older. Shoulders slumped under a frayed brown cardigan. Her shoulder-length graying hair was brittle, in need of a conditioner and a good cut, and her face had those deep wrinkles typically incised through years of smoke and alcohol. An overweight tabby cat wound itself around her ankles until she gave it a gentle shove with her foot, causing it to mew loudly and run off down the hall.

She led me into a small living room that was sparsely furnished, but crowded with books. Shelves along one wall sagged under the weight of them and a stack of hardbacks substituted for a missing leg of the coffee table. The table's surface was littered with volumes of different colors and sizes, topped with an empty wine glass. She picked up several magazines from the couch and patted the cushion into shape, sending up a cloud of dust.

"Tea?" she asked. "Or a glass of wine?"

"Tea, please, if that's not too much trouble?"

"Come with me then and we can talk while I make it."

I followed her down the narrow hallway to the kitchen. It was cleaner than I'd expected, and compact, with appliances lined up along one wall under a row of white laminate cabinets. Most of the doors were chipped on the corners, the fiberboard underneath showing through. After filling the kettle, Eliza took some teabags from a metal canister with a picture of a cat on it and put them in a brown teapot that didn't appear to have a lid.

"So, tell me again why the mighty Colin didn't come here himself?" she asked. The smell of stale smoke hung around her like a shroud.

"Do you know Colin personally?" I asked, confused. I knew he'd written an article about her, but she spoke of him more as though she knew him well. He'd mentioned that there was some history now I came to think of it, but he hadn't elucidated. Then again he hadn't really explained anything much.

"He didn't tell you how we met?"

I shrugged.

"He's a friend of my sister's. I met him ages ago when my sister was trying her hand at match-making. That was a big waste of time. The men she thought I'd be interested in, oh my God. Anyway, Colin was one of them and we liked each other well enough, I suppose, but not like that. I hadn't seen him for years before the scandal erupted. Then he turned up and offered to write my side of the story. I think my sister begged him to do it."

"The scandal being the issue with the vaccination?"

Eliza sighed. "Yes, of course. That scandal."

She poured tea and milk into a couple of beige earthenware mugs and handed me one. "Let's go sit down," she said.

I sat on the dusty couch, while she settled into a brown velour armchair that looked like a dog with mange, mottled with worn shiny patches and unidentifiable stains.

"Do you mind?" I asked, putting my mobile on top of a book on the coffee table. "If I can record our conversation, I won't need to take notes."

She shrugged. "Okay." She was tapping a fingernail against her mug. I thought she seemed nervous, so I tried to ease into a conversation.

"You have a lot of books. You must collect them."

"Obviously."

"Any particular genre?"

"Not really. A lot of them are medical books, boring as hell." She pointed to the bookshelf. "But those are my favorites; poetry, novels, short stories. I can't stand watching television, so I read instead."

I nodded. "I don't like television either."

She didn't respond. Eager to begin the interview, I checked the recorder was working and leaned back against the lumpy sofa cushion.

"Why don't we just start with what it is that you wanted to tell Colin Butler?"

"There are some things about Simon Scott," she said. "Things that people should know before they decide to vote for him."

I waited but she didn't say anything else.

"Can you tell me about them?"

"Of course. That's why I invited you to come. But you will publish what I tell you, won't you? I want this to be in the paper so everyone can read it."

Although she had the impression that I worked for Colin's newspaper, this didn't seem like the time to clarify the situation. "All I can do is take notes," I said. "The editor decides if and when to publish. But I have a question for you. Why aren't you talking to the tabloids? They'd love to get their hands on rumors about Scott. You'd be sure of widespread coverage that way."

"I'm not telling you rumors," Eliza snapped. "I'm telling you the absolute truth. And I hate the tabloids, almost as much as I detest Simon Scott. You know what they did to me."

"I saw the stories from a couple of years ago, yes," I said.

"So you must see why I don't want to talk to any of those scumbags." She drank some tea and grimaced. I sipped at mine and it tasted fine.

"Why don't you give me a quick rundown on everything leading up to this moment?" I asked. "It's best if I hear it from you directly."

She sighed. She seemed to do that a lot. "Let's start at the beginning then, as it will make more sense that way. Scott and I were at Cambridge together, medical students. Scott was one of those golden boys, good-looking, smart, popular. You know the type." She paused and peered at me. "Or maybe you don't. You're not Oxbridge, are you. Let me guess. One of the modern places in the Home Counties?"

Stung, I felt the blood rush to my cheeks. "University College London, actually."

"Oh, well, good for you," she replied. I was stunned at the way she threw her prejudices around so casually, but she either didn't notice my reaction or didn't care.

"Anyway," she continued. "Simon was one of those. Everyone liked him. I wasn't in his league in terms of looks and popularity, but we were in the same classes and became friends. Turned out that our fathers knew each other vaguely as they both worked in Whitehall."

She stopped when the previously shunned cat jumped on to her lap. She let it settle in before going on. "In our final year, Simon offered to proof-read a paper for me. It was really important, so I was thrilled that he was willing to help. I wasn't quite so happy when he pointed out what he called some specious arguments. But I knew he was right, so I made the revisions he'd suggested. That took a couple of weeks. Not long after handing it in, my professor called me to his office. He accused me of cheating."

Eliza's hand started shaking. She slammed her mug down on the rickety table, which trembled under the onslaught. "Cheating. Can you believe it? He said my paper was almost a copy, and not a very good one at that, of a thesis submitted the previous week by Scott. I was given a fail and that meant a couple of residency positions I'd applied for were revoked."

She stood up suddenly, and the cat adroitly jumped to the back of the chair, where it perched with its tail bushed out in annoyance. "I'll be back," she said.

Alone, I checked that my recording app was still working. It was, but I considered turning it off. Everything Eliza had said sounded like the rantings of a failed scholar. This trip was beginning to feel like a waste of time.

She came back with a glass of red wine in her hand and settled back into the chair. "Want one?" she asked lifting the glass up. I shook my head.

I really didn't want to hear any more of her ramblings. The story was pathetic. A plagiarized paper from twenty-five years ago was hardly likely to deal a fatal blow to Scott's political ambitions.

"I'm not sure I see where this is going," I said. "Some academic cheating, even if it happened—"

"It did happen," she said. "But that's not the point. I told you about it to explain why I dislike Scott so much. And it illustrates his character, not that people seem to care much about character nowadays. They only care that whoever is in power promises to cut taxes and the price of petrol."

I didn't want to get drawn into a discussion about politics so I asked her what had happened after the debacle with her final paper.

"I couldn't get into the cardiology residency program I was trying for," she replied. "I ended up being a general practitioner." She made it sound as though she'd become a child molester.

"Family care is very important," I said. "Think of all the people you've looked after. I'd think that would be a great way to practice

43

medicine."

She threw me a look of utter disdain. "Try it," she said. "Snotty-nosed kids, obese mothers, rashes, coughs, sprained wrists. It's not the stuff of dreams for someone who wanted to save lives in a cardiac unit."

I shifted on the scarred sofa. Her self-pity grated on me. "I'm sure you could have worked your way into a cardiology program if you cared that much about it," I said, then tried to soften my words. "I mean, there must be ways to do that?"

She shrugged, the movement causing wine to splash out of her glass and on to the brown velour. She didn't seem to notice. We were losing direction.

"So—?" I prompted.

"Two years ago, I made a mistake. I gave a kid the wrong dose of a vaccine and it made him sick. Not dangerously ill, but the parents complained and the press got hold of it. Within a day, I was splashed all over the papers, made to look like a monster. They said I was a drunk and unfit to practice. I was fired, my license was taken away. That's why I hate the tabloids. The only newspaper that gave me a fair trial was Colin Butler's. He wrote a piece about the pressure of overworked family doctors. He stood up for me. So I want him to handle this story because I trust him to do it properly. Otherwise it will be a twenty-four hour extravaganza of tabloid sleaze that no one with any intelligence will read."

A little shocked, both by her story and her tone, I pressed on, anxious to finish the interview and start the journey home. Self-pity is corrosive and Eliza was swimming in a deep pool of it. It was her own life she was destroying. No one else was doing it for her.

"So, is there more?" I asked.

"Yes and this is the important part." She drained the last of her wine, but gripped the stem of the glass as tightly as a lifeline. The cat remained on the back of the chair, making her look like a witch with a demon on her shoulder. "Simon fell in love with a Greek girl, another medical student who was one year below us. Her name was Phoena Stamos. She was beautiful, exotic, and brilliant. From what I heard, her family had made big sacrifices to make it possible for her to come to Cambridge. She and Simon made a stunning couple. But when his family heard about her they told him to finish the relationship. They had someone far more suitable in mind apparently, a woman called

Tiffany Holden, whose father was a Member of Parliament.

"I think Simon resisted for a while, during which time, Phoena got pregnant. At that point, Scott senior was so angry he was threatening to pull Simon out of college. Simon gave Phoena money for an abortion and that was the end of it. I know that Simon, against his father's wishes, offered to go with her to London for the procedure, but she refused. She didn't return to Cambridge."

"Did you know if she was all right? What happened to her?"

"Simon told me he got a postcard from Greece saying she was fine but not coming back. Within a few months he was engaged to Tiffany. They married and that lasted about two years, I think. Just enough time for him to benefit from her father's connections." She leaned forward in her chair to put the empty glass on the table. "And then he dumped her."

In the silence that followed, I heard kids laughing and talking out on the street, and the explosive sound of a motorbike revving up. My mouth was dry and my throat burned as though I'd ingested some of the acid that Eliza was spewing.

"Then as you probably know, he married Melody Blake, the heiress, which gave him the funds he needed to run for office."

The room felt airless and close, and it was growing dark. Eliza and her story weighed on me, as though her depression was contagious. I didn't know how much was the truth and how much was the fantasy of a bitter and vindictive woman.

"So you can get that into print, can't you?" she was saying when I started listening again. "Let people see what kind of man their Prime Minister elect really is?"

"I thought you said yourself that no one values character any more," I said carefully. I didn't want to offend her, but I wasn't going to encourage her illusions. "And to be honest, I'm not sure why anyone will give a damn about something that happened all that time ago. He was just a kid, really. I'm sure there are plenty of fifty-year old men with errors in their pasts, like broken relationships and unintended pregnancies. This may not have the effect you are looking for."

Besides, I thought, Scott's aura means he has far bigger issues to deal with than an old romance gone bad — but I couldn't tell Eliza that.

She reached out to switch on a floor lamp that stood at a tilt next to her chair. The lamp- shade was stained and the weak bulb threw a puddle of thin light on the velour chair. I imagined her sitting there in the evenings, reading a book, nurturing her grudges and resentments. I felt sad for her, but frustrated too. The cat opened its eyes and looked at me for a few seconds before jumping to the floor and stalking out of the room.

"I want you to promise that you'll write it up," she said, standing up.

"I'll do my best," I said, turning off the recorder application on the phone and pushing myself up from the couch.

"You have to do better than that." She raised her voice. She was almost shouting. "I'm counting on you. It's not fair that a liar and a cheat gets to be Prime Minister, don't you see?"

"I do." Picking up my bag, I made my way out of the room, stepping around piles of books on the floor. I couldn't wait to get outside.

"If you don't get this done, then I will," Eliza said, lowering her voice to a whisper that felt more threatening than the yelling. "If I have to, I'll take this into my own hands."

The hair rose on the back of my neck. Was she the threat to Scott? She was obviously unbalanced. She walked me through the hallway that was now murky with the gloom of early evening. When she closed the front door behind me, I stood on the step for a few seconds, breathing in fresh air and enjoying the tingling sensation of rain on my face.

The street lamps flickered on, their orange light dimmed by mist and rain. I walked quickly, anxious to put some space between me and Eliza's dreary house. The road was surprisingly quiet, unlike London at this time in the evening, when the pavements were crammed with commuters. I missed the feeling of being part of a bigger entity, and felt a pang of nostalgia for the tube trains crowded with wild and assorted representatives of humanity.

This glimpse into Eliza's life had been a stark reminder that I wasn't making the most of my education or my skills either. My life as a freelancer was beginning to feel less entrepreneurial and more unemployed. Protecting my phone from the rain, I called Alan Bradley, and left a voicemail, asking if I could talk with him about coming back to work.

I left a voicemail for Colin Butler too, to say I'd met with Eliza and would send him more details later. By the time I reached the station, I'd decided to call the police as well. I'd start with the detective chief inspector who'd headed the investigation into my friend's death the previous year. I wouldn't tell him about the auras. I'd just pass on the information Eliza had given me and let him take the next step.

***

In the early evening, back at home, I sat at my computer, sifting through dozens of websites, looking for information that would verify Eliza's version of events. The first searches brought up the stories in the tabloids two years earlier. I thought about what it would be like to see your name plastered across the papers, every sordid detail punctuated with exclamation marks and bad photographs. I reread the piece that Colin had written, which was measured and reasonable, extending sympathy to the parents of the child, but also suggesting that they perhaps overreacted.

My searches for Phoena Stamos didn't bring up anything. There were, as I'd imagined, thousands of people with that surname in Greece but nothing on Phoena, so it was possible that she had married and changed her name. What had happened to her? Had she taken up her medical studies somewhere else, in Athens perhaps? I hoped that she was a happy and successful doctor now, as she had dreamed when she went up to Cambridge.

Closing my laptop, I leaned back on the sofa, thinking about Simon Scott. I hadn't found anything that linked anyone else to his aura. The only clear threat was Eliza; she obviously loathed him. I picked up the phone to call Clarke again. This time he answered; we exchanged pleasantries and checked on each other's health before he asked what I wanted. I explained it all as succinctly as I could, without mentioning Scott's aura. Clarke might have guessed that an aura had been the catalyst for my call, but he didn't say anything. In fact, he seemed unimpressed by my story. "I can't investigate everyone who disagrees with a political candidate," he said. "But thanks for the call."

The line went dead.

9

My phone rang while I was eating a sandwich for dinner. It was Alan Bradley.

"You called earlier?" he asked.

Typical Alan, always brusque and to the point. I'd always thought of him as the boss from hell, but he'd softened over the last few months. His partner's arrest had, for a while, driven him into a depression so profound that it had seemed the company was doomed to close. Then he'd had the idea of promoting Josh. Now, with an impressive roster of new clients, Alan was back to his irascible self.

"I was thinking about coming back to work now," I said. "If you have enough for me to do?"

"Can you start tomorrow?" he asked. "We can go over the project list together. Glad to hear that Josh has talked some sense into you at last."

"I need a couple of weeks to finish up my work for the gardening magazine," I said, ignoring his comment about Josh. It wasn't true that I needed time to finish the projects. I could complete them in a day or so, but I still wanted enough freedom to investigate the auras over Scott and Dr. Reid.

"How about a week from Monday then?" he countered. I said that would be good. If I were to help Reid or Scott, it would have to be soon anyway.

Alan rang off, with no farewells or expressions of joy, but I was excited about going back. And Josh would be thrilled. I'd tell him when he called later in the evening.

I rang Anita to let her know. "Thank God," she said. "I never understood why you left in the first place. You have talent, Kate. I want to work in a hospital building designed by you one day."

"How are you?" I asked. "How's Dr. Reid doing?"

"Good. No issues at all. He seems to be back to his usual self, actually."

"I'm glad."

"Can you come over tomorrow?" she asked. "To see if his aura is still there?"

"I thought you didn't believe in auras?"

"I don't," she said. "But you do, and if you can really see one over Dr. Reid, then you can also see if it's disappeared. If you think he's going to be okay, then I can relax a bit."

"I suppose that makes sense," I said, pleased that Anita was finally acknowledging the fact that I could see auras. "I'll come over at lunchtime again tomorrow if you think Dr. Reid will be available for a viewing at that time?"

She laughed. "I'll make sure he is. It will be good to see you. What did you do today?"

I hesitated. Telling her about my trip to Cambridge would raise the whole issue of the aura over Simon Scott, and she was in such a good mood that I didn't want to spoil it. I settled for telling her that I was almost done with my projects. "And you've had no more problems with being followed?" I asked.

"No, I was just imagining the whole thing, I'm sure."

"Ok," I said, not convinced.

The next day, I arrived at the hospital at noon, and went to the fourth floor to find Anita.

"Dr. Banerjee is finishing up with a patient," a nurse at the reception desk told me. "If you go to the waiting room, I'll let her know you're here—" Her head jerked round at sudden beeping sound and, without a word, she hurried away, leaving me standing at the desk. My phone buzzed with a text from Anita. "Sorry to be late. Already downstairs, so let's meet in the cafeteria."

"Coming now," I texted before heading towards the lift, just as a figure in a white coat turned into the corridor ahead of me. It was Dr. Reid. His aura was very visible, spiraling over his grey corkscrew hair. I watched him go, sad that the aura was still there. Anita would be disappointed when I told her.

When I reached the cafeteria, it was busy, but there was no sign of Anita, so I grabbed a tray and got in line. A minute later, hands clamped over my eyes and a voice whispered, "Guess who?"

I laughed and turned. "Late again, Anita—" I stopped.

Her smile faded. "What? What's wrong? You look as though you've seen a ghost."

"Nothing, I'm fine. What are you going to eat?"

Pushed forward by impatient customers behind us, we advanced through the line, picking up salads and bottles of water. Only when we were seated did Anita ask again. "What's wrong, Kate?"

How could I tell her that she had an aura?

I looked at her salad. "Yours looks far more appetizing. Do you want mine?" It was a futile attempt to distract her.

"No thank you. And we're not eating until you tell me what's going on," she said.

"You have an aura." There was no point in trying to soften the blow. Anita swore by telling and hearing the truth, however unpalatable.

"I don't believe in auras, remember?" she said, pouring dressing over her salad greens.

We sat in silence for a couple of minutes while I pushed pieces of lettuce around in the plastic tray. Anita looked up at me. "So how will I die and how long do I have?"

I shook my head. "I don't know how it will happen. Your aura is faint, so maybe a few weeks, a month. But, listen, you won't die. I won't let you. We've got time to work it out. Remember, my nephew had an aura, and he's fit and healthy now."

"Because you got him to the hospital in time," she said.

"That's not your problem," I said, forcing a laugh. "You're already here."

She grinned, forking food into her mouth. I doubt I could eat if someone had just told me I was going to die. But then she didn't believe me.

"I think there has to be a link with Dr. Reid," I said.

"But I'm hoping his aura has gone. He's been better again today. We need to go check on him."

I told her that I'd already seen him upstairs and that his aura was still there. "If anything, it's moving faster. That's not good."

"Damn," she said.

"So you both have auras. We need to analyze what the connection could be. It's highly likely that the danger to you both is from the same source." I pushed my uneaten lunch away. "Can you think of anything?"

"He and I are pediatric doctors and we work together," Anita said, ticking off the items on her fingers. "And we have offices on the same floor."

"Yes, but there are other doctors who work on your floor and they don't have auras. Is there anything that's specific to just you and Dr. Reid?"

She shook her head. "I don't think so. I'm Indian, he's white. He's married and I'm not — yet anyway." She grimaced, no doubt thinking of her father's plans for an arranged marriage. "He's old, I'm young. We have the same blood type. That came up in conversation once. Oh, I know. We both love chocolate-covered cherries. A patient gave me a box and Dr. Reid and I fought over it like ravenous wolves."

She wasn't taking this seriously. I wanted to shake her, to make her see it was real. "Do this for me," I said. "Have as many health checks as you can, MRI, blood test, cardiogram. Let's try to eliminate the obvious risks. And keep thinking about any possible relation between you and Reid. Do you ever go off-site together, for example? In a car, an ambulance?"

"No."

"Okay, what about your patients? Do you both care for a patient who could in some way be a threat?"

"What? One of the kids is going to jump on us both with a coloring crayon?"

"I'm serious. Maybe a parent who's unhappy with the care a kid received?"

She shrugged. I knew I wouldn't get much further with her. She needed time to internalize what I'd told her and I could only hope she wouldn't take too long.

"There's something else," I said. "I wasn't going to tell you, but Simon Scott has an aura as well. And his colleague, Kevin Lewis."

She was staring at me, her fork halfway to her mouth.

"Scott?" she said. "Bloody hell, Kate. Your aura-seeing capability knows no bounds. Look around, how many people here have auras?"

I didn't want to see any more darn auras, so I shook my head.

"Probably a few, given that we are in a hospital."

She finished her salad in silence, and I kept quiet too. There was nothing to be gained by trying to convince her of something she didn't want to hear. When her pager buzzed, she put her empty salad container on the tray. "That's Dr. Schwartz. I'm sitting in on a consultation with him in ten minutes. I should go."

She stood up. "Are you coming to the campaign office tonight?"

"Yes," I said. "I'll see you there."

She left without our customary hug, striding off in her starched white coat, looking the picture of health and energy.

It seemed obvious to me that her aura and Reid's were linked in some way. If I could find out more about a potential threat to Reid, perhaps I could pinpoint the danger to Anita too. Checking my watch, I leaned back in the chair and waited for ten minutes. Then I went up to the pediatric floor. Although it was a long shot, I wanted to find Dr. Reid while Anita was out of the way. I wasn't sure what I could learn from talking to him, but anything was worth a try.

When the lift hissed to a stop, I stepped into the hallway and looked up and down. There was no sign of Anita. Two nurses I didn't recognize were talking with a man in a suit near the reception desk, the man young and good-looking with dark brown hair and a dimpled chin. The nurses were laughing at something he'd said. Hoping they'd be too preoccupied to notice me, I walked past the desk towards Dr. Reid's office, which was just a few doors up from Anita's.

"Can I help you?" one of the nurses called out.

"I have an appointment with Dr. Reid," I said, turning around. Reluctantly, I made my way back to the reception desk. "At one o clock. The name is…" I hesitated. These nurses didn't know me. "Sophie Harrison."

"Let me find you on the schedule," the younger nurse said, typing on her keyboard. Trying to appear relaxed, I flashed a smile at the man in the suit. He was wearing a name tag on a lanyard. Audley Macintyre, followed by a company name, LB Pharmaceuticals. So he was probably a drug rep like the oleaginous Eric, the one Anita didn't like.

"Busy day?" I asked.

He nodded, returning my smile with a multi-watt one of his own. "Always, but I love what I do, so time goes quickly."

"Ms. Harrison, I can't find your name here. Are you sure your appointment was for today?"

"I'm positive," I said. "There must have been a mix up? If Dr. Reid is free, could he see me just for a couple of minutes? I've traveled quite a long way to get here. It's about my son."

I cringed as I rolled out the lies, one after another. Perhaps I should have just waited near the lift and hoped for Dr. Reid to make an appearance.

"Well, he has an appointment in five minutes," said the nurse. "And I'm busy…" she glanced at Macintyre.

"Don't worry. No rush," said Macintyre. "You sort this out. I'll go grab a cup of coffee if that's okay."

"Thank you so much," I said to him.

After he'd walked off, the nurse escorted me in silence to Dr. Reid's office. The tempo of her footsteps on the lino floor was a staccato echo of her annoyance. When she opened his door and introduced me, he looked a bit confused, but invited me to sit down. The aura was moving around his head very quickly, the rippling air blurring the picture of a Provence landscape hanging on the wall behind him, rendering the lavender fields and golden sunflowers indistinct and formless.

Seeing Reid close up for the first time, I was struck by his eyes, which were brown and soft. I imagined that they had often comforted the parents of sick children.

"Ms. Harrison? I'm afraid I don't recall your case?" he said, glancing at his computer screen.

"Dr. Reid, I'm actually a journalist doing a story on surgeons and stress. You're a leading surgeon here and you work with children and young adults. I imagine you experience stress every day. Would you be willing to talk to me about it?"

"I really don't have time," he said with a quick look at his watch. "Which publication did you say you work for?"

"I'm a freelancer. I'm working on the story for the *Messenger*." It was a huge lie but now I'd come this far, I'd keep going. "I would just need a couple of minutes of your time."

He leaned forward in his chair. "Go on."

"Statistics show that doctors suffer, on the whole, a disproportionately high incidence of depression, alcoholism and substance abuse," I said, recalling the research I'd done when I'd first learned about Reid's aura. "Surgeons in particular work under intense pressure, which leads to a high burnout rate and suicide."

I stopped, looking at him, searching for a reaction. To my surprise, he nodded. "I know the numbers," he said. "And I know some doctors who've experienced 'burnout' as you call it, which is in fact a clinical syndrome characterized by emotional exhaustion and a reduced sense of personal accomplishment — among other things. But most of us, in my experience, love what we do. We are extremely well trained. We think on our feet, we have positive interaction with our peers, and we save lives. I can't imagine getting burned out, to be honest."

"So you're not unduly stressed?"

He smiled. "No. But I will be if I'm late for my next meeting, so if you'll excuse me?"

"Do surgeons have regular medical check ups?" I blurted out as I stood up.

He laughed. "I know a few hypochondriacs who do. Practicing medicine can do that to you. You get one little symptom and extrapolate from there. Before you know it, that slight cough is TB and a headache is a brain tumor. But no, in general, I'd say we get checked out much like anyone else does."

I desperately wanted to keep him talking. "So you're feeling good?" I smiled, trying to make a joke of it. "All healthy? No particular pressures?"

For a microsecond a frown crossed his face. Not a frown so much as a moment of introspection, while he thought about his answer.

"Nothing specific," he said. His aura was moving fast. Based on what I'd seen in the past, death could arrive at any moment.

"Good. I really appreciate your time. If you have anything else you'd like to contribute to the story, will you contact me?"

He pushed a pen and notepad across the desk towards me. I scribbled down my fake name and my real mobile number.

"Goodbye, Ms. Harrison," he said, turning back to his keyboard.

I walked out of Dr. Reid's office just as Anita turned into the corridor. She stopped dead, staring at me. I pulled the door closed behind me.

"What are you doing here?"

I was feeling lied out, unable to think of a single plausible explanation. I shrugged. Taking a couple of strides forward, she grabbed my arm and tugged me towards the small staff kitchen, which was empty. Macintyre, the drug rep, must have taken his coffee somewhere else to drink it. She closed the door, leaning against it to stop anyone else entering.

"What are you doing?" she asked again. Her aura moved around her head, slow but distinct. I looked down at the floor, not wanting to see it more than I had to. It felt like it must have done when people saw the telltale signs of the bubonic plague on a loved one, except that back then death was inevitable. I was going to fight to save Anita.

"I wanted to talk to Dr. Reid, just to see if I could get any hint about what's causing his aura."

"And did he actually speak with you? Did you tell him about the aura? What did he say?" Not waiting for me to answer, she carried on. "I can't believe you'd do this, Kate. Dr. Reid is my boss. You can't just go swanning into his office, talking rubbish about auras. He'll think I'm crazy too. It's bloody ridiculous."

I moved a couple of steps away from her, propping myself against the countertop, shaken by her anger. We'd never fought before. For one thing, I knew she'd win if we did, so I'd always managed to defuse potential conflicts before we reached the point of arguing.

"He doesn't know I'm your friend, Anita. I told him I was a journalist and gave him a false name. He'll never connect the two of us. And, I never mentioned auras."

She glanced at the door as though expecting him to appear. "I still don't get it. What's the point? You have no idea what *might* happen to him. Or to me. You say there's a threat. We're going to die but you know nothing about when or how. It's useless and stupid. Why scare people when you can't do anything to help? It's like yelling fire in a theater."

"That's why I wanted to talk to Reid. I'm trying to help, can't you see that?"

"Not really no. I don't see that at all. I have to go. It'd be best if you left now too."

10

Smarting from the fight with Anita, I hurried home under black clouds that swirled above the rooftops. Inside, I turned on the lamps in the living room and sat on the sofa, staring at my laptop. My chest was tight and my heart bounced around as though I'd drunk too much coffee. Already reeling from the shock of seeing Anita's aura, I'd been thrown even further off balance by our argument. But I had to stay calm if I were to have any chance of helping her.

Falling back on routine and practicalities, I sent an email to Colin Butler telling him about my interview with Eliza Chapman, relaying my concern that she might be a danger to Scott. Then I sat down to tackle my final magazine assignment. Thirty minutes later, Butler sent back a message thanking me for following up. I got the impression the case was closed as far as he was concerned. I wondered if he would feel differently if he knew about the aura over Scott, but that wasn't a conversation I ever planned to have with him.

Engrossed in my project, I didn't notice the time until I got a text from Josh saying he was on his way home. When he arrived he was carrying a bag of Chinese takeout.

"Delivery for the beautiful girl in Flat 4," he said, handing me the steaming, fragrant bag. "And a bottle of your favorite wine."

For the first time that day, I felt the tension in my shoulders give a little. When we were settled on the sofa with our plates and glasses, I asked Josh about work. A dose of normality was just what I needed. Josh gave me a colorful account of his latest project, his rather wacky client, and the shenanigans of the team working on it.

"Everything's going great, but I miss you," he said. "It will be good when all this traveling is over." He paused. "I talked to Alan earlier and he told me that you're coming back to the firm in a week. That's wonderful." His voice trailed off. "I'd rather have heard it from you, though."

"Oh Josh, I meant to tell you. I'm afraid I've been a bit preoccupied with things. Aura things."

"Simon Scott? I thought we'd agreed there's nothing you can do about that."

"Not Scott. Anita."

"Anita? Oh shit. Have you told her? What's going on? Is she ill?"

I put my empty plate on the coffee table and curled up in a corner of the sofa, my legs tucked under me. Although we talked for an hour about Anita, we weren't able to resolve anything. I wasn't expecting that, but I did feel a little better when I went to bed.

Maybe it was just my brain needing a break from auras, but I woke up the next morning thinking about the postcard from Josh's old girlfriend. He'd picked up the stack of letters when he got in the night before, and had taken it to the kitchen to sort and read. Then nothing. He hadn't mentioned the postcard.

He was still sleeping, so I slipped out of bed, went to the kitchen, and opened the recycling bin. There, on the top, were empty envelopes, fliers and offers for credit cards with outrageous interest rates, but no sign of the postcard. I assumed that meant he'd kept it.

I put the kettle on and clattered around pulling cups from the cupboard and making toast with butter and marmalade. When the tea was ready, I carried a tray back to the bedroom, to find Josh awake, sitting up in bed, with his hair sticking up in a way that I usually found endearing. Right now, it just irritated me.

I set the tray down on my side of the bed. "You got all your post then?" I asked, handing him his tea and toast. "Anything interesting?"

He looked at me over the rim of his teacup. "Er, no, just the usual junk and one bill I need to pay."

I couldn't help myself. "I thought you got a postcard."

He waved a piece of toast in the air. "Oh, yeah, and a postcard."

"The picture was pretty. Where was it?"

He put his cup down, placed the toast back on his plate. "Munich, from a friend who's just moved there."

"Anyone I know?"

"No."

Perching on the edge of the bed, I munched on my toast to give myself some time to think about whether I was going to pursue this further. The fact that he was keeping the card, and that he wouldn't talk about it, seemed evidence that he was hiding something. I imagined a massive hand slapping my face. *Hello? Anyone there? What do you think is going on? He gets a postcard from an ex-girlfriend and he doesn't tell you about it?*

Josh glanced at the clock. "I should get going."

"Where?"

"I've got a short meeting at the office, just to go over our presentation slides for a big client meeting on Monday." Odd that he hadn't mentioned that before. Was he really going to work? I stopped right there. I had to trust him.

He got out of bed while I sipped my tea, admiring, in spite of my bad mood, the view of him from the back. He had the shoulders of a swimmer and a slender waist. Forcing my eyes upward, I sighed at the way his dark, glossy hair curled against the nape of his neck. Then I reminded myself that I was angry with him, and with good reason.

"Why don't you come?" he asked, sliding hangers around in the closet, looking for a shirt.

"Why would I do that?"

"I thought you'd agreed to come back to work. Why wait? If you came in today, it would show Alan that you're anxious to get started. Besides, you haven't got anything else to do, have you?"

I stood up suddenly, tilting the tray on the bed, tea splashing out of my cup on to the white duvet cover.

"Damn." I hurried to the bathroom, grabbed a towel and rushed back to mop up the mess.

"Do you know where my leather jacket is?" Josh asked, still flipping hangers. He found it and put it on over a black t-shirt. No need for suits and ties for weekends in the office. "Look okay?" he asked, turning round. He looked great, but I was in no mood to tell him that.

"What do you mean, I have nothing to do?" I asked, taking another stab at scrubbing out the spot on the duvet. "There's an assignment to finish and I do have a small problem to solve, like saving a few lives."

He pulled a scarf, Stewart tartan of course, from a drawer. "You should look out for Anita," he said. "But you can't worry about the others. You'll drive yourself crazy."

"Maybe, but you know what does drive me crazy? Is you not telling me the truth about that postcard. It was from your old girlfriend, Helena, or whatever her name is. I don't know why she's getting in touch with you and I don't understand why you kept the card and didn't tell me about it. What's the big secret?"

Josh zipped up his jacket. "I'll call you later," he said. "I'm late and you need to calm down before we talk."

I waited until I heard the front door close quietly — Josh never slammed doors — and then I threw myself on the bed and gave in to a storm of tears that had been brewing for days. I felt as though I was making a mess of everything. I'd interrupted my career for no good reason, I wasn't solving the threat to Anita or Dr. Reid, and I had no way of warning Scott. A sense of failure descended over me like an impenetrable fog.

My dad always said that there was no substitute for hard work. As a lawyer, he'd commuted every day from our family home in Dulwich to his offices in Temple Bar, where he worked long days handling some of the most challenging cases with the toughest of clients. Yet he always looked forward to going to his office. I'd inherited his work ethic and resorted to it that morning. Within a couple of hours, I'd finished my assignments, and reviewed the project notes that Alan had sent me. I'd be able to go back to Bradley Associates with a running start.

Normally, a clean desk would comfort me, give me a sense of accomplishment and a feeling of control. But today, I felt as though my world was still hurtling towards disaster.

11

Josh and I got through the rest of the weekend without mentioning the postcard or Helena, staying busy with our visit to the theater and a Sunday brunch with friends. He left on Sunday evening for a trip to Edinburgh, leaving me to stew alone about our quarrel and my fight with Anita. I'd checked in with Anita by text and phone and received only monosyllabic responses. At least I knew she was alive, but I hated that we weren't speaking. So when she texted me early on Monday to ask me to go to the campaign office that evening, I jumped at the chance. She didn't mention our quarrel, but I took her text as an attempt at reconciliation.

The office was already crowded when I arrived, the atmosphere electric with excitement and urgency. I wondered what the enthusiastic volunteers would think if they knew about Scott's past transgressions. Nothing, probably. Everyone saw what they wanted to see. And the opposition choice was probably just as bad, if not worse.

Anita was on the phone when I arrived. She looked up and waved when she saw me, her aura still trembling over her dark hair. I wasn't thrilled to see her working the phone bank, as we wouldn't get to talk if she stayed there all evening, but I found a group in need of help with another banner and made myself useful. Trying to secure an enlarged photo of Simon Scott to a piece of fabric, I dropped a tub of glue on the floor where it rolled under a nearby table. A young man bent down to pick it up and walked over to give it back to me. He was tall and slim, with dark curly hair and fair skin. He was in his late twenties, I'd have guessed, about the same age as me.

He stuck out his hand to shake mine. "Chris Melrose," he said.

I introduced myself and asked if he could help me finish the poster. While we worked, he told me he was a postgraduate student studying chemical engineering. "And I work three nights at Smithfield Market," he said, "to pay for my studies. So, if you ever need a side of beef or a venison steak, I'm your man."

I laughed. "That sounds like hard work."

"It is, but I only work about five hours a night and I finish at three a.m., when the Market opens to customers."

When we finished the poster, he suggested a coffee, so I followed him to the small kitchen, where we poured treacle-thick coffee into paper cups and sprinkled powdered creamer on top. Leaning against the counter, we sipped the vile stuff.

"So what will you do when you finish your doctorate?" I asked.

"I have some job opportunities lined up," he said. "Or maybe I'll stay in academia, but that's all in the future. Who knows what will happen?"

He tipped the remainder of his coffee into the sink. "It was good to meet you. I hope to see you again soon. In fact, are you coming on the campaign rally tour this week?

I shook my head.

"You should come. It could be interesting," he said.

I doubted it. I couldn't think of anything worse than listening to the same speech repeated multiple times. We said goodbye to each other, and I went back into the office, where I offered to help a small team of people who were stapling packets of information together.

It was late by the time Anita finished on the phones. To my relief, she came straight over to me, wrapping her arms around me. "Sorry I got so mad yesterday. I was just wiped out and not thinking straight. I need a coffee."

She steered me to the kitchen. I declined a second cup, feeling the first one roiling my stomach.

"How are you doing?" I asked.

"Good, great."

"Did you think any more about your aura?"

"Not really," she said. "It was a busy day." She sighed. "I'm sorry, sweetie. I wish I could believe in premonitions and all that mumbo jumbo. But I can't. I deal with real life and death situations every day. I don't need to see an aura over a kid with a failed kidney or a collapsed lung to know that he's in danger." She tipped creamer into her coffee. "Who was that you were talking to earlier?"

I told her about Chris.

"I've seen him here before," she said. "Never talked to him. I wouldn't kick him out of bed, though."

She sipped the coffee and threw the rest of it away, filling the cup with water. "You know," she said. "It's a good idea of Chris's to go to all the events. That could be fun. What do you think? I have a couple of days' holiday due, which I should take before they expire. The people here are organizing a bus to transport everyone to the rallies. Want to go?"

"Of course," I said. I'd go anywhere Anita was going. Political rally or a visit to the zoo, it didn't matter as long as I kept her in my sight.

12

The following morning I boarded the charter bus outside the volunteer office and waited impatiently for Anita to arrive. Hearing the swish of closing doors, I hurried to the front, begging the driver to wait a few more minutes. While he complained about being late, I stood at the door, looking up and down the street. My pulse raced. What if something had happened to her?

When she jogged into view, I felt weak with relief. Helping her with her bag, I led the way to the back of the bus, away from the mutterings of the impatient driver.

The first rally was in a renovated barn west of London, with the stone ramparts of Windsor Castle visible in the distance. The barn smelled of wood and straw. Drafts swirled through knotholes in the planks, but we'd all come prepared in our parkas and anoraks. We joined the locals, giving a huge cheer when Scott appeared with Lewis and a covey of bodyguards in tow. Scott gave a rousing speech, greeted enthusiastically by his fan club.

His aura, invisible to everyone else, danced over his head while he talked. His past, also invisible to his supporters, nagged at me. Plagiarized papers, pregnant girlfriends, marrying for influence and money. None of it was attractive, but I wasn't sure how much it would sway the electorate against him even if they knew. It seemed unlikely that Eliza Chapman's accusations would ever see the light of day. I kept an eye open for her. It was hard to imagine her summoning enough energy to leave her wine and her books, but revenge and hatred are powerful forces.

Anita was in a good mood, excited by the spirited crowds and the snappy speeches. I glimpsed Chris, standing by himself near the back of the crowd, unwilling to push through to a better viewing point at the front, unlike Anita, who'd had no qualms about elbowing her way to the first row.

Our next stop, in a city center square, felt like a replay, although the turnout was even higher, and the audience more vocal. After that stop, we traveled to Oxford, where Scott addressed a largely student audience in a cavernous hall with wood paneling and old, murky oil paintings on the walls. Once the speeches were done, our busload of supporters adjourned to a nearby pub for dinner. Anita and I sat with Chris, ate chicken pies and drank white wine, listening to the ebb and flow of political debate. When we'd heard enough, we said goodnight to Chris and wandered up the high street to the small bed and breakfast where we'd spend the night before getting back on the bus in the morning.

Our diminutive room was nestled in the attic of an old Tudor building. The beamed walls, bowing under the weight of the roof, were papered in green, sprigged with white blossoms. The ceiling, covered in the same botanic wallpaper, sloped over two single beds covered with pink and green flowered bedspreads. It was like an Alice in Wonderland version of Kew Gardens. I propped a pink pillow up against the bed head and leaned back. The day hadn't been particularly demanding, but I felt exhausted, as I often did when dealing with an aura.

Anita pulled a half bottle of wine from her bag and poured some into two paper cups. She took a sip. "Astringent with a hint of cardboard," she said. "My favorite."

I sipped mine. "It's not that bad."

She held up her cup. "To us," she toasted. "Auras and all."

After taking a big swallow, she cocked her head to one side.

"When you look at me, do you just see this big circle of impending doom?" she asked.

"Of course not. When I look at you, I see *you*, my wonderful, irritating friend. I hardly notice the aura. Besides, it's just a warning, an admonition to be vigilant. You're not going to die any time soon. We'll make sure of that."

She raised her paper cup again. "I'll drink to that."

We stayed awake until the early hours. I told her about my fight with Josh, she described the growing hostilities with her father over a marriage she didn't want. Leaving those painful topics behind, we talked about our careers. By the time we'd finished the wine and turned out the lights, I felt a renewed bond between us, the attachment we'd formed as freshman students just as strong now as it was then. I lay awake in the dark, listening to the old house creak, thankful that Anita and I had put our quarrel behind us. I could protect her better if we stayed close.

The next morning, we bundled up in our warmest clothes for another day of outdoor speeches. While we were on the bus to Tewkesbury, my phone buzzed. Seeing that it was Eliza Chapman, I answered at once. Her raspy voice seemed to breathe smoke down the phone. "When will the story be in the paper?" she demanded.

"I'm not sure," I said. "Let me find out and I'll get back to you."

"That's not good enough," she said. "Give me the name of your editor. I'll find out for myself."

"No," I said. "I'll check in with him and get back to you."

She put the phone down without replying. I called Colin and left a voicemail to warn him that Eliza was likely to be in touch.

For the rest of the day, we followed Scott from one market town to another, traversing the English countryside like the traveling court of a medieval king, journeying from castle to castle. But these courtiers wore jeans and puffy anoraks, ate cheese and pickle sandwiches, and drank tea from thermos flasks.

As the crowds increased in size, so did the number of auras I saw. Many months ago, I'd realized I couldn't handle the emotional toll of trying to analyze every aura, and I'd developed what I called selective recognition. I only took notice of auras over people I knew or who were connected to people I knew. It worked, mostly. Apart from Scott and Lewis, of course, but that was different. Scott was a public figure. His premature death would leave his party without a leader, generating a degree of chaos that would be bad for the country. I felt compelled to do something.

In a car park at the Mini factory in Cowley, we huddled against the cold for the final rally of the weekend. I took my digital camera out of its protective bag and took some shots of the crowd, working on my camera technique. Through the lens, I noticed a man I'd seen several times the previous day. I felt I knew him from somewhere else and it was only when it began raining that I realized he was the birdwatcher I'd seen on the lake in Hyde Park. He was wearing a sage-colored

Barbour jacket, lined with a distinctive tan and black plaid. When he was struggling in the wind to pull his hood up, it caught my attention. Of course, the jackets were popular, but I was still certain it was the same man. Now his earlier presence on the lake seemed ominous. Had he been watching Scott, not birds, through his binoculars?

I snapped a few shots of him. I'd share them with DCI Clarke. Not that he'd rushed to do anything about Eliza, it seemed.

Late in the afternoon, with daylight fading and the temperature plummeting, we stood near the front of a large crowd, shivering through Scott's last speech of the day. Even his enthusiasm was waning. His voice was hoarse, and, if his feet hurt as much as mine did, then he had to be in some discomfort.

Someone behind us shouted; I turned to see a man in a black hoodie shoving his way forward towards the platform. A few people in the audience yelled at him to stop pushing, but he barreled on, using his elbows to move everyone in his way. Suddenly, he stopped. I saw a small dark object arc through the air, and watched in horror as the projectile struck Scott on the head. Two bodyguards leapt towards Scott as he collapsed. They broke his fall, lowering him to the platform floor. Lewis threw himself in front of Scott, shielding him from further attack and from view.

The mayhem on the stage was mirrored by the frenzy in the audience as supporters grabbed hold of the attacker and pinned him to the ground. Several security guards jumped off the platform, clamped handcuffs on the assailant, and dragged him to his feet while sirens wailed and several police cars slid to a halt near the platform. The handcuffed man was pushed into the back of a car, which sped away with lights flashing.

Scott lay still on the dais floor, with Lewis and a group of others kneeling or crouching around him. The crowd waited in complete silence. My legs felt like jelly.

At last, Lewis helped Scott to his feet. Scott held a handkerchief to his head and, for a moment, looked unsteady. Then he straightened up, standing unaided, to look out over the hushed audience. His aura circled above him, just as it had before.

"It was only a stone, folks," he said. "Nothing to worry about."

He looked down at his white shirt, which was spattered with drops of blood. "Nothing except a ruined shirt and my favorite tie, that is."

Everyone clapped and cheered as he left the platform, escorted to a black sedan with Lewis at his shoulder. The crowd began to disperse, everyone talking about the assault. The stone throwing was a petty offensive, no more than a statement of disgust or contempt, but it slammed home to me just how vulnerable Scott was, campaigning like this in such public venues. I felt I had no chance of averting whatever danger threatened him.

Walking back to the bus, I looked around for binoculars man, but saw no sign of him. Typical, I thought, that I'd been worrying about the wrong person. Maybe binoculars man was just a supporter after all.

"So is Scott's aura still there?" Anita asked when we'd boarded the bus. "Or was that the threat that didn't turn out to be one?"

"It's still there," I said, letting her take the window seat. As soon as we sat down, she put on her headphones and leaned against the glass, leaving me to my thoughts, which weren't good company. After a while, I tried to read, but it was hard to concentrate. I stared out of the window, watching the sky fade from pink to grey to charcoal and the glass transform into a black mirror that reflected colorless images of the passengers. The bus smelled of damp clothes. Everyone was quiet, shocked by the attack on Scott, and tired after two long days of traveling and cheering. Chris sat by himself on the seat in front of me, reading a textbook.

For a while, I worked on an Italian language app on my phone. After ten minutes of staring at the same word, I gave up. My mind was teeming with thoughts of auras. The bus slowed in traffic when we reached the outskirts of London, where the driver started letting the volunteers off close to bus stops and tube stations. It was raining hard. Anita got off near Ealing Broadway, heading to to her parents' house for dinner.

"Wish me luck," she said. "Mum was tight-lipped about it all, but I think Dad's invited a potential suitor over. It'll be a nightmare. I'll talk to you tomorrow."

Almost everyone had left the bus by the time we approached the campaign office. Chris stirred and called out to the driver.

"Can you drop me here? I live on that street."

He stood up, hefting his backpack on to his shoulders as the driver pulled the bus to a halt at the curbside.

"Bye, Kate," Chris said. "Let's hope for the best on election day. Maybe I'll see you in Eastbourne for the acceptance speech."

Climbing down from the bus, he strode away, collar turned up against the rain. He turned up a side road, disappearing into the darkness. The driver had changed gears and was about to pull back into traffic when I caught sight of Chris's book on the seat he'd just vacated.

"Wait!" I called to the driver. "Chris left something. I'll run and give it to him."

"Okay. Shall I wait for you?"

"No, it's fine. I'll just go straight to the tube station."

Picking up the book, I hurried off the bus and along the street Chris had taken. I could see him in the distance, a dark figure appearing and disappearing through pools of orange light from the street lamps. He turned off the road, disappearing from view. I broke into a run, hampered by my overnight bag and the heavy book, but, when I reached the place where I thought he had turned, I couldn't tell which house he'd gone into. The semi-detached houses, fronted by short driveways, were all identical. I hesitated, feeling the rain dripping down the back of my neck. Just then a light came on downstairs in the house to my left. Guessing that would be him, I walked to the front door and rang the doorbell. A broken gutter above poured a steady stream of water on to the doorstep, and I backed up, braving the rain rather than the leak.

When the door opened, Chris peered out, looking wary. Even when he saw it was me, his face didn't seem to relax.

"Your book," I said holding it out to him. "You left it on the bus."

"Oh, thanks. Those books are really expensive."

He took the heavy volume, one hand still holding the front door half open. "See you next week maybe," he said after a long pause. He was obviously in no mood to chat.

"Which is the quickest way to the tube from here?" I asked.

He nodded left up the street, the way I'd come.

"Okay, thanks. But could I use your loo before I go? I drank too much tea today."

He hesitated long enough to make me regret asking. I realized I'd assumed he lived alone, but maybe he shared with other students or a girlfriend and it wasn't a good time. He hadn't told me much about his personal life.

"Don't worry. I'll make it," I said quickly, turning away.

"No, come in," he said. "The place is a mess, so you'll have to excuse it."

I followed him inside. The front door opened directly into the living room, which was small and cluttered with furniture. A flowery three-piece suite took up most of the space, arranged around a tiled fireplace with an electric fire retrofitted into it. A table holding a small, old-fashioned television lurked in the corner. Dusty silk flowers in a cheap-looking vase were the only decoration. It didn't look like a room furnished by a young male student.

"There's just one bathroom and it's upstairs," he said. "I'll show you."

I was about to say I was sure I could find it, but he led the way up the narrow, pink-carpeted stairs to a small landing with three doors. He closed one of them and pointed to the furthest one. "That's the bathroom."

The bathroom was shabby but clean, with lavender carpet flattened from years of use, and pink fixtures that bloomed with lime scale. Maybe Chris was renting the house from a landlady with a penchant for pastels and no money for repairs.

While I washed my hands, I thought about his reluctance to let me in. The house wasn't exactly Architectural Digest, but it wasn't anything to be embarrassed about. My curiosity piqued, I tiptoed from the bathroom towards the door that he'd closed, pushing it open a few inches. It was dark inside.

My brother Leo had been known to call me nosy and meddling, but I preferred to think of what I was about to do as investigating. My curiosity had got me into trouble on more than one occasion. I tried not to think about that right now.

Light from a street lamp outside illuminated the room enough for me to see a single bed neatly made with a white duvet and matching pillowcase. An old wooden armoire stood against one wall. The room was very neat and revealed nothing particularly interesting, which made me wonder why Chris had bothered to pull the door closed. The headlights of a car passing on the street briefly flooded the room with light and illuminated the far wall. It was covered from floor to ceiling with pieces of paper attached with thumbtacks and tape. I crept in to take a closer look. Not wanting to risk switching on a lamp, I held up my mobile, which shed enough light for me to see that the papers were press clippings and magazine pages, and every one of them featured Simon Scott.

Chris was truly a supporter, I thought, until I peered more closely at one clipping and saw deep slashes across a photo of Scott's face. I looked at another and saw similar gouges across Scott's eyes. Large black Xs criss-crossed some of the photos and there appeared to be yellow highlighter on some of the text, but I didn't have time to read any of it. My heart was thumping against my ribs and I was finding it hard to breathe. Struggling to make sense of what I was seeing, I also knew I had to move before Chris became suspicious. I crept out to the landing, carefully pulling the door closed. When I reached the top of the stairs, Chris was standing at the bottom looking up at me. Pulse racing and my legs trembling, I made my way down.

"I feel much better now, I said. "Thanks."

He nodded. "I made some coffee. Do you want some?"

What I really wanted was to get out of the house, but rushing away seemed rude, so I followed him into the kitchen, my hand shaking when I took the cup of coffee he offered me.

"Are you all right?" he asked.

"I think I'm coming down with something, actually," I said. "What with the rain and being in close quarters with all those people, it's not surprising I suppose."

I drank the coffee fast even though it was hot, burning my tongue and throat as I took several big swallows.

"I'd better go," I said, handing him the empty cup. "It's getting late. I hope I'll see you next week."

"Perhaps," he said, following me to the door. I heard him bolt it behind me before I hurried under relentless rain to the tube station.

13

Jittery and perplexed, I found it hard to sleep, and was wide awake long before dawn, listening to the faint hiss of tires on wet asphalt and the steady beat of rain on the windows. I climbed out of my warm comfortable bed for just long enough to make tea and toast and then hurried back with my breakfast and laptop. Searching online for Chris Melrose brought up half a dozen results, all confirming what he had told me about his postgraduate student status. I couldn't find anything else on him. General searches on Melrose filled the screen with pages of information, but nothing that was helpful.

After a while, I got up, put on a robe and went to the living room to look through the photos I'd taken at the campaign events. I printed some of them; a shot of the man with the binoculars, a couple of Chris, and even a decent one of Simon Scott standing on stage with his arms raised in the air. Spreading them out on my desk, I added a photo of Eliza Chapman that I'd printed from one of the old articles on the Internet. In the lamplight, I stared at the images, trying to see the relationships between them. If I could work out the links, perhaps I could save some lives.

Chris was working in Scott's campaign office and going to all his campaign events. Was he doing that to support him, as appeared to be the case, or to watch him, the way I suspected the binoculars man was? And if so, with what objective? Revenge, like Eliza Chapman? Chris, Eliza and binoculars man were all possible suspects if Scott's aura indicated death by murder.

I checked the time frequently, wondering when Anita might be free. I wanted to make sure she was all right, and tell her about Chris, but she'd told me she was on duty until mid-afternoon. I moved the photos around, shuffling them like cards to see if I could wheedle any information out of them. After a while, I got up and made more tea, throwing on jeans and a sweater while the kettle boiled.

Cup in hand, I walked back towards the desk, happy to see there was a break in the rain. Pale sunlight filled the room. The light gave substance and depth to the photos, and I stared at them for a full minute, wondering if I was imagining things. Picking up the two pictures that had caught my attention, I carried them to the window for a closer examination. Chris resembled Scott. He had the same eyes, hazel with a gold-colored ring around the iris. Could they be related?

I went back to the desk to send an email to Colin Butler, telling him that I had some news and that I needed his help. To my surprise, he responded almost at once. When he suggested meeting in a pub not far from where I lived, I jumped at the chance to get out of the flat.

I arrived at the pub before Butler did, and took a mineral water to a table near the window. The bar was packed with lunchtime patrons, their chatter competing with the sound from two televisions showing replays of the previous weekend's football matches. Black beams held up sagging plaster ceilings. The floor undulated and creaked underneath tired red carpeting. When Butler arrived, I gave him a little wave, not sure that he would recognize me. In brown cord trousers and a brown jacket belted around a substantial gut, he reminded me of a bear. He shambled to the bar and then joined me at the table.

"So, Kate, what did you make of Eliza Chapman?" he asked, taking a long swallow of his drink.

"Well," I said carefully, "She has a good reason to dislike Scott for cheating, but her hostility to him is extreme. She seems a little unbalanced, to be honest." I'd told Butler by email about Eliza's account of the pilfered thesis, but I hadn't mentioned her story of the pregnant girlfriend. That seemed like malicious gossip, not something that a journalist at a serious newspaper would be interested in. But my discovery about Chris changed all that.

"There was something else," I said. "She said he got his girlfriend pregnant, and then dumped her when his family told him to."

Butler's bushy eyebrows ascended towards his thinning hairline. "Tell me more."

I gave him a brief summary of what Eliza had told me about Scott's relationship with Phoena Stamos. "So Scott behaved badly, but why did it bother her so much?" I mused. "I mean, I've had friends who've shown significant lapses in judgment, but it doesn't mean I hate them for it. Her reaction seems irrational."

He wiped foam from his lip and nodded. "I think she was in love with Scott."

I hadn't thought of it, but it made sense in terms of explaining her animosity towards him. The woman scorned and all that.

"What makes you think so?"

"Just something she said when I interviewed her about the scandal with the vaccine dosage," he said. "She didn't name Scott, just mentioned the pain of some unrequited love in her past. She never married, you know. I daresay she didn't really mean to talk about her personal life like that, but it came out during our conversation."

I smiled. "I'm sure you're a better interviewer than I am. And that makes me curious as to why you sent me to talk to her?"

Butler's eyes blinked rapidly behind his thick-lensed glasses. "Yeah, that's a fair question. The decision to not pursue any rumors came from high up and I really did have a pile of other articles to write, but I was curious. So I thought if I sent you to meet Eliza, I'd find out what she knew without directly contravening instructions from my editor. When I heard what she'd told you, I decided that there really isn't a story there. So, I have to say, my editor's happy, I'm happy. Eliza won't be, but that's life."

"I think we need to be careful," I said. "She made a threat. Said she'd take things into her own hands if you didn't put her story in the paper. I think she could be a danger to Scott."

Butler took another drink of his beer before answering. "You're conflating two things, it seems to me. She seems to hate Scott. She resents his success. She'd like to see the details of his past indiscretions covered by a serious newspaper. That's not the same thing as being a danger to him." He took another long swallow from his glass. "I don't like to be harsh about a fellow human being, but Eliza is a sad fish. I did my best for her once and that's as far as it goes."

I sipped my mineral water, which tasted flat. Butler's words depressed me for some reason.

"But you said you have something new to tell me?" he asked.

I sat up straighter. "According to Eliza, after Scott broke off the relationship, Phoena left for London to have an abortion." I said. "Eliza told me that Scott later got a postcard from Phoena saying she was back in Greece. But I think it's possible she had the baby, and he's here in London."

I was gratified to see a flicker of excitement in Butler's eyes. He set his glass down on the sticky tabletop. "And what is the basis for that hypothesis, may I ask?"

It took a while to explain how I'd met Chris, the chance visit to his house, and the discovery of the hate wall in the upstairs bedroom.

"I didn't see it before, but now I've caught a glimpse of the similarity in the photos, it seems obvious. Chris has darker hair, but the same fair skin and light eyes. He has the same nose as Scott, and they're about the same height. I believe he could be Scott's son."

"Very interesting," Butler said. "And by 'interesting' I refer to your investigative methods. Snooping around people's bedrooms and finding a casual resemblance between two photos doesn't exactly present a cast iron case."

I pulled the photos out and put them on the table facing him. "Take a look for yourself."

He studied the photos for a while. "You may be right."

When I grinned in self-satisfaction, he held up a hand. "But I still don't think the story is newsworthy. An illegitimate son makes an appearance just before the election." He turned his hands palms up. "So what?"

"You don't think that would cause a scandal?" I asked. "I'd take a bet Scott's wife doesn't know about Phoena. If Chris went public, it might be enough to upset Scott's supporters. Women might decide not to vote for him."

"Well, that is possible, but the putative son is leaving it awfully late if he wants his grand entrance to influence the election."

"What about the mangled press clippings? Do you think Chris intends harm to Scott?"

Butler drained the rest of his beer. "Not really my field of expertise. It sounds a little melodramatic, actually."

If he thought that sounded melodramatic, what would he make of a death-predicting aura?

"So that's it? You said you needed my help?"

"Do you have access to databases, records, anything that might show if Phoena Stamos had a baby and lives in England?" I asked him.

"I know you don't think it's newsworthy, but I'm still interested. I'd like to know but I already searched the Internet and nothing showed up."

He nodded. "Well, I do, but I can't give you access," he said.

"You could look it up for me, couldn't you? It wouldn't take long and I just feel that I need to know more about Chris before I see him again, even if he's not a danger to Scott."

"I do owe you for doing that trek up to Cambridge," he said slowly. He leaned over to retrieve a laptop from a black canvas bag on the floor by his feet. I was surprised. I'd thought of him as a paper and pencil man. He smiled at my expression. "I'm very handy with a keyboard. While I get this booted up, why don't you buy another round?"

It was hard to suppress my excitement. I jumped to my feet and headed to the bar. When I got back to the table, I pulled my chair round to sit next to Butler, who was looking at a website I didn't recognize. He might look like a slow and lumbering bear, but his fingers flew across the keys and he seemed to read at a great pace, putting screens away and pulling up new ones before I'd got much past the top few lines.

"Aha."

I peered at the words on the screen as he pointed a finger at an entry halfway down. "Marriage certificate for Phoena Stamos and William Melrose, dated 14th September 1993 at the Islington office."

"I knew it! Phoena must have settled in London after she came back from Greece, assuming that she ever went back there. And she married Melrose about five years after leaving Cambridge. Chris must have taken his stepfather's name. Look up William Melrose."

"Pushy, pushy," said Butler, but he carried on typing. "What makes you think that Chris isn't William Melrose's son by birth?"

"The timing. Chris is in his late twenties. If Melrose and Phoena had a child together, he'd only be early twenties, five years too young to be Chris."

"Ok, give me a minute. There are lots of listings for William Melrose, but let's see if I can whittle down the list a bit." He glanced up at me. "Drink your water or something. I can't work with you breathing down my neck."

I sat back in my chair, giving him some space, and checked my watch. It was only one in the afternoon, at least another hour before Anita would be free.

"All right," murmured Butler to himself. "This could be our man. Oh dear, yes it is. Death certificate dated November 2005. So he and Phoena weren't married for very long." He stopped typing, cracked every finger on both hands and then took a big swallow of his beer. "Did you get any snacks?" he asked. Obediently, I went back to the bar and bought two bags of salt and vinegar crisps.

"Mmm, thanks. Love these things," he said. "Wife tells me not to eat them but she doesn't understand that I need salt to focus my brain."

"Any more details on Phoena?" I asked.

"I've checked and there aren't any records of other children nor did Phoena remarry. However, when she and Melrose were married, they bought a house in their joint names at Morgan Street in Shepherd's Bush."

"That's where Chris is living," I said. "And that would explain the pink carpet and the flowery sofa. I wonder where Phoena was last night?"

"Dead," said Butler. It felt like a punch to my stomach, even though I hadn't known her. "Death certificate dated, let's see, just under two months ago."

"Poor Chris," I said. "So he's all alone now. He must be grieving."

Butler looked at me with an eyebrow raised. "You're quick to jump to conclusions and that's not good journalistic methodology. Maybe Chris was happy when she passed away. Now he gets the house and any money she had, and doesn't need or want your sympathy at all."

"I don't think there was much money going round that household. Chris told me he works a night shift to pay for his college fees, and the house was pretty shabby." I crossed my arms, a little miffed at Butler for criticizing me.

He smiled. "Okay, okay, my comment was uncalled for. But you have to review every fact and decide if it's relevant to the story and you have to dig deep for the truth, not take things at face value."

I nodded. "All right. And there's one more thing." I gave him the photo of the man with the binoculars and told him I'd seen him watching Scott in the park and then at the rallies. "Is there any way you can find his name?" I asked.

He shrugged. "Unlikely, but I'll see what I can do." He looked at his watch. "I should get back to the office before my editor sends out a posse to find me. Let me know how things go, and be careful. Don't make assumptions and don't run around putting yourself in danger."

76

He closed his computer, pulled on his anorak and wrapped a beige scarf around his neck. We left the pub under charcoal clouds swollen with rain.

14

On my way to the tube station, I called DCI Clarke, eager to share my latest information with him. He sounded distracted when he answered the phone, but said he could meet me if I went straight over to his office.

Twenty minutes later, I stood waiting for him in the entry hall of the police station. He arrived in a flurry of activity, with several people in tow, one of them taking notes. It was usually like that with him. He was the source of energy at the center of a massive machine. Although he wore a traditional tie and oxblood loafers, his fair hair was stylishly cut. He resembled a wrestler more than a police officer, with wide shoulders under a leather bomber jacket and thigh muscles that looked ready to burst out of his jeans. As always, I was struck by how young he was to be a Detective Chief Inspector.

"I thought we'd get out of the office and walk for a while, if that's okay?" he asked, wrapping a scarf around his neck.

"Sounds good," I said, falling into step beside him. We strolled towards St. James's Park, turning in through the ornate iron gates. A few young women pushed strollers or trailed after toddlers, everyone bundled up in coats and hats and scarves. The park was one of my favorite places in London. In summer, the old plane trees offered pools of welcome shade for visitors who sat in striped deck chairs and admired the views to the lake. And, even in the winter, I usually found the park appealing, with its broad sweeps of lawn, assorted evergreen shrubs and the constant activity of dozens of species of water birds. Today, though, the water sat flat and dull, and the leafless trees were black and menacing, their branches swaying in the blustery wind.

When we reached the lake, Clarke indicated a bench. "Let's sit down and you can tell me why you wanted to meet."

The wooden slats were cold, so I pulled my coat tighter around me. "Did you get in touch with Eliza Chapman?" I asked.

"Yep. One of my men is working on it."

"Really? When she and I last talked, she didn't say anything about the police contacting her. I think she'd have told me because she'd know I was the one who put you on to her."

Clarke sighed. "I'll check into it. Remind me, how did you meet her?"

I decided not to tell him about Colin Butler. I didn't want to drag the journalist into anything after he'd been so helpful. "Friend of a friend," I said. "She drinks, she's demented, but she's angry enough to do damage, maybe."

"Is that it? We could have covered this on the phone."

I took the photos out of my bag. "There's more." I showed him Chris's photo. "This man has a motive to be a threat to Simon Scott. His name is Chris Melrose. He's a graduate student studying chemical engineering here in London. He knows how to make explosives."

Clarke shrugged. "I don't get the connection."

"He's Simon Scott's illegitimate son."

It was good to see an expression of surprise flit across Clarke's face. "He has a hate wall in his house," I continued. "Press clippings and photos of Scott, all mutilated, slashed with a knife or disfigured with a marker."

Clarke turned so he could look at me. "Tell me exactly how you know Scott has an illegitimate son. And stick to the facts please. No embellishments."

"I did some research. Well, a journalist and I did it together. We found records online. Based on what Eliza told me about Scott's girlfriend at Cambridge, we were able to trace her. She married someone called Melrose when Chris was about five."

I gave Clarke a photo of Simon Scott. "Compare that and the one of Chris. The resemblance is obvious."

Clarke tapped Chris's photo with his forefinger. I could almost see the wheels spinning as he wrestled with his natural desire to know more, in spite of the highly untrustworthy source.

"How do you know this Chris Melrose?"

"He's volunteering on Scott's campaign, as am I. We met at a local campaign office. That's the point. He's volunteering in order to be close to Scott."

In the silence that followed, I heard the distant hum of traffic, the wind in the trees, and the splashing of a water bird on the lake. I took a copy of the photo of binoculars man from my bag. "There's one more person you should look into. He keeps turning up wherever Scott is. I saw him in a rowboat on the Serpentine when Scott was jogging, and again at a campaign rally."

"Good God, Kate. Anyone else on your roster of villains?"

I decided not to grace that with an answer.

Clarke flipped through the three photos one more time. "So my next obvious question is, why are you so sure anyone means harm to Simon Scott?"

"He's running for office. He could be our next Prime Minister. It's inevitable he'd be a target."

There was a chance that Clarke would accept my explanation at face value. But he didn't.

"Inevitable?" He cocked his head to one side, his green eyes narrowed. "Please don't tell me this has anything at all to do with your, how can I put this, psychic abilities?"

I clutched my bag to my chest. I hated talking to Clarke about auras, but there was no choice. "Simon Scott has an aura. So does Kevin Lewis. There is a real danger. I'm not imagining it."

Clarke failed to suppress a sigh. "Kate, I know you mean well, but I can't take action based on these aura things. They don't really tell us anything useful. Nothing about how and when. They're not much more than monsters in a closet and are just as ephemeral as those childhood fears. They come, they go, they're indeterminate, and only you can see them."

I closed my eyes for a few seconds, willing myself to stay calm and not say anything that would give Clarke an excuse to get up and walk away.

"You know I'm not imagining them," I said. I twisted on the bench to look him in the eye. "A person with an aura will die. And the faster the aura is moving, the sooner death will occur."

"Yes, I remember you telling me all this last year."

"And I was right! You can't deny it. I helped you find the killer."

He held the photos out for me to take. "There's nothing I can do. I can't just drag people in off the street to interrogate them without cause."

"The police are always asking the public to report suspicious activity, for God's sake. What's the point if you won't follow up?"

He gave me a sidelong grin. "You're tetchy today."

"And so would you be if you were being ignored and patronized."

"Scott has a security detail everywhere he goes," he said. "He's already as protected as it's possible to be."

I shook my head. "I was at a rally earlier this week. A man threw a stone at him. It hit him in the head and drew blood. What if the assailant had had a grenade or something else more deadly than a rock? Scott was completely exposed."

Clarke nodded. "I heard about it," he admitted.

"So…"

"I'm going to lose my job one day. If my boss knew I was even listening to you, I'd be out on my ear."

"Your boss needs to widen his horizons."

Clarke smiled and stood up. "How about a hot chocolate?"

Without waiting for an answer, he started walking again, forcing me to stride fast to keep up with him. Passing a woman and a little boy feeding nuts to two squirrels, we soon reached the stand that sold drinks and sandwiches. Once I had the warm cup in my hands, I followed Clarke as he strode out again, apparently determined to do a complete loop of the huge park. I'd finished my rich, creamy chocolate by the time we reached the exit.

"Thanks for listening to me," I said.

"Yes, well. You take care of yourself. Don't approach any of these people. Leave it with me."

"Ok, but time is running out."

"I'll see what I can do," he said by way of farewell.

15

I was on my way back home when Anita called me. "Lunch?" she said. "I'll bring sandwiches. Let's go the British Museum. I haven't been there for months."

We'd often spend a few hours together there or at the Tate or National Gallery, chatting quietly in front of a Turner landscape or a Caulfield still life. Anita had a theory that we'd absorb knowledge and culture just by being close to the artworks. Osmosis, she called it.

We found a bench in the Egyptian rooms, where we gazed at painted and gilded coffins and linen-wrapped mummies. It was quiet, mercifully free of groups of schoolchildren on field trips. Most of the visitors were elderly locals or American tourists in tennis shoes. A few auras drifted past over grey-haired ladies, but I ignored them.

Anita's aura, on the other hand, demanded my full attention, although it hadn't changed much from the day before. It was strong but no worse, moving sinuously around her hair. The sight of it made me feel nauseous. She leaned back against the wall, legs stretched out in front of her.

"I'm knackered," she said. "I barely slept last night in spite of going to bed early, and I was back in the hospital at the crack of dawn. I'm not sure what's wrong with me. I can usually keep up the pace with no problem."

"Did you get all the check-ups I asked you to?"

"Yes, I did. EKG, blood work, all the standard stuff. I'm fit as a fiddle, Kate. Just a little tired. And Dad's driving me crazy."

"Anita, I know it seems far-fetched, but let's just run through some scenarios. Think about those suitors your dad is lining up. Have you had any strange interactions with any of them?"

"All the interactions are strange. Completely bizarre. My mum cooks a fabulous meal, which I don't eat because I'm too worked up about the stranger sitting opposite me. My dad conducts the Indian equivalent of the Spanish Inquisition, bombarding the poor chap with questions about his education, his job, his prospects. And whatever his name is can't eat because he's too occupied answering my father."

"That does sound weird," I said. "But seriously, has any of these potential *inamorati* behaved inappropriately? You know, like stalking?"

"No, of course not," Anita said, but then she frowned. "Well, there is Kai. I have to admit he's odd. He inundated me with texts for a while until I told him to stop or I'd call the police. And I saw him lurking outside the hospital a couple of times."

"When was that?"

She shrugged. "I don't remember exactly. Six months ago, I think."

"Ok, then keep an eye open for him."

"He might be weird, but he's not going to do me in, Kate. That's more than just far-fetched, that's absurd."

I sighed. "It's all absurd at some level," I said. "But humor me and promise to watch out. Please?"

She shifted on the bench to find a more comfortable position.

"Was Dr. Reid at work this morning?" I asked, still clicking through possible connections in my head.

"No, he's on duty this afternoon and evening. Why? Do you want to check on his aura again?" She said "aura" as though it was a swear word.

"I do, actually," I said. "Maybe I'll come over there tomorrow. Has he been okay? No more incidents?"

"No. He's been fine. Maybe he just had a touch of flu or something, because he's back to his normal self now." She frowned. "Oh, and he asked to meet with me tomorrow. It was a little odd, actually, because he looked really uncomfortable about it. That kind of look your boss has when he's going to fire you. I hope he's not going to tell me I'm doing a bad job. I'm giving it all I can."

"Did you ask him what it was about?"

"I tried, but he was in a hurry. I'll just have to be patient until ten tomorrow morning."

"It's probably nothing important. Try not to worry."

Anita stood up suddenly. "Come on, let's go to Asia. I've had enough of staring at dead people."

We strolled slowly to the Asian gallery and found another empty bench. In front of us was a group of painted earthenware figures, guardians of a tomb from the Tang dynasty. It seemed that getting away from dead people was a bit of a challenge in the British Museum.

"I have some interesting news for you," I said. I told her about Chris Melrose. She sat up straight and looked at me, all signs of fatigue gone. "Chris is Simon Scott's son? You've got to be kidding me."

"No really."

She grabbed my hand. "We have to go talk to him, don't you think? I want to see that wall for myself."

"I don't want to go back to his house," I said. "Seeing those mutilated pictures was really creepy. He could be dangerous."

Anita patted her Burberry handbag. "You know me. Always prepared. I've got my pepper spray with me. If he tries anything, we'll take him down. That would be quite enjoyable actually. I could do with working off some pent-up aggression."

"You should go to the gym and hit a punchbag then." I said, images of a fight between Chris and Anita darting through my head. Chris didn't have an aura, which meant that Anita would lose. My pulse began to race at the thought. "No way. We're not going to the house. In fact, we shouldn't talk to him about it at all. I've already told the police."

Anita looked at me in surprise. "You went to the police?"

"Of course. Scott is in danger. I'm sure that Chris is a threat. Think about it. Scott abandoned his mother when she got pregnant. She died just a few months ago, quite young and after what sounds like a tough life. Chris wants revenge."

"Will the police arrest him?"

"I doubt it. There's no evidence. But my detective friend said he'd look into it."

"We could get evidence," Anita said. "We could take a photo of the hate wall. You could give it to your policeman friend."

"No. We'll leave it to the police."

"For crying out loud, Kate. You're no fun," said Anita, wrapping her scarf around her neck. We were looking at Viking treasure when

Anita tried again. "Let's contact Chris and suggest a drink or something. I want to see for myself if you're right. Does he really look like Scott? We'll invite him out for afternoon tea and I'll be frightfully proper, I promise."

Anita had put Chris's number on her mobile when we were all traveling on the bus, in case we got split up. She rang it as soon as we got outside and he answered, somewhat to my surprise. I'd imagined him, knife in hand, in the bedroom, pinning Scott to the wall, intent on destroying him, one slash at a time.

"Okay," Anita spoke into the phone. "How about that tearoom just round the corner from St. Paul's? How long do you need? Good, see you there."

Thirty minutes later, we were seated at a table in the cozy cafe, where white tablecloths provided the only respite from the profusion of pink, gold and blue porcelain teacups, saucers, and teapots that adorned every level surface. Most of the tables were full, and a quiet hum of conversation offered a soothing counterpoint to Vivaldi playing in the background.

"When you said afternoon tea, I thought you were joking," I said to Anita, who grinned, obviously happy with her chosen meeting place.

Chris arrived not long afterwards, bringing a rush of cold air in with him.

"Chris, we have something to ask you," I said when the tea had arrived. "Was your mother Phoena Stamos?"

He lifted his eyes to meet mine. "What?"

"I came across some information on her when I was doing some background research on Simon Scott for a story," I said. "I learned that she was a friend of Scott's when they were at Cambridge together."

He shrugged. "So what? That was a long time ago."

"Because I think you're Simon Scott's son."

Chris's hand trembled and he put his teacup down slowly. "That's ridiculous," he said. "My father was William Melrose." His cheeks were flushed and his eyes glittered.

"No, he wasn't. Melrose married your mother when you were, what, five or six years old? It's okay, Chris. I'm just interested, that's all."

"Interested? Sounds like more than that to me. This is none of your business."

I glanced at Anita, hoping she would say something. This had been her idea, to talk to Chris. Now she didn't even seem to be listening.

"I'm sorry, Chris. You're right. It's none of my business. Forget I said anything."

We were all silent for a minute. I crumbled a piece of scone into small pieces on my plate, wishing we hadn't come.

"Tell me why you want to know," Chris said. "What difference does it make?"

"It could maybe demonstrate what kind of man Simon Scott is," I said. "Does he know about you? Did your mum ever tell him?"

"No, she didn't."

He looked at his watch, then poured more tea into his cup. His hand steadied and the flush was fading from his cheeks. "I really don't want to talk about it, Kate. Everything that happened is old history. It caused all sorts of problems for my mother, but I'm not letting it affect my life. I've moved on."

"So why are you volunteering on Scott's campaign? That doesn't seem like moving on."

His cheeks reddened again. "My mum died a few months ago. I don't have any other relatives in England and very limited contact with my family back in Greece. I talk to my grandmother, and one of my aunts, but that's all. I don't know, maybe I wanted to reach out, to make a connection. Anyway, I hadn't realized that Scott would never come to the campaign office or meet with the volunteers. I thought I'd have a chance to talk to him at some point, but that was just wishful thinking on my part."

"Have you tried to contact him? To tell him he's your father?"

"I wrote to him once, hoping to get him to apologize to my mother or something, I don't know. I was only sixteen when I wrote the letter. I never heard back from him."

"So he does know you exist," I said. I felt that information settle like a rock in my stomach. I couldn't imagine what would drive a man to refuse to acknowledge his own son.

He shrugged. "Like I said, it's ancient history. I'm not going to make the same mistake my mum made, living in the past, full of regret. She was happy with my stepfather for a while, but after he died, she just seemed to give up. We never had any money. She wouldn't look for a job. She didn't fight back. That's why I'm working so hard to get my doctorate."

I thought of Eliza Chapman and her derailed career, asking myself how it could be that Simon Scott had done so much damage to the lives of two bright young women. Was he to blame? Were they?

Anita moved her chair back. "I need to go to the loo," she said. "Do you need to go, Kate?"

I was about to say no, but she squeezed my arm. Not sure what was going on, I nodded. "Okay. We'll be straight back, Chris."

I followed Anita, tripping over a step in my haste to keep up. I was worried that she was ill. But when we reached the pink-papered bathroom, Anita didn't rush into a stall. Instead she turned and looked at me. An air freshener pumped out the scent of lavender.

"Are you all right?" I asked her.

"Did you see the stains on Chris's fingers?"

"I didn't notice anything," I said, although now I was thinking about it, I realized that he did have orange marks on both hands.

"Nitric acid can cause that kind of marking on the skin. It starts off yellow but turns orange when it is diluted with water. You know, if you got drops of acid on your skin, you'd run your hands under water to neutralize the acid burns? And when he took off his coat, there was an odor. I've been trying to place it, something like acetone or peroxide."

"So? He's a chemical engineering student."

"I know he is, but those elements I mentioned can be used to make explosives."

"Explosives?"

"Yes, Kate. Isn't that why we're here? To find out what he's planning against Scott? Well, I think he's planning a bomb attack of some kind."

16

When we went back to our table, Chris had gone. He'd left a twenty-pound note tucked under his plate, more than enough to pay for his share of our partially-consumed meal.

"That's a definite sign of guilt," said Anita. "Running away."

I wasn't so sure. Chris had been blindsided by my interrogation and by Anita's silence. If I were him, I'd have left as well. Anita gathered up her things. "Come on, I think we should tell the police at once."

"Just give me a minute," I said, digging in my pocket for a clean tissue. I put on my leather gloves to pick up the note Chris had left, wrapped it carefully in the tissue and put it in my bag. An elderly couple at the nearest table watched me closely.

"Are you a detective?" the lady asked. "Did that nice young man do something wrong?"

"He works for Russian intelligence," I said. "But we'll catch him, don't worry."

The lady turned to her husband in excitement. "Did you hear that, George?"

"Can you leave money for the bill?" I asked Anita. "I'll pay you back later."

"I will if you tell me why you took the note?"

"We can have it tested to see if you're right about the kind of chemicals Chris had on his hands. It's possible that some traces would have transferred to the paper when he took the note out of his wallet."

"Not if he washed his hands thoroughly," she said. "But it's worth a try."

"Let's go past the police station and drop off this note," I suggested.

When we got there, the desk sergeant told us that Clarke was out. I was disappointed; I wanted to introduce him to Anita. I left a short message, explaining the bank note, feeling a little nauseous as I wrote it. I really liked Chris and this felt like a betrayal. But if I could stop him from doing something stupid, I was doing the right thing.

We left the police station, immediately pounded by needle sharp rain and a blustery wind that blew my hair into tangles. Anita tucked her arm through mine. Together we hurried through the darkening streets, past brightly-lit shop windows full of mannequins and dresses and shoes. Normal pursuits like shopping for clothes seemed like a vague and distant dream.

We were cold and wet by the time we reached my flat, where I turned on lamps and music, and closed the blinds against the increasingly vile weather outside. Anita poured two glasses of wine while I checked the fridge and cupboards for dinner ingredients. Once we'd decided on fettuccine with mushrooms, we divvied up the preparations, falling seamlessly into the way we'd cooked together for years when we were students. We hadn't done this since Anita came back from a one-year residency at a hospital in Boston. I often cooked with Josh, though, and wondered how he was doing. We'd only exchanged a few texts since our argument the previous week. It was time to mend the rift. Using my phone to take a picture of Anita and me together, I sent it to him. "Missing you," I texted.

He sent a message straight back "I miss you too. Out with clients talking work. I'll ring you later."

"So, I'm still waiting to hear how you came to make friends with a detective," Anita said.

"He investigated the death of my friend Rebecca. She and I took the same structural design classes at university, but you never met her, I don't think. Anyway, she was one of my first aura sightings. I did what I could, but…" I trailed off, the silence broken by the rhythmic knife strokes on the chopping board as Anita diced onions. She put the knife down and looked at me, eyes wide.

"She died? Was she murdered?"

I nodded. Even now, it depressed me to think about it.

"And she had an aura? Like mine?"

"Yes.

Anita picked up the knife and attacked the mushrooms, slicing them with surgical accuracy.

My mobile buzzed. I picked it up, expecting it to be Josh again. Instead it was a text from Colin Butler. "Check your email. Got a hit on that photo."

Anita replenished our wineglasses while I opened my laptop and logged on.

"Hey, look at this," I said, glad of a reason to change the subject. "This is the man who was watching Scott with binoculars in the park. I gave his photo to Butler to check it out. He says the guy's name is David Lowe, and he was once arrested for threatening Scott with a knife. That's why his picture is on file."

"Let me see." Anita turned the laptop so she could view the screen better. Colin's email went on to say that Lowe's wife had died during an operation performed by Simon Scott. The hospital had denied any wrongdoing but when Lowe had turned up at Scott's medical office brandishing a knife at him, he had to be subdued by two porters. No charges were pressed because no injury had been inflicted, but Lowe was put under a restraining order.

Anita sat back and took a big gulp of her wine. "That was eight years ago. You think he's still holding a grudge against Scott after all that time?"

"Maybe," I said. "Wouldn't you, if you'd lost your spouse, and the doctor who did the surgery was about to be elected to the highest political office in England? You'd probably be resentful and angry. So now we have three possible suspects, assuming that Scott's aura indicates death from a violent act of some kind."

"Three?"

"Chris, Lowe and Eliza Chapman. A long shot, but she's mad enough."

"All the more reason to talk to Clarke," said Anita. She looked at her watch. "I suppose he doesn't work late?"

"He'll get my message and call me, I'm certain," I said. I yawned. "If he doesn't ring back by nine, I'll try again. For now, I think we should try not to think about all this and enjoy dinner and a movie. What do you want to watch?"

"Anything as long as it's not a romantic comedy," said Anita. "No happy ever after, no cute but awkward scenes where everyone except the girl knows the boy's going to get the girl. Nothing with kissing in it."

I squeezed her arm. "Love really isn't that bad, you know."

"Your dad isn't trying to set you up with an 'appropriate' suitor. He never stops. Really, he's turned it into a bloody full-time job. Amin, Ash, Atri. We're still on the A's and we've got twenty-five more letters to go. I'll have lost the will to live by the time Z comes around. Then Dad can marry my corpse off to poor Zev or Zulfikar."

She unzipped her boots and threw them behind the sofa. I'd always gone around cleaning up after her when we shared a flat. "We had another dinner week this where I couldn't swallow a mouthful because I was so nauseated by the whole process. Maybe I'll end up expiring of malnutrition."

I wished Anita wouldn't joke about dying. It made me feel queasy, so I stood up to go finish dinner. "Find the remote and look for a movie," I said. "Let's stick to a classic. No violence, no terrorists, and definitely nothing creepy. My nerves won't take it."

"Then I think we're going to end up with Sesame Street reruns," she said.

I heard Anita's phone ring while I was pouring pasta into a pan. A minute later, she rushed into the kitchen, pulling on her boots. "I have to go to the hospital. The nurse on duty said to get there quickly."

"A patient emergency?" I asked.

"Probably. She said something about Dr. Reid, but I didn't really catch it." She bent down to zip up her boots. When she straightened up, she looked worried. "She sounded a little panicked, which is really unlike her."

"I'll come with you," I said, turning off the gas under the pasta.

"Don't be daft. There's nothing you can do. Finish making dinner and I'll be back as soon as I can."

I hesitated. Anita was probably right. There was nothing I could do at the hospital, but her mention of Dr. Reid had alarm bells ringing in my head.

"You'll need to get a taxi. I'll come to keep you company on the ride." I was counting on her being in too much of a rush to argue. With a slightly exasperated sigh, she nodded. We grabbed our coats from the hall cupboard and ran down the three flights of stairs. I lived on a quiet residential street without much chance of a taxi going by, so we sprinted to the corner of Bayswater Road, my heeled boots threatening to turn my ankle at every contact with the rain-slick pavement. Almost immediately, an empty taxi approached. Anita flagged it down. "London General," she said. "Fast as you can. It's an emergency." She held up her ID badge.

"Will do, doc," the driver responded, pulling into traffic.

"What else did the nurse say?" I asked.

"Nothing. It was Pauline. She's a good soul and a great nurse. But it must be something important or she would have just paged me."

17

My stomach was in knots. I stared at the blurred lights blinking red and amber through the rain-soaked windscreen, jiggling one leg up and down. Anita shifted closer to me on the bench seat, taking my hand in hers.

"Kate, you should have stayed home. You don't need to deal with whatever this is. I can see it's unnerving for you. We're trained to handle this kind of stress. You're not."

I didn't answer. Anita had no idea how much stress I suffered when I saw an aura over someone. My first reaction was always guilt. Guilt that I knew something incredibly personal about that person. What could be more intimate than knowing that death is hovering, ready to strike soon, often far sooner than anyone could imagine or expect? Following guilt, I ran through a gamut of emotions, from outrage and anger to anguish and despondency.

Self-hatred raised its head occasionally as well, when I thought about how I could be proactively using my gift to save more lives. If I tried harder, surely I could stop awful things happening to innocent people. I could travel the world, watching for signs that would foretell a mass disaster, like tsunamis in Asia, terrorist bombs in the East, train crashes, plane crashes, school shootings in America. But I also knew that thinking that way could quickly drive me crazy, certifiably insane. So I stuck to merely coping with my gift. Enough trouble came my way without my going to look for it.

This wasn't the time to explain any of this to Anita, so I remained silent, wanting the ride to be over. When we reached the hospital, there were several emergency vehicles, including a police car, parked outside. That was perfectly normal for a hospital with an emergency facility, of course, but they made me even more uneasy. We took the lift to the fourth floor, which was awash with lights. Four nurses, gathered at the reception desk, were talking with a uniformed police officer. I saw that, further along the hallway, all of the patient room doors were closed.

A tall brunette in pink scrubs looked in our direction and came to meet us, her shoes squeaking loudly on the lino floor.

"Pauline, what's going on?" Anita asked.

"I'm really sorry." Pauline's eyes brimmed with tears.

"What happened?"

Pauline held her hand to her mouth, not answering.

I was ready to strangle Pauline. "What happened?" I asked, repeating Anita's question.

"Dr. Reid's dead," she said.

Anita blanched. "What?"

"They're saying he committed suicide."

"Never," breathed Anita. "Dr. Reid would never take his own life."

"No," said Pauline. "I don't think so, either."

"Where?" Anita asked.

Pauline looked confused. "Where is he? They rushed him down to Emergency to see if they could resuscitate him but..." Her voice broke as tears spilled down her cheeks.

"No, where was he when he was found?"

"He was in one of the examination rooms, 2B, I think. The janitor found him."

My lungs were having trouble functioning. They felt as though a heavy weight were lying on them. Dr. Reid had an aura. Now he was dead and I hadn't done anything to stop it happening. All that guilt and helplessness welled up inside me, stopping my breath.

"I have to go. The nurses are all upset but they need to get back to work." Pauline turned back towards the reception desk. I grabbed Anita's hand, but she shook it free and walked down the hall. I followed close behind.

"Where are we going?" I asked.

She didn't answer. We came to a stop outside Dr. Reid's office. The door was open and blocked by a uniformed policeman. Peering around him, I saw two men in white jumpsuits. They seemed to be dusting for fingerprints. The chair behind the desk was pushed up against the wall but everything else looked as tidy as when I'd visited Reid a few days earlier.

"Who are you?" The policeman's voice was gruff and unfriendly.

"I'm Dr. Anita Banerjee. I work here and I need access to Dr. Reid's computer." She took her badge out of her purse and showed it to him.

"You can't go in there," he said.

"I have to. I have sick children to care for and will need to check on Dr. Reid's patients."

"I thought it was a suicide," I said, wondering why the police were there at all.

"We're obliged to review all instances of unattended death," he said. "Just routine."

With a final glower at the officer, Anita turned away, walking fast in the direction of her office. I hurried after her. Closing the door behind us, she sank into her seat, burying her face in her hands, her shoulders heaving. I knelt down next to her chair, putting my arms around her, feeling her tremble. We stayed like that for a couple of minutes until the shaking subsided. She wiped tears from her cheeks with the back of her hand. I stood up to grab some tissues from a box on the credenza behind her desk.

"He wouldn't have committed suicide," she said. "That would go against everything he believes in. He was dedicated to making kids better. He'd never abandon his patients. The children mean everything to him."

I pulled out the visitor chair and sat, elbows on the desk, facing her. "But everyone seems to think he did. Kill himself."

She shook her head. "I don't believe it."

"Okay, maybe it wasn't suicide," I said. "Maybe it was an accident. Perhaps he was having a heart attack or some other health issue. Was he on medication? Maybe he overdosed by mistake. Won't the autopsy show if he had a serious medical event? There'll have to be an autopsy, won't there?"

Anita nodded. "Yes. God, this makes no sense."

The lights in the ceiling buzzed gently in the silence that followed. I didn't know how to comfort her.

"And I'm scared," she said.

I swallowed hard but couldn't shift the lump in my throat.

"Kate, you said he was going to die and he did." Anita's voice shook. "And you say I'm going to die too. I don't want to die. I want you to make the aura go away."

I didn't know what to say. I was terrified too of what might happen to her, and the risk seemed all the more real now that Dr. Reid was dead.

18

Finally Anita seemed to collect herself. She stood up, bent her head from side to side as though working kinks out of her neck, and walked to the small washroom adjoining her office to splash water on her face and comb her hair.

"Let's find out what's going on out there."

Back at the reception desk, she stopped to talk with Pauline. While they discussed Dr. Reid's patients, I wandered along the corridor to see that the men in white jumpsuits were finishing up in Dr. Reid's office. Closing the door, they pinned yellow tape across it. There was no sign of the policeman we'd talked to earlier.

Unsure what I could do, I walked back to the nurses' station.

"There's nothing on my schedule this evening," said Anita. "Everyone is tucked in and sleeping. We may as well go home." She looked at Pauline. "I'll come in first thing in the morning. Call me, though, if anything at all comes up, okay?"

When we got home, I suggested Anita take a bath to relax. To my surprise, she agreed. Relaxing wasn't usually high on her priority list, but she was moving slowly, as though her muscles were tired and tight. Hot water would be good for her.

I gave her a pair of my PJs and went to the kitchen to make chamomile tea, while thoughts of Dr. Reid swirled in my brain. A bath suddenly seemed like a bad idea; I imagined Anita drowning or falling and hitting her head on the tile floor. Leaving the tea to brew, I went to the bathroom door to listen for any sounds of trouble, then sat down, leaning against the door. Over the last year, I'd developed an arsenal of techniques to keep myself calm when faced with an aura and all its implications. Taking some deep breaths, I felt my heart rate slow down.

Encounters with the dead and visions of auras that predict death have made me realize that there are forces that humans don't understand. I don't pretend to know more about the mysteries of existence than anyone else, but I do believe that coincidences are always worth investigating. Dr. Reid and Anita both had auras. Now Dr. Reid was dead and I was certain that Anita's fate was connected to his in some way.

When I heard the water draining. I stood up and moved away from the door, waiting until Anita emerged with a towel wrapped around her. She looked at me suspiciously. "What are you doing in the hallway?"

"Just cleaning up," I said, adjusting a framed photo of my parents on the wall. "That's better."

"Good, because I'd hate to think you were listening out for sounds of drowning or anything like that," she said with a hint of a smile. "You can't protect me, Kate, and I don't want you to try. I can look after myself. Death is not going to lay its ugly hands on me just yet."

We took our tea into the living room. I turned on a lamp, its soft glow warming the room.

Anita settled on the sofa, pulling a throw up to her shoulders. "Kate, I want to know everything about the auras. I need to understand them so that I can deal with them. They say ignorance is bliss, but not for me. The more I know, the better I feel."

It felt good to talk, to tell Anita everything that had happened, starting with how guilty I'd felt about my mother's death a year ago. I'd been texting with her when she was run over in a pedestrian crossing by an elderly motorist. Everyone said it wasn't my fault, but I'd always had a predisposition to guilt. My baby brother, Toby, had drowned in a pool when I was supposed to be watching him. The burden of thinking I could have saved him had weighed on me for the last seventeen years.

"I sometimes think now that if I'd seen an aura over Toby that afternoon, I would have known to pay more attention," I told Anita. "I'd never have been distracted or left him alone even for a second."

"You think that's why you can see auras now?" Anita asked. "As a way of compensating for losing Toby? Or your mum perhaps?"

I shrugged. I didn't know why I could see auras. I only knew that my life had been turned upside down for the last year.

Anita sipped her tea. "Have you ever wondered if seeing an aura is what actually causes death?" she asked.

"What? You think I make the danger appear? That's ridiculous."

"Maybe, but think about it. There's something called the observer effect in physics. The very act of observation changes the object being observed. Like, if you measure the temperature of water in a beaker, the presence of the thermometer affects the temperature. Or, say, if you want to measure an electron, you have to shoot a proton at it."

"And of course, the proton changes the position and movement of the electron. I did physics in school too," I said.

"It's worth considering," Anita went on. "It's just statistically unlikely that you see so many people about to die."

"No, it's not. Wait here." I went to the kitchen to get my laptop. Coming back to sit next to Anita, I opened a local news website. "Look at this," I said, scrolling through the headlines. "Teen stabs man to death on bus. Motorcyclist killed in collision with car. Toddler killed by stepfather. Multi-car crash on M25 kills four. Man dies after falling through open window."

I closed the laptop. "That's just one day, Anita, all here in London. And it doesn't include the hundreds of non-newsworthy deaths from heart attacks and other diseases, accidental falls, or overdoses. Most people don't choose to acknowledge that death is so pervasive. I have no choice."

She put her hand on my arm. "I'm sorry. I really didn't mean to imply you were responsible. I just find the idea of a physical manifestation of impending death so—"

"Unbelievable," I said.

She nodded.

Further conversation was, thankfully, interrupted by the ringing on my mobile. It was Detective Clarke. For a moment, I was confused, unsure why he was calling me. Then I remembered the message I'd left about Chris, and the twenty-pound note we'd left at the police station. All that seemed like a long time ago now, completely overshadowed by Dr. Reid's death. But it would be rude to brush him off.

He asked me for more information and asked if I'd heard anything at all from Chris. I'd tried calling Chris a couple of times since his abrupt departure from the tearoom. He wasn't answering.

"Call me if you hear from him," Clarke said. "We're doing what we can to trace him."

I promised I would.

19

It was hard for me to watch Anita leave the next morning. I wanted to stay close to her, to protect her from whatever threat was out there, but I couldn't follow her around all day. She had to go to work, to be with her patients and their families. Nobody wanted me hanging around, getting in the way. After working on some illustrations for my dad's book for a couple of hours, I was relieved when Anita texted me, asking me to bring sandwiches for three and to meet her in the hospital lobby. When I got there, she was waiting. She looked tired.

"Are you doing all right?" I asked.

"Well enough," she said. "It's been so busy, I've barely had time to think. But I've got a break now and want to go down to talk with Grace Trillo. She's head of the Forensic Pathology department."

I shook my head. "I don't want to meet a pathologist."

"Come on, Kate. She's fun. You'll like her."

I wouldn't have put the words "fun" and "forensic pathology" in the same sentence, but I followed Anita to a bank of lifts at the back of the building. Using a keypad where the call button would usually be, Anita entered a number. The doors immediately opened to reveal a large cabin, big enough to hold a gurney or two. The metal walls were dinged in multiple places and the overhead light flickered ominously. I tried to ignore the creaking and jolting of the battered cage as it lurched downwards. When we reached the basement, we stepped into a corridor with green walls and tan lino floors, lit by buzzing fluorescent lights. I followed Anita to a set of double doors, where she pressed buttons on another keypad.

"I can't imagine that the security is to stop people getting out," I joked, clutching the sandwich bag closer to my chest. I'd seen my first dead body a year ago and I wasn't relishing the thought of seeing any more.

We entered an autopsy room dominated by two stainless steel operating tables. Steel cabinets lined the walls. The floor and ceiling were covered in white tiles. A strong smell hung in the air, sharp and sweet. My knees began to shake.

A slim woman in a white coat was lining up scalpels on a stainless steel counter. She appeared to be in her mid-forties and had pixie-cut blonde hair, with striking blue eyes under perfectly groomed eyebrows.

"Anita, love, how are you doing?" she asked, striding across the room to give her a hug. "I'm sorry about Dr. Reid. I know you two were close."

When Anita introduced me, I shook hands with Grace, noticing her perfect French manicure.

"Did you bring sandwiches?" Grace asked. "I'm starving."

When I held up the bag, she smiled. "Great. Let's eat."

"Here?" I asked.

"Well, we could. The place is spotless. You could eat off the floor and it'd be safer than your average kitchen counter."

"No thanks all the same," I said, eager to get out of the cold, hard room.

We followed her next door into a cluttered, untidy office, where we sat on uncomfortable straight back chairs grouped around her desk. I handed out the sandwiches and water but didn't open my own. The morgue had twisted my stomach into knots and killed my appetite. I couldn't imagine how Grace worked here every day, with dead bodies for company.

Anita took a bite of her shrimp on rye. "Who's the coroner on the case?"

"Margerison," said Grace. "That's good. He's a detail freak. Everyone is really upset about Dr. Reid, and they're throwing the most senior resources at the investigation. Margerison has tons of experience."

"And they gave you the autopsy because you're the best," said Anita. "What did you find out?"

Grace washed her beef sandwich down with a large gulp of water.

"Not much yet. I've sent all the samples for testing. They've been given high priority, but you know toxicology analysis can take a while. We probably won't know anything for at least a couple of weeks."

"But do you have an idea of what happened?" I asked. "How did Dr. Reid die?"

"My guess is that a lethal cocktail of insulin, digitoxin and midazolam, or substances like them, were delivered by an IV into his left arm. The IV was still attached, the drip bag empty, but forensics can analyze the traces to pinpoint the exact medications. It certainly supports the suicide theory."

Grace brushed some crumbs off the desk on to the floor. Obviously, cleanliness wasn't as important in the office as it was in the autopsy room.

"And those drugs are lethal?" I asked.

"In that mix at a sufficient dose, yes. Midazolam knocks you out, which has the additional benefit, if you can call it that, of not allowing you to change your mind. The digitoxin causes arrhythmia and the insulin, in a high dose, induces a hypoglycemic coma. So, you're unconscious, your heart beats erratically, and the result is a cardiac arrest. You never wake up. It's not a bad way to go, if you're intent on going."

"Damn." Anita slumped forward, elbows on the desk.

"Where would Dr. Reid have got hold of those medications?" I asked.

Grace and Anita exchanged looks. "It's not hard," Anita said. "Doctors write prescriptions for them every day. Cardiac drugs, insulin, sedatives. All of them are common enough treatments for our patients."

"It wouldn't be the first time either," added Grace. "I've seen two other cases like this one, both of them doctors and obvious suicides."

I twisted off the top of my water bottle but didn't drink. "Was there a note?" I asked. "Don't suicides usually leave notes?"

"I followed up on that this morning," said Anita. "Pauline spoke to Dr. Reid's wife briefly and there was no letter at the house. No one has found anything here either."

"Inconclusive," said Grace. "A sudden wave of depression, no time to think about penning a goodbye missive. It's not unusual."

Anita shook her head slowly. "Not Dr. Reid. He wouldn't kill himself. I'm sure of it. He always said that our goal, as doctors, is to be useful. And you can't be useful if you're dead."

We sat in silence for a minute. "Are you sure there was nothing else?" Anita asked finally. "No signs of a struggle?"

Grace shook her head. "Nothing. The body was remarkably clean..." She stopped when she caught sight of the look on Anita's face. "Sorry, I know Dr. Reid was more than just a body. But other than the puncture for the IV needle, there no other signs of abuse, drug use, nothing."

She finished her sandwich and crumpled up her paper napkin. Shaping it into a ball, she lobbed it across the desk. I turned to watch it drop into a wastepaper basket behind me.

"Played netball at school," she said with a grin.

"What was the time of death?" Anita asked.

"I put it at about eight p.m. Possibly as early as seven-thirty. His body was discovered at eight forty-five."

I put my uneaten lunch back into the plastic carrier bag. Grace looked up hopefully. "What kind of sandwich do you have there?"

"Egg salad."

"Great, I'll have it."

I handed it to her. She opened the packet, gave a section of the sandwich to Anita, and took a big bite of the other half.

"The nurses change shifts at eight," said Anita. "There would have been a fair amount of coming and going at that time, but the examination rooms wouldn't normally be in use that late in the evening."

"So Dr. Reid found a quiet space where he wouldn't be disturbed," said Grace.

"Why at work?" I asked. "Why not at home?"

Grace shrugged. "Maybe he'd have even less privacy at home. And at work, he had access to the drugs and the equipment. It makes sense to me."

"I still don't believe it was suicide," Anita was folding her paper napkin into a tiny triangle. "He wouldn't do that. I saw him earlier in the afternoon and he was absolutely fine. In fact, he was telling me about his plans for the weekend, going to a niece's wedding in Oxford with his wife."

"I don't know, Anita," said Grace. "Suicides can be very good at pretending, at making plans, feigning happiness. Relatives will say afterwards that they had no indication their son, or daughter, or husband was contemplating killing themselves." She looked sad. "But it happens, more often than you'd think."

"I suppose you get plenty of opportunities to investigate causes of death?" I asked her.

She nodded. "Yes, though it's not my job, of course. The coroner officially heads the investigations, but he trusts my opinion and I've helped him a few times. In my spare time, I read masses of forensic reports, and study different areas of forensic science, like blood spatter patterns, toxicology, ballistics. I love it all."

"And then there's Egypt," said Anita, somewhat cryptically. I raised an eyebrow at Grace.

"Well, that's my real area of interest, my passion really," said Grace. "I know all about embalming and burial rites. Which isn't surprising given that I was an Egyptian embalmer in a former life."

I laughed, but stopped when her expression remained completely serious.

"Really," she said. "I lived in the Twentieth Dynasty during the reign of Rameses III. I was the chief embalmer at the massive funerary complex, Medinet Habu, adjoining the royal palace in Thebes, and I was responsible for the preparation and burial of members of the royal family. That's what made me go into this business of being a forensic pathologist. I knew when I was about five years old that it was what I wanted to do."

She stopped talking and stared at me. "Anita thinks I'm crazy. I expect you do too."

"No, I don't," I replied. "Not at all."

"Kate can see auras that predict death," Anita said.

Grace's face lit up. "Fascinating."

Only two other people had ever greeted that revelation so matter of factly: Sister Chiara, in Tuscany, who had helped me accept my new "gift" and Olivia, my brother's lovely wife. Funnily enough, Olivia looked like Cleopatra with her straight black hair and heavily-kohled eyes. She and Grace would probably get on like a house on fire.

"But the worse thing is that Anita has an aura too," I said.

Grace's eyes widened and she stared at Anita. "I can't see anything."

"No, but it's there. That's why we have to work out how Dr. Reid died. If it was foul play, then Anita may be at risk from the killer."

"All right," said Grace, pulling her chair closer to the desk and leaning forward on the fake wood surface. "Let's assume that this wasn't suicide. You think he was murdered? By whom and why? More importantly, how? Dr. Reid wouldn't just lie there waiting for someone to stick an IV in his arm."

"I don't know about the why," replied Anita. "So let's start with who and how. We've just agreed that there were people about, other doctors, nurses and patients."

"What about visitors?" I asked. "Do you have visiting hours?"

"We encourage visitors to come between ten in the morning and six in the evening," said Anita. "But many parents are present twenty-four hours a day. They stay overnight, sleeping in chairs next to the kids' beds. So, yes, there are always people around. But why would a parent want to kill the doctor who's treating his child? That doesn't make sense."

"Maybe someone pretending to be a parent then," I said.

"That's a thought," said Grace. "Although I still don't see how. Dr. Reid wasn't going to lie there meekly while someone put a needle in his arm."

"Maybe he was incapacitated somehow," I ventured. "Knocked out for long enough to get the IV running?"

"There was no damage to the head or any other organ, so he wasn't physically punched, stabbed or assaulted with a weapon of any kind."

"Another drug then," I said.

"That could be the answer," said Anita. "What do you think, Grace? Flunitrazepam? A couple of tablets of that would dissolve easily in a cup of coffee and have an almost instantaneous effect."

"What is it?" I asked.

"It's best known as Rohypnol," Grace said. "The date rape drug."

"Oh." I couldn't think of anything to say. A cornucopia of terrifying concoctions circulated hospitals, it seemed. Drugs that could save lives, but take them too.

Grace cupped her chin in her hands, her slender fingers cradling her cheeks. "The Grand Vizier, Aat, was murdered by men who thought he had too much influence with the Pharaoh. He was stabbed to death by five different weapons, but first he was drugged. They put a sleeping potion in his wine. That way he couldn't resist, or make a noise that his guards would have heard. He was assassinated in complete silence, in his room, with eight bodyguards standing just beyond the curtains. By the time his body was discovered, the murderers had dispersed, making their way to their rooms throughout the palace. None of them was ever caught. Back then, of course, we didn't have the tools to show that a drug had been used. My master knew, though, how it had happened. His brother was one of the assassins."

Images flashed in front of my eyes. Candles casting a flickering light on the gruesome scene. A group of men, each with a sharp blade, bowing over the unconscious man, the arc of the knives, the sound of iron plunging into unresisting flesh, the splatter of hot blood.

Anita broke the silence, pulling me back into the twenty-first century. "So who would want to murder Dr. Reid?"

"It would have to be a medical professional," Grace said. "Someone who knew that particular mix of drugs would cause death very quickly, and who also knew how to set up an IV."

I looked at her in surprise. "You mean you think it was another doctor?"

"A doctor, a nurse, a pharmacist. Or anyone who knows how to google "ways to kill people."" Grace looked indignant. "You can find anything on the web nowadays, even how to build bombs, for God's sake."

For a moment, my attention was diverted to Simon Scott. A bomb seemed like a highly likely form of threat to him. I hoped that Clarke was working on it.

"Yes, but you still need access," Anita said. "Those are all regulated drugs. You can't pick them up over the counter. Of course, a doctor could get them at the hospital pharmacy."

"We should go talk to Ted," said Grace. She glanced at me. "He's the head of hospital pharmacy. I've worked with him on a few overdose cases. He's very knowledgeable."

"Right," said Anita. "But first, I'd like to ask a few more questions up on the fourth floor."

Grace stood up. "Let's get to work then."

Up at the Pediatric Unit, I paused to look out of a window. The sky was still grey and overcast but, after the windowless gloom of the basement, the light felt pure and invigorating. I paused for half a minute before following the others towards the nurses' station, where I recognized Pauline, the nurse who had discovered Dr. Reid's body. She looked distraught and red-eyed.

"Pauline, we need to talk to you," Anita said. "Do you have a minute? Come with us."

We all crowded into the small kitchen, where Grace poured herself a cup of coffee. "The coffee's better up here," she said. "Downstairs, it's always treacly and disgusting. Must be something to do with the particles in the air." She waved the carafe around. "Anyone?"

My stomach was doing flips at the description of the coffee in the autopsy suite. "No, thanks."

"Dr. Margerison has already been up," Pauline said. "Asking questions and taking notes. A detective too. What's going on? I thought Dr. Reid committed suicide?"

"Everyone just wants to be sure of what happened," said Grace, taking charge. "You were the one the janitor came to when he found Dr. Reid, right?"

"Yes, I was here at the nurses' station. Maurice rushed up the hallway in a panic. We called down to Emergency at once."

"And you didn't see anyone else go into that exam room or come out of it?"

She shook her head. "I was busy supervising the evening medication rounds. And we had an alert in 4C that was a false alarm, but it caused a bit of chaos, happening right then during the shift change."

"So who was here before you began the medication rounds?"

Pauline seemed to think for a minute. "I can check the roster, but there were four nurses. And Dr. Schwartz. Dr. Reid of course. Dr. Marks was just going off duty. A couple of sales reps were still here, hoping to grab one of the doctors before they left for the day. Macintyre from LBP and Eric Hill from PharmAnew. I remember because that Hill chap was complaining we'd run out of coffee. And a half dozen visitors."

Pauline dabbed at her eyes. "I wish I could help more. Dr. Reid was a fine man. I'll miss him. Can I go? We're very busy today."

After she hurried out of the kitchen, Grace finished her coffee. "Off to the pharmacy then," she said as she tossed the paper cup into the rubbish bin.

We followed her to the other end of the building where we found a middle-aged pharmacist working at a computer behind a high counter. The only access to his workspace was through a closed door that bore the sign "Strictly No Admittance."

"Hey, Grace," he said. "I didn't know they let you out during daylight hours."

"Haha. Listen, Ted, we need a favor. Could you check your records for prescriptions filled in the last couple of days, for flunitrazepam, midazolam, insulin, and digitoxin or an equivalent, and who they were prescribed by?"

"It would take a while. Most of those are standard issues. There'll be dozens of records."

"How long?"

"I could do it in two days, maybe a little less. I'll work on it after hours tonight and tomorrow. Will that work?"

"The faster the better," Grace said.

"Can you search by the prescribing doctor?" Anita asked.

Ted nodded, his bald head catching the light. "Yep."

"Can you look up all recent prescriptions requested by Dr. Reid?"

He frowned. "What's going on?"

Grace leaned across the counter. "I have two tickets to the English National Opera's production of *Othello*."

He grinned. "You'd go with me?"

"No, I'd give you both the tickets. You can take your girlfriend or boyfriend or anyone you like. You won't have to put up with me for the evening."

"Okay. But you know Dr. Reid was fastidious about medications. He always did everything by the book, writing out proper prescriptions and usually only for a small amount. Just enough to get his patient through the first couple of days. And those drugs you mentioned? Not on his usual list at all."

"But you could check."

"Sure, anything for opera," he said, and began typing on his PC keyboard. He clicked away for a minute or two, the frown lines on his forehead deepening into chasms under the overhead lights.

"Nothing," he said, looking up at us. "Dr. Reid never requested any of those meds. The last one was just his usual, a three-day supply of vicodin. Notes say it was for Joey Nelson, age sixteen."

Anita nodded. "Joey came in with complications from a damaged spleen, after a bad fall. He was discharged two days ago."

"Is that all? I should get back to work," Ted said.

Grace thanked him, promising to come back with the opera tickets later in the day. The three of us retraced our steps to the lobby where she hugged us goodbye and made me swear I'd come back sometime to talk about auras.

20

My afternoon was open and unplanned. It was tempting to go visit Bradley Associates, which was close by. I'd be welcomed back like a prodigal daughter. Alan would be happy, even though he wouldn't show it. I could review the projects, catch up with the team, maybe go for drinks after work. A haven of normalcy shimmered like a gold citadel on a distant hill.

My mobile buzzed. Without checking the caller ID, I answered.

"What the hell is going on, Kate?" It was Eliza Chapman. "It's been days since we talked and I'm not seeing anything in the papers. When is the story coming out?"

"It's on the schedule," I lied. "I'd have to check with the editor to find out exactly when."

"Do that and call me back. If I don't hear from you, I'll follow up on my own."

The phone clicked off. I stared at the blank screen, then slid the phone into my bag. To hell with Eliza, to hell with all of it, I thought, walking with intent towards Paternoster Square and my office. I'd go back to work, look after Anita, and leave Scott and Lewis to the professional ministrations of the police and security forces. But, while my feet were doing my bidding, my mind wasn't cooperating.

I was worried about Eliza. What did she mean by following up on her own? Did she intend to call the editor of the *Messenger* and tell him all about a journalist on his staff who had promised a story? A journalist who in fact wasn't a journalist and wasn't on his staff? Or did she mean that she'd take some sort of action against Scott? I stopped suddenly, a bad idea, as two people barreled into me from behind, both looking at their mobiles. One of them muttered "idiot" as he circumnavigated the obstacle in his path. I moved to the side, leaning against the solid limestone wall of a Lloyds TSB Bank and dialed Clarke's number. He didn't answer, so I left a message telling him what Eliza had said. Then I called Colin Butler. The least I could do was warn him that his boss might hear from her.

"I appreciate the warning," he said after I'd explained. "Not to worry. I'll claim journalistic immunity if Eliza mentions my name."

There was a pause. In the background, I heard the click of a keyboard. "Was there something else, Kate?"

"Not really," I said. "Well, yes, actually. I'd like more information on Simon Scott. I told a detective, a friend of mine, about Eliza, Chris Melrose and the binoculars man but I'm not convinced he's doing anything with the information."

"Hmmm." I guessed Butler was concentrating on something else. Then he spoke. "I'm about to take a lunch break." The clack of the keys stopped. "Let's have a beer, or whatever you young things drink. How about the Mitre? You know it?"

"Of course." We agreed to meet at two. The clacking resumed just before Butler rang off.

I checked my watch. It would be too rushed to get to the office and still make it to the pub, so I set off, weaving my way through the crowds. The pub was a quaint and ancient landmark, popular with locals and tourists, tucked away in a narrow street. When I arrived there, Colin was just going in. "I'll grab a table if you get drinks," he said.

Getting to the bar was like swimming against the tide. "Lemonade and a pint of something good on tap," I shouted above the din. The bartender nodded, returning quickly with both the drinks. Wending my way carefully through the crowd, I found Butler at a small table near the door.

He took a deep swallow of beer before speaking. "What do you need?"

"All the background on Simon Scott," I told him. "His political career, his years as a doctor, his marriage, family, everything."

Butler shifted on his chair, tapping his fingers on the table. "Can I ask why?"

I knew he was going to ask that and had come up with an answer of sorts. "I have it on good authority that there's a serious threat to Scott. Maybe not Chris Melrose, although I have my concerns about him. Nor Eliza Chapman, or that binoculars chap. But someone means him harm. So I'm doing some research to see if there's anything else in his past that might show up as a motive now."

Butler tilted back in his chair, raising the front two legs from the ground. I winced, thinking of all that weight on two spindly supports. He rocked back and forth several times before coming in for a gentle landing. "And this 'good authority' of which you speak? Who would that be?"

"I can't name my sources," I said, thinking I'd heard a phrase like that in a movie I'd seen recently.

Butler's face creased in amusement. "Uh huh. So why don't you tell me the real reason you're digging around, Kate?"

"You want the truth?"

"It's always a good place to start."

I took a swallow of my drink, which was cloyingly sweet. It was all or nothing now. "I have an unusual gift. I can see auras that predict death. Scott has one. So does Kevin Lewis."

To be fair to Butler, he didn't get up and walk out. He ran his finger around the rim of his beer glass several times before looking up at me. "I've heard a lot in my long and checkered career, but this is a first. Do you find it amusing to take the mickey out of a grumpy old journalist?"

"Colin, I'm telling you the truth. The problem is that almost everyone reacts like you. They don't believe me and therefore they don't take any action that might save a life. My only option is to identify what the source of the threat to Scott is. If I can come up with a credible scenario, maybe I can persuade the powers that be to take me seriously."

Without saying a word, he got to his feet, carrying his empty beer glass to the bar. He returned with a replenished pint. "Let's talk," he said. "Tell me more about these death-predicting auras. What do they look like?"

My glass, sweating with condensation, was slippery in my hand. I put it down, carefully positioning it in the dead center of a cardboard coaster. Then I told him everything. Good journalist that he was, Butler listened without interrupting, just nodding his head occasionally. The lenses of his glasses shone like yellow headlights when they caught a ray of the pale lemon sun coming through the bottle-glass window.

When I finished, I hunched forward over the table. Describing my ability always left me exhausted, as though I was using all my energy up in an effort to convince my listener to believe me.

"Remarkable," he said. We sat looking at each other. I was suddenly aware of noise around us, the hum of voices and the clink of glasses, as though someone had turned the volume dial. "So, let's talk about Scott and what you hope to find?"

"Does that mean you believe me?"

"I have no reason not to. Based on our acquaintance, brief though it is, I believe you to be an intelligent and responsible young woman. This gift of yours would explain several things, like your rather pathetic attempt to be a journalist at the event when we first met and your willingness to go to Cambridge to visit Eliza Chapman. This gift is a rather better rationale for your recent behavior than your sudden purported interest in politics."

"I am interested," I protested.

"I think it's very hard to be interested in something you know nothing about," he said. "It would be like me expressing an interest in quantum mechanics."

"*Nothing* is rather harsh," I said. "I know as much as any average voter."

"True. Sad, but true. So let's get on with it then. The best place to start is at my office. We'll have access to a range of resources there."

He drained his beer, wiped a foamy moustache from his top lip and stood up.

"Now?" I asked

"I'm under the impression that there is some urgency to the matter, so yes, now."

It turned out that the *Messenger* offices were only a couple of blocks away, a short walk passed in silence. When we arrived, we walked through a spacious lobby, which was surprisingly and rather disappointingly modern, with a massive "Messenger" logo on the wall behind a reception desk. Comfortable couches, interspersed with plants in shiny black pots, gathered comfortably around coffee tables holding glossy magazines and back copies of the *Messenger*.

My disappointment lasted only a few minutes though as we turned out of the lobby into a narrow corridor with a tan lino floor and beige walls. It led into a large room crammed with cubicles, most of which were occupied. A general buzz of noise hovered like a swarm of bees, the sound of dozens of people on phones or talking loudly over the cubicle walls to their neighbors.

The days of ink and cigarettes were long gone, replaced by computer keyboards and the stale odor of burned coffee, but the flickering light and the cramped workspace had something satisfyingly Dickensian about it.

Colin led the way to his cubicle, set down his bag and draped his huge brown jacket over the back of a rickety chair. His computer screen filled the tiny area with blue light.

"Take a seat," he said. "I'll be back."

He returned a few minutes later with a stack of folders. "Work your way through these," he said. "If anyone asks what you're doing here, tell them you're my intern. I've got some things to finish up. Just take your time."

Opening the first folder, I found a stack of papers that were creased and coffee-stained, pierced with staples or held together with paper clips. The name Scott was highlighted in yellow throughout. It didn't take long to realize that sometimes his name was mentioned only in passing or that the article related to something where he was only marginally involved.

I'd already spent hours researching him on the Internet, and nothing new jumped out at me from the contents of the first folder. I skimmed the second folder and opened the next one, already feeling the disappointment of wasted time. On the second page, I found a collection of news clippings about his wife, an heiress who ran in the same circles as some of the minor royals. Her father, I learned, had founded a luxury food company. Her money and connections had been of huge benefit to Scott when he first went into politics. It seemed from some of the later clippings though, that Daddy had been losing money. He was selling the family house in Hertfordshire as well as several racehorses.

Was it possible that money was the source of the threat to Scott? I wrote some notes on a pad I found on Colin's desk, and moved on to the next file. More clippings, describing Scott's climb from Member of Parliament to Under Secretary of State for Health, a long and tedious analysis of his political platform, quotes from his speeches, a schedule of his public appearances leading up to election day and what seemed to be a calendar of his other appointments. I typed the dates into the notepad on my smartphone. Knowing where he was going to be each day for the next week might be useful.

By the time Colin lumbered back to the cubicle, I'd finished reading all the files. "Find anything?" he asked.

I held the phone up. "I took notes. I'll review them at home. Thanks, Colin. I really appreciate that you let me do this. There was more material than I could have imagined, far more than I found on the web."

"Digital is overrated in my opinion," he said, tapping one of the folders. "Write it down, file it away. You never know when something might come in useful. It helps, of course, to have a team of researchers on hand to do all the legwork."

I held out my hand to shake his bear paw. "Thanks again. I'll let you know how things go."

He nodded. "My pleasure."

I had taken a few steps when he called me back. "Kate?" he said, cocking his head to one side. "I don't have an aura, do I?"

21

I'd turned my phone off while I was sitting at Colin's desk. When I remembered to turn it back on, I had three voicemails from Eliza, each one ratcheting up the threat level. The last one was delivered at high volume. She sounded unhinged. "Last chance," she said. "That story hits the headlines tomorrow, or I will do something that will make you sorry." I tried calling her back but I just reached her answering machine.

When I opened the door to my flat, the lights were on and music was playing. Although it seemed unlikely that an intruder would make himself so at home, my heart pounded as I edged into the hallway. Then I remembered it was Friday. Josh must be back.

"Kate?"

"Josh." We hadn't spoken much during the week. His excuse would be that he'd been busy with work. Mine was that I'd been busy with auras. And I hadn't been able to put the postcard out of my mind.

He crossed the kitchen to give me a hug. I stood stiffly in his arms, not ready yet to forgive him.

"Tea?" he asked, stepping back. "Maybe wine would be better?"

I nodded, taking off my scarf and coat.

We sat, Josh on the couch, me in an armchair, glasses of wine on the coffee table between us. After an awkward silence, I spoke. "How was your week? Are you home all weekend?"

He winced. "Actually, Alan needs me to go to Cambridge for meetings on Sunday and Monday. It's a pain, I know, and I'm sorry.

You know he's on a mission to restore the company to its former glory. When a client says jump, he leaps. And he expects the rest of us to as well. But you and I can do something nice tomorrow."

He picked up his glass and took a drink. "Before that, though, I need to explain about Helena."

"You don't have to explain anything. It's none of my business."

"I want to. I've been thinking about it a lot for the past few days. You were right to be upset that I kept the postcard. I…" He paused, put his glass on the table. "I've been trying to work out what to do about it."

"Are you really sure you want to talk about this?"

I shifted in my chair, trying to get comfortable.

"Let me tell you the history, just so you understand. Helena and I dated all through college. We'd planned to move to London together when we graduated, but her mother got very sick about two weeks before graduation. Helena said she needed to go home to Berlin to be with her and asked me to go too. She said we could hold off on getting jobs for a couple of months. I wouldn't do it. I already had an offer from Alan Bradley, and he wanted me to start right away. I started just a couple of weeks before you did, right?"

I nodded, remembering how kind he'd been to me when I first joined the firm. We'd been the newbies together, deciphering the politics of the company, reading up on clients, working extra hours to convince Alan he'd made good choices. I think I'd fallen in love with Josh then, but I'd kept my feelings to myself because he seemed so inaccessible.

"I told Helena that I'd start work and go flat-hunting on weekends. As soon as she was able, she could come back to London. It never happened." He was tapping his fingers on his knee, a nervous habit of his. "I should have gone with her."

Tears burned my eyes. His words were like slashes at my heart.

"I don't mean it that way," he said, reaching out to take my hand. "I don't wish I was with her. I just think it would have been the right thing to do. She needed me and I abandoned her. I didn't even make time to visit Berlin to see her at weekends because I was too busy at work."

"What happened? Why didn't she come to London?"

"When her mother died, her father was distraught. She stayed on to look after him. It was supposed to be just for a few weeks, but it dragged on. I flew to Berlin then, to talk to her, but it was too late, I suppose. We broke up officially, even though at that point we hadn't seen each other for months anyway."

"It doesn't seem to me that this is your fault," I said. I didn't mean to criticize Helena, but I wanted to reassure him.

He shrugged. "I've always felt guilty that I left her to deal with things by herself at such a critical time in her life. God knows how I'd feel if my mother were sick. It was selfish of me. And I put my work first. Who does that?"

"Don't be so hard on yourself."

Pulling my hand away, I stood up. My body felt tense and twitchy. "So now she's moved to Munich," I said. "That must be a good sign, don't you think? That she's getting on with her life?"

"I suppose so." He pulled the postcard from his inside jacket pocket. I gasped, a sharp intake of breath. He was carrying it around with him?

"Do you still love her?" I asked. I hated hearing my voice tremble when I said it.

"Of course not. I love you." He looked at the card. "I've been trying to decide whether to email her. Just to wish her well. It would be the right thing to do. Wouldn't it?" He looked at me, eyebrows raised as though seeking my permission.

"Of course," I said, even though I felt as though I had a lead weight pressing against my chest.

***

On Sunday morning, we woke late and moved slowly. Josh planned to take an early afternoon train to Cambridge for his meeting there. I decided to make brunch, something to keep my mind off postcards and auras. I'd texted Anita a half dozen times the day before to make sure she was safe. Finally, she'd told me she was applying for a restraining order against me and to stop stalking her at once. At least that had made me smile.

I peeled some oranges, careful to remove every piece of white pith, and swept the nubbly skins into the rubbish bin. The citrussy smell reminded me of my last trip to Spain's central coast, where orange groves stretched for miles beside the azure Mediterranean Sea. Maybe Anita and I could go back there together, when this was all over. It would be good to focus on something positive for the future. I cracked eggs into a bowl, snipped chives, and ground salt. The motions of cooking were soothing and distracting. By the time the food was ready, I was feeling calmer.

"Want a glass of bubbly?" Josh asked, looking in the fridge.

"I think we finished it last night," I said. "Coffee's fine for me." I rarely drank during the day, except at weddings or funerals. Not like Eliza Chapman, I thought, as I remembered her mid-afternoon glass of wine. I had an idea.

"I'll come with you to Cambridge," I said to Josh, handing him a plate. "I think Eliza Chapman is planning to make trouble. I want to find out what she's thinking."

I was glad to see his face light up. "Excellent. We'll get another few hours together that way."

We were able to find good seats on the train and used the time to prepare Josh for his meeting. I found myself enjoying the work talk. It took my mind off Helena, the postcard, and auras. When the train pulled into the station, Josh went off to find a taxi to take him to his first appointment and I decided to walk to Eliza's house.

The residential roads were quiet. One or two sleepy-looking students rode past me on bikes, but mostly, the streets were empty of pedestrians or moving cars. When I reached Eliza's house, I traversed the short, narrow path to the front door and rang the bell. Inside, her cat meowed loudly but no one came to the door. I waited a couple of minutes, then pushed the letterbox open and peered into the hallway. The cat was sitting in the middle of the hall, its eyes shining green in the gloom. Obviously, Eliza wasn't home, which was strange. I'd got the impression she never went anywhere.

I crossed a strip of scrubby lawn and leaned on the windowsill to take a look through the window. The book-filled living room was empty. Just as I turned away, the cat sprinted into the room, jumped on to the back of the sofa and stared at me. There seemed to be nothing to do but wait. Maybe Eliza had gone to the shops. I tried calling the number I had for her, but heard the phone ring inside the house. She either didn't have a mobile phone or she hadn't used it to call me.

I walked up and down the long street twice, trying to decide if I should give up and go back to London. It was bitterly cold. I remembered someone telling me that the winds blew straight from Siberia across the Fens to Cambridge. On a day like today, it was easy to imagine the boreal temperatures of the faraway tundra.

When I passed Eliza's the second time, I noticed the lace curtains twitch at the window of the house next door. A dog barked as I ventured up the path to the front door, and a woman in a pink robe and curlers opened it before I had a chance to knock.

"You looking for Eliza?" she asked, holding the dog by its collar. It was large and brown with lots of teeth bared in my direction.

"Yes, I am. Do you know when she'll be back?"

"She said she was going on a trip. Couple of days, she said. I'm feeding the cat for her 'til she gets home."

"Did she say where she was going?"

The woman frowned. "Not really. She said it was very important. She was going to meet a man, I think?"

What did that mean? Was she going to London to talk to Colin Butler? Or was she going after Scott herself? But what would she do? Hit him over the head with a book? Thanking the neighbor, I began the walk back to the station.

On the way, I called Detective Clarke to tell him what the neighbor had said.

"I appreciate the help," he said. "But I hope the list of people you suspect doesn't get too much longer. Have you heard from Chris Melrose at all?"

Chris. I'd almost forgotten about him. "No. Nothing. Have you?"

"Would I be asking you, if I had? I've put out an alert for him. I expect we'll pick him up soon, but if you hear from him, let me know immediately, all right?"

"Of course."

22

I made my way back to the station and caught the next train back to London. I felt as though I'd done all I could about Eliza. I'd notified Detective Clarke and could only hope that he'd take my concerns seriously.

Standing in the main concourse of Kings Cross station, I texted Anita. She said she was working an afternoon shift at the hospital, but had an hour or so free and wanted me to go over. Grace had an update on Dr. Reid's death.

When I got there, Anita led the way to the keypad-protected lift, where I braced for another encounter with the autopsy room. In fact we bypassed it, going to Grace's office, where a faint odor of antiseptic and Chanel Number Five hung in the air.

"Glad you're here," said Grace. "I'm supposed to have today off, but I have a ton of reports to write, so here I am. I can't stop thinking about Dr. Reid."

She glared at her computer screen as though it was guilty of preventing her from writing.

"I wanted to give you an update. First of all, the analysis of the drip bag turned up more or less what we expected. There were traces of insulin, digitoxin and barbiturates."

"And did you hear back from Ted?" Anita asked.

Grace nodded. "Yes. Ted says that no one doctor ordered that mix of drugs. There were lots of individual prescriptions for insulin and for digitoxin, and a wide array of sedatives, of course. So, it's almost impossible to pinpoint a specific physician who could have gained access to all of the medications."

"But someone must have acquired all three drugs," said Anita. "Which means they either stole drugs from somewhere in the hospital, or they bought them through outside sources."

Grace nodded her agreement. "Neither is hard to do. We're talking about very small amounts needed to achieve the desired effect. A vial here and there."

She tapped her fingernails on the desk. "There's something else. They tested the IV and the vials for fingerprints. Dr. Reid's showed up."

Anita shook her head. "That's inconclusive. Whoever did it wore gloves."

"And pressed Dr. Reid's fingers against the IV bag and the bottles," I said. "It would have been easy enough to do."

Grace nodded. "Agreed."

Anita pressed her forehead to the desk in a dramatic show of frustration. "So where does that leave us?"

Grace went to a small refrigerator in the corner, and handed us each a bottle of water.

"We have to come at it from a different angle," I said. "If we can't pinpoint who might have done this, we have to look for motive. *Why* would anyone want to kill Dr. Reid? It sounds as though any one of the medical staff in the hospital could have set up an IV, but why would anyone want to? If it was murder, it wasn't random. It was premeditated, which means that whoever did it had a reason."

"The staff all admired Dr. Reid," Anita said. "No one would want to do him harm."

I put my hand on her arm to get her attention. Her fingers were beating out a staccato on the desk, and she kept crossing and uncrossing her legs. "Maybe we shouldn't talk about this," I said. "It's just too upsetting for you."

She took a deep breath. "No, we have to talk about it. I'll be all right."

"Well, can you think about anyone with a motive?" I asked. "A rivalry with another doctor perhaps? Had Reid threatened to fire a nurse recently, or had a falling out with someone?"

Grace's eyes lit up. "Good idea. Anita, did you ever see him arguing with anyone?"

Anita began to unscrew the top from her bottle. She stopped and looked up at us. "What about Eric Hill? The sales rep. Remember I told you, Kate, that he was meeting Dr. Reid late one night about a week ago? That was very unusual and Dr. Reid was in a foul mood that evening. He and Eric could have been fighting about something. And Eric would have access to all those drugs. We should talk to him."

"Not so fast," said Grace. "You can't run around accusing people of murder. And if Eric did have something to do with it, then it could be dangerous. It's better that the police handle it, which they will if anything shows up in the toxicology report."

"But it's still a couple of weeks away isn't it?" I asked. That was far too long. Anita was in danger. We had to move more quickly than that.

"Kate's good at charming people into talking to her," said Anita. "I'll introduce her to Eric and we'll see what we can find out."

I took a big gulp of water. Anita was right that Eric might be a good lead and Grace was right that it could be a rash move. We risked warning him that we were on to him, or worse, we could provoke him into some kind of retaliation. Still, we had few other options.

"Let's give it a try," I said, draining the last of my water.

"We'll find him first thing in the morning," Anita said. "He's always here early."

Grace looked at her watch. "I think I'll call it a day then. A hot bath and a glass of wine are beckoning."

Anita stood. "I have to get back to work."

Just then, Grace's pager went off. "So much for that great idea," she said. "There's an incoming body. Come on, I'll walk you out."

In the corridor we met two orderlies pushing a gurney towards the autopsy room. A white sheet covered a figure underneath. There was no aura over the dead body, but that was normal in my experience. The auras always disappeared when the person died. Somehow that made me feel better. When I'd first started seeing them, I'd thought of auras as alien beings, attaching themselves to victims, sucking the life from them. Later, I'd realized that they were organic, a living part of the body. On my best days, I thought of them as visiting angels, ready to accompany the fated person from this life when the time came.

"This one is yours, Dr. Trillo," one of the men said.

Grace gave me a quick hug. "Be careful tomorrow, Kate, and let me know how it goes."

Turning, she followed the orderlies back to the autopsy room, one skewed wheel on the gurney clicking rhythmically in the silence.

23

We found Eric the next morning, pouring himself a cup of coffee in the fourth floor staff kitchen.

"Hi Eric!" I heard the fake warmth in Anita's voice and hoped he wouldn't notice. "This is my friend Kate. She's taking me out for lunch as soon as I'm off duty." She made a show of looking at her watch. "Good lord, I'm late. Must run. Can you pour some coffee for Kate? I'll be back in fifteen minutes."

He raised an eyebrow, but turned to take a cup from the shelf. "Milk?" he asked.

"Yes please, but I can do it. You don't have to."

"I'll do anything Anita tells me to do," he said. "She normally avoids me like the plague."

I took the cup from him, noting the gold links threaded through his pristine white shirt cuffs. His dark blue suit looked expensive, as did his red silk tie. It was a shame his appearance was marred by his bad skin, which had a greasy sheen under the kitchen lights.

"Why would Anita avoid you?" I asked. "Aren't you a doctor, a colleague of hers?" I'd decided that appearing to know nothing about him might elicit the most information.

His laugh was dry, like desiccated leaves scraping along a pavement. "No, I'm not a doctor. I'm a sales rep from one of the pharmaceutical companies that supplies drugs to the hospital."

He took a business card from his pocket and gave it to me. "PharmAnew," I said, reading the company name out loud. "How long have you worked there?" I tucked the card into my wallet and put it in my shoulder bag.

"Ten years, more or less," he said. "It's good job, apart from having to deal with doctors." He gave another dry laugh.

"You don't like doctors?"

"Not really. They look down on drug reps. To them, we're just like car salesmen. I have a Chemistry degree from Imperial College, but that makes no difference."

"So why do you do it then?"

"Because the money is good— really good— and there are plenty of perks. I don't mean to complain. It's not that bad. And some of the people I deal with are nice. Here, for example, the nurses are a decent lot."

"Do you spend much time here?"

"A fair amount. This place is one of my key accounts. I have a couple of other hospitals in London and I do a lot of work with private clinics. But yeah, sometimes I feel like I live here." He looked around the cramped, ill-lit kitchen. "Although thank God I don't. I have a penthouse in Canary Wharf with views up the river." He smiled. "One of the perks."

I sipped my coffee. It wasn't awful. "What other perks?" I asked. "Apart from the money?"

"Sales conventions in exotic places. They're boondoggles, really, for the doctors who attend. Lots of free booze, free food, fancy hotel rooms and rounds of golf or casinos and nightclubs, depending on where they're located." He shrugged. "It's good advertising. Keeps our products front and center when a doctor's prescribing."

He eyed me suspiciously. "Why? Are you looking for a job?"

"Maybe," I said. "I'm always looking around for something interesting to do. My dad says he should have called me Kat, not Kate. You know that phrase, curiosity killed the cat? That's me. I'm just the nosy type."

He smiled. "I get paid to be interested in other people. The more I know about a doctor, the more likely it is that I'll convince him or her to use our products."

"So you know personal stuff about all the staff here?"

Eric poured himself another cup of coffee. That was a good sign. He wasn't rushing off.

"Depends on how you define personal. Mostly, I know about their kids, their hobbies, that kind of thing."

He flicked back a cuff to look at his watch, even though there was a clock on the kitchen wall. The watch was big and gold, rather gaudy for my taste, but it probably sent the right signals to anyone who cared about that sort of thing.

"So you talk to doctors directly about drugs?" I asked.

"Of course. I also talk to nurses, pharmacists, and anesthesiologists. Heck, I'd talk to the office cat if there was one." His face took on an intent look, eyes slightly narrowed and focused on me. "Unlike in the USA, we can't do direct to consumer advertising, so the only way patients know about the drug options available to them is via their doctor. That's why it's so important that we educate all medical professionals, let them know what's out there, what's new, what's working. We share study data with them, that sort of thing. If we can make people's lives better, or save lives, then I'm doing my job right."

"That's wonderful," I said. "It must be so rewarding to know you're helping people." I paused. "Like poor Dr. Reid. Anita says he was an amazing doctor. Did you know him?"

Eric's eyebrows came together, and his mouth tightened. "Yes, I know all the doctors here."

"That's right, of course," I said as though just remembering. "I thought I'd seen you somewhere before. I shared a lift with you and Dr. Reid, about a week ago."

He didn't respond, so I carried on talking, watching his face. "It's so sad. To be under so much pressure that you'd commit suicide. I can't even imagine how that must feel."

He took another swallow of his coffee. "So, they are saying it was suicide?" he asked finally.

"Apparently, yes. Isn't that awful? Right here, in the hospital."

Eric remained silent, lips clamped together.

"I suppose Dr. Reid never asked you for any advice on medications like anti-depressants?" I asked. "I mean, you're the expert. I'm sure you could have helped if you'd known what was going on?"

He put his cup on the counter before pulling his cuffs straight. "Not my job. I don't prescribe, I promote. Nice to meet you, Kate."

He strode out of the kitchen. Even from the back, he looked angry. What did that mean? That he was guilty? Or just that he was offended by my questions? He certainly seemed to have a chip on his shoulder about the lack of respect shown him by the doctors. But that wouldn't be enough of a motive to kill one of them, would it?

24

Despondent, I went to find Anita. I hadn't learned much from Eric. If he were involved, I'd just waved a big red flag in front of him. I saw her at the reception desk, chatting with a couple of nurses. She excused herself and came over as soon as she saw me.

"Well, what did you find out?"

"That Eric has a big chip on his shoulder," I said. "But that's all."

"Damn. Well, it was worth trying. Listen, I really do have patients to see. Why don't you go home? I'll come over after work."

"Will you be all right? I hate leaving you alone."

Anita waved her arm around, encompassing the hallway, which was busy with patients and visitors, and the nurses' station where a doctor had joined the nurses.

"Alone? I wish."

"Okay. Text me when you're leaving, then I'll know you're on your way home."

"You sound like my mother."

Just as I turned to go, a short, pudgy man in a tweed jacket and creased tan pants hurried towards us. "Dr. Banerjee, can I have a word please?"

When he reached us, he stuck his hand out to shake Anita's. "Detective Parry," he said. He was in his fifties, with sandy hair combed over to hide his pink scalp. He smelled of smoke.

"I'd like to ask you a few questions, doctor," he said. "Can we use your office? It won't take long. Just a minute or two."

Anita grabbed my hand. "Come with me," she whispered.

When we were seated in Anita's office, Parry pulled a notebook from his jacket pocket.

"I expect you have everything on computers nowadays," he said, "But I prefer the old-fashioned tools. Just as efficient."

"So are you investigating Dr. Reid's death?" I asked.

He frowned at me. "And you are a doctor too?" he asked.

"No. A friend. The name is Kate Benedict."

He raised his sandy eyebrows. "I see."

Jotting some notes in his book, he asked me a few questions about where I lived and if I worked. When he'd finished, he looked up at Anita.

"Can I ask where you were on Tuesday night?" he asked Anita.

"I was with Kate at her place. I got there at about 6 p.m. We both rushed straight back here when I got a message from one of the nurses."

"And what time was that?"

"Nine-fifteen, more or less. I didn't really pay attention."

Tapping his pencil against his notebook, he asked if I could confirm that Anita had been with me on the evening of Dr. Reid's death.

"Yes," I said. "So you're treating this as a murder?"

He leaned forward, lowering his voice. "No, actually not. Just going through the motions on orders from higher up, to let the staff know that administration is taking this seriously. No one wants their doctors committing suicide. It's bad for morale, not to mention the hospital's reputation."

"Well, heaven forbid that Dr. Reid's death be allowed to upset anyone." Anita's voice was heavy with sarcasm.

"It's better for the hospital's image to have a doctor killed on the premises than to commit suicide?" I asked.

He shrugged.

"But we do think it was murder," I said.

"What makes you think that?"

"He wouldn't have killed himself," said Anita. "There was no note. And those drugs that killed him? He didn't request them from the pharmacy, not on the day he died or any day before that. So where did they come from? We think someone else used them."

"Someone stuck an IV in the doctor's arm?" Parry's tone was incredulous. "And how would that work?"

"We think he was drugged. The killer gave him something or used ether to knock him out for long enough to get the IV started."

"Uh huh." Parry snapped his notebook closed and stood up. "Interesting theory. I'll give it some thought. Thanks again for your time, ladies."

"Idiot," muttered Anita after he'd left the office. "We should march to the police station and demand that a real detective take over the case."

Standing, up, she retied her hair in a tight bun. We reached the door just as Pauline arrived. Her face was pale. "Anita, I thought you should know. It's Isaac Kaminski."

"What?" Anita hurried away with Pauline, leaving me alone in her office. I kept the door open so I could see everyone coming and going and, when that got boring, I watched pretty pictures of babies floating across her computer screen while I tried to analyze everything Eric had said. Fifteen minutes later, Anita came back to the office. Her mascara was smudged and her eyes looked red.

"What's wrong?" I asked. "Can you take a break?"

She nodded, taking a seat on the visitor chair. "One of our patients died. He was only fourteen." Anita rubbed her eyes. "Dammit. We're not supposed to lose them like that."

My nephew, Aidan, was fourteen. I couldn't imagine losing him, although we'd come close the previous year when he'd had peritonitis. He'd also had an aura, which had helped me get him to a hospital in time. Still, he'd been very sick for a while. I shivered, remembering the agony of watching him suffer.

"I'm sorry, Anita." I said. "What happened?"

"I saw Isaac when he first came in. He'd been diagnosed with end-stage renal disease, which meant he needed a kidney transplant. I wasn't part of the surgical team for that one but I saw him at a follow-up appointment a month after the operation. I seem to remember that he wasn't responding well to the post-operative medication. It was an immunosuppressant, a drug designed to prevent the immune system from rejecting the new organ. He was showing some symptoms of side effects. High blood pressure, increased BUN values. It wasn't my case of course. I was just an observer."

"Er, what's a bun?"

"Blood urea nitrogen. We can measure nitrogen in blood to assess kidney function. Here, change places with me." She came round the desk to sit in her own chair while I moved to the visitor chair. She typed on her keyboard. "If you look at the EPR — that's the electronic patient record — there's no mention of negative side effects. In fact, it says here that he was making good progress."

"Who wrote that on the patient record?" I asked.

Anita typed for a few seconds. "What? That can't be right. According to this, it was Dr. Reid."

She sat back in her chair, drumming her fingers on the desk.

"Why couldn't that be right? Was Dr. Reid one of the doctors looking after Isaac?"

"He was overseeing the team because he's head of department. The senior physician was Dr. Schwartz. But I'm sure Dr. Reid wouldn't get it wrong. If there were side effects, he'd have been certain to see them and record them."

She leaned down to open the bottom drawer in her desk. I heard papers rustling before she pulled out a sheet of creased lined paper covered in writing. "Because I'm still learning, I keep my own notes on some of the more complex cases," she said. "I write down my observations of the patient and then review them from time to time. Hence, my complete lack of any kind of social life."

She put the paper on the desk, smoothed it out with the palm of her hand. "That's what I thought," she murmured. "On January 10th, I wrote here that Isaac was not responding well to post-operative treatment. Darn, it's hard to make out exactly. Sometimes I can't even read my own writing."

A vertical line appeared between her beautifully arched brows as she read on. "This doesn't match at all with what is on Isaac's electronic file. Why would Dr. Reid record inaccurate information?" She carried on typing, murmuring to herself.

"Anita?"

"I'm sorry." She turned the screen so that we could both see it before she opened another patient record.

"Mark Jacobs, another teenager in for a transplant. The operation went well but the kid fell ill afterwards and was moved to intensive care." She looked at me. "Don't you dare tell anyone I'm showing you this. Patient confidentiality and all that."

"Of course not."

Anita pulled another sheet of paper from the drawer. "Falling hematocrit and hemoglobin levels," she read out loud. "See," she pointed at her notes. "This is what I recorded when I saw him. Nausea, diarrhea."

She pointed at the screen. "Here, it shows HCT and HGB at normal levels. Blood pressure normal, no GI issues."

"And was Dr. Reid the doctor who wrote that up too?"

She pressed a few keys. "Dr. Schwartz was the presiding doctor and I assisted. Dr. Reid made the last few entries." She leaned back in her chair, tapping one finger against the file.

She extracted another sheet of paper and read through it. "Danny Boyd. Let's see. Danny was in urgent need of a transplant when he came in. Kidney function was failing, as measured by his creatinine and blood urea nitrogen levels. He had potassium levels of 6.5, which is high. He couldn't pee. The transplant seemed to go well, but then, three days later, he was also transferred to the ICU."

She flung herself back in her chair and rubbed at her temples.

"How didn't I see any of this before?" she said. "I should have noticed these discrepancies." She put her hands flat on the desk and looked at me. "Do you think this has anything to do with why Dr. Reid died?"

"I don't know. What do you think you should do? Report it to another doctor?"

"If I do, I open up an investigation into Dr. Reid and why he altered these records. I'd hate to do that. He was a good man, Kate. Besmirching his name after he's dead just seems wrong. And if he was doing something unethical, well, he can't do any more harm now, can he?"

I stood up, stretched my arms over my head. My whole body felt tense.

"I'll think about it," Anita said, putting the notes back in her bottom drawer and shoving it closed with a thud. "Promise not to say anything until I decide what to do. Maybe I'll do some digging around, see if anyone else has noticed anything."

"I'd be careful who you talk to. If there is a connection between these files and Dr. Reid's death, and if he was in fact murdered, you don't want to alert anyone to how much you know."

"Which isn't much, yet," she said. "But later on, I'll go through all these notes. Maybe something will jump out at me."

A knock at the door was followed by the appearance of the nurse, Pauline. "Dr. Banerjee, emergency in room 42."

Anita jumped to her feet. "I'll see you at your place later."

I followed her out of her office, turning towards the lifts through a constant stream of patients and visitors, doctors and nurses. I saw Detective Parry, who raised a hand in greeting on his way towards the nurses' station. Knowing he was there made me feel better about leaving Anita behind. I headed out into the chilly afternoon. Dark clouds to the west were rimmed with pink and gold, which meant that the sun had to be shining somewhere. I just couldn't see it.

25

I walked slowly from the hospital to the tube station, thinking about what Anita had shown me on the patient records. Was it possible that the discrepancies between the electronic records and Anita's notes were related to Dr. Reid's death? And what did that mean for Anita? Was her aura signaling a danger that tied into the three patient records we'd looked at?

Realizing that I'd walked right past the station, I carried on towards the next one. In front of me, the Millennium Bridge, fictionally destroyed in a Harry Potter movie, stretched across the Thames to the South Bank. To the west, the London Eye soared, its glass pods glowing orange in the strange half-light of the hidden sun.

This was the view I used to see every day from my office window. I looked at my watch, tempted to make a detour to see if anyone was still there. I was impatient to get back to work. Just a few more days, I thought. But my excitement was tempered by fear. Every hour that passed brought Anita closer to death.

I turned towards the Victoria Embankment, carried along by the strengthening crowd of early evening commuters. At the Temple tube station, I took the escalators down from the street to the platforms below, suddenly in need of a cup of hot tea and anxious to be home.

When I got back, I tidied up the already spotless flat, straightening throws and cushions, and scrubbing the granite counters in the kitchen. I could have been doing something useful like reading the project files that Alan had emailed me, but folding towels and rearranging jars in the refrigerator in order of size seemed far more suitable to my frame of mind. After straightening all the wine bottles in their rack, I picked out a sauvignon blanc and put it in the fridge to chill. I was missing Josh, but I looked forward to spending another evening with Anita.

I checked the time at seven and again at five past, feeling my stomach churn. Anita was late. She didn't respond when I rang her mobile, so I scrolled through my contacts and found the number for the nurses' station. Anita had given it to me once when her phone was broken. When one of the nurses answered, I asked for Anita.

"She's not here, sorry. I think she left about an hour ago."

"Could you just double check that she's not in her office?" I asked. "It's really important that I reach her."

"All right pet, give me a minute."

While I waited for the nurse to return, I stared at my reflection in the blackness of the kitchen window. Bereft of color, it was only a shadow outline, like a ghost hovering on the other side of the glass. Finally, the nurse picked up the phone. "Sorry to take so long. The lights in her office are out and her coat isn't there. As I said, I'm sure she left already."

"Thanks," I managed to say before clicking off. I decided to call Anita's parents. I didn't want to worry them, but there was a chance that Anita had stopped by to see them on her way over. For all that Anita complained about her dad, she was close to her mother and often dropped in for a cup of tea and a chat.

"Hello, Mrs. Banerjee," I said. "I was wondering if Anita is with you? I have a question I need to ask her."

"Kate, dear, how lovely to hear from you. I was just thinking about you, actually. I'm making tarka daal for dinner and I know that's one of your favorites."

"It is, when you make it." Anita's mother was a terrific cook. "So, is Anita there by any chance?"

"No, I'm sorry, she's not. Have you tried her mobile? She's so busy, I never know where she is. She promised to come over for dinner this week though, so perhaps you could come with her? You know we'd like to see you. Oh and before you go, can you explain again how to change the ring tone on my phone? You're so good at that technical stuff, but I tried what you told me and it's not working."

"I'm in a bit of a hurry," I began and then relented. "Go to Settings and we'll take it from there."

It took five minutes, at the end of which Mrs. Banerjee happily announced that her ringtone now played Mozart's Symphony number 40 in G Minor.

"Come for dinner soon, love," she said.

"I will," I promised. "Thanks Mrs. B. I'll see you soon."

I rang off quickly, anxious to try Anita's cell again. There was still no answer. My heart was beating fast and I felt short of breath. I tried to calm myself. If she were on the tube, there'd be no cell signal. But the journey should only take twenty minutes or so. I looked at my watch again. I checked the news on the television to make sure nothing had happened to disrupt the tube service. I ran through various scenarios in my head, and considered walking down to the station to see if she was on her way. Perhaps her phone had run out of power. Maybe it had been lost or stolen.

The sound of someone on the landing outside the front door dispelled all my fears. She was here. I ran to the door and threw it open.

"Josh!"

He had been looking for his key, slightly handicapped by the huge bouquet he held in one hand. His bag and briefcase were on the floor and he put the flowers down on top of them before wrapping his arms around me. "The meetings finished early enough for us to get a train back this evening," he said.

When I burst into tears, he grasped my hands in his. "What's wrong?"

"Nothing. I'm so glad to see you." I couldn't talk properly through the tears, and he gently steered me into the living room. "Sit down and I'll make some tea," he said. He went back to the door, brought his things inside and then I heard the clink of cups in the kitchen.

After a minute of sitting alone on the sofa, I jumped up and went to join him. He was running water into a vase and I picked up the flowers to sniff them. "I love these. Thank you," I said.

"Can you tell me what's wrong?" he asked again. "You seem very upset. Didn't you want me to come over this evening?" His eyes were shadowed with concern and I felt a huge upwelling of guilt.

"Of course I did. I'm just really worried about Anita."

I brought him up to date on the events of the day, telling him about Grace, her analysis of Dr. Reid's death, and Anita's concern about the altered patient records. "I haven't heard from her and she seems to have left the hospital." I felt tears welling in my eyes again and rubbed them away.

"I'm sure she's all right," said Josh. "Maybe she went down to see Grace again, or stopped to talk to someone else in the hospital."

"But she'd answer her phone if she saw it was me calling," I objected.

"Cell service goes out all the time," he said, stretching the truth in an attempt to console me. "Or it might be a delay on the Underground. She could be stuck between stations."

I imagined a marooned tube train in a dark tunnel. A crash or a terrorist attack? The options didn't make me feel any better.

"Mechanical problems," Josh said as though reading my thoughts. "Don't assume the worst, Kate."

He took my hands in his. "You say that her aura hasn't changed much since you first saw it. That means that she's not dead, not even close to dying yet. So we have time to find her if she's missing. Okay?"

I leaned into him, drawing some comfort from the feeling of his arms around me. When we heard the kettle come to a boil, I pulled back and looked at him. "Thank you. I'm so glad you're home."

26

While we drank our tea, there was a lull in the storm raging in my head. Life felt normal. I was safe. Josh loved me. For just a minute or two, I convinced myself that I was over-reacting. But then I felt the panic returning. Josh sensed it, took my cup and put it with his in the dishwasher.

"Where do you want to start?" he said. "Should we go to the hospital or her flat?"

"Her flat is closer. Let's go there first. None of this makes sense, though. She would have called if she planned to stop off at home."

We were soon ready to leave, dressed warmly against the night-time chill. While we waited outside for a taxi, I filled in more details for Josh, telling him about Anita's fear that she'd been followed home a few nights earlier. Traffic was light along the Westway, which gave our taxi driver the opportunity to show off his Formula One driving skills. I grabbed the door handle each time he took a corner fast, but we finally arrived in one piece outside Anita's flat in Marylebone, which was on the ground floor of a modern low-rise.

Anita had given me a set of keys when she first moved into the flat. I found the larger key, which unlocked the front door. A light turned on automatically when we walked into the small lobby.

Unlocking the door to her flat, I pushed it open. It was dark and she obviously wasn't home, but I flipped on a light switch just to check. At the sight of the chaos inside my stomach contracted as though I'd been punched. The living room had been ransacked. Sofa cushions were strewn on the floor, and all the books had been swept from shelves. Magazines littered the carpet like colorful confetti. The flat panel television was still in place and intact, which made me think this was no common burglary. Josh grabbed my hand and we made our way to the kitchen. Every drawer and cabinet door was open, many of the contents lying in pieces on the floor. The room was cold, a draft moaning through a broken window in the back door that led to a tiny patio. Glass shards littered the linoleum floor.

My mouth was dry as we tiptoed up the short hallway to Anita's room. I prayed that she wasn't here, hurt or worse. Josh flipped on the bedroom light to reveal more evidence of a thorough search. There was no sign of Anita. Every drawer was open and there were armfuls of clothes on the carpet. The wardrobe gaped open, most of its contents puddled on the floor. The bedclothes and pillows formed a small white hill on one side of the stripped bed. But Anita's jewelry was still on the dressing table.

Retracing our steps to the living room, we looked for signs of anything that had been stolen. "Her laptop," I said, finally. "Usually she leaves it on the coffee table. She never takes it to work."

We searched for it amidst the detritus on the floor but found nothing, not even the charging cable.

"Theft then," said Josh.

"It seems like a lot of work for one computer?"

A noise from the hallway sent my heart rate rocketing. Josh put his finger to his lips and we both ducked down behind the sofa.

"Who's there?" came a woman's voice.

I peeked around the end of the sofa. A middle-aged woman in purple sweats and slippers stood at the front door, with one hand on the doorknob.

It was Anita's neighbor from across the hall. I recognized her but didn't recall her name.

I got to my feet, raising my hand in greeting. "I'm Kate. You might remember me?" Josh stood up next to me. "This is my boyfriend. We just got here and found all this."

"What's going on?" she asked, still waiting at the doorway.

"We don't know. Someone broke in through the window in the back door. Did you see or hear anything?"

The woman shook her head. "No, I had the telly on and it's hard to hear anything. Anita works all hours, you know, so I never know when she'll be here."

She took one step into the room, which I took as a sign that she believed we weren't dangerous intruders. "I'm Nancy, by the way. I was just on my way to put the rubbish out and saw the door was open. We should call the police, shouldn't we?"

"Yes, I was just about to do that." I took out my mobile to call Clarke's number. It clicked over to voicemail, so I left a message asking him to call me urgently.

When I'd finished the call, Nancy was looking at me, her eyes narrowed. "Aren't you calling 999?" she asked. "That didn't sound like emergency services."

"No, I called a detective. It's complicated, but you're right, we should call the local police too. Would you do that? We have to go."

"You're leaving?"

I glanced at Josh. If we stayed until the police came, we could be stuck here for hours. We needed to keep moving.

"Nancy, we have to go. We believe that Anita is in danger. Okay?"

"Here." Josh pulled one of his business cards from his wallet. "You can give this to the police so they know where to contact us."

She looked very dubious, but we left, dashing across the lobby to the front door. The block of flats was in a quiet side street, so we hurried to the corner and turned on to the busy City Road, which thronged with cars and buses. Outside a bustling pub, we flagged down a taxi.

"London General Hospital," I told the driver. "As fast as you can please."

27

As soon as we pulled into the turnaround in front of the hospital, I jumped out while Josh handed the driver a ten-pound note, telling him to keep the change. Hurrying up to the fourth floor, and heading towards Anita's office, we found Pauline at the nurses' station. Quickly introducing Josh, I explained that we were worried about Anita.

"I haven't seen her for a couple of hours," said Pauline. "She was due to go off duty at six. Give me a minute. Let me ask the other nurses if they have any idea where she might be."

She disappeared while Josh and I waited impatiently. After a few minutes, Pauline came back accompanied by a short, black-haired nurse in pink scrubs. "This is Suzy. She saw Anita leave the building."

Suzy nodded. "I was just coming in for my shift when I saw Anita walking out with a man. They got into a car. I only noticed really because she didn't speak to me. She's usually so friendly."

"Did you recognize the man?" I asked. "Had you seen him before?"

"No. I think maybe he was a boyfriend or something because they were walking arm in arm, very close."

"Could you describe him?"

Suzy shook her head. "Not really. It was pitch black in the car park. You know they are always saying they'll put more lights out there, but it never happens? He was quite tall, but I really didn't see his face."

"What was he wearing?"

"I don't know. A dark jacket, dark jeans or maybe cords. I'm sorry I can't be more help."

"What about the car?" asked Josh. "Did you see what kind of

vehicle they got into?"

Again Suzy shook her head. "I'm not good with car models. It might have been a BMW, but I'm not sure. It was a dark color though."

If she said "dark" one more time, I'd scream. I knew the sun had gone down and that the lighting was bad, but surely she'd seen something that would be useful.

"Suzy," I said. "It's really important. We think that man kidnapped Anita."

Eyes wide, Suzy gazed at us. "Kidnapped? Then why didn't she shout for help when she saw me?"

"Because the man was probably holding a knife against her neck. It's hard to scream when you're under that kind of threat."

I knew that from personal experience.

Suzy looked at Pauline. "Can I go?"

When Pauline nodded, she scampered away.

"Is that detective still here?" I asked.

"Detective Parry? No, he left a few hours ago, maybe around five. He didn't say he'd be back and he took down the tape from over Dr. Reid's office door."

"Did Anita leave the ward with this man Suzy described?" I asked. "Did you see anyone?"

"No, I didn't. That doesn't mean he wasn't here though, because I'm usually in one of the patient rooms and don't see much of what's going on out here. Or he could have met her downstairs in the lobby."

She paused. "I have to go back to work. But will you let me know when you hear from Anita? She's a good doctor, you know, and a wonderful person."

Frustrated by the lack of information, I turned towards the lifts.

"Now what?" asked Josh.

"Let's go check the car park."

Outside, the air was clear and very cold. The sky was full of stars, but they were faint, struggling to shine through the blanket of light from the city's buildings, street lamps and neon billboards. I thought of the sky over my father's house in Tuscany. There, the stars were so bright that they looked close enough to touch.

We walked around the car park, peering in through car windows. All of them were empty.

"Kate," Josh said. "It seems as though we need to report Anita missing."

I leaned up against a car. My legs were shaking. "I'm scared," I said. "What if she's been …" I couldn't even finish the sentence.

Pulling my phone from my purse, I tapped in Clarke's number. "Who're you calling?" Josh asked.

"Clarke again," I said.

"Why Clarke? Why not that detective who's been investigating Dr. Reid's death?"

"You haven't met Parry. Believe me, Clarke will be more helpful."

The detective answered on the first ring. "Yes, Kate?"

"Did you get my voicemail? Anita's missing. Her flat was broken into. Someone said she left work with a man, but no one knows who it was."

"Calm down," he said. "Tell me who Anita is." I explained, my voice shaking. Josh put his arm round my shoulder.

"When did she go missing?"

"A few hours ago," I said. "She was supposed to come to my place, but she never turned up. And her flat has been ransacked."

There was a long silence and then I heard papers rustling in the background. "Usually we can't process a missing person report until she's been gone for twenty-four hours."

"Her flat was turned upside down." It was hard to keep my voice down. "And a nurse saw her leave the hospital with a man. I think she was being abducted."

"Can you come to the police station and make a statement? Give me half an hour to finish up some paperwork and then we can have as much time as we need."

I began to object and then changed my mind. I wanted Clarke to mobilize the police force to search for Anita. I knew that, realistically, that wasn't going to happen yet.

We did one more round of the car park before heading back to the hospital building. It was cold and I was glad to step back into the warmth of the lobby.

"Hello there!" A man was walking towards us with a big smile on his face. After a couple of seconds, I remembered that he was the young drug representative who'd been chatting with the nurses the day I'd faked my way into Dr. Reid's office.

"Hi," I said, hoping that he'd just keep walking. He didn't.

"I hope your son's doing okay," he said. "The staff up there are amazing. He's in good hands."

Josh opened his mouth and I cut him off. "Yes, thank you. He's fine now. We've just been up to see him."

The rep stuck out his hand to shake Josh's. "Audley Macintyre," he said. "Good luck with your boy."

I grabbed Josh's arm, pulling him across the lobby towards the exit doors.

"What the heck?" Josh asked once we were out on the pavement.

"It's a long story."

Josh suggested we take the bus to the police station in Westminster so that I could tell him all about it. The commute rush was over and the bus was only half full. We sat together upstairs at the back, so that I could make my confession in private. I told him about lying to Dr. Reid and my fight with Anita.

"It was the day I first saw her aura," I said. "I hoped that I could find something out from Dr. Reid that would give me a clue about whatever it is that threatens her. I didn't get much out of it though, except to learn that Dr. Reid was a very nice man." I felt tears burning my eyes.

The brightly-lit interior was overheated and smelled of dusty upholstery and fast food. I thought of the hundreds of bus rides I'd taken with Anita when we were students and my chest throbbed with pain. I was so scared for her.

At the police station, we were directed to a meeting room where Clarke joined us a few minutes later. He shook hands with Josh. "Good to see you again."

After we were seated, a policeman came in with a tray of coffee and biscuits. Josh took two shortbreads. "I haven't eaten since breakfast," he said.

"So, tell me everything you know," Clarke said to me. I went through the events of the last few days, starting with Dr. Reid's death, Grace's preliminary findings, and the alterations Anita had found on some of the patient files. Clarke took notes on an iPad, looking up at me from time to time as though to check that I was telling the truth.

"I'm sure, well reasonably sure, that Dr. Reid was killed. It wasn't suicide," I said. "There was a Detective Parry at the hospital, making some enquiries, but a nurse told us he's cleared the area, so it sounds as though he's finished. From what he told us, the whole investigation thing was just window dressing to make the staff feel that the hospital was taking the death seriously."

"Give me a few minutes," Clarke said, leaving the room. When he came back, he tapped something else into his iPad.

"I can request further investigation in the light of Anita's disappearance," he said. "Detective Parry will be the lead."

I rolled my eyes. "I'd rather you handled it."

"It's not my jurisdiction." He held up a hand when I began to protest. "But I'll talk with Parry, make sure he gets onto it right away. I've put a call in to him. He's on his way in. I'll give him your report and he'll get in touch with you."

I leaned towards him. "Did you get an official report about the break-in at Anita's flat?"

He nodded. "That's one of the things I went to check on. It certainly sounds to me as though she was taken under duress. We'll find her. Is there anything else that might help us?"

"I just want her to be safe."

Tears filled my eyes again and I blinked them away, angry with myself for being so emotional. There was a long pause and then Clarke asked if I'd heard from Chris. My throat was so choked up with tears that I couldn't answer.

"What's the problem with Chris?" Josh asked. I'd told him about Chris and his relationship to Scott, but hadn't brought him up to date about Chris's mysterious absence.

"We've put out an alert for him," Clarke said. "But no sign of him so far." He looked at me. "It's funny, the way people you know keep disappearing."

"It's not funny at all," I said.

"No, it's not. I'm sorry," he said, standing up. "Try not to worry, Kate. If you hear anything at all from or about Anita, call Detective Parry. I'll work with him on this."

He came with us to the front entry and said goodbye. Josh and I walked slowly towards the bus stop.

"Why would anyone take Anita?" I asked. "This has to be connected in some way with Dr. Reid's death."

"Well, the police are on it now," said Josh. "They'll find her."

It was after ten by the time we got back to my flat. I unlocked the front door, and switched on the hall light. Just inside, on the hardwood floor, lay a white envelope. Someone must have pushed it under the door. Puzzled, as my post was usually delivered to the box downstairs, I picked it up and turned it over. There was no name on the front.

"Open it," Josh said.

I pulled out a sheet of standard white copier paper. The message on it was typewritten. "We have Anita."

28

After a nauseating rush of adrenaline subsided, I read the note out loud to Josh. "We have Anita. Bring the patient notes. No police or there will be consequences. The meeting location will be sent by text to your phone in two hours."

"What notes?" Josh asked. He took the paper, which fluttered in my hands like an injured bird.

"I don't know." I tried to get my shaking fingers under control so that I could check my phone. There was no text yet.

My knees suddenly felt weak, as though the bones in my legs had dissolved. "Josh, whoever has Anita knows where I live." The thought of a stranger at my door brought back all the memories of the intruder the previous year.

He took my hand, leading me to the kitchen. "We should let the police know about this."

"The message says not to," I said. "But I know we can't handle this without them. I'll call Parry."

When he didn't answer, I left a voicemail for him.

Josh put the piece of paper down on the counter. "Do you know what it is they're looking for?"

I thought back to the records I'd looked at with Anita that afternoon. "Patient files, I think, but they're on the hospital computer system. There's no way to access them from here."

"Let's go, then."

Before we left, Josh went to my desk in the spare bedroom and found a USB flash drive.

At the hospital, lights shone in some of the windows, but many were dark. The lobby was almost empty, the silence broken only by the squeak of a wheel as a tired-looking woman pushed a man in a wheelchair towards the cafeteria.

Fortunately, Pauline was sitting at the nurses' station when we got there. The lights were turned down and she was filling out a form by the glow of a small lamp on the desk.

"What are you two doing back?" she asked, jumping to her feet. "Have you found Anita?"

We'd agreed on the taxi ride that we'd tell Pauline what was going on. We needed all the help we could get. I quickly explained the kidnapper's note and the urgency to find the patient files.

Pauline's fair skin turned a shade whiter. "Anita's been kidnapped?" She slumped back into her chair. "Which patient information do you need?"

"I only remember one name for sure. Isaac Kaminski. There was another one, which I think was Jacob? No, it was a surname. Jacobs."

Pauline tapped on the keyboard of the computer on the desk. "Let me see what I can do."

She looked up when a young nurse walked towards the desk and sat down in a chair next to Pauline. "What a night," she said. "I'm run off my feet."

"Why don't you go to the kitchen? Grab a drink and a snack?" Pauline said to her. "I'll cover you for a few minutes."

The nurse shook her head. "Thanks, but I'll just sit here for a bit."

We stood, looking at each other, not sure what to do. "Well, as you're free," said Pauline, "Please accompany these visitors to the waiting room."

Sighing, the younger nurse got to her feet. "Follow me," she said. She left us in the small waiting room with the yellow walls and boxes of kids' toys. We waited until she'd been gone for two minutes and then tiptoed back up the hallway until we could see the nurse's station. Pauline was alone and typing. She waved us over when she saw us.

"Do you have a flash drive? I'll copy the files for you."

We all watched while the files were copied to the drive, the progress bar moving painfully slowly.

"And you don't know the name of the third patient?" Pauline asked.

"I know it began with a B. Something short. I wasn't really paying attention to the names."

Pauline did an alphabetical search and started reading out names beginning with B. "That's it," I said, when she read out Boyd, Danny.

"I'll just add this to the flash drive," she said.

"Can I ask what's going on here?"

We turned to see a doctor in a white coat watching us. He was short, barely as tall as me. The overhead light reflected on his eyeglasses so I couldn't make out his expression.

"Good evening, Dr. Schwartz," said Pauline, her tone unflustered. "These are friends of Anita's. She asked them for copies of a couple of patient records so she could review them before her appointments tomorrow."

"I believe you know that's against the rules," he said. "You can't give medical information to unauthorized members of the public. If Dr. Banerjee wants to study patient records, then she can come in here to do it."

"She's not feeling too good," I said. "Not well enough to travel anyway."

"Then I suggest she gets a good night's sleep and also that she only comes in tomorrow if she's completely free of symptoms. We can't have sick doctors seeing patients."

"We were just trying to help," I said. "We'd give her the drive. We'd never read anything on it."

"It's out of the question," he said, turning those gleaming eyeglasses on Pauline. "And you, nurse, will be reprimanded for making unapproved copies."

"Please, it's not Pauline's fault," I said.

"I'd like you to leave now," he said, swinging his head back to me. "Nurse, you will come with me to my office while I write up a formal complaint against you."

Pauline's mouth was set firm. She looked angry, but she said nothing. I was veering between frustration and despair. Could we tell Dr. Schwartz why we really wanted the files, throw ourselves on his mercy and beg for his help? It seemed to be the only solution. But he was glaring at me with such intensity that I couldn't bring myself to say anything. "I will call security if you don't leave," he said.

Resisting the urge to grab the flash drive and make a run for it, I grasped Josh's arm and we hurried away towards the lift. When the doors closed behind us, I beat against them with my fist. "Damn,

damn."

"Good to see that you're staying cool and collected," said Josh, leaning forward to take my hands and shake them. "You always do that when you're stressed," he said.

"What?"

"Clench your hands together until your knuckles go white. It's not good for you."

I looked at my hands and then at Josh. "What do we do now?"

"We get a cup of coffee and think about it for a few minutes."

We headed to the cafeteria, which was surprisingly busy considering the late hour. Illness and injury don't stick to timetables. Soon we were seated in the cafeteria with cups of coffee. I felt as tense as an over-wound clock, ready to fall apart at any moment.

Josh rubbed at damp spot on the table with a paper napkin. "Perhaps we should go back up and explain everything to that doctor," he said. "Maybe he'd help us. I mean, he's a colleague of Anita's and won't want any harm to come to her. What do you think?"

I considered that for a moment. "I don't know. He was obnoxious, the way he was ranting at Pauline. Classic Napoleon complex. Little bully."

"That theory's been disproven actually," said Josh, stirring creamer into his coffee. "Short people are no more aggressive than tall people. And it's said that Bonaparte was actually of perfectly normal height for that time period. The British government just made up stories about his small stature to diminish his image in the eyes of the public."

A smile formed on my lips in spite of myself. "You're a veritable encyclopedia."

Josh gave me a sheepish grin. "A mine of useless information." His expression changed. "So what do you think? Do we go back up and talk to him?"

Suddenly, I remembered something. Anita had said that Schwartz was the senior doctor on at least two of the cases we'd looked at that afternoon. That meant it was possible he was involved in some way. I explained it to Josh, who looked confused. "If he's involved, why's he asking you to bring the files when he has direct access to them? It makes no sense."

I drummed my fingers on the edge of the table. "I don't trust him. We should try to do this without him." I pulled my phone out of my pocket. "I have a number for the nurses' station. We can call Pauline and have her bring the drive down here to us."

"Worth a try."

I called the number but got no answer and tried again. The second time, a male voice answered. "Dr. Schwartz speaking."

Damn. I hung up quickly. "We'll just wait for a few minutes and try again," I said. "Maybe Napoleon will go away and Pauline will answer next time."

Josh took a sip of his coffee, glancing at a television that hung from the ceiling in a corner of the cafeteria. "Simon Scott," he said. "The election is only a week away."

"There's nothing we can do about him," I said. "We have to focus on Anita."

"Of course," Josh replied. "It's just weird that I'd forgotten all about him. I assume his aura is still there?"

I twisted in my seat to look at the television. Scott was standing at a podium as a camera zoomed in for a close-up. "I can't tell." I'd never been able to see auras on television or in photos.

For a few moments, I thought about Scott, and about Chris. What a mess that was. I liked Chris, and I felt badly about reporting him to Detective Clarke. At the same time, I hoped that Clarke would find him before he had a chance to do anything stupid.

"It's too bad because I'd planned on voting for Scott," Josh said. "Maybe I should give my vote to that Independent, what's his name?"

I let him ramble on about politics for a few minutes. I knew he was giving me time to calm down, which I did gradually. My hands stopped shaking and my brain settled down to where I could think in a more orderly manner. Just as I was about to try calling the nurses' station again, my phone buzzed and a text appeared from a blocked number. It gave an address and a time, midnight. The witching hour. That was creepy. I pulled up my maps app and keyed in the address. It was for a building on the outskirts of Slough, a town about twenty miles west of London. So now we had a place to go but no files to take with us.

"Oh God," I said, momentarily overcome with anxiety for Anita.

"It's all right, sweetheart." Josh reached out and touched my cheek. "She's going to be okay, I promise."

I took a moment to pull myself together. "It seems to me that we have to risk a smash and grab," I said.

"Great, I'm ready for some action." Josh drained his coffee. "We need a decoy. I have an idea."

By the time we reached the fourth floor again, we had a plan. There was no sign of Pauline, but Dr. Schwartz was standing at the nurses' station looking at a computer screen. He didn't look up when the lift door pinged shut behind us. We darted along the corridor into the men's washroom. I pulled the door closed and locked it. Josh splashed water on his face and slicked back his hair. We were hoping the moisture would look like pain-induced sweat. Putting down the toilet lid, he sat on it, head in hands. "I'm ready," he said.

I nodded, pushed the door open and ran up the corridor to where Dr. Schwartz was standing. "Help!" I called. "Please help. My friend is very ill."

He looked up. "You," he said. "I thought you'd left."

"No, my friend wasn't feeling well and needed to use the lavatory. But he's getting worse. I think it's his heart."

Schwartz pushed past me and hurried along the corridor. I knew it was a matter of minutes before he realized Josh was faking his illness. There was no sign of Pauline. I stepped over to the desk to look around, but couldn't see the drive. I opened a drawer to see if she'd put it away. There was nothing. Perhaps Schwartz had confiscated it. A shadow fell over the desk and I looked up in fear of seeing the doctor again. It was Pauline.

"He took the drive," she said. "But we can make another one."

She opened another drawer and pulled out a bright blue flash drive. "One of the drug salespeople was giving these out," she said. "Keep an eye open."

She plugged it in and went through the same process as before. The copying process seemed to take forever. My heart was pounding in case Schwartz came back.

"Done," she said, giving me the drive, which I slipped into my jeans pocket.

"Thank you."

I ran back down the corridor. Schwartz was holding a stethoscope to Josh's chest when I pushed the door open.

After a minute or so, the doctor straightened up, frowning. "Your pulse is a little high," he said to Josh. "But your heart sounds fine. Can you tell me again where the pain is?"

Josh glanced past Schwartz to me. I nodded and patted my pocket to confirm I had the files. "Actually," Josh said, "The pain is easing. Perhaps it was just indigestion because I ate dinner too fast. I think I'll be fine."

"Stand up and let me know how you feel," the doctor instructed. Josh stood, stretched his arms out and nodded.

"Yes, much better. I'm sorry to take up your time."

"I'd like you to go down to Emergency and get checked out," said Schwartz. "They can run an EKG just to be sure. Here." He pulled out a pad of paper and a pen and scrawled something on it. "Better yet, let me take you down. Sit there until I can get a wheelchair."

"It's really all right," Josh protested. "We can find our way there."

"Yes you could, but if you pass out on the way, I'll be responsible." Schwartz pressed some buttons on his pager.

We were silent under the bright overhead light, which gave off an irritating buzz. I didn't know if Dr. Schwartz was really being solicitous or if he suspected we were up to no good. I glanced at my watch. It was nearly eleven o clock. Time wasn't on our side. I pushed the door open when I heard the susurration of wheels on the hallway floor. A young nurse backed in the wheelchair and helped Josh into it.

"Where does he need to go, doctor?" she asked. "I can take him."

"That's okay. I'm about to go on break, so I can escort our patient to Emergency on my way to the cafeteria," replied Schwartz, releasing the brakes. "What's your name?" he asked me.

"Kate," I said, deciding that the less I said the better.

He nodded. "Off we go then."

We rode the lift down in silence. My heart was flinging itself at my ribs so hard that everything in my chest hurt.

I was grateful when the lift came to a halt and the doors slid open. Schwartz pushed the wheelchair into the Emergency department, bypassing the registration desk. He helped Josh on to a bed in a curtained cubicle, where another doctor joined us. While they talked quietly, I stood next to Josh, holding his hand tightly. Finally, Schwartz finished talking and nodded to us in farewell. "You'll be in good hands here," he said.

Relief flooded through me when I watched him walk away, but we still had to get away from the ER doctor. A nurse wheeled in a portable EKG machine and started to set it up. The doctor watched for a few seconds, then muttered something about coming back later and disappeared through the curtain.

"Take off your shirt and lie down," the nurse said. "I'll be back in a second." We really didn't have time for this. The minute she'd gone,

Josh got up from the bed, and we slipped out of the cubicle, pausing for a moment, unsure which way to go. Seeing an Exit sign, I pulled Josh in that direction. Dr. Schwartz was in the corridor talking to another doctor. There was nothing for it but to keep going. We walked as fast as we could without breaking into a run, past the conversing doctors and into the ER registration area. I heard a voice behind us.

"Wait! Where are you going?" Napoleon was on the war path. We pushed our way through the crowd of people waiting at the reception desk and out through the double doors. Then we ran. After a hundred yards or so, we stopped and checked, but I couldn't see anyone pursuing us. I was sure we weren't the first to bolt out of an emergency room to avoid unwanted attention, but I was relieved that the doctor hadn't given chase.

"Ok, let's find a taxi," I said, trying to catch my breath.

"Better be quick then. There are two security guards coming this way," said Josh.

We ran out of the hospital grounds on to the main road, waving frantically until a black cab pulled over. When I gave the driver the address, he looked surprised. "That's a fair trek," he said. "It'll be expensive."

"That's all right. And please go as fast as you can. It's an emergency."

It seemed to take forever to cross London. We drove past shuttered shops and streets crowded with young men going home after late night pub crawls. As the taxi wound through the quieter streets of Earls Court and Hammersmith, I found it hard to sit still. I kept checking my watch.

It was close to eleven forty-five by the time we got on to the M4, where the driver was finally able to put his foot down. When we pulled off the motorway at junction six, my mobile rang. It was Detective Parry. "You said there's a note? Tell me what's going on."

I explained about the patient files on the flash drive. "We're supposed to hand them over in a few minutes," I said, looking at my watch again.

"I can't get anyone out there in that timeframe," Parry said. "You'll have to no-show. He'll get back in touch." I heard voices on his end of the line. "I have to go," he said. "Let me know when you next hear from the kidnapper."

"This man is a moron," I said, staring at the blank screen on my phone. "I don't think he gives a damn about Anita. He said we just had to no-show."

"Well, we're not doing that," Josh said, squeezing my hand.

29

The taxi driver pulled off the main road and drove slowly into an industrial estate, a network of streets flanked by two-story warehouses with roll-up doors and loading docks. In daylight, the area was probably a hive of activity, but now the silence and darkness were oppressive.

"This is it, folks," said the driver, pulling to the side of the road. "Are you sure you gave me the right address?"

I knew I had, but I checked the address on my phone screen again and showed it to Josh. *21 Spring Meadow Road.* It was hard to imagine a place less like a meadow in the spring.

"This is it," said Josh. "How much do we owe you?"

"Sixty pounds, guv." Josh pulled some notes from his wallet and handed them over.

"Could you wait for us for a while?" I asked. "We'll need a ride out of here."

The driver shook his grizzled head. "Sorry, miss, but I should have gone off duty at midnight. I'll bet you can call a local cab company and they'll be out here in a jiffy. You got a mobile, haven't you?"

We watched the taxi drive away, its orange lights fading like the dying embers of a fire. I shivered, feeling the cold and damp already seeping through my jacket, and fear permeating my bones.

I turned to look at the building, a squat flat-roofed block of concrete with a rusting roll-up door. We approached slowly, unsure of how to make our presence known to whoever might be inside. There was an entry door next to the roll-up. Josh knocked on it. We listened for sounds, any sign that the place was occupied, but heard nothing. Josh banged on the door more loudly, but still there was no response.

"Let's go round the back," he suggested. The ground at the side of the building was unpaved and covered with knee-high weeds that stank of urine. I wondered briefly if it was human or animal, then tried not to think about it at all. We turned the corner to an expanse of crumbling asphalt. A skip crouched in one corner, its patches of peeling paint like animal markings in the moonlight. The back wall of the warehouse reminded me of a face, with two windows like old eyes, filmy and impenetrable, and a single metal door in the center. Josh turned the knob and, to my surprise, the door creaked open. Inside, it was completely black. I stepped into the doorway and felt around on the wall for a light switch. There was one but it didn't turn anything on. The darkness seemed to intensify the more I looked into it.

Josh pulled a small LED torch from his pocket.

"Don't tell me you were a Boy Scout," I whispered.

He grinned. "Nope, but my grandma always told me to be prepared for anything. She gave me this for Christmas. A few years ago, she gave me a Swiss army knife." He patted his coat pocket. "I always carry them with me."

"Cool grandma," I said. The Christmas gift washed the hallway in white light. Stepping inside, we walked along the corridor past several closed doors. I pushed the last one open but the room was empty, so we kept going until we reached a large open space. There was no shelving, no machinery. It looked as though the place had been abandoned for a long time. When I scuffed the floor with the toe of my boot, dust flew up like a swarm of insects in the beam of Josh's torch.

"There's a mezzanine," I nodded in the direction of a metal staircase in the far corner. "Should we go look up there?"

Josh nodded. We tiptoed across the warehouse floor and climbed the steps, the metal ringing under the tread of my boots. Fearful of what we might find at the top, I felt my heart speed up. The stairs opened on to an open area enclosed with a half-height wall. A few scraps of newspaper littered the bare plywood floor and a pile of blankets lay in one corner.

"Nothing," I whispered. "Let's check those rooms on the ground floor." It was hard to talk out loud, even though it seemed obvious that there was no one around. We went back down the stairs, crossed into the hallway and opened a door. Like the warehouse, the room was covered in dust. No one had been in there for a long time. But, in the next room, we found signs of recent occupation. A plastic table and three chairs sat in the center, and there was a blanket on the floor. In the beam of the torch, we saw footprints and drag marks in the dust. I was sure that Anita and the kidnapper had been here.

Venturing into the room, I took a good look at the table, hoping that Anita might have left a clue of some kind. Josh shook out the blanket, but all it shared with us was a dense cloud of sepia-colored dust that made my eyes itch.

"We should go back outside," I said between sneezes.

The asphalt at the back of the building was corrugated from years of use, edged on one side by a metal link fence, festooned with papers that had caught in the mesh. Josh swung the light around. There was a small puddle on the tarmac not far from the back door. He bent down and ran his finger across the surface. *Please don't let it be blood*, I thought.

"Looks like fluid from a car," he said. "Water, like evaporation from the heater, perhaps."

"So there was a vehicle here fairly recently," I said. "Why did they leave before we got here?"

We shivered in the cold night air. It felt unreal to be in such a desolate place in the early hours of the morning but, however bad I felt, Anita must be faring worse. I stared around the lot for a minute, looking for clues. My eyes came to rest on the dented skip. It was big, more than big enough to hide a body.

"We need to look inside," I said, the bile rising in my throat. I hung back when Josh lifted the lid and peered in.

"Anything?"

"No." He started to let the lid fall and then stopped. "Wait, come and look. What do you think that is?"

I took a step forward to peer inside. The metal container was empty apart from a small white box, which was lodged in the far corner.

"I think we should check it out," he said.

"I'll do it. Just hold the light steady."

Before he could argue, I pulled myself up on the metal rim, swung one leg over and jumped down into the container. It smelled awful. I reached for the white box and stopped. "We shouldn't touch it without gloves on, should we? It might have fingerprints that the police could use."

"We don't have any choice," Josh said. "Just lift it by a corner."

I nodded, picking it with my thumb and forefinger, and handing it over to him. He waited until I'd clambered back out of the skip before opening the box. Inside was a single used syringe and a small square of white cotton dressing. There was no label or print on the outside of the carton, nothing to indicate what the contents of the syringe would have been.

"Too tidy for a casual druggie," I said. "Do you think our kidnapper left it here?" My thoughts were running faster than my words. "Oh God, they're drugging Anita."

"We don't know that," said Josh. "But we should keep it to show to the police, just in case." He slipped it into a pocket of his overcoat. "Now what?"

"Back to the main road," I said, already leading the way back to the front of the building. When I turned the corner, I ran straight into a man with a beard. He yelled. I screamed.

The man shoved me against the wall. "What are you doing here?" he shouted at me. "This is my place. You're trespassing, that's what you're doing."

"Back off, mate." Josh had found his Swiss army knife, which he pointed in the man's direction. Not surprisingly, my assailant laughed.

"You need one like this, my friend." He pulled a knife from his pocket and held it out in front of him. It was a kitchen knife with a red plastic handle. Still, the blade looked lethal enough.

I watched Josh lower his pocket knife, but he kept it in his hand. When I looked back to the bearded man, he'd moved closer, his face just inches from mine. He pushed the point of the knife against my neck. His skin was dirty and his hair was matted. He stank. For an instant, I felt relieved. This was no kidnapper, just a homeless man. But then my relief dissolved. He might be a vagrant, but he had a knife at my throat.

"What do you want? Money?" asked Josh, digging into his pocket for his wallet.

"What would I do with money? You shouldn't have been trespassing on my property."

"Please let her go," Josh said, moving a few steps closer. "We'll move on. We don't want to disturb you."

"Nah," the man exclaimed, enveloping me in a cloud of foul breath. "Second time in one night you've been here. You'll just come back again."

"We haven't been here before," I said. "Did you see other people here earlier? A young Indian woman with black hair? A man, perhaps more than one?"

He took the knife away from my neck, breathed on it and rubbed it against his coat. "Nice and shiny," he said, looking at the blade.

"Please? Did you see her? She's in danger."

He nodded. "All that frizzy air. Lot of danger."

"Her hair is straight…" I had a strange sensation, a tingling that ran from my head to my toes. "Wait. What do you mean? Frizzy air? You mean wavy air? Around her head?"

"Yep. Means she's going to die."

I leaned against the wall, dropped to my haunches. The shock took all the strength from my legs. They felt like jelly.

"Have you seen the moving air before? On other people? How long have you been able to see it?" I had a hundred questions, but the bearded man moved a few steps away from me, looking at me from under drawn brows. "What's it to you?"

"I can see it too."

He laughed, long and loud, the sound of it grating like chalk on a board. "Good luck with that. Look what it did to me."

"What do you mean?" asked Josh, helping me back to my feet, keeping his arm around my shoulders.

"They did it to me in the army. Put something in my head. That's when I started seeing them. Hundreds of 'em. Drove me crazy. I mean, it was Afghanistan. We all knew some of us were going to get shot or blown up, but I knew exactly who wasn't coming back each day. Couldn't stand it after a while. I got myself shot, got sent back home. I thought they'd go away but I still see 'em. I need to get this thing out of my head."

He started rubbing his scalp, pulling at his tangled hair. Josh and I looked at each other. I felt faint, but we needed to keep moving. "Who was with the woman?" I asked.

He shrugged. "A man."

"Just one?"

"Maybe two. No, there were three. Using my place. Bastards."

"Did you see a car? What kind it was?"

He tugged at his ears, and beat one fist against the side of his head. "Big white car," he said.

"Can you describe the men? Did you get a plate number?"

"One of them was a lizard." The head bashing continued.

Josh took my hand. "We're going now," he said. "Thank you for your help."

We began walking fast through the weeds to the front of the warehouse. Just as we reached the road, the man shouted after us. "Green car, big. One man."

We walked down the middle of the road, keeping some distance away from the dark structures that loomed along both sides of the street. I hadn't noticed on the taxi ride in, but realized now that all the warehouses were abandoned, with broken windows and weed-strewn lots. There was something disturbing and post-apocalyptic about the place. And I was still shaking from the encounter with the man who could see auras.

30

We came to an intersection and stopped, unsure which way led back to the main road. Without speaking, we both turned to the right. After half a mile or so, we left the derelict warehouses behind and entered a newer development of three-story, glass-fronted office buildings. Many of them had signs out front indicating company names. Street lamps revealed swathes of neatly manicured lawns and pruned shrubs, a display of normality that helped me breathe a little more easily. After another turn, we were surprised to see the twinkling lights of an all-night cafe, fifty yards up the road.

A bell tinkled when we walked into the brightly-lit cafe, where several tables were occupied by men in overalls and work boots. Two men in navy blue security uniforms ate heaping plates of bacon and eggs. A Bollywood musical ran on a TV on the wall, the soundtrack barely audible. A bald man behind the counter smiled at us. "What can I get you?" he asked.

"Just coffee please," I said.

We carried white mugs of steaming coffee to a table for two in the corner. The wooden surface was scratched and dinged, but was immaculately clean. No one took any notice of us, but I was glad to have people around after the dismal emptiness of the warehouse. I wrapped my hands around the hot cup to warm them and to stop them shaking. An electrical storm was raging in my head. The man who could see auras. Signs that Anita had been in the warehouse, signs that she'd been drugged.

"That man…" I started. "Anita."

"Listen, we didn't find Anita, but at least we know she's still alive," Josh said. "And next time, we'll be early, and we'll have police back-up. You should call Parry to let him know what happened."

I made the call and got Parry's voicemail again. "He never answers his goddamned phone," I complained while I waited for the beep. I left a message before taking a swallow of coffee. It was surprisingly good.

"We'll call in the locals if we have to," Josh said.

As if divining that he was about to be superseded by the Slough police force, Detective Parry called back right at that moment. Quickly explaining what had happened, I told him we were waiting for further instructions from the kidnapper.

"Sit tight and let me know the minute you hear from him," he said. "Give me the warehouse address. I'll get a team out there to take a look. Maybe we can get some fingerprints."

"That's a surprise," I said to Josh, when Parry rang off. "He's actually going to do something useful this time."

For the next five minutes, I stared at the phone screen, willing it to flash another message.

"Why did the kidnappers leave so quickly?" I mused out loud.

"The homeless man probably scared them off," Josh said. He looked at me over the rim of his cup. "That was weird, huh? Him being able to see auras?"

"Very," I said. "I wish I could have talked with him about it. He was crazy though. What did he mean about one of the kidnappers being a lizard?"

Josh shrugged, signaled to the man behind the counter to bring more coffee.

"I just realized something," I said, when I felt the caffeine hit my tired brain. "Most of those businesses we walked past were medical. One was surgical devices, and another was imaging. Does that seem like a coincidence or do you think there's a connection? I mean, given that Anita is a doctor, and someone wants to get hold of patient records?"

Josh nodded. "Yeah, I was thinking about that too."

I kept checking the phone to make sure it was on and the volume was up, but it remained maddeningly silent. After a while Josh yawned, pushing his metal chair back on the scuffed linoleum floor so that he could stretch out his legs.

"I'm sorry, I know you have to get to work tomorrow," I said, feeling guilty that I still had a few more days off before returning to the office. "Why don't you try and nap, and I'll wake you if I hear anything."

"I'll be all right," he said, but within a couple of minutes he was asleep. The cafe was quiet now that most of the customers had left. The bald man came out from behind the counter with a tray and a tea towel. He wiped down the tables and stacked mugs and plates on the tray. I followed him and leaned on the counter while he piled the dishes in a sink.

"Not from around here, are you?" he said, over the gurgle of water from the tap.

"No, we're meeting someone here," I said. "Do you know anything about the warehouses on Spring Meadow Road?" I asked. "Are they all derelict?"

"Yeah, most of them. There were some problems with water drainage out there, foundations all started rotting out and the tenants all gave up their leases one by one. Developers came in and built a new industrial estate on higher ground. Full of medical companies so there's lots of money going around. At night we serve the janitors and security guards, and the office folks come at lunchtime. We're famous for our rhubarb pie. Do you want a piece?"

"No, thank you. I'm not hungry. But can I get a bottle of mineral water please?"

"So, what, you interested in buying them warehouses?" he asked, turning to take a chilled bottle from a glass-fronted refrigerator.

I laughed. "No, just curious, that's all."

He gave me the bottle and a glass. I went back to the table and took my scarf off, folding it and tucking it under Josh's neck so he wouldn't be too uncomfortable when he woke up. Every few seconds I looked at my phone, but there was no message.

Sipping water from the bottle, I thought about the homeless man. I'd never met anyone else who could see auras like I could. But then I didn't exactly go around publicly announcing my ability, so maybe there were many others, who saw and kept quiet, or who saw but never understood the significance of what they observed. To acknowledge the auras meant accepting that the universe is infinitely more complicated and mysterious than we humans would like to believe. It's terrifying.

Terrifying enough to drive someone mad? I thought so. The homeless veteran could have lost his mind when he started seeing the auras. Or perhaps losing his senses was a natural result of the horrors he experienced in the war. Either way, I doubted he had anything implanted in his head.

Suddenly the phone buzzed and Josh jumped at the noise.

"What?" he asked before realizing where he was and coming fully awake.

I snatched the phone from the table and stared at the screen. There was a short message from the blocked number. "Wait for instructions."

I showed it to Josh.

"Well, that's good," he said. "As long as we are hearing from them, that means Anita is okay, and they still want to make a deal."

I didn't want to think about what Anita was going through. She had to be scared and uncomfortable. She might even be unconscious if the syringe had been used to sedate her.

"What's the time?" Josh asked.

It was just after three in the morning. He took a sip of my water. "Let's call Parry again, warn him that we're going to need some help when the instructions come through from the kidnapper."

I called Parry and left a message. He rang back fifteen minutes later, sounding as though he'd been asleep, which was a perfectly normal thing to be doing at three a.m.

"I'm sending a team to meet you," he said. "Give me a few minutes and I'll get back to you with more information."

It was hard to sit still. I was impatient for the phone to buzz again, desperate to get moving, to find Anita. Josh leaned over, took my phone and tapped on some keys. When he gave it back to me, the screen showed a sudoku puzzle. "Give your brain something else to think about," he said.

I'd solved two puzzles by the time Parry called back. "Officers Grey and Ibori will meet you at the cafe in about thirty minutes. Do exactly what they tell you. They're experienced officers."

The door opened, letting in a rush of cold air. Four men walked in, all in overalls and boots. They were loud, making jokes, yelling their orders to the owner. I was glad of the distraction. They'd almost finished their middle of the night breakfast when the door opened again. A young man in jeans and a parka came in, scanned the cafe and nodded when he saw us. He came over to our table. "Kate Benedict?" he asked. "I'm Officer Alex Grey."

I'd just introduced Josh when another man entered. He was black,

164

muscular and wearing chinos and a cream-colored turtleneck, which seemed a little underdressed for the arctic night. "Steven Ibori," he said, shaking our hands. The two officers sat down, signaling to the man behind the bar that they wanted coffee.

"Tell us everything you know," Grey said. "Then we'll be ready when the kidnapper gets in touch."

I talked while they drank their coffee and had their mugs refilled. When Ibori had finished his second cup, he got to his feet and went outside.

"Sneaking a fag," Grey said. "I keep telling him to give it up."

Ibori came back in, trailing cold air and the smell of smoke, and rejoined us at the table. He raised an eyebrow at Grey, who shook his head. "Nothing yet," he said. The two of them checked their watches.

"I thought that only happened in movies," I said.

"Synchronizing watches?" Ibori grinned. "We do it all the time. Makes us feel important."

Grey's mobile rang. He went outside to take the call. When he came back in, he told us that Parry had sent a team out to check the warehouse. There was no one there, apart from the homeless man. I felt sad for him. He'd fought in a war and now he was sleeping in an abandoned warehouse. When this was all over, I'd go back and talk to him. For now, all my attention was on finding Anita.

I picked my phone up from the table where it lay, a useless chunk of anodized aluminium, the empty screen like a black hole, sucking in all my energy. "Say something," I said to it. After a minute or two, Grey took it from me and stared at it, as though willing it to burst into life with a new text. There was nothing.

We waited until just after five in the morning, when a new round of customers poured in, ordering their full English breakfasts and pots of tea.

"We need to get back to the station," Grey said. "My advice is that you two go home, get some rest. Do you need a lift somewhere?"

I looked at Josh, feeling helpless. We couldn't stay in the cafe indefinitely, but leaving felt as though I was abandoning Anita.

"You're right," Josh said. "Can you take us to the train station?"

We all piled into their blue Mondeo for the drive and I napped on Josh's shoulder, but only for twenty minutes. When Grey opened the back door to let us out, the cold jolted me awake. The street was empty apart from a road sweeper and a bus with its windows so fogged with condensation that I couldn't tell if anyone was inside or not.

"Good luck," Grey said. "Don't forget. Let me know when you hear something. We're on duty for another couple of hours. We'll get right on it."

"What if I don't hear anything?" I said, concentrating on keeping my voice down even though I wanted to scream. "What if he gives up and just kills Anita?"

"He won't do that. He needs something from you, which means he'll try again."

31

After Grey and Ibori drove away, Josh pushed my hair back from my face and stroked my cheek. "The kidnapper will be in touch, Kate. It'll be fine."

I nodded, trying to focus on the fact that Anita was alive while I followed Josh to the platform. The early morning light was dull and flat, threatening another wintry day. I shivered in the icy blast that swept along the tracks.

Josh tackled the ticket machine, succeeding in printing out two one-way tickets just seconds before the train rolled into the station. We jumped on, happy to find that it was early enough for there to be plenty of seats. Even better, we were right next to the buffet car, where we found bacon sandwiches and fresh tea. Fortified by our breakfast, I scrolled through the news on my mobile to pass the time until we reached London Paddington. The breaking news was about a gas explosion in Portsmouth. Josh found it on his phone at the same time.

"Did you read this?" he asked, showing me the headline. I nodded, wondering why he was interested. Clicking on a link, I streamed live coverage from the BBC site. A studio announcer was talking about the explosion. "It's not clear at this time what the cause of the explosion was, but it appears to have been a gas main. At least one person is dead and there are a number of casualties who are receiving aid from early responders. We'll bring you more on this story as we receive information. In other news, the stock market—"

I clicked my phone off, but Josh carried on looking at his.

"What's wrong?" I asked.

"I don't know," he said. "I must be jumpy, but I thought there was a connection somehow to you, to us."

His jaw was set firm and I could see the muscles flexing in his cheeks. It was so unlike him to react that way that I shivered. If Josh thought there was something wrong, there probably was. But it was a gas explosion in Portsmouth, which was more than fifty miles away on the south coast. This couldn't have anything to do with Anita.

"Scott?" I said.

"Maybe," Josh said. "Although they're not saying that."

The ticket inspector came past to check our tickets. He was chatty, sharing his opinion about whether we'd get sleet or snow later in the day. As soon as he'd gone, I checked the news again. This time, the headline reported a bomb detonation in a parking garage. The next line made my heart jump around. "The whereabouts of Opposition Leader Simon Scott are not clear at this time."

Remembering the schedule I'd found during my research at Colin Butler's office, I pulled up my notes to check. There it was, an early morning speech at a convention center in Portsmouth.

Josh looked over at me. "Are you all right? You've gone white as a sheet."

"Simon Scott is in Portsmouth. And now the news is describing the explosion as a bomb."

My fingers trembled as I tried to find Detective Clarke's phone number in my contacts list.

"Clarke," he said when he picked up.

"It's Kate. I heard the news. Do you know if Scott is safe?"

"Not yet," he said. "The explosion happened in the underground garage where his car and driver were waiting for him."

My stomach lurched. "Is he all right? The news said someone was dead."

"I don't have any more details yet, I'm sorry."

"Will you call me when you know more?"

There was a pause. "If I have time." He rang off.

I tuned back into the news station that was broadcasting interviews with people who'd heard the blast. The lack of information was maddening. My frustration compounded by the lack of contact from the kidnapper, I found it hard to sit still and kept shifting in my seat.

My phone rang. It was Colin Butler. "I expect you've heard?" he said without introducing himself.

"Yes," I said. "Is Scott safe?"

"Yep. He was late getting to his car because he stopped to talk with a couple of campaign volunteers. Those few minutes probably saved him."

"What about Kevin Lewis?"

"He's okay too. He and Scott were together. Their driver was killed, and half a dozen others were injured. It's a shambles down there."

"Was it a car bomb?"

"That's the rumor certainly, although it's speculation at this point. I'll let you know when I find out more."

"Thank you." I said, wondering why he'd called me.

"It seems as though you were right about there being a threat to Scott's life, Kate. Whether it turns out to be a bomb or a gas leak, he was right in the vicinity and it sounds as though he was very lucky. Did you turn anything up in your research at my office that would have predicted this?"

"Only that Scott was due to be in Portsmouth today."

"Hmm. So your aura thingy doesn't tell you anything about where, when, or how?"

"Sadly not."

"That's tough," he said. "Knowing something bad is going to occur, but not being able to stop it happening."

"Tell me about it," I muttered.

"Well, I'll keep you updated on what I find out."

The line went dead. Colin was a strange bird, but I was glad he'd called me. I settled back in my seat. Scott was safe, but Anita wasn't, and there was nothing from the kidnapper.

I called Clarke again. "Do you have any updates?" I asked.

"Initial analysis by the first responders at the scene suggests a small incendiary device, pretty rudimentary. It only did the damage it did because it was in the confined space of the garage." Clarke paused. "I just want to let you know. You were right about there being a specific threat to Scott. I did my best with what I had, but it was just sheer damn luck that it wasn't worse. I wish I'd been able to do more."

I didn't blame him for not taking my warning more seriously. He'd done what he could, but he could hardly risk his career on the word of someone who saw death in rippling air. His superiors wouldn't take kindly to his acting on such imperfect information. I sensed, though, that a bridge had been built across the chasm that had divided us and that he would listen to me more carefully from now on.

"You tried," I said. "I'm sorry about the people who've been hurt down there, but I'm happy Scott wasn't harmed. It sounds as though it was a close shave."

"Closer than it should have been. Warning or no warning, no one should have had access to that garage."

"No," I agreed.

"I heard what happened at the warehouse," Clarke said. "Parry just brought me up to date. I'm sorry it didn't work out, but it will next time."

"That's what everyone tells me," I said, just before he rang off.

I sank back in my seat, staring out at the passing scenery. The ticket inspector had been right. It was sleeting, the freezing, watery mix hazing the windows. When we stopped at West Drayton, the platform was glazed with ice. I glanced at my watch. Once we reached Paddington, we'd get the tube back to my flat. It was an hour's journey at most, but it felt infinite, because going home served no purpose. We were in limbo, waiting for instructions from the kidnapper.

Listening to the rhythmic clicking of the wheels, I felt something tugging at my brain, trying to tell me something. Finally, I realized what it was.

"I have to see Scott."

Josh glanced over at me. "Why?"

"To make sure his aura has gone. If the bomb was what was supposed to have killed him, then his aura will have disappeared and he'll be safe."

This was what happened, in my previous experience. Once the threat to life had been avoided or nullified in some way, the victim's aura vanished.

"Can't you assume that it's gone?" asked Josh. "Besides, you can't be in two places at one time, and we need to wait to hear from the kidnapper."

Darth Vader's signature tune suddenly filled the carriage, coming from Josh's phone. I knew that ringtone. It was Alan Bradley. Josh pushed the phone along the table towards me. "You answer it," he said. I picked it up.

"Where's Josh," Alan asked, without bothering to say hello.

"Driving," I lied. "So nice to hear your voice, Alan."

He grunted. "I might have known he'd be gallivanting around with you. Tell him I need him in the office straightaway to be briefed for a client meeting this evening. No excuses. Oh and Kate, two more days and you're at your desk at nine. Not a moment later."

"Yes, of course," I said, but Alan had rung off at 'yes.'

"Remind me why I'm so excited about coming back to work?" I asked Josh. "Alan is such a prick."

"You know he loves you, really. He just doesn't show it."

"Hmm. Anyway, you need to get back to the office for Alan's 'vitally important client briefing,'" I said, twisting in my seat to look at him. "Not too bad. You'll pass inspection. It's lucky that stubble is in."

"I don't want to leave you alone," he said. "What if you get another message from the kidnapper while I'm gone?"

I didn't want him to go to work either, but Alan was going to be mad if he didn't turn up.

"I'll call Detective Parry. It'll be fine, I promise."

32

After thirty minutes home alone in my flat, I was feeling Josh's absence, wishing that he'd been able to come home with me. I couldn't sit still. My feet kept moving, but my brain seemed to be paralyzed by fear for Anita. I couldn't think straight. I was sure there was something I could or should be doing to find her, but I never got past two coherent thoughts in a row before everything fell apart and I found myself staring at the toaster, not sure why I'd come to the kitchen at all.

I was making my second cup of tea when the phone rang. It was Detective Parry. "Do you have a minute?" he asked.

"Of course." I stirred some milk into my tea and took the cup to the kitchen table.

"We found very little at the warehouse," he said. "Apart from one piece of paper with the word "kitchen" scrawled on it. Someone here seems to think it was written with mascara, which could indicate that Dr. Banerjee was being held there and that she wrote it. Does it mean anything to you?"

I thought about it. "Was there a kitchen at the warehouse?" I said. I didn't remember seeing one.

"No, so it must refer to somewhere else."

I looked around my kitchen. Could Anita have left something here that she wanted me to find? But why would she hide something here without telling me?

"Your people checked the kitchen at her apartment?" I asked. "The intruder must have been looking for whatever it was that she hid."

"Yeah, they looked. There was nothing obvious, but we don't even know what we're looking for."

I thought for a moment, but I couldn't work it out. "I'm sorry. I have no idea. And there's been no word from the kidnapper. I'm really worried." My voice caught in my throat, so I coughed a couple of times to get it back under control. "What if he doesn't contact me again?"

The silence at the end of the line was so long that I thought we'd been disconnected. "Detective Parry?"

"He will," Parry said. I didn't think he sounded very convincing.

As soon as he rang off, I sat down to think things over. Why wasn't the kidnapper contacting me? After a few minutes of driving myself crazy imagining the worst possible scenarios, I took the flash drive out of my bag and plugged it into my laptop to re-read the patient files. Maybe something would jump out at me.

I scrolled through Isaac Kaminski's record and then the one for Mark Jacobs, but as I tried to access the third file, my laptop froze. When I tapped on the keyboard, the screen flashed bright for a moment before going dark. I hammered the keys. No response. How could my computer misbehave just when I needed it most? I was ready to throw it across the room, but common sense prevailed.

I hurried to the bedroom, knowing that Josh had left his personal laptop there. I took it back to the kitchen counter, turned it on and plugged in the flash drive. As I clicked on it to open the patient record for Danny Boyd, a notification flashed in the top left hand corner, warning me that there was only ten percent power left. Dashing to the living room, I found the charger and hurried back to plug it in.

While I watched the screen to check that the charger was properly connected, I noticed that Josh had three unread emails. And they were all from the same sender. 'Hdunst.' That was Helena Dunst, Josh's old girlfriend. My stomach clenched. I knew that Josh had planned to email her in response to the postcard she'd sent, but he hadn't said anything more about it, so I'd assumed that she either hadn't responded, or that there hadn't been anything to say.

Clicking on the email application, I saw half a dozen emails addressed to Helena, and more then a dozen back from her. I took my hands off the keyboard and stood up. At the window, I looked out over the slate rooftops, black and ice-slicked under grey clouds that towered like battlements in the air. I thought again of the pure blue skies on the postcard from Munich.

Why was Josh corresponding with Helena? I supposed that when he acknowledged her card, it was reasonable that she might write back with more news, and he'd feel compelled to respond to that too. But a dozen emails back and forth over the course of a few days? The last one had been sent yesterday.

Blood roared in my ears. I felt cold. I desperately wanted to open the emails and read them, to find out what Josh and Helena were saying to each other, but I couldn't do that. Going back to the computer, I quit the email application quickly, before temptation got the better of me.

For the next few minutes, I tried to focus on the patient records, but the words seemed indecipherable. I stared at the screen, not really seeing anything, my hands clamped together in my lap. I was falling to pieces. Should a short correspondence between two old friends trigger such an extreme reaction? Maybe not, but I was insecure when it came to Josh. Even now, after we'd been dating for a year, I wondered what it was he saw in me. There was a long list of things I loved about him. He was kind and smart, thoughtful and generous. He loved his parents. At work, he'd help anyone who needed it. Alan Bradley obviously valued his design talent and business skills. What would he say about me if anyone asked?

After a couple of minutes, the screensaver activated and showed a picture of Josh and me together in Tuscany, drinking vernaccia in the Piazza della Cisterna in San Gimignano. I remembered every minute of that day, our drive down from my dad's house near Florence, Josh's excitement at his first view of the town's medieval towers in the distance. We'd climbed up the fortress ruins to look out over the narrow, cobbled streets to the church of Sant'Agostino. Beyond the walls of the city, the rolling hills were dotted with farmhouses and fields of sunflowers. It had been a perfect day, full of love and sunshine.

My phone buzzed. It was a text from the blocked number. "Bring the notes. Time and place to follow."

33

I held the phone so tightly that it hurt my fingers as a brief wave of exhilaration at hearing from the kidnapper quickly gave way to anger. What was he playing at? It had been nearly twelve hours since I'd last heard from him and he was still making me wait. I wondered how Anita was holding up.

I stared at the message as though reading it ten times would make it say something revealing, give me a hint as to who was holding Anita, or where. Then I remembered that I needed to ring Parry to let him know, not that I had much to tell him. I made the call anyway.

"I've heard from the kidnapper," I said. "He said to bring the notes and he'll let me know the time and place later."

"And you have the notes, right?" Parry asked.

"Yes, on a flash drive." I tapped on Josh's laptop keyboard to bring the screen back to life, and double-checked that the three patient records were definitely on the drive.

"Call me the minute you get a location," Parry said. "I'll get a team briefed and ready to go."

"That will be great, thanks."

I closed down Josh's laptop. My concerns about Helena and the emails would have to wait. As I put the flash drive in my bag, I thought again about the kidnapper's demands. In the first written message and now again in the text, he hadn't referred to patient records or files. He'd said "notes."

It hit my brain like a flying sledgehammer. He must mean the notes

175

in Anita's desk drawer. The ones she told me she'd kept on all the cases so that she could review them as part of her continuing education. It fit. He'd taken Anita specifically because of her notes. How did he know about them though? Surely Anita wouldn't have told him.

I didn't have much time to work it out. I needed to get to the hospital to retrieve the notes before I got the next text message.

I jumped to my feet. As I was putting on my jacket, I realized I had a few taxi rides ahead of me and I was low on cash. A kitchen drawer full of scissors, tape, and old Chinese takeaway menus also held a couple of twenty-pound notes that I put there for emergencies. If solar flares ever took out the power grid, at least I could buy a few bottles of wine and tins of tuna to sustain me for a while. The twenties were tucked under a Stanley retracting knife that I used for opening boxes. On a whim, I put that in my bag too. Then I locked up and ran down the stairs to flag down a taxi. When I told the driver to get to London General as fast as he could, he took us up side streets that I'd never seen before and got us to the hospital in record time. I kept an eye open for Dr. Schwartz as I took the stairs up to the fourth floor. A nurse I didn't know was on duty at the desk.

"I wonder if I could check something in Dr. Banerjee's office?" I asked her.

She looked uncertain. "Visitors aren't allowed in without, you know, someone to accompany them."

"I understand. Do you know if Pauline is on duty?"

"Yes. I'll let her know you're here."

I paced back and forth, and rushed towards Pauline when she approached the desk a few minutes later.

"I need something from Anita's office," I said. "I know it's an unusual request, but can you help me? It's to do with the kidnapping."

"Of course. We're all worried about Anita, so do what you have to do. Whatever it takes to get Anita back safely. Do you need any help?"

"I don't want to cause any more problems for you," I said. "I can manage alone, and, if Dr. Schwartz makes an appearance, you can pretend you had no idea what I'm up to."

I walked to Anita's office, passing the kitchen, where a couple of nurses were standing chatting. I opened Anita's door and turned on the lights. The room felt desolate, its emptiness making me miss her more than ever. Sitting in her chair, I pulled open the bottom drawer. There was nothing in it. My heart clattered around in my chest. Where were the notes?

I quickly went through the other drawers. The first revealed only a generous supply of pens and post-its, together with a stash of dark chocolate bars. In a shallow top drawer, nestled on a bed of cream tissue paper, lay a small Paddington bear, a gift I'd given Anita when we were in college. I hadn't realized she still had it. Running my finger over the soft fabric of the bear's face, I felt a lump in my throat.

Thinking back to when we'd looked at the files together, I tried to imagine where the notes could be. Had Anita moved them? If so, where? They can't have been in her flat, or the kidnapper would have found them. Had someone else been in and taken them?

I rushed back to the nurses' station, glad to see that Pauline was still there. "Has anyone been into her office?" I asked. "There were some papers in her desk when I was here last, but they've gone."

Pauline frowned. "Not that I know of. But I can't say for sure."

My brain felt scrambled. I was sure the kidnapper was asking for those notes, but now I didn't have them. If I didn't bring them to him, what would he do to Anita? Tears burned my eyes. Pauline noticed at once. She linked her arm through mine. "Come and sit down in the kitchen for a minute and I'll make us a cup of tea while we think about where those papers might be."

The kitchen! That's what Anita had written on the piece of paper that Parry had told me about.

"Pauline, you're a gem. I think the notes are in the kitchen."

I hurried there with Pauline in tow, relieved to find the two nurses gone. Pauline stood at the door so no-one would come in, while I started opening doors and drawers. In addition to cups and plates, there were cartons of coffee, filters, sugar, creamer, and several boxes of biscuits, but nothing that looked like Anita's papers. I felt sick to my stomach. Without the notes, I had nothing to bargain with, and who knew what the kidnapper would do to Anita?

My phone buzzed. Another message from the blocked number. "Come to St. Katharine's dock at 4 p.m. No police."

I checked the clock. It was just after two. I had time, but not much. "We have to find those notes," I said to Pauline. "It's urgent."

"Let me help. I have an idea."

Pauline came over, knelt down in front of a bank of lower cabinets, and started to pull out some of the larger cartons of coffee. She reached into the back of the cupboard.

"My dad keeps his will and stock certificates in an old biscuit tin at the back of his saucepan cupboard," she said.

It was in the third cabinet that she found a shoebox-sized plastic crate full of paper. With trepidation, we took off the lid and removed a few pages. They were all covered in Anita's scrawl. What was it about doctors that their handwriting was always illegible?

She put the lid back on the box and gave it to me. "I have to get back to work. What are you going to do now?"

"I'll call Detective Parry. He's setting up a team to accompany me to the meeting point."

When she'd gone, I made the call to Parry and got his voicemail. While I waited for him to ring back, I had an idea. There was about an hour remaining before I needed to leave for St. Katharine's dock, so I called Grace, using the cell phone number she'd given me at our first meeting. She picked up immediately and, five minutes later, met me in the hospital lobby. I explained about the kidnapper's texts as we made our way down to the basement through the secure doors.

In her office, Grace swept everything off her desk, making space for us to spread out Anita's notes. We were going to look for anything that might give us a clue as to who the kidnapper might be and why he was holding Anita. It seemed to me that would give the police a better chance of successfully rescuing her.

"The kidnapper can't want all of this, can he?" asked Grace, looking at the blizzard of paper on the desktop.

"I suspect he just wants the notes relating to the electronic patient records I looked at with Anita." I said. "So, we should look for all pages with one of those three names on them."

After ten minutes, we'd made several neat piles.

"These three pages," I tapped the top of one of them, "are notes relating to patient Kaminski. And this one is Jacobs. The third patient record I looked at with Anita was for Danny Boyd, but I haven't found any notes on him yet."

"Here," Grace said, handing over a single page. "This one says Boyd on it." She straightened up a tall pile of pages. "And these seem to be random musings about specific symptoms, but not related to any particular patient."

For a moment, we looked at the neatly sorted sets of notes.

"So, tell me again," Grace said. "You and Anita looked at these three patient records, all of which appeared to have been edited by Dr.

Reid. And Anita thought that was strange. Did she say why?"

"Because those three patients had all experienced complications from side effects of medication, but the electronic records didn't show details of those side effects. Dr. Reid noted that all were responding well to treatment."

"That would rather change the scenario, wouldn't it? If Reid were up to something?"

I thought back to my conversation with the doctor, his soft brown eyes, and his courtesy to me even though I'd lied my way into his office. It was hard to imagine that he was capable of doing anything criminal or even unethical.

"Maybe we just found our motive," Grace continued. "If Dr. Reid were involved in something bad, maybe someone killed him to stop whatever he was doing?"

"Or maybe he really did commit suicide. Either because he felt guilty, or because he knew he was about to get caught. That's a really depressing thought. Anita would never get over it."

"But if that's the case, then who would have taken Anita? — and why?"

I rolled my shoulders, trying to release the tension in them. "I don't know. It makes no sense. All we do know, really, is that Anita suspects that the medical records relating to three renal transplant patients have been tampered with. The kidnapper wants the notes and we assume he means Anita's notes relating to those three patients." Panic rolled through me, contracting my muscles, roiling my stomach. "What if I'm wrong? What if these aren't the notes the kidnapper's expecting?"

Grace stood up and went to the coffee machine in the corner. She waved a mug at me. "Want some?"

When I shook my head, she poured one cup and came back to the desk. "It's going to be all right, Kate. I'm sure we're on the right track."

With trembling fingers, I picked up a page with Isaac Kaminski's name on it, took a seat and read it all the way through, struggling with the bad writing and the medical terminology. I dug into my bag for the flash drive.

"Can we look at these files on your computer?" I asked.

Grace took the flash drive, plugged it into her computer and opened the file. It all looked familiar, but I read it through again. "These are the differences," I said, pointing them out to Grace. "See here, this set of blood test results? And these vital statistics? They're not the same as the ones recorded by Anita in her notes."

Grace looked at the figures, then sat back in her chair. She pursed her lips, tapping her fingernails on the edge of the keyboard.

"Anita's my friend," she said finally. "But isn't it more likely that if one of the versions is wrong, it's hers? She's a junior resident without Dr. Reid's experience. And these notes are, well, just that, hand-scrawled notes."

Her pager vibrated. She frowned when she looked at it. "I've got about thirty minutes, then I'll have to start prepping for an autopsy."

I nodded and we stared at the screen again.

"What made Anita think it was Dr. Reid who made those entries in the electronic records?" she asked.

When I moved the mouse to hover over the provider notes icon that Anita had shown me, a box popped up over a line that read 'blood urea nitrogen - 12.'

"See here? This little box shows who typed it in. These are Dr. Reid's initials, DWR, Daniel Walter Reid."

I pushed the page of Anita's notes towards her. "You know more about this stuff than I do but, if you check the BUN value for that date, according to Anita, the number is 34."

Grace looked it over. "So, assuming Anita's notes are accurate, they show something different from the official patient record," she said. "If Anita decided to share these notes with anyone, they would see the discrepancy. And that discrepancy must be a serious issue, something that Dr. Reid wanted hidden."

"Or maybe it wasn't Dr. Reid," I said. "Is it possible that someone just used his login and password to make the entries?"

Grace nodded. "That's possible. But who?"

"Dr. Schwartz? He was the physician leading the team on those three cases. But if it is Schwartz, why on earth does he need me to give him the notes?"

"Because they'd already gone missing," Grace said. "Anita had hidden them and he didn't know where."

I thought back to the encounter with Schwartz, when Josh and I had first tried to download the electronic patient records at the hospital. "You know, I want it to be him because he's a jerk. And I don't want it to be Dr. Reid. I liked him. But I can't see how Schwartz is involved with the kidnapping."

Grace's pager vibrated again. "Give me a minute." She left the office. I carried on looking at the patient record, but there was nothing new to be learned from it. I closed it and unplugged the flash drive. I didn't like being alone in the windowless office, with corpses next door. A sudden draft of air from a vent in the ceiling ruffled the notes, setting them fluttering and rustling on the surface of the desk. I stared at them. They were our only leverage with the kidnapper, the reason he'd kept Anita alive so far.

As though he knew I was thinking about him, he sent another text. "Same place. New time. 3.30. Don't be late."

I realized that Parry hadn't called me back. I rang him again and heard his same stupid voicemail message. Then I called Clarke. There was no answer. It seemed to me that the alien invasion could start in London and there wouldn't be a single policeman around to stop it. In a panic, I started to gather up the notes.

Grace came back in a rush, a frown creasing her forehead. "Sorry about that. My boss is on his way down. I need to get back to work. How's it going here?"

I told her about the revised time for the meeting. "And I can't reach Parry," I said, the papers trembling in my hands. "Do you have any large envelopes?"

"Of course."

She rummaged in her desk and gave me two brown letter-size envelopes. I stuffed the pages relating to the three patients into one of them, and put the remaining notes into the other.

"This one has the real notes, the ones we think the kidnapper wants," I said, holding up the first envelope. "Is there somewhere safe we can hide them?"

"Come with me."

Grace led me to the morgue, where she pulled open one of the metal drawers used to store bodies. "Safest place in the hospital," she said. "No one can get down here without a pass, even if they thought of looking here, which they won't."

I put the other envelope in my shoulder bag. "I'll give these to the police to use as bait." I said. "It'll take a few minutes for the kidnapper to realize they're not the notes on those three transplant patients. Hopefully, that will be enough time for the police to do whatever they do to capture kidnappers."

"So what next?"

I looked at the clock on the wall. "I'll start heading towards the meeting place and join up with the police there."

"I wish I could come with you," she said, glancing in the direction of the autopsy room next door. "But duty calls."

I gave her a hug. "Thank you for doing this. I'll be back as soon as it's over."

In a taxi, I headed further east. Traffic in the City slowed us down and it was three twenty-five when we reached our destination. I jumped out, shoving a ten-pound note at the driver. "Keep the change."

34

St. Katherine Docks, originally a working port, had been redeveloped with modern offices, shops, restaurants, and flats overlooking the river. The place was bustling with office workers and tourists taking pictures of Tower Bridge.

I scanned the crowds, looking for someone who could be a kidnapper. How were we supposed to connect? He was hardly going to be wearing a sweatshirt with Kidnapper printed on it. I jumped when my phone rang. It was Parry. "The officers are on their way," he said. "Plain clothes. Owens and Walsh. You can't miss Owens. He's got red curly hair."

"Wait," I said, but Parry had already rung off. I looked at my watch again. It was exactly three-thirty. I searched through the people nearby, straining for a glimpse of anyone trying to attract my attention. As another minute ticked by, I began to panic. Perhaps I'd misunderstood the instructions; or the kidnapper had changed his mind.

My phone buzzed again. "Take the next boat to Greenwich. I'll meet you there."

Heart pounding, I found the pier where the river boats stopped, and managed to find one that was just leaving. It was a thirty-minute trip to Greenwich. As soon as we boarded, I called Parry to let him know of the change of plan. "Have the officers meet me at the Greenwich pier," I said. They could get there faster by car than I was going by boat. Parry said he'd make sure it happened.

When we pulled up to the dock, I was the first to disembark, pushing my way through a throng of excited Italian tourists and a slow-moving elderly couple. A man with a shaved head marked with tattoos stood to one side of a queue of people waiting to board. He didn't look like a tourist. He caught my eye and raised his hand. I didn't move. I wasn't going anywhere until the officers arrived, but there wasn't a single red hair in sight.

My phone buzzed again. "Follow me."

Still I didn't take a step forward. I had to stall until Owens and Walsh arrived. Passengers from the boat pushed past me, one of them banging into my shoulder. The strap of my bag slipped and that gave me an idea. I let the bag slide to the ground, and knelt to pick it up, taking my time. When I straightened up, the tattooed man was glaring at me. He turned, striding away up the long narrow walkway that led to the road. Seconds later, another text appeared. "Last chance. Follow me or Anita dies."

My heart was thrashing around so hard I thought it would crack my ribs. But there were plenty of people around, so I felt safe enough to follow him. Out on the street, I stopped, to the irritation of a large tour group behind me. About twenty people pushed past me, all wearing yellow bandannas and headphones. By the time they'd gone by, I couldn't see the kidnapper any more. But I did catch sight of a tall man with red hair. About a hundred yards away, he and another man were walking fast towards the pier. Thank God. While I was trying to decide whether to go to them or wait, someone else bumped into me from behind. Damn tourists. I felt pressure against my ribs and looked down to see a tattooed hand holding a knife.

"Keep walking if you ever want to see your friend again," the kidnapper murmured in my ear. I stumbled along beside him, painfully aware of the point of the knife against my side. We were heading away from the officers. When I glanced behind to see if they were following, the kidnapper pressed the knife harder. I was sure it had broken the skin, but was too scared to check. After a few more steps, I decided I had to scream for help. I guessed the kidnapper would run away, but the officers were close enough to see him. They'd catch him.

I opened my mouth and yelled just as a horn from the boat blared. No one even glanced in my direction. Intent on getting to the Cutty Sark or the Observatory, everyone was busy talking, laughing and taking photos.

"You scream again and I'll use this," he said, jabbing the knife at my side. This time I felt a hot stab of pain. He turned off the main road on to a smaller street lined with parked cars. Stopping next to an old green Land Rover, he opened the back door.

"Get in."

I hesitated. I couldn't get in the car. The officers wouldn't know where to look for me. My mobile vibrated in my jeans pocket. It was probably Parry. It took a lot of self-control not to answer it. If I did, I knew the kidnapper would just seize the phone. And if I didn't answer, Parry would know something was wrong.

"Get in the fricking car." The man pushed me towards the open door. I could see now why the homeless man at the warehouse had called him a lizard. His neck was covered with tattoos of green and brown scales, as were his muscular arms, which bulged from a short-sleeved army green T-shirt. He wore camouflage pants and boots.

"Goddammit," he muttered. He grabbed me and threw me head first into the back seat. My skull hit the door on the other side. For a second my vision blurred. He leaned in, grabbed my wrists and wound a zip tie around them. Then he tied a piece of fabric around my eyes as a blindfold. It was itchy and smelled of petrol.

"Get this off me," I said. "It's disgusting."

"We're not going anywhere without it on."

He hurried to the driver's side and started the car. It was an old and basic model that banged and jolted along. Either the transmission was dodgy or Lizardman was a bad driver. The engine revved high, followed by a loud clank when he changed gear.

Occasionally, we stopped, presumably at a traffic light or intersection. It seemed to me that the stops became less frequent and our speed increased, which must mean that we had left the city behind, but I had no idea in which direction we were going. After a while, we slowed down and made a sharp turn. The tires made a crunching sound and I guessed we were on a gravel road. That scared me. Gravel roads often led to quarries or wastelands, easy places to dump a body.

By the time Lizardman stopped the car and opened the door, I was trembling. He took the blindfold off first, for which I was grateful, and then he cut the ties that bound my wrists before dragging me out of the back seat. It was dusk, that time of day when the sky was more violet than blue, not yet dark, with a few stars making an early foray into the sunless sky. Expansive lawns, black in the twilight, stretched as far as I could see. Standing a few yards from the edge of the driveway was a deer with antlers, so still he looked like a statue. He watched us for a few seconds and then bounded away, vanishing among the trees that bordered the lawns. I wished I could follow him.

Lizardman tugged at my leather bag, which hung from my shoulder. "Show me the notes," he said.

"I want to see Anita first. That's the deal. No Anita, no notes." I shivered in the cold evening air. Without a word, he pushed me towards a huge house that stood at the end of the driveway. More than a house, I realized, it was a mansion, a Victorian version of a French chateau, with tall windows that formed symmetrical patterns on both sides of a massive double door under a limestone pediment. Ornate brick chimneystacks rose high above a mansard roof, and a conical turret stood to one side like something out of a fairy tale. Focusing on the building helped reduce the fear. My trembling subsided. I needed a clear head to have any chance of rescuing Anita.

We walked up a short flight of limestone steps to the front door, which he opened to reveal a grand hallway, furnished with Persian rugs and antique tables. A graceful archway led to a dining room, where I glimpsed a table, a long slab of gleaming walnut, set with flowers and candlesticks. We walked the length of the vast entry hall, past a wide staircase, to a door set in the back wall. He opened it and pushed me forward on to a small landing. Poorly lit, narrow wooden steps led downwards. We clattered down two flights, passing a landing that led to more doors. I kept gathering the details, going over them in my head in case I needed to take this route back in a hurry.

The stairs ended in a claustrophobia-inducing corridor with green-painted walls and a low ceiling lined with bulky metal pipes. We passed through a fire door only to find that the corridor continued. It must run the length of the house, I thought, providing access for water pipes and heating ducts. At the end of the long corridor was a metal door. Heaving it open, Lizardman shoved me forward into a small, gloomy cellar.

Anita sat, tied to a chair, her head lolling forward. Her aura was dense and moving fast. I stumbled towards her, knelt next to her and put my hand on her cheek. "Anita? It's me, Kate."

With relief, I saw her eyes open, grow large when she realized I was there.

"Kate," she whispered. "Thank God."

She was wearing the same grey wool pants and black jacket that she'd been wearing on the day she'd been kidnapped. Her hair was pulled back in an untidy ponytail. Keeping my fingers against her cheek, I surveyed the room. With stone walls, and a flagstone floor, it had probably been used as a storage cellar sometime in the mansion's past. Apart from Anita's chair, it was furnished with three other chairs grouped around a small square table, which held a tray of dirty plates and a roll of duct tape. A single window, high up and out of reach, was opaque with grime.

Lizardman pulled me away from Anita and pointed to a chair facing her. Before I realized what he was doing, he zip-tied my wrists to the arms of the chair. "What are you doing?" I demanded. "I'm here to give you the notes. You have to let Anita go now."

Silently, he wound ties around my ankles, pulling them tight. I couldn't move my legs. He stood, and picked up my leather bag. From it he withdrew the envelope, took out the papers and flipped through them. I held my breath, but he just nodded, slid them back in the envelope and put it on the table.

"You've got what you want, so let us go," I said again.

"All in good time." He settled into a chair, sticking his booted feet out in front of him, arms folded, eyes closed. He didn't appear to be planning on going anywhere anytime soon.

"Are you all right?" I whispered to Anita. She nodded, even though she looked terrible, tired with dark circles under her eyes, her shoulders slumped.

"No talking or I'll use the duct tape," Lizardman said, without opening his eyes.

I looked around the cellar, which felt more like a prison cell with no possible avenue of escape. Iron rings fastened to the walls looked like something out of a medieval dungeon. It was cold, even colder than outside. A good condition for storing meat or wine, perhaps, but very uncomfortable for humans.

There was a smell that I recognized, although I couldn't place it immediately. I'd first noticed it when we got out of the car. A melange of vegetation and wet earth, it wasn't unpleasant. Then I realized it was the Thames. That meant we must still be close to the river, but where exactly?

I wriggled my wrists against their bonds, but the plastic ties held tight.

"What are we waiting for?" I asked Lizardman.
He opened one eye. "My boss," he said.

35

I exchanged looks with Anita. When she shook her head, I guessed she hadn't met the boss yet.

"This wasn't the deal," I said. "You said to bring the notes and I did."

"Shut up," he said. "You talk again and I'll tape your yappy mouth."

"You shouldn't have come," Anita whispered to me. "It's my fault. I shouldn't have led you to the notes."

This time Lizardman moved, sitting up to aim a kick at her shin. "I said no talking."

"Touch me again and you'll be sorry," she said.

He laughed. I don't know how long we sat there. It seemed to be an eon before we heard noises at the door. For the briefest of seconds, I allowed myself to hope it was the police.

The man who entered was dressed in tight jeans and a black leather jacket over a black T-shirt. He looked very different from the last time I'd seen him, in his suit and tie, in the lobby at the hospital.

"Audley?" Anita sounded as shocked as I felt. "What are you doing here?"

It was Audley Macintyre, the drug rep. At once, all the pieces fell into place, or some of them did anyway.

He smirked, his white teeth glowing in the gloom. "I couldn't pass up the chance to see this for myself," he said. "Can't let Phil here have all the fun." He nodded towards Lizardman, who'd jumped to his feet and was standing at attention.

Macintyre came to stand in front of me. "Hello Kate," he said, bending briefly to touch my cheek. "Or should I call you something different? Sophie, wasn't it? With the poor sick son that you just had to talk to Dr. Reid about?"

Anita looked at me in confusion, while he picked up the envelope, slid the papers out and began to read them. I wasn't ready for the blow when it came. His hand connected with my jaw and jolted my head sideways.

Anita screamed at him. "Stop it!"

He threw the papers on to the floor. "Really, Kate? You thought you could fool me? These may be some of Anita's notes, but you know full well that they're not the ones I want. Where are they?"

"I don't know what you mean," I said, my cheek smarting. "You said you wanted the notes and that's what I brought."

Macintyre turned a chair round and straddled it, resting his elbows across the back. "We have all night. You can tell me now or you can tell me later. But you will tell me where those notes are."

"And if I do, then what? Will you let us go?"

He cocked his head to one side. "Good question. I don't know yet. I might let you go, or I might kill you."

"Did you kill Dr. Reid?" Anita asked, her eyes still wide in shock.

"Reid? Yes, although I didn't want to. He was stubborn, the old fool. All he had to do was keep his mouth shut, but no. Why do some people have to stir up trouble?"

Anita struggled against the ties around her wrists, almost tipping her chair over. "You bastard. You cowardly bastard. How could you?"

"Kill? It's easy. And it just gets easier the more you do it. I'd have no trouble killing either of you. I want you to know that."

He tapped his fingers along the back of the chair. "You know, I've never understood soldiers who spend a lifetime regretting a death they were forced to inflict. Or a murderer who suffers remorse while languishing in a prison cell. Killing is part of the natural order of things. And in my personal experience, people who are murdered have usually done something to deserve it."

He leaned over and picked up a page from the floor. "Interesting, but useless. So, one more time. You tell me where the real notes are, and I'll let you go. Maybe. That's just a chance you'll have to take."

There was no way he was going to free us. He'd just confessed to killing Dr. Reid. All I could do was play for time, and hope that the police would arrive soon. I'd turned on GPS tracking on my mobile. Parry had my number. I was sure he'd be able to find us.

"The notes are in Anita's desk drawer," I said.

"No, they're not. We looked there already."

He looked from me to Anita and back. "No? Nothing?"

Nodding to Lizardman, he cradled his chin in his hands. "Well, I like to watch."

Lizardman approached Anita with a knife. The blade was long and wide, narrowing to a razor-thin point, which he held against one corner of Anita's mouth.

"One little slice and those beautiful lips will never be the same," Macintyre said. "You'll look like the Joker in Batman. Except that you're brown, of course."

My arms and legs felt terribly cold, as though all my blood had rushed to some deep part of me to hide from this monster.

"Leave her alone. We don't know anything. Someone must have moved the notes from Anita's drawer."

The grimy window was black now. The only light in the room was from a dim bulb hung above the table, populating the corners of the cellar with murky shadows. I shuddered, a deep muscular contraction running from my toes to the top of my head. I wasn't scared of the dark, but I was terrified of Macintyre.

"So, here we are," he said. "A little cooperation would go a long way."

I glanced at Anita. She was still staring at Macintyre in horror.

"Why did you kill Dr. Reid?" she asked. "Because he was about to expose you?"

"Yes." He nodded at Lizardman, who pressed the knifepoint against Anita's upper lip. A single drop of crimson blood appeared. It rolled slowly over her lips and down her chin.

"Leave her alone," I pleaded.

Macintyre grinned at me. "Ah, Kate, you're adorable when you want something."

I pressed myself against the back of my chair, trying to put more space between us. He repelled me.

"Let's play a game," he said. "I'll show you mine if you show me yours. You start. Tell me what you think you know."

I clamped my lips together. I didn't even want to breathe the same air as him.

"Go ahead, Phil," he said. Lizardman moved the knifepoint to the corner of Anita's mouth.

"Okay, okay. I'll tell you."

"Good," he said. "Phil, stand down. Let's hear what the little lady has to say."

"Don't tell him anything," Anita said. "He's going to kill us anyway."

I was thinking fast. If I talked, maybe they'd leave Anita alone. Maybe Parry would have worked out how to track my phone. Maybe Owens and Walsh were about to burst through the door.

"Someone used Dr. Reid's login and password to change the data on the electronic patient records," I said. "Was that you?"

"No. But you're on the right track."

"Dr. Schwartz then."

"Keep going."

"Schwartz was trying to hide something," I said, trying to work out what it was.

"He was falsifying data on the side effects of LitImmune," Anita said. "Which is a drug developed by your company."

"And what makes you think that?" Macintyre was smiling.

"The edits that Schwartz made were on records of patients who'd had kidney transplants."

"Good, good." Macintyre sounded like a teacher coaching a student. "And where do you come into the picture, do you think?"

"There were differences between the electronic patient records and my notes. Anyone who saw the two of them side by side could easily identify the false entries."

"Hence my need to secure the notes," Macintyre said, looking at me.

"I think Reid was worried that maybe Anita was the one making the edits," I said. "He'd set up a meeting with her to discuss it. But that meeting never happened."

Macintyre clapped his hands together slowly. "Bravo."

"How did you do it?" Anita asked. "How did you manage to get an IV hooked up to Dr. Reid?"

"I told him I had a problem I needed to discuss in private," he said. "Once I had him in an examination room, I gave him Rophynol in a cup of coffee to knock him out long enough to get the meds going. His brain might have been robust but physically, he was weak."

Anita closed her eyes. A tear rolled down her cheek.

"Don't stop, ladies. I'm enjoying your little narrative."

He looked from Anita to me and back again. "Come on," he said. "You must know more."

When neither of us spoke, he nodded again at Lizardman. With an expression of deep satisfaction, Lizardman stroked the point of knife across Anita's lips before jabbing it into the corner of her mouth. She whimpered as blood streamed from the cut.

"Stop it, for God's sake," I said. "Stop it."

Macintyre raised an eyebrow at me.

"We thought that Eric Hill was involved in some way," I said. "That he—"

"Eric." Macintyre interrupted. "What a loser. He actually believes he's helping doctors save lives and all that crap. It'll be a pleasure to shut him up once and for all."

"Why?" asked Anita. "Why do you need to shut him up?"

"Because Reid talked to him. Eric's too stupid to have realized that LitImmune was the problem, but he'll connect the dots at some point. So he has to go."

I gazed at Macintyre, trying to understand. "You're working for someone else, aren't you? Someone at LBP? Maybe the researcher who was responsible for LitImmune's initial tests?"

"A researcher? God, no."

"The CEO of LB Pharmaceuticals?" I threw out the suggestion, hoping for a response, even an involuntary one like a nervous tic, a twitch of an eye. But Macintyre was far too professional to give anything away.

"You can't really believe I'm going to tell you who I work for," he said, standing up and pushing the chair to one side. The screech of wood on the flagstone floor was deafening in the dreary confines of the cellar.

"I don't really understand one thing," I said, still aiming to draw more information from him. "There must be other hospitals using LitImmune and other doctors who've noted side effects. What good would it do to silence Anita?"

"The drug is still in trial. A double blind trial, as luck would have it, which makes things easier for me. There are other hospitals testing it, and other doctors willing to compromise their medical ethics to reap the financial reward of cooperating with me. And, sadly, there have been a couple of tragic accidents involving doctors who insisted on sticking to their moral principles."

I wanted to ask what the hell a double blind trial was, but my voice was stuck in my throat.

"You've killed other people?" Anita asked. "Not just Dr. Reid?"

He shrugged. "All in a day's work," he said. "You are the annoying fly in the ointment. By keeping notes separate from the official records, you've made my life rather more difficult. But I'm about to solve the problem, because Kate is going to tell me where the notes are."

He walked towards me, his black clad figure melding with the dark shadows. "Where did you put the notes, sweet Kate?" He bent down, putting his face close to mine. His eyes were like dirty ice, translucent, almost colorless. If eyes are windows into the soul, his gave away nothing; maybe there was no soul to be seen. I turned my face away from his. I really didn't want to die in this horrible cellar.

"Don't tell him," Anita said. I'd almost forgotten she was there. Lizardman too. Macintyre took up all the space. He absorbed the weak light, sucked all the oxygen from the air. It was like being locked up in a tomb with him.

"Other people know about the notes," I said. "Even if you kill us, they will find you."

Macintyre laughed. "I don't think so. These other people, whoever they are, won't know who I am or where I am. I have resources beyond your wildest imaginings."

"They won't give up." I felt the need to keep talking. It was better than listening to his creepy voice. And there was still a chance the police were on their way. I glanced at my leather bag, thinking of my phone. Macintyre noticed. He picked up the bag, shook it upside down.

"You're looking for this?" he asked. He held my phone up so I could see the screen. "No signal, dear heart. We're in a basement with twenty-four inch stone walls."

"You won't get away with it," Anita said quietly.

"You say that in hope, not in fact." He turned to look at Anita. It was as though a glaring light pointed at me had been turned off. "You're the type who thinks that evil will always be punished, that good will be rewarded. But life isn't like that. Not at all. Murderers and rapists stroll the pavements of our fair city next to mobsters, swindlers and thieves. The good people, as you think of them, walk the streets deaf and blind, unaware that the man next to them on the bus is a terrorist, or the barista serving them coffee is a pedophile."

I was finding it hard to breathe, scared beyond reason. The man was a psychopath.

Macintyre straightened up. "I've had enough of this. It's time, ladies. Tell me where the notes are."

My thoughts were darting around like fish in a bowl. If I told Macintyre where the notes were, he might keep us alive while Lizardman went to find them. Once he had them, though, we'd be dead. "The notes are in a cabinet in the kitchen on the fourth floor at the hospital."

That would throw some obstacles in his way. Lizardman couldn't just walk in there and pick them up. In the early evening the wards would be busy, with plenty of staff and visitors still around to make access difficult. Anita looked at me with a faint smile. She knew now that I'd found them in the kitchen, and that they weren't there any longer.

Macintyre came to stand close to me again. I recoiled when he reached out and stroked my hair. "If you're lying, Kate, I'll take great pleasure in getting the truth from you. It won't be quick, I promise you. Where exactly are they?"

"They're in a manila folder with a K on the front for Kate. In the cabinet furthest from the sink, behind some boxes of coffee." I hoped that embellishing the details would make him think I was telling the truth.

Macintyre ran his finger along my aching jaw. He straightened up, stepped away. "Phil, keep an eye on them. We'll deal with them when I get back."

With several long strides, he was gone, the metal door clanging closed behind him. I had to restrain myself from smiling. He'd taken the bait and, even better, he'd gone on the errand himself. If we had any hope of escaping it would have to be now, with only Lizardman to contend with.

Anita's tears had dried and she straightened up in her chair. She gave a slight nod towards me, a sign that she was thinking the same as I was. I had to do something to get Lizardman to untie me. I began to cough and convulse, the ties on my wrist and ankles digging into my flesh every time I jerked against them.

"She's seizing," Anita shouted. "You have to help her."

Lizardman looked at her blankly.

"Now, you idiot," she yelled at him. "Get her horizontal, with her head turned to one side. Do it now."

"What the hell?"

"You don't want to let her die. Macintyre will be furious if you do. He's going to need her to tell him where those notes really are."

"She lied? I need to call Macintyre."

"Later. You can call him later. Now do as I say before she swallows her tongue and suffocates."

Lizardman bounded towards me, knife in front of him. He began sawing through the zip ties around my wrists, freeing my arms from the chair. When he cut the tie on my right ankle, I brought my fists together on each side of his head, battering his ears. He yelped in pain, pushed away from me and fell backwards just long enough for me to aim a kick at him. It was luck, not skill, that my foot connected with his face. I heard a loud crack. Grasping the knife in one hand, he used the other to cradle his nose. Blood poured through his fingers.

His temporary lack of attention gave me the time I needed to retrieve the Stanley box-cutter from the table, where it lay amongst a mess of make-up containers and old receipts. My fingers were shaking, but the blade was razor sharp, able to cut through the tie on my left ankle with ease. I stood up, holding the box-cutter in front of me.

Lizardman was already climbing to his feet. When he saw the blade in my hand, he paused, but only for a second. Then he came at me, his knife raised and aimed at my chest. I knew I couldn't beat him in a knife fight. I moved behind my chair, putting more space between us.

Instead of charging at me, as I expected him to do, he moved towards Anita, who was still bound hand and foot. She was the easy target, of course.

"Put the weapon down, Kate," he said, pointing his knife at her. His voice sounded raspy and nasal as though he had a bad cold.

I grabbed my empty chair, held it high with the legs pointing at him, and ran. The chair hit him in the torso, barely making an impact. He merely grabbed one of the legs and pulled, bringing me with it. We were close now, with just the chair between us. I whipped the box-cutter around, stabbing at thin air until suddenly, miraculously, the blade hit his upper arm. I felt it sink through the flesh and hit bone. Swearing loudly, he dropped the chair and grabbed at his arm, his knife hanging loosely in his hand.

Behind me Anita yelled, urging me on. I picked up the chair again and swung it at his injured arm. The knife flew out of his hand and clattered to the floor. I flung the chair around again, aiming for his head. The edge of the wooden seat made contact with his broken nose with a satisfying crunch. He wavered for a few seconds before falling to his knees, his hands covering his face.

I wasn't thinking very clearly, but I knew we only had seconds to act. He was disabled, but not for long. I cut through the ties on Anita's wrists and thrust the box-cutter into her hand. Skirting Lizardman, I rushed to retrieve his knife from where it had fallen.

By the time he was back on his feet, Anita was free, and armed with the box-cutter. I stood next to her with the knife in my hand.

"Stay back," I said to him. "I'll use this if I have to."

Even through all the blood, he smirked, which made me mad. I raised the knife, preparing to throw it. I'd thrown javelin in school one year when I was too injured to run. At this distance, he was an easy mark.

His eyes widened. "What the…" he said, holding his good hand in front of him.

"Back on your knees," I said.

When he was on the floor, Anita crouched down next to him, holding the box-cutter at his neck. "Don't think I won't do it," she said. "I'm a surgeon and I know exactly where your carotid artery runs." She stroked the blade along his skin, leaving a thin red line.

"Tie him up," she said to me. "Check his pocket for zip ties."

I dug into his pocket and pulled out three ties, then sat on his legs while securing his ankles to the table legs. There was only one tie left so I bound his wrists together.

"We need to go," I said. "Macintyre could come back at any moment."

Anita nodded, still holding the blade against Lizardman's throat. I grabbed my bag and threw all my stuff back in it, including my useless phone. Looping the strap across my body, I followed Anita to the heavy iron door, which squealed on its hinges when she pulled it open. I checked quickly but there was no lock, no way to block it. We'd just have to move fast.

The long corridor stretching ahead was our only way out. If we met Macintyre coming the other way, we were in trouble. When we reached the wooden staircase at the other end, we paused to listen for any sounds from above. It was quiet and we had no choice anyway. We had to go up. My pulse raced. I wasn't going to tell Anita, but her aura was still there, spinning over her head. That meant we weren't out of danger yet.

We reached the top of the staircase and pushed open the door that led into the spacious lobby, where I fumbled around until I found a light switch. Soft lamplight revealed wood paneling and dozens of framed paintings of horses or flowers on the walls.

"What is this place? It looks like an aristocrat's country house, but we're in London." Anita turned to look at me. "Aren't we? I'm so confused. I have no idea where I am."

I didn't know either, except that I was sure we were near the river. "We need to keep moving," I said. As I led the way across the hall towards the front doors a table near the staircase caught my attention. It was covered in glossy brochures.

I picked one up. "Welcome to Litton Bernhoff Hall," I read out loud. "Now it makes sense. This place must belong to LB Pharmaceuticals. Maybe a conference center or a hospitality center where they entertain customers?"

"There's nothing very hospitable about this place," Anita said, unlocking the front door. "Let's go."

We ran down the steps to the gravel driveway, and past the Land Rover that I'd arrived in. "Damn," I said. "We should have got his keys so we could drive out of here."

"No time to go back," Anita said. "Keep moving."

An amber moon appeared from behind a bank of clouds, giving us just enough light to see where we were going. We'd walked about ten yards, when a sudden sweep of headlights in the distance made my heart pound. I pulled Anita off the driveway, finding shelter behind a thick and prickly bush. The lights soon faded, and I stood up.

"That's good," I said. "We must be closer to a road than I thought. I say we make a run for it. A straight line along the driveway. Can you do that?"

She nodded and stood up, leading the way around the shrubs back to the gravel. Suddenly a hand grasped my shoulder. I turned to see the bloody, wrecked face of Lizardman.

"You should have killed me when you had the chance," he said. "Because I certainly intend to kill you."

He swung at me, his fist connecting with my cheekbone. Pain ricocheted around my head, coming to rest at my lower temple.

Staggering, I fell to my knees. He seized the knife from my hand. The moon reflected in the blade as it curved towards me, aiming at my neck.

He was so focused on me that he didn't see Anita move behind him. She jumped up, wrapping one arm around his neck, her legs around his waist. He flailed around, trying to throw her off, the knife in his hand whipping to and fro, perilously close to my face. I wanted to move but I couldn't; there seemed to be no muscles left in my legs or arms. Anita yelled at me to get up. As I clambered to my feet, Lizardman lunged forward, throwing Anita off. He raised the knife again, poised to stab me in the neck.

With a scream like a warrior going into battle, Anita ran at him and stabbed the box-cutter repeatedly into his shoulder. For a second, I thought he hadn't even felt it. Then he fell forwards in slow motion, his bloodied features looming over me before he collapsed on top of me.

Adrenaline fueled a burst of strength, helping me to push him off so that he rolled on to his back on the gravel. Blood flowed freely from his nose, like ink in the light of the sallow moon. A puddle collected near his shoulder.

Anita bent over him, holding a finger to his neck. "He's alive," she said. "What do we do with him now?"

"Nothing. We leave him and keep going," I said, moving my head from side to side, trying to dislodge the pain.

Suddenly, there was a flood of white light at the end of the drive, the revving of an engine as tires gained traction on the gravel. It had to be Macintyre.

"Help me," I said to Anita, grabbing Lizardman under his arms. She raised his feet a few inches off the ground and we dragged him off the driveway, over the grassy verge and behind the bush where we'd sheltered before. I prayed that Macintyre couldn't see us from the drive.

A black Audi flew past us, the tires spitting up small stones. The second I saw its tail lights, I grasped Anita's wrist. "We're going to run for it. Ready?"

She glanced at Lizardman. "We can't leave him here. He could die without attention to those wounds," she said.

"Who cares? We don't have time. As soon as Macintyre sees that we're gone, he'll be out here looking for us."

We ran. The driveway ended at a set of wrought iron gates, flanked by stone walls about six feet high. I grabbed the handle, but the gate was locked.

"It's on some kind of motion detector," Anita said, pointing to a wooden post set eight feet back from the gate with a small box mounted on it. I ran back, waving my hands in front of the box. "Not enough mass to make it work," I panted. "Now what?"

Without hesitation, Anita ran at the wall, jumped up and gripped the ledge at the top. I followed her and held both her legs, pushing her upwards until her waist hit the ledge and she was able to scramble up on top of the wall. She leaned down to grab hold of my outstretched hands as I used my feet to clamber my way to the top. We dropped to the other side, onto a bank at the edge of a road. I pulled my phone from my bag, almost crying with relief that we had service back now we were out of the basement. I called Parry.

"Where the hell are you?" he asked.

"Where the hell were your men?" I responded. "Listen, we need help urgently. Dr. Reid's killer is at a place called Litton Bernhoff Hall. I don't know exactly where it is, but it's close to the river, probably east of Greenwich."

The roar of an airplane engine drowned out his reply.

"And I think we're close to City Airport," I said. As the engine noise faded, Parry told us to stay where we were.

Help was coming, but when he clicked off, I felt nervous and vulnerable. There were no streetlights, just thick woods opposite us and the wall at our backs. If Macintyre came out, he'd see us at once. We crossed the road to the trees on the other side. Picking our way across fallen branches and through brambles, we found a clear grassy area with a good view of the road. We crouched down to wait. Less than a minute later, there was a sweep of headlights on the mansion driveway, which meant that Macintyre must be leaving. The lights stopped moving for a while, giving me hope that the police would arrive in time to cut off his exit. But then the lights came closer. Seconds later, the gates swung open and the Audi turned out of the driveway, accelerating up the road. He was getting away.

After a minute or two, I pulled Anita to her feet. At least with Macintyre gone, we could wait at the gates for the police. Five more minutes passed before two squad cars arrived in a rush of flashing lights and wailing sirens. A WPC grabbed a first aid kit from the back of one car and tended to Anita's cut in the light from the headlamps.

"It's not as bad as it looks," she said. "You won't need stitches."

While she worked, I stared at the aura that still swirled over Anita's head. Damn, damn, damn. We'd escaped, but she was still in danger. From Lizardman? From Macintyre? Or something else I wasn't aware of yet? She looked exhausted, and there was a bruise on one cheek that I hadn't noticed in the gloom of the cellar. Her hair had come loose from its ponytail and hung limply on her shoulders.

I told one of the police officers that Macintyre had gone already. He talked on his radio to someone, maybe Parry, while another officer worked out how to open the gate.

When the WPC had finished tending to Anita, she helped us into the back of one of the cars. "The driver will take you to Detective Parry's office now," she said. "Take care of yourselves."

The back seat smelled of sweat and something musty, a vestige perhaps of a previous occupant.

"What was going on today?" I asked the driver. "I was supposed to get police support hours ago." I hoped I didn't sound too whiny.

The officer nodded, looking at me in his rear view mirror. "I'm sorry, miss. Did you hear about the bomb? We were all put on high alert."

"A bomb?" My mind immediately went to Simon Scott. "What happened?"

"Someone called in a message about a bomb in central London. I think they were targeting a politician. Scott, the leader of the opposition, was due to drive right past where they said the bomb was. He was diverted."

"Was it a hoax or was there really a bomb?"

"Not sure. They don't tell us everything. If it was, they must have defused it. But it was most likely a hoax, just to make the security forces jump."

I leaned back in my seat, thinking. If it had been an actual bomb, who'd set it? Someone on my list, or some third party I didn't know about? I hadn't heard from Chris for a couple of days and, of course, we hadn't exactly parted on friendly terms. The memory of those chemical stains on his hands stuck with me.

I glanced at Anita. Sad to see that aura still spinning, I sank back in my seat, with my hands over my eyes. Anita didn't notice. She was already asleep.

36

Anita dozed as we sped through the outer reaches of East London, past the O2 arena, which was brightly lit for an event. The moon that had helped us find our way to freedom was completely obscured now by dark clouds. Rain beat against the windows. It wasn't the first time I'd ridden in the back of a police car, which was surprising, given my law-abiding nature. Only sort of law-abiding, I amended. Last year, I'd almost strangled someone and tonight I'd stabbed Lizardman. It was all in self-defense, but I wondered what it meant, that I could resort to violence when necessary. Are all humans inherently violent? A propensity that, for most, remains dormant until provoked? That certainly wasn't true of Macintyre. He seemed to need very little reason to hurt or kill. The memory of his flat, colorless eyes still made my heart pound.

I shook Anita gently, impatient to get answers to a million questions. At first she grumbled, but then sat up straight. "I need coffee," she said.

"We'll get some as soon as we reach the station, I promise. First you need to call your mother. She must be frantic with worry."

"You and my mum could be the same person, you know that?" she said, taking my mobile. The call didn't last long, but I heard Mrs. Banerjee crying and yelling at her husband that Anita was safe. Anita rang off after swearing up and down that she was absolutely fine and would see them soon.

"Tell me more about your notes," I said when she gave me back my

202

phone. "How the hell did Macintyre even know they existed?"

She stretched her arms above her head. "God, I ache all over. The notes? Macintyre saw them in my office. I feel like such a fool, but I had no idea at the time. He'd asked to meet me to talk about a blood pressure medication from Eric's company, PharmAnew. Obviously, Macintyre wanted the hospital to replace it with the version from Litton Bernhoff. Our computer system was down for maintenance, so I dug through the notes in my drawer to check some data. He asked me what the notes were all about and I told him. He was charming and complimentary, telling me how impressed he was that I was advancing my learning, blah, blah, blah. I never gave it another thought until Dr. Reid asked me about the notes, at the same time he said he needed to meet with me. That was the day before he died."

"And how did Dr. Reid know about the notes?"

"I'd often take notes when we were working together, and I'd told him why. He thought it was a good idea too. But when you and I had compared them to the electronic files, I got nervous, so I found a plastic box in the store room and hid them in the kitchen until I'd have time to go through them properly."

Anita turned to look at me. "Where are they now? The real ones that Macintyre wanted?"

"In the morgue. Grace hid them in an unused refrigerator drawer." I grabbed my mobile. "Oh, damn. I need to call her to let her know we're okay."

Grace picked up as soon as I rang. I explained that we were safe and that the police were tracking down Macintyre, but I skipped the gory details of Macintyre's threats and our escape.

"I've been so worried," Grace said. "I can't wait to see Anita again. The morgue is all locked up for the night. You can retrieve the notes tomorrow, if that's okay."

"We'll see you in the morning. Thanks again, Grace." I clicked off, vaguely worried that Macintyre might still work out where the notes were. But it seemed unlikely. And, even if he did, he couldn't break into the morgue.

Anita picked at a nail she'd broken during the scramble over the wall. "Do I still have the aura?" she asked. "Has it gone?"

"It's still there."

"That makes no sense," she said. "We escaped. Lizardman didn't kill me."

"I know. It means we have to continue to be careful."

My heart ached for her. She'd already been through so much, and it obviously wasn't over yet. We slowed in traffic as we came into the City.

"Take a nap," I told her. "I'll wake you when we get there."

Anita closed her eyes, leaning her head against the back of the seat. While the car idled at a traffic light, I watched the rain form rivulets on the window. They wound in serpentine patterns, their motion dictated not by the laws of gravity, but perhaps by infinitesimal flaws in the glass that disrupted their flow. Two rills eight inches apart curved as though irresistibly drawn to each other, creating one larger stream that meandered to the bottom of the window.

I traced its path with my finger on the inside of the glass, imagining that I could feel the cool water on my skin. The car pulled away, but I didn't hear the engine or the hum of tires on wet road. It seemed that all sounds had stopped except a rushing noise in my head like the roar of a waterfall.

The two cases, Simon Scott's and Dr. Reid's, were connected. There was a common link between them, I was almost sure. I tried to shake Anita awake. She gazed at me for a moment through heavy-lidded eyes before going back to sleep.

Macintyre was looking for records that implicated his company, Litton Bernhoff Pharmaceuticals, in a cover-up of side-effects. In the back of my mind, I recalled seeing the company name somewhere else recently, somewhere outside the hospital. I pulled out my phone, looking back through the notes I'd taken when reviewing Simon Scott's files at Colin Butler's office.

There was one annotation, more cryptic than I'd have liked, of an appointment with the CEO of Litton Bernhoff. Someone in Colin's office had noted that the meeting was on Scott's agenda, but I couldn't recall any details.

Maybe I'd been on the wrong track the whole time, by assuming that the threat to Scott was from someone with a grudge against him. My initial meeting with Eliza, and my concerns about Chris and the binoculars man had convinced me that Scott was in danger from someone who resented his rise to prominence, someone he'd harmed in the past. Perhaps that was all wrong. It could have been Macintyre who'd planted the bomb in the underground car park.

When we got out of the car outside the police station, my legs were shaking. I linked arms with Anita and took a few deep breaths of cold, damp air. To my surprise, it was Clarke who was on the steps waiting for us. He handed me a thin beige raincoat, which I put on and buttoned up to hide the bloodstains on my jacket.

"You look as though you could do with a hot drink," he said to Anita, who nodded her agreement. We followed him through the rain to a café around the corner. No one spoke until we were sitting with cups of steaming coffee in front of us.

"Where's Parry?" I asked.

"He's busy. I told him I'd stand in for him for a couple of hours."

"Macintyre got away," I said. "Did you find Lizardman? Macintyre calls him Phil."

"Not yet," he said. "Tell me what happened."

I summarized everything we knew about Litton Bernhoff and gave him descriptions of Macintyre and Lizardman. Clarke nodded occasionally, tapping notes into his smartphone.

"I think that Macintyre is going after Simon Scott because Scott knows something about that drug, LitImmune. It could have been Macintyre who set that bomb off."

Clarke shook his head. "It wasn't. We have that person in custody."

"Who? Not Chris Melrose?"

"No." He paused, looking as though he was trying to work out what to say. "The man we have in custody is your binoculars man, David Lowe. He confessed to making and detonating a small bomb in the car park in Portsmouth."

"I did warn you about him," I said.

"We're very grateful." Clarke didn't sound grateful. He sounded ticked off that I'd been right.

"What about the bomb scare in London? Was it real?"

"I don't know yet. All I know is that it'll have generated a mountain of paperwork, so I need to get back to the office."

He drank the rest of his coffee. "You haven't heard from Chris Melrose, I take it? We have to consider him a suspect for the London bomb, given what you told us about him."

"Did you test that twenty-pound note?" Anita asked.

Clarke shook his head. "I don't have the results yet." He looked at his watch. "I'll be handing you off to Parry when we get back to the station. He's in charge of the investigation into Macintyre."

"No way," I said. "You have to do it. Parry's an..." I was going to say 'idiot' but Clarke wouldn't appreciate my insulting his fellow officer.

Anita looked at me, then at Clarke and back. "You two obviously know each other fairly well."

"Unfortunately, yes," Clarke said, but the corners of his lips moved upwards in the faintest of smiles. "That's the way it works, Kate. I can't barge in on someone else's case. Parry was in charge of the investigation into Dr. Reid's death. He'll reopen the inquiry and go after Macintyre."

"Parry said that Reid committed suicide. He didn't investigate anything." Anita raised her voice enough that several customers turned to look at us.

"I'll make sure Detective Parry has all the right resources at his disposal." Clarke's tone was firm.

"We don't trust him," I said.

"There's no choice, Kate. Work with him, tell him everything you've told me. The more you can help him, the quicker he'll pick up Macintyre." Clarke's malachite eyes stared into mine as he looked for my agreement.

I nodded.

We trailed after Clarke along the rain-doused street to the police station, where rows of well-lit windows made it look almost welcoming. Telling us he'd be in touch, he left us to wait on uncomfortable plastic chairs near the front desk. It took fifteen minutes for Parry to make an appearance, looking as bald and pink as I remembered him.

He led us to a small meeting room, where a uniformed officer typed up our statements, while Parry prompted us with questions or clarified an answer. We related everything that had happened, including Macintyre's confession that he'd killed Dr. Reid. Parry made no comment on the news that Reid's alleged suicide was in fact a murder. I wondered what it would take to elicit a reaction of surprise or anger from him. Or an apology for being so dead wrong.

After we'd made our statements, we had to wait for a technician to retrieve DNA samples from my blue jacket.

"What about Lizardman?" Anita asked Parry. "Phil whatever his name is. Did the police find him? He was on the driveway."

Again, Parry looked back through his notes. "Give me a minute," he said. While he was gone, a young officer brought in tea and biscuits. Anita ate three chocolate digestives, barely pausing in between each one. I needed to get her home and make her something to eat.

Parry huffed back into the office. "I got a report. There was no sign of your Lizardman when the local police got there, but there was blood on the gravel. I'd guess that Macintyre picked him up and they left together. We've alerted the hospitals. From what you've told me, he'll need medical attention."

I massaged my jaw, wishing the pain would go away. It was an unpleasant reminder of Macintyre. That reminded me to tell Parry about my theory that Macintyre could be going after Scott. I explained what I knew about Scott's scheduled visit to Litton Bernhoff the next day.

"We're aware of Mr. Scott's agenda," he responded. "He has plenty of security, I promise you."

"What if Macintyre tries something?"

Parry sighed. "As I said, Scott will be well protected. The police have a description of Macintyre. But as of now, I haven't seen any evidence that links Macintyre and Scott."

Pompous prick, I thought, but I was too tired to argue.

Parry checked his notes. "Where were we? Oh, yes. We'll be able to match DNA and fingerprints to what we picked up at the warehouse."

"Did you find anything else useful there?" Anita asked. "The kidnapper, Phil, had a key to the place, but we were only there for a half hour before some homeless guy came charging in, threatening to report us for trespassing."

She closed her eyes for a moment as though remembering. "I tried to use the distraction to run away, but Lizardman stuck a needle in me. I don't remember anything from then until I woke up in that cellar at the mansion."

While Parry consulted his notes, flipping through pages in his spiral-bound notebook, I thought about the homeless man at the warehouse. When this was all over, I'd go find him, see if I could do something to help him.

"Ah yes," said Parry. "We did find your message about the kitchen," he said.

Anita's face brightened. "I was proud of that. Phil left me alone for two minutes because he had to pee. I used a scrap of an old receipt and a mascara from my purse. I tucked the message under the table leg so he wouldn't see it."

Parry nodded. "Very enterprising," he said. He sipped his tea and then looked at me. "Where are the notes now?"

I explained that they were in the morgue, under lock and key. "We'll pick them up tomorrow morning. They'll be safe there until then."

"Good. We'll need them for evidence, to back up this story of yours."

"Story?" Anita demanded. I put my hand on her arm. There wasn't any point in picking a fight with Parry.

"Can we go?" I asked. I was tired, everything hurt, and I smelled of sweat, blood and whoever had been in the back of the police car before us.

Parry tapped a pencil on his desk. "I don't feel good about letting you wander off by yourselves," he said.

Anita raised an eyebrow. "You're going to keep us here? Put us in a cell?"

"I'm concerned for your safety," he said, which seemed to be the most sensible thing he'd ever said. "I'm going to assign you a police escort, just until we find Macintyre. Sound good?"

"Definitely," I said, glancing at Anita's aura. The more protection she had, the better.

Finally, we were able to leave, and Parry led us to the exit, where we waited until our police officer arrived. His name was PC Wilson. He would be our driver and escort until further notice.

"DCI Clarke is very busy," Parry said, as we shivered on the doorstep. "Please call *me* if you see any sign at all of Macintyre or his accomplice. I'll keep my mobile switched on 24/7."

Back at my flat, PC Wilson said he'd wait just outside the front door. I invited him to come in but he said he had a good book and was used to being on duty so I took a kitchen chair and a cup of tea out to him. Anita and I took it in turns to shower and prepare dinner. The normal routine of it all made the time in the cellar feel like a dream, a nightmare. Still, I couldn't settle. Even with the police involved, I couldn't help feeling nervous that Macintyre was still out there and that he knew where I lived. I stared at my reflection in the bedroom mirror, turning my head from one side to the other, straining to catch any telltale sign of an aura, perhaps a slight disturbance of the air seen from the corner of my eye. There was nothing. For now, I thought, I'd take that as a positive. I needed all the reassurance I could get.

While Anita showered, I texted Josh to let him know she was safe and at home with me. I owed him that much at least, even though I was still confused and angry about all his emails with Helena.

"Fantastic," he wrote back. "Still with my clients. I'll text you when done."

Anita and I sat at the counter to eat, but my spaghetti tasted so bland that I only got through a couple of mouthfuls before pushing my plate away. Anita ate all of hers before starting on mine.

"That whole thing with my notes," Anita said, twirling her fork in the pasta. "I'm feeling really awful about it."

"Why? You didn't do anything wrong, apart from letting yourself get abducted in the first place."

"Very funny. But the fact is that I was getting desperate. Phil, the Lizardman as you call him, was becoming more and more brutal. He gave me a granola bar for dinner, a glass of water for breakfast. He ordered pizza and Chinese for himself and never shared with me. When I complained loudly, he gave me a sedative." She pulled up her sleeve to show me bruises and puncture marks in her lower arm. "Moron. He didn't even know how to inject properly. I really began to think he didn't care if I died. It seemed that getting the notes to him was my only way out. I wrote that message, hoping that you or the police would eventually work out which kitchen I meant."

She frowned. "I never intended for you to get embroiled in this, Kate. You should have given the notes to the police, not come after me by yourself."

"Believe me, I tried," I said.

"You could have been killed, and it's all my fault."

"Don't be daft. None of this is your fault."

"You're the daft one," she smiled. "What were you thinking to let yourself get taken by the Lizard bully? You're a bloody idiot, if you ask me."

I gave an exaggerated look around the kitchen. "Are you still in the cellar? Did Lizardman kill us? And does Macintyre have his precious notes? Or are we sitting at home, eating dinner in perfect safety?"

She waved a fork in the air, her mouth too full to speak.

"I'll take that as no, no, no, yes," I said.

Anita swallowed. "Thank you for rescuing me. You're still a bloody idiot, though."

37

When Anita had finished eating, I gathered up the plates and put them in the dishwasher.

"Do you want to watch television for a while, or go to bed?" I asked her. "It's only nine o clock, but maybe an early night would do you good."

"Television," she said. "I'm tired, but I'm so wound up, I won't be able to sleep yet. I think I'll call the hospital to see if Pauline's on duty and let her know I'm okay. Can I use your mobile?"

She wandered off to the bedroom to talk while I started the dishwasher and put the kettle on. Ten minutes later, she was back. "I have to go in. Pauline said one of my patients is on his way to the ICU. Dr. Schwartz didn't come in today, and neither did Dr. Marks. It's chaos over there."

"Schwartz is probably on the run," I said. "I wonder about Marks. Is he involved too?"

Anita nodded. "It's possible. He was part of the team for those three kidney transplant patients, and he's tight with Schwartz. They play squash together three or four times a week."

I let that information sink in while I wiped down the counter. "You can't go into work, Anita. You're tired and hurt. You need to rest."

We debated back and forth, but the result was a foregone conclusion. Ten minutes later, we were in my room, getting dressed to go out. I threw on jeans and a wool coat. Anita was transformed in a pair of my black wool pants that fit her better than they did me, and a lavender-colored shirt. Her long hair was wound in an immaculate bun. Apart from the bruise on her cheek and the cut near her mouth, it was impossible to imagine the terrible ordeal she'd been through.

If PC Wilson was surprised when I went out to tell him we were heading to the hospital, he didn't show it. He walked down the stairs with us and waited until we'd both put on our seat belts before he started the car. At the hospital, he accompanied us up to the fourth floor, where Pauline hurried towards us.

"Oh my God, Anita! Are you all right? We thought you'd been..." Tears in her eyes, she looked at me. "Good to see you too, Kate."

"I'll tell you everything later," Anita said. "Right now, can you bring me up to date on patients?"

"It's pandemonium. I've brought in as many off-duty nurses as I could find but, without enough doctors, we've been struggling all day." She looked over her shoulder. "And there are a couple of police officers here, asking questions about Audley Macintyre, that drug rep, and about Dr. Schwartz and Dr. Marks. What's going on?"

Glad to hear that the police were already on site, I slightly revised my opinion of Detective Parry.

"I'll probably work for quite a while," Anita told me. "Are you sure you want to wait?"

"Of course. If I get tired, I'll sleep on a chair in a waiting room."

When Pauline and Anita walked away towards the patient rooms, PC Wilson took a seat close to the nurses' station. I felt better about letting Anita out of my sight, knowing that he was there. Wandering towards one of the small waiting rooms, I tried sleeping, but the chair was too uncomfortable. It was like trying to sleep on a plane, something I'd never achieved. Giving up on that idea, I realized that I hadn't thought to bring a book or my laptop. This was going to be a long and boring night if I had to rely on the muted television for distraction. Perhaps I could find something to read in the hospital gift shop on the ground floor.

The glass-fronted store displayed flowers and stuffed animals in the window and stocked more practical items inside. On my way to the book racks at the back, I passed a shelf of over-the-counter medications and immediately thought of Eric Hill, the PharmAnew rep. Macintyre had made threats against him at some point in his crazy rant. It seemed as though I should warn him. And it was possible he'd know something about Litton Bernhoff that might help me work out what

Macintyre would do next. I found a paperback and paid for it, then dug in my purse to see if I still had Eric's business card. When I found it, I called his mobile.

"I'm finishing dinner with a client at the Grill, just round the corner," he said. "I can meet you in the hospital lobby in about ten minutes."

I hung out in the lobby until Eric appeared through a set of glass doors and strode towards me, dressed in a well-cut suit, white shirt and green silk tie. He didn't have an aura, which made me feel better, given Macintyre's nasty threats against him. "Let's go to the cafeteria," I said. "I need caffeine."

"Tell me about Anita," he said, while we waited our turn to be served. "Is she really safe?"

Assuring him she was, I watched his face blanche when I told him that Audley Macintyre had kidnapped her.

"But why?" he asked.

"It's all to do with a drug manufactured by Litton Bernhoff Pharmaceuticals," I said. "Let's sit over there, where no-one can overhear us."

We sat at a table in a quiet corner.

"Do you know anything about LitImmune?"

Eric looked startled. "LitImmune? Well, yes. The damn drug has the potential to erode sales of my company's current immunosuppressant medications, so I've been keeping a very close eye on it. It's in trial right now at several hospitals in the UK. It's in an RCT, which is a randomized control study, where some patients are receiving LitImmune and some are receiving a different, but proven and known medication — one from my company, actually. They're using a double blind trial where neither the provider nor the patient know which medication is being administered."

"So how can the drug's effectiveness be tracked if no one knows who's receiving it?"

"Generally the trial continues for a predetermined number of cases and then the results are tabulated. Certain people have access to the ongoing data in case there are unusual results. Although uncommon, sometimes a drug is so beneficial that every patient receiving it has good results, in which case the trial is stopped early. Dr. Reid, as head of the department, and the Chairman of the Research and Investigation Committee would have had access to the data."

"And what does it do? LitImmune?"

"It's basically a new class of immunosuppressant. It eliminates the need to combine multiple drugs to achieve the same result, which is to ensure the body doesn't reject the new organ. In theory, its side effect profile is good and its post-transplant success rate is superior to anything else on the market. That's what Litton Bernhoff is saying anyway."

"Did Dr. Reid talk to you about it?"

Eric's face contorted. He almost looked as though he would cry. "Yes, he came to me to talk about concerns he had. He didn't say much, just that he thought side effects of LitImmune weren't being fully reported. I had no idea he was so upset about it. I mean, upset enough to commit suicide."

"He didn't. Macintyre killed him."

Eric sank back in his chair, eyes closed.

"Did Dr. Reid tell you who was doing the under-reporting?" I pressed on.

Eric opened his eyes. "No. He was rather tight-lipped about it. I got the impression that he knew, but didn't want to point fingers. It must have been a doctor on his staff."

"Yes, we're reasonably sure it was Dr. Schwartz. And possibly Dr. Marks was involved too. Neither of them turned up for work today."

"So you're telling me that Macintyre and Schwartz were working together? They killed Reid and kidnapped Anita?"

"Macintyre did the dirty work. I think that Schwartz was being paid by LB Pharmaceuticals to mess with the reporting. He somehow obtained Dr. Reid's login and password and used them to hide his trail when he made edits to the patient records."

"Damn." Eric ran his hand over his eyes. "There's something else that might be pertinent then. Pending final approval of the drug, LBP has secured contracts to supply LitImmune to several European countries, including Germany. It's quite a coup. The German health services hold medications and manufacturers to very exacting standards, and they've rejected many other drugs in the last couple of years. And of course, LBP really needs all the help it can get. Profits are way down for them right now."

"So, it would be bad timing for LBP if Dr. Reid had told anyone about the alleged side effect issues?" I asked.

"Absolutely. The Germans would withdraw approval immediately."

"Who would Reid have talked to?" I asked. "If he had decided to tell anyone?"

Eric thought for a few seconds. "He could have gone to the MHRA. That's the regulatory agency for drugs and healthcare. They would have investigated."

We stopped talking while an elderly woman shuffled past with a tray of tea. I leaned forward towards Eric. "Does Simon Scott have a connection to LBP?"

Eric looked surprised. "Scott? The politician?"

"He has a meeting with the Managing Director of Litton Bernhoff late tomorrow afternoon. Is there any way he'd know what it is that LBP is trying to hide?"

Drumming his fingers on the table, Eric appeared to ponder the question.

"Scott was a doctor before he went into politics," he said eventually. "And he was still practicing when LitImmune was in initial trials. Also, as Shadow Secretary for Health, he would probably be aware of any significant contracts for overseas sales of UK-manufactured drugs. And I think he's friends with the head of the MHRA. They went to Cambridge together."

"So it's possible he would have heard if there were any irregularities, like unreported side effects?"

Eric nodded. "It's possible."

A young couple wandered towards our corner. The woman, who was very pregnant, was giggling, leaning into her partner. For a moment, I was sad, remembering Josh's emails to Helena, and the conversation he and I still needed to have.

I dragged my attention back to Eric. "Macintyre has been hired to stop any leaks of bad reports on LitImmune," I said. "The question is who hired him? The Managing Director of LBP?"

I pressed my fingers to my temples. A headache was brewing and I could do with an aspirin.

"My guess would be Gerald Hunter," Eric said. "He resigned from my company, PharmAnew, about four years ago. Resigned under pressure, which means he was fired, but it didn't show up on his resume that way. There'd been an internal investigation into test result manipulation and my company wasn't happy with the findings. They didn't bring any charges against him, but they made it clear he had to move out. LBP took him on, specifically to develop channels for

LitImmune. He's Executive Director, New Products Worldwide or some such title. If anyone can prove that he's been hiding negative results, his job is on the line and he would almost certainly be charged and fined. There's a lot at stake for him, not to mention a huge fine for the company."

"Yeah, but from what I've read," I said. "Drug companies pay massive penalties all the time, and it doesn't seem to slow them down."

Eric nodded. "It's true. These drugs are worth so much money that a manufacturer will take risks. If they get caught, they just pay up. Last year, Barton Pharmaceuticals paid almost five hundred million in fines for marketing its antipsychotic drug for uses that hadn't been approved. It happens more often than the public realizes. But LBP is short of cash right now, mostly because of some bad management decisions over the last few years. They almost certainly don't have enough to pay a large fine. More to the point, I think there would be more than just money at stake. The LBP Managing Director has a reputation for being a real tyrant. He'd turn Hunter over to the authorities in a heartbeat. I'd think Hunter would be terrified of facing criminal charges and prison time."

I pushed my empty cup around on the table. Was I right that Audley Macintyre could be after Scott? The link was tenuous. Macintyre hadn't mentioned Scott at all during his self-aggrandizing revelations in the cellar.

"This is a lot to take in," Eric was saying. "And what about Macintyre? Is he really a sales rep who also happens to be a contract killer?"

"I was thinking about that too," I said. "Have you talked to him much? Does he know what he's talking about when it comes to LBP's drugs?"

"Hard to tell. It's not very difficult to read the literature and spout it all back, especially if you have a good memory. All he needed to do was dress up in a suit and tote a bag full of samples around. Gerald Hunter would have been able to get him an ID and some false paperwork. Come to think of it, Macintyre's only been around for about six months. I assumed he'd just transferred in from a different territory."

Eric took a swallow of his coffee, which had to be cold by now.

"So going back to Scott," he said. "If you really think Macintyre is after him, you have to go to the police straightaway."

"I have. And I'll tell them about Gerald Hunter too. There's one other thing. Macintyre was making threats against you. He knows you talked with Dr. Reid and he assumes you know about the altered records. You should be cautious, perhaps lie low until the police catch up with him."

Eric swallowed back the rest of his coffee, stood, and buttoned up his jacket. "Thanks for the warning, but I don't think so. If Anita can carry on working through all this, I damn well can too. Bloody Macintyre. I never did like him."

"Thanks, Eric. I appreciate your help."

Wending my way back across the lobby, I called Parry to give him an update. He greeted my news with a long silence. "Are you there?" I asked.

"Yes, yes. Thank you for sharing this with me." He sounded distracted. "I appreciate the call, Kate." As I disconnected, I wondered if he was a drinker or had problems at home.

I pushed open the front door to a blast of cold air just as my phone rang. I moved back into the warmth of the lobby to answer it. It was Chris Melrose.

"Kate. It's Chris. I'm back in London and I'd like to see you. Can we meet?"

"When?"

"Now, if you can. I just got off the train. Where are you? I'll come wherever you want me to."

38

Chris walked through the front doors of the hospital in jeans, hiking boots and a fisherman's sweater, with a battered backpack hanging from one shoulder. He shook my hand before we crossed the lobby to the cafeteria. My day just kept getting longer.

"Why did you want to see me?"

"Apparently the police are looking for me," he said. "Something about explosives? Did you send them after me?"

"Yes."

We stood at the counter, waiting for someone to serve us. "I can't believe it," he said, scooping up a handful of sugar sachets from a basket near the till.

"I'm sorry, Chris, but you had those orange stains on your hands when we saw you at the teashop. Anita said they were probably caused by nitric acid, which is a component of an explosive."

"Anita said that? Well, she's right. It was nitric acid. I study Chemical Engineering. That's what I do, for hours every day. I mess around with chemicals."

"You're volunteering on Scott's campaign, which seems suspicious. Besides, where have you been? I rang you a few times and you never answered."

"I was up in Scotland, in a place where there was no signal," he said.

We stopped talking when a young blonde server asked us what we wanted. Another coffee seemed like a good idea. We carried our cups to the same chairs that Eric and I had vacated thirty minutes earlier.

217

"I don't understand," Chris said. "When my phone service came back on, I had voicemails from someone called Clarke telling me to report to the nearest police station. My friend, the chap I was traveling with, made some discreet enquiries and was told that there's an alert out for me. Bloody hell, Kate. All that because of some stains on my fingers?"

"And the photos," I said. "That wall of clippings upstairs. What's that all about?"

"You snooped around my house?" He got to his feet, looking down at me sadly. "I thought we were friends."

"So why all the mutilated photos?"

"My mother did that." Chris sat back down, his handsome face tight with anger. "After Scott dumped her, my mother went back to Greece, to her parents' home in Arachova, but her father was furious about the shame she'd brought on the family and put her more or less under house arrest. She kept house for her parents and three brothers, and she looked after me. Her mother tried to help her, but apparently her father was the driving force in the family and everyone did as he said. After three years, Mum packed up and left. We came back to London, and she got a job as a clerk for a building supply company."

Chris stopped talking to drink more of his tea. His hand trembled slightly. "She managed the office job for a few years," he continued. "It paid for our rent and a babysitter for me. I stayed with a neighbor during the day. Mrs. Gleason. She smelled of mothballs but she was nice enough to me, in the way that kids measure nice, which meant that she let me eat sweets and watch television all day. I was a pudgy little kid."

"That's hard to imagine," I said.

"Yeah well, then I went to primary school and stopped eating junk food. My mum married William Melrose about that time. They bought a house and did it up. He had a decent job, so there was more money to spend. We even went on vacation for the first time, to Cornwall, and he built sand castles on the beach with me. We had a good few years and then things started to go wrong. He lost his job and then he got sick. He died when I was fifteen. My mother went to pieces. She started blaming Scott for everything that had gone wrong in her life."

"So she put those pictures up and defaced all of them," I said.

He nodded. "I haven't had the heart to go in there and make any changes since she died."

"I'm sorry," I said, meaning it. It was a terrible outcome for a bright young woman who'd wanted to be a doctor.

Chris put down his cup. "I need you to tell the police I'm not building a bomb. You started this. You have to make it stop."

"Did you hear about the bomb scare in London yesterday?" I asked. "The police think it was aimed at Scott. Were you involved?"

He shook his head. "Of course I bloody wasn't. My mate Kurt and I were hiking near Loch Lomond. There was no phone, no tv." He must have seen the doubt on my face. "This was a trip we planned weeks ago. I work with Kurt at the meat market. He's into all that camping, hiking, mountain climbing stuff. I don't mind it, and I enjoy his company. So, no, I didn't hear about a bomb." He paused, picking at a thread on the sleeve of his shirt. "Is Scott okay?"

I nodded. "He's fine."

"Kate, I don't know why you think I want to hurt him. I can't ignore the fact that he's my father. It's impossible to forget what happened to my mother. To some extent, we are all products of our past. But what I can do is change my future. By being educated, and working hard to save money, I can avoid living the life that my mother led. To me, that's the best way to keep my past firmly where it belongs. To even think of doing something to harm Simon Scott would destroy everything I'm working for."

"I realize that now," I said. "But with the photos in your house and the explosives residue on your hands, it seemed sensible to warn the police. Then you disappeared after leaving the restaurant. I didn't know what else to think."

He shrugged. "Why were you so convinced that there was a threat? You seemed awfully sure there was something specific."

Unwilling to pursue that discussion, I looked in my bag for my lip balm. My certainty came from seeing Scott's aura, and that wasn't something I could share with Chris.

He looked at me, waiting for an answer.

"I have a source, a sort of inside track," I said. He raised his eyebrows, but that was as much I was willing to say.

"Do you believe now that I'm innocent?" he asked after a pause.

"Yes."

He shrugged. "Not sure why I care what you think. Damn, Kate."

I grasped my coffee mug in both hands, looking down at the beige liquid, which was the same color as the table top.

Chris's hand touched mine. "Friends?" he asked. When I looked up at him he grinned. His eyes crinkled at the corners just the way his father's did.

"Are you all right?" he asked. "You look exhausted, if you don't mind my saying so."

I realized that he had no idea what had happened to Anita, didn't know about Macintyre or the drug cover-up. I gave him a succinct version of events. When I'd finished, he sat back, shock on his face. "My God, I'm really sorry," he said. "I like Anita, you know. It makes me mad that anyone would try to harm her."

Did Chris have a crush on Anita? It was possible, now that I thought back to the way he acted around her, angling his chair to face her, walking next to her when we were at the campaign rallies.

"Or you, of course," Chris added.

"Yeah, well. We're both fine now." It wasn't true. Anita still had an aura.

"You really think this Macintyre character might be going after Scott?"

I shrugged. I honestly didn't know what to think. Even though Macintyre hadn't set off the bomb, I still had a feeling that he intended to stop Scott from talking to the Managing Director of Litton Bernhoff. But maybe I was completely off track. Or perhaps binoculars man was working with Macintyre. I should call Parry and suggest he look into that.

"I'll call Detective Clarke about the alert," I said. "And I think you should go see him and give him your side of the story."

He nodded. "I'll do that tomorrow. For now, I want to get home to change. I'm planning on going to Scott's campaign speech at the Wentworth hotel in the morning. It's the last one before the election."

"Haven't you had enough of political speeches?"

"I've been thinking about it," he said standing up and hefting his backpack over his shoulder. "I feel that this could be my last chance to talk to him. If his party wins and he becomes Prime Minister, I'll never get near him. At least tomorrow I can see him up close. If that's the best I can do, then it's better than nothing."

"I really think you should talk to DCI Clarke before you do anything else," I said. "We need to get that alert lifted, or you could be arrested at any moment."

Half an hour later, we were at the police station, waiting for Clarke.

He'd gone off duty but was on his way back in. It was nearly midnight and the waiting room felt like something out of a Grimm tale, full of strange characters: a youth covered in tattoos, an old man with a bandage over one eye, and a woman with wild ebony hair, a very short red dress and very high spike heels. When Clarke arrived, he bypassed them all, beckoning us to follow him. Soon we were seated in a gray room at a gray laminate table, drinking tea from mugs with the Chelsea football club logo on them.

I'd seen Clarke in full DCI mode once before, when he was interviewing me after my friend's murder. Tonight, he was back in force, focused, serious, taking rapid notes on his tablet. He gave no sign that we'd known each other for a year. It was impressive and a little scary.

When he'd interrogated Chris for a while he leaned back in his chair. "Here's the situation. We have the man who set off the bomb in Portsmouth. We don't yet know who called in the hoax message about the bomb in central London, but I have no evidence that it was you, Mr. Melrose. The twenty-pound note that was turned in for analysis does indicate you or a previous owner of that note had been handling chemicals that can be used to make explosives."

Chris hunched forward across the desk. "I told you, it was a lab experiment for my thesis. I can show you round the lab and give you a copy of my report if you like."

Clarke nodded. "I understand. The net is that, for now, I have no reason to hold you. I appreciate that you came in of your own volition. You are free to go. But my advice is that you stay away from Scott. Don't give anyone any reason to doubt you."

Five minutes later, we were standing on the doorstep of the police station, looking out at the pouring rain.

"Thanks for coming here with me," Chris said. "It's good to have it all sorted out."

"I'm sorry I suspected you." I turned up the collar on my coat, contemplating a dash to the tube station. "I hope we can still be friends."

"Of course. And you'll tell Anita that I'm not a crazy bomb builder, won't you?"

His cheeks reddened when he said her name. I was right. He definitely had a crush on her.

"I'm going to make a dash for the tube station," he said. He looked at his watch. "Or maybe not. The trains will have stopped running by now."

"Darn. We can't even share a taxi. I'm going back to the hospital to wait for Anita. I assume you're heading back to Shepherd's Bush?"

"I was, but I think I'll find somewhere to hang out closer to the Wentworth, as it's already so late." He shifted his backpack.

I stared at him. "You can't go to the speech. You heard what Clarke said about staying away from Scott. You should just keep a low profile for a few days."

"I'm going, Kate. I hope you won't feel compelled to let DCI Clarke know that. Good grief."

"It's not a good idea."

"Then come with me. You can keep an eye on me and if you think I'm behaving suspiciously, you can call your detective to let him know."

I was cold and tired. The lack of sleep was already weighing on me, but I'd deal with it. If Anita was going to work all night, the least I could do was stay awake as well.

"All right. Let's go back to the hospital. We can stay warm in the cafeteria until it's time to go to the speech."

39

By the time we reached the hospital cafeteria, I was starving. I'd eaten almost nothing since the previous morning. After we'd ordered, I texted Anita to let her know where I was. She responded with a quick okay. Once I had a cup of tea and a large plate of sausage, eggs and toast in front of me, everything seemed a little less grim. But I was still worried about Chris's plan to go to the hotel after Clarke had told him not to get too close to Scott.

"What do you really hope to get out of being there?" I asked him. "Scott's giving an important speech. He's going to be surrounded by VIPs and bodyguards. I don't think there's any chance he'll talk to you."

About as much chance as flying pigs, I thought. Chris drank his tea, gazing somewhere over my shoulder.

"It'll work out. I'm sure of it. My grandmother always told me I can achieve anything I want, as long as I work hard and occasionally attempt the impossible. Maybe reconnecting with my father is impossible. But I won't know until I try."

"I just don't want you to be disappointed," I said, making a mental note to call my own father as soon as we got home. I loved him so much and had done nothing to show it recently.

We ate slowly, ordered more tea, and managed to drag out the meal for a couple of hours. Finally, Chris looked at his watch. "We should go over. They'll start letting people in very soon and I want to be near the front."

A frisson ran down my spine when I remembered the man who'd forced his way to the front of the crowd in the Oxford car park in order to throw a projectile at Scott. I picked up my bag and, before putting my gloves on, I sent another text to Anita, telling her I was going out for a couple of hours. I sent the same message to PC Wilson. Anita answered. Wilson didn't, but I assumed Anita would let him know when she saw him. Outside, the rain had stopped but the wind had picked up, whining through the telephone wires, pushing scraps of paper along the street.

The Wentworth Hotel was a six-story limestone building fronted by a grand entry with a portico and two sets of double doors. Lights shone from all the large, multi-paned downstairs windows, and doormen in bottle-green uniforms stood under a Union flag that cracked in the wind. We walked through the marble-floored lobby towards the ballroom, passing through a security checkpoint where we surrendered our bags to uniformed staff and an x-ray machine.

Inside the ballroom, a hundred or more people stood in groups, drinking tea and talking. On a stage at one end, a podium waited under a massive banner with Scott's name on it. The one that I'd worked on was puny in comparison. I looked at my watch. It was just before eight, still more than an hour until Scott was due to speak.

Chris told me he was going to find the men's room. "Wait right here," he said. "If you move, I'll never find you again."

Alone, I looked around the room, wondering what drove supporters to get up at the crack of dawn to listen to a political speech. I wandered towards the front to save a couple of seats, sat down and waited for Chris. After ten minutes, when he hadn't returned, I started to worry. What was he up to? I stood up, pushing my way back through the growing crowd towards one of the two sets of double doors.

Eliza Chapman walked in through the other door. In the mass of business suits, polished shoes and well-groomed hair, she stood out in her frumpy beige clothes and hair in need of a comb. Remembering her frantic voicemails threatening to take matters into her own hands if the newspaper didn't publish her story, I watched her shove her way forward through the crowd, making for the front row. As soon as I found Chris, I'd call Detective Parry to warn him that she was here.

After passing through the lobby, I found the toilets near the escalators. Even in my anxious state, I couldn't bring myself to go into the men's room, so I waited for someone to come along so I could ask them to check on Chris.

Scott's supporters continued to pour in through the front doors, standing in increasingly long lines to pass through the security checkpoint. On the far side of the lobby, a man in the hotel's green uniform caught my eye. I thought I recognized him. He disappeared through a door marked Employees Only and it was only as the door closed that I realized the man was Audley Macintyre.

Two men in black suits, each with a telltale earpiece, stood at the doors to the ballroom. They had to be secret service so I hurried towards them.

"There's a man here who plans to kill Simon Scott," I said to them. "I can point him out to you."

The men exchanged glances. One of them spoke into a microphone on his lapel. Thank God they were taking me seriously.

"Please come with me, miss."

I followed him, with my heart pounding. Just seeing Macintyre again had taken my breath away. I glanced back towards the toilets. Still no sign of Chris. The security men had sandwiched me between them, uncomfortably close, with our elbows touching as though they thought I might run away. We advanced in formation along the side of the lobby towards a uniformed police officer, who was talking with a security guard.

"This young lady says there's someone in the hotel who plans to kill Scott," one of my escorts told them. "I'll leave her with you."

Without waiting for an answer from the policeman, he and his mate strode off.

"Come this way, please, ma'am," the officer said.

"I'm not going anywhere. You have to listen. There's a man here who kidnapped my friend and me, but we escaped. He'll kill Scott. If you don't believe me, phone DI Parry. I have his number right here."

It sounded ridiculous, even to me. The officer regarded me with an expression of pity.

"Let's move to a quieter place," he said. "And we'll make that call, all right?"

While we walked, I pulled my mobile from my purse and pressed Parry's number. After three rings, the line clicked over to voicemail. So much for his promise of 24/7 accessibility.

"Damn," I said. "He's not answering."

The officer nodded as though he'd expected it.

"Listen," I said to him. "Do you have instructions to look for a suspect called Audley Macintyre?"

The officer's face was blank. "Audley who?"

There was nothing else to be done. "I'm sorry. I must have made a mistake."

I turned and walked away, praying he wouldn't come after me to arrest me for wasting police time or just for being crazy in a public place. When I glanced back, he was talking to the security guard again, both of them laughing.

I angled back towards the door where I'd last seen Macintyre.

"Kate!"

Chris hurried towards me, pushing his way through the crowd. "Where were you? We should go find some seats."

"Where've you been?" I asked, although it was obvious he'd been sprucing himself up. He had on a clean shirt, and loafers replaced his hiking boots. "I need your help," I rushed on. "Macintyre is here. We have to find him and stop him doing whatever it is he plans to do."

Chris's eyes widened in shock. Grabbing his arm, I hurried towards the Employees Only door. It opened to a corridor with beige walls and a tan lino floor, a stark contrast to the marble and gilt of the ballroom. At the far end was a door with a small glass window in it.

"Come on," I urged Chris, who'd stopped in the doorway.

"We're not supposed to be here," he said. "Just tell the police."

"I tried that."

Moving ahead of him, I jogged along the corridor. When I reached the door, I paused for a second, worried that that I might have been mistaken. But I was sure that the man I'd seen was Macintyre; there was something about the way he held his shoulders. The window in the door revealed a large commercial kitchen where a dozen people in white coats and checked blue pants worked at stainless steel work surfaces, peeling, paring and chopping. Large pots boiled on a massive stove, steam curling above them. I opened the door, and sidled in, expecting to be stopped, but no one even looked up.

I was glad when Chris slipped in beside me. "Now what?" he whispered.

"I don't know. Macintyre's wearing a hotel uniform. Green trousers, waistcoat, long sleeved tan shirt. Medium height, dark hair, cold eyes."

No one seemed to take much notice of us as we skirted the main work area. Staying close to the wall, we came to a corner. Peering around it, I saw what seemed to be a staging area for plates of food. Macintyre was there, putting items on a tray, a pot of coffee and a plate of tiny pastries that reminded me of my favorite pasticcheria in Florence.

"That's him," I said to Chris, who craned his head around the corner to look. "I don't know what he's up to."

Macintyre picked up the tray and headed for a swinging door at the far end of the serving area. Chris and I dashed after him. Over the bang of metal pans and clink of dishes, someone called to us, but we kept going, easing through the swinging door into the corridor beyond. It led to a bank of three service lifts. The indicator above the middle one was moving upwards, and stopped on the sixth floor, which I guessed was at the top of the building.

I pressed the call button, jamming my finger against it several times. It seemed to take forever for a lift to arrive.

"What are we going to do?" Chris asked while we waited. I noticed that his backpack was missing. Why would he leave it somewhere? I didn't have time to pursue that line of thought, however, as our lift arrived and transported us quickly to floor six.

The doors opened to a wide corridor with light blue wallpaper, deep blue carpets, tasteful wall lights and gleaming double doors with plaques indicating suite numbers. It was easy to see which one was Scott's. The door was guarded by two men in black suits, just like the jokers down near the ballroom. Even from ten yards away, I saw the bulge of holsters under their jackets. They reminded me of Tommy Lee Jones and Will Smith in the Men in Black movies.

"Stop right there," Jones ordered. Smith was talking into his mouthpiece. At any moment, I feared, a posse of gunmen would appear.

We stopped. The lift doors slid closed behind us. "Did a man go in with a tray of coffee?" I asked them.

"You need to leave this floor immediately," Jones said, just as the door to the suite opened. Macintyre walked out, his hands empty.

He didn't even glance at the bodyguards, but walked straight towards me. It only took a few seconds for him to cover the ten yards to the lift, where he pressed the call button.

"You have to stop this man," I shouted at the guards. They didn't move, not even a muscle twitch.

The lift pinged open behind me. Macintyre was close to me, close enough that I could feel the heat coming off his body. "Anita next and then it's your turn, if you survive this little episode," he said softly.

"You have to stop him," I yelled again.

"That's it." Jones pulled out a gun and pointed it at me. I'd been through a lot, but I'd never had a gun aimed at me before. It was terrifying. All I could see was the sleek iron-gray barrel and the round hole that threatened death. "Put your hands up in the air."

Beside me, Chris put his hands up. When I hesitated, the guard wiggled the gun. I complied. Behind me, Macintyre whispered "Sayonara." He stepped into the lift.

I remained frozen, feeling like an insect caught in amber for all eternity. Macintyre was going after Anita, and I was stuck on the wrong side of a gun. I almost cried with frustration.

Seconds passed, feeling like minutes. Smith was still talking into his microphone, possibly calling for reinforcements. Maybe a SWAT team was about to descend from the ceiling. And Macintyre was getting away.

"Listen," I tried again. "That man, the waiter who just left. He's an assassin. You have to stop him."

Jones told me to shut up, with another twitch of his gun to make his point. I did, trying to work out what Macintyre could have done in the suite. Obviously, he hadn't pulled a gun or a knife on anyone. He'd gone in and walked back out. There was no shouting, no alarms, nothing to indicate that he'd done anything more than deliver coffee. *The coffee.* I'd take a bet it was poisoned.

"Macintyre is trying to poison them," I said to Chris. "We have to do something."

Chris looked at me, his lips pressed together so hard they were white. I felt sorry for dragging him into this. I was still trying to work out what to do when the door to the suite opened and a man in a navy suit came out.

"Five minutes before we go downstairs," he said to the bodyguards. Then he noticed Chris and me. "Who are they?"

Chris moved. He crossed the hallway to the door so fast that the guards didn't have time to stop him. Pushing the man in the navy suit to one side, he dashed inside. Smith and Jones pursued him, followed by the man in the suit, leaving me alone. I heard a gunshot.

Shaking from head to toe, I ran to the open door. Peeking in, I saw a room full of men in suits and ties. Jones had his gun pointed at Chris

228

and was yelling, "Stand down, now."

Ignoring him, Chris ran at Scott and knocked a cup from his hand. I was terrified that the bodyguard would shoot, but Chris was so close to his father that it would have been too dangerous. Instead, Smith leapt at Chris, pulling him to the ground, mashing his face into the carpet.

Kevin Lewis was standing just a couple of feet away, a look of horror on his face. Suddenly, his legs buckled. As he sank to the floor, his legs and arms jerked and yellow foam spewed from his mouth. Everyone started shouting at the same time.

There was nothing I could do there. I turned back into the corridor and ran towards the fire exit. Another gunshot in the suite behind me made my pulse race. What if they had shot Chris? Clattering down the staircase, my rapid breath echoing against the concrete walls, I tried to make sense of what I'd seen. Kevin Lewis had drunk some or all of his coffee. Had Scott? Was he back there, writhing, like Lewis, in pain?

Three floors down, I stopped for a second. I needed to formulate a plan. If I found Macintyre, what would I do? I pulled my phone from my bag, but my fingers trembled so much that I kept pressing the wrong numbers. I carried on running, almost turning an ankle on the concrete steps.

He could be heading to the hospital to find Anita. I got my phone out, noticing that the power was down to less than two percent. I hadn't charged it for nearly twenty-four hours. Frantic, I typed a text. "be careful macintyre's coming" and pressed send just as the screen went blank.

I dashed through the car park to the street beyond, realizing that it was just an access road to the back of the hotel. Even at this time in the morning, there were no pedestrians in sight. I ran to the right, unsure of where I was. At the corner, I found myself on a main road lined with shops, not yet open, and a few people out on foot. I thought of asking someone if I could use their mobile, but I knew what the response was likely to be.

Catching sight of a sign for a pub, I hurried towards it. The Rose and Crown was a shabby-looking place, but it was open, serving breakfast. The smell of last night's beer mingled with the cloying odor of deep frying. Still, I wasn't there to eat. When I asked the girl behind the bar if they had a public phone, she jutted her chin in the direction of a narrow, purple-painted hallway that led to the loo. A phone hung on the wall. Ignoring my reservations about hygiene, I picked up the greasy receiver. While I scrabbled through my purse, looking for change, I realized I didn't have Parry's number written down. I'd put it directly into my contacts list on my mobile. Anita's personal phone had been destroyed and I didn't recall the direct number for the Pediatric Unit. In this golden age of electronic communications, a dead battery had severe ramifications. The only number I knew off by heart was Josh's. I crammed some coins into the box, but he didn't answer, so I left a message asking him to contact Anita urgently to let her know Macintyre was looking for her.

Next I called 999, trying to explain to the operator that I needed to get a message to DI Parry at the Westminster station.

"You've reached the emergency line," she said. "You should call him direct."

"This is an emergency. Send police to London General to the pediatric unit. There's a killer on the loose."

She asked me a few questions that seemed to take forever. Finally, I jammed the receiver back in its cradle and ran outside. It is a universal truth that when you don't need a taxi, the streets are full of them. When you do, they disappear. I stood at the curb waiting for an empty taxi to pass by, gave up, walked a hundred yards, and tried again. Five minutes later, one pulled over. As we headed towards the hospital, I sat rigid in the back seat, willing the wheels to turn faster and the lights to be green.

40

By the time we reached the hospital, I was so wound up I thought my bones would crack under the weight of my tense muscles. My breathing exercises weren't helping. I paid the driver, took the entry steps two at a time and ran up four flights of stairs to the Pediatric Unit.

"Anita?" I asked the nurse at the desk.

"I'll page her."

My knees went weak with relief when Anita appeared just then at the far end of the corridor. I hurried towards her.

"Did you get a message from Josh?" I asked.

Anita's face was blank. "Josh? No, why?"

"My phone is out of power, and I asked Josh to warn you — Never mind, it's a long story. Have you seen any sign of Macintyre or Lizardman?"

Her face paled. "No, should I have?" She looked as exhausted as I felt. I didn't want to scare her, but I knew we needed to be extremely careful.

"Where have you been?" she asked. "Did you see Chris?"

"Yes, but I'll explain it all later." I didn't even know what I'd tell her, as I had no idea if he was okay. He could be dead or in a police cell. But her safety and the risk of Macintyre making an appearance were more pressing issues right now.

"We should go pick up the notes to get them out of Grace's way," I said, walking back towards the nurses' station. "Let's ask PC Wilson to come with us. He can be responsible for getting the notes to Parry. I'll feel better once they are in police hands."

I glanced around. The desk area was quiet, with only the one nurse on duty. "Where is Wilson?"

Anita shook her head. "I'm not sure. He was here the last time I walked by, but I've been in a consultation for the last hour or so. I'll page him."

There was no answer.

"Can you call Parry?" I asked. "He needs to know that PC Wilson's not responding. My mobile is dead."

Anita pulled Parry's card from her trouser pocket and used the phone on the nurses' desk to call. This time, the detective picked up immediately. She told him that Wilson wasn't around and hadn't answered our page. After a short exchange, she hung up.

"Parry said he'll get a team over here right now. And that we should stay together here in the Pediatric Unit."

"I called for police support nearly half an hour ago. What the hell is going on? I thought the hospital would be swarming with officers by now."

Anita rubbed her eyes. She was almost asleep standing up and I felt the same way. "This makes me really nervous," she said. "We should talk to Grace."

Grace didn't answer her page either.

"She's probably working," I said, trying to be reassuring, even though the hair was standing up on my arms. The lack of contact with Grace and PC Wilson had set alarm bells ringing in my head.

"We need to go check on her," Anita said.

"We should wait for the police."

Anita pushed away from the desk she'd been leaning on. "I'm going. Are you coming with me?"

"If we go down there and Macintyre is watching us, we'll be leading him right to the place where the notes are hidden."

"It's a risk, but the morgue is a secure area. We'll be safe there until the police arrive."

She was right. And I was anxious to see Grace. Too impatient to wait for the lift, we ran down the stairs and crossed the busy entry hall. Never my favorite place, the hospital seemed especially depressing today. Under bright lights intended to replicate sunshine, auras hovered over a number of patients in wheelchairs or with walkers. I was jumpy and watchful until we reached the lift with the keypad. On the slow, creaking journey down, I told myself I was being ridiculous. Macintyre wasn't in sight. There was no way he could know where we were going.

When we reached the basement, I relaxed. Several secure doors now protected us from the public spaces of the hospital. We hurried along the beige corridor to Grace's office. It was empty.

"What do we do now?" I stood by Grace's desk. A full cup of coffee sat on a coaster next to her computer, which was switched on, with images of pyramids floating across the screen. A stack of papers next to it was secured under an iridescent glass scarab beetle paperweight. I picked it up, attracted by its luminous wash of gold and crimson. It was surprisingly heavy.

Anita went to the door that connected Grace's office to the autopsy room. She pushed it, but it didn't open. Turning to lean on the door, she paged Grace again but there was no response.

"If she's working, she won't be able to answer," I said. I touched the coffee cup. It was warm. "Or maybe she just went to the loo?"

Anita pushed on the door again. It didn't budge.

"Why would the door be locked?" I asked.

"I don't know. We'll have to go in the other way," Anita said, heading out of the office into the corridor, where a set of wide swing doors gave access to the autopsy room. My heart raced. I had no desire to walk in midway through an autopsy.

Anita gently pushed one of the swing doors, which opened quietly. After a quick peek inside, she took a step back. "Oh my God," she whispered, motioning me to come to her.

The door had swung back silently to the closed position, so I eased it open a couple of inches. A body lay on the stainless steel table, covered with a sheet. Velcro straps crossed the torso and legs. That was weird. Bodies don't get up and walk away.

A man was bending over the table. Even from behind, I knew who it was. And I guessed who was under the sheet. When I turned round, Anita was pale and shaking. I sank down to a crouch, my back against a wall.

"Call the police," she said. "But do it quietly."

I got up and tiptoed back into Grace's office. My fingers felt like balloons and it took two attempts to dial the emergency number. The operator was confused at first about exactly where we were, but she finally seemed to understand and promised help was on its way. While I talked, I picked up the scarab paperweight and put it in my coat pocket.

It wasn't much of a weapon, but a quick glance around the office didn't reveal any other possibilities.

A sudden shrill scream came from next door. Horrified, I ran back to join Anita. She was holding the swing door open a couple of inches. Inside, Macintyre had a scalpel in his hand. I watched in terror when he slid the blade the length of Grace's arm, leaving a thin red line that slowly blurred as blood seeped from the wound. Grace was trying to thrash her way out of the straps that held her.

"We have to go in," I said. "She could be dead before the police get here."

We pushed the door open, creeping up behind Macintyre. I thought we were going to take him by surprise, but he swung round, scalpel in hand. "Ladies," he said. "So glad you could join the party. I appreciate your thoughtfulness. Now I won't need to come and find you."

"Let Grace go," I said. "She doesn't know anything."

"Oh, she does. She knows exactly where those notes are and she'll tell me after another little cut or two." Grace's face was deathly white, her pupils black pinpricks under the harsh fluorescent lights. "Such a beautiful woman. It would be a shame to ruin that flawless skin."

"I'll tell you where the notes are," I said. "Just leave her alone."

Macintyre cocked his head to one side as though pondering his options. He held the scalpel directly over Grace's abdomen. "Tell me."

"I'll show you. They're in a drawer in the morgue next door." I had no intention of lying to him. All I wanted to do was get him away from Grace and Anita.

Grace was quiet now, still as a cadaver. She also had an aura. I hadn't noticed it at first, as it was almost transparent against the stainless steel table where her head rested. But it was moving very quickly, which meant she was in grave danger. I glanced up at Anita. Her aura was swirling too.

"So many pleasures, so little time," Macintyre said, running his hand down Grace's slashed arm. He lifted his bloodied fingers to his mouth and licked them. I felt like throwing up.

"Let's go," I said, desperate to get him away from Grace. He didn't move, but stood looking at her, the scalpel still raised over her. I saw the muscles in his hand twitch. He was going to kill her. "If you touch her, I won't tell you where the notes are," I said. I made a point of looking at my watch. "I'm sure you'd find them eventually, but you're running out of time. The police will be here any minute now."

He shook his head as though coming out of a trance.

"Don't go anywhere," he said to Anita. "Any trouble and you'll never see Kate again."

I made eye contact with Anita, willing her to take Grace and get out of there. She gave a slight nod of understanding while Macintyre thumbed something into his mobile with one hand. I wondered who he was contacting, but had no time to finish the thought because he grabbed my arm and forced me towards the door that led to the morgue.

Walking into that room alone with him felt like stepping into hell itself. There were no raging fires, no devils with forked tails. This was the underworld of the Greeks, dark and cold, a pit of despair from which there was no hope of escape.

Macintyre squeezed my arm. "Where are they?"

On one wall, six stainless steel drawers gleamed, reflecting distorted, ghostly images of us both. It seemed like a long time since Grace and I had hidden the notes. Was it the second or third drawer down?

"Don't mess with me. Which drawer?"

"That one." I pointed. He slid the drawer open to reveal a man's body, partially covered with a sheet. His feet were grey. I swallowed the bile that rose in my throat.

"It must be the next one down," I said. Macintyre seemed amused to hear the shake in my voice. "Are you scared of dead people, Kate?" he asked, putting his hand under my chin and gazing into my eyes. I turned away, not wanting to hear any more of his rantings on death and dying. When I didn't answer, he slammed the drawer closed and opened the next one.

There lay the envelope, holding Anita's handwritten notes.

"Is it really worth it?" I said to him as he grabbed the envelope. "All this to stop some creep in management from going to prison? What do you get out of it?"

He slid the drawer closed. "Why does anyone do anything?" he said. "It always comes down to money and power. They go hand in hand. Money buys power. Power generates wealth. I love the simple synergy of it, don't you?"

Although I hated breathing the same air as him, I needed to give Anita time to get Grace out of harm's way.

"So you're getting paid a lot to derail an inquiry into a drug that is known to have negative side effects," I said. "A drug that has actually

235

killed people. Doesn't that make you feel bad?"

Macintyre laughed. "I never feel bad. It's a weakness, Kate. Expunge the word from your vocabulary. There is no bad. There is no guilt. I feel good about everything I accomplish."

"Even an attack on our elected politicians?"

"Of course, when the end justifies the means. The means in this case being poison. A fatal dose in a coffee pot. With a vast panoply of drugs at my disposal, I found great enjoyment in selecting the right one. Too bad I couldn't wait to watch the results."

Shivering, I asked myself if he knew something I didn't. He looked very self-satisfied, with a hint of a smile on his lips. Had Scott and Lewis died?

I glanced up at the clock on the wall. The red second hand didn't move smoothly but flicked and jarred its way around the face as though reluctant to keep moving. I wondered why the clock was there at all. Time meant nothing for the inhabitants of this bleak room.

It had only been a minute since we left the autopsy room. Not enough time for Anita to free Grace.

"How did you know to come down here?" I asked Macintyre. "And how did you know the access codes?"

"Always so many questions, Kate. Snooping around, meddling in things that don't concern you. There's something about you that I don't quite understand. That's why I find you so interesting. Alluring, almost. We'd make a good team."

"So answer the question."

"Ted was kind enough to help me out."

"Ted the pharmacist? But he's friends with Grace."

"Yes, and he's also addicted to barbiturates. I've been able to supply him with what he needs so that he no longer has to steal drugs and risk discovery. In return, he told me you and Anita spend time with Grace and that the three of you had been asking him questions. The minute I heard that, I knew. The morgue would make an excellent hiding place. You and I think alike, Kate."

"Hardly."

A sudden scream from the autopsy room sent chills skittering down my spine. I moved towards the door. I had to go help Anita. Macintyre grabbed my arm and backed me up against the wall of drawers. "Sit down on the floor." He brought the scalpel within an inch of my eye. All I could see was the cruel tip of stainless steel, filling my vision. "If you move, I won't hesitate to use this," he said.

I sat, my back against the front of a steel drawer, my legs out straight. Cold seeped into my jeans and coat, feeling damp against my skin. I heard more sounds from next door, a crash, another scream. Macintyre ignored it all. Crouching at my feet, he put the scalpel down close to him, out of my reach. Then he pulled the notes from the envelope, six pages in total, and started to look through them. Another shout from next door made me jump. I shifted my weight, getting ready to move.

Without warning, Macintyre grabbed the scalpel and stabbed it into my thigh.

"I said to keep still," he said.

I felt no pain, but blood darkened my jeans, a spreading circle of glistening black. I panicked. If he'd cut an artery, I could bleed out fast. Macintyre saw the look on my face and he laughed. "You're not going to die, not from that wound anyway. I need you for a little longer."

"It's all pointless," I said, willing myself to ignore the blood. "I took photocopies of the notes and left them in a safe place." It wasn't true. I hadn't even thought of making copies.

"Perhaps you did," he said. "Although I suspect not."

"That means we'll still have evidence to give the police."

"You're assuming, wrongly, that you or Anita or Grace will be alive to hand over that evidence."

"Not necessarily. There's someone else who knows where the copies are," I lied.

"Really?" He didn't seem concerned. "Are you going to tell me who that is? I can probably guess. Your boyfriend perhaps?"

Macintyre's words were like a bucket of ice water over my head. The last thing I'd intended was to send him after someone else. He'd done enough killing already.

I slumped back against the drawer front. "There are no copies."

"I thought not. It doesn't matter to me anyway. My part in all this is almost done."

Spreading the pages out on the floor, he used his mobile to take a photo of each page, his eyes flickering between me and the notes. After typing something into his phone, he gathered the papers into a pile and pulled a small gold lighter from his pocket. The mini-bonfire crackled, the smell of burning paper replacing the stink of disinfectant. A fire was good, I thought, hoping it would set off an alarm. But the papers burned bright for less than a minute before collapsing into a little heap of charred scraps.

It had gone very quiet next door. My guesses at what had happened left me numb with despair. I imagined that Lizardman was in there. Perhaps he'd already killed Grace and Anita. If so, I was next.

Macintyre's phone beeped. When he looked up at me, he was smiling. "We're done here, Kate. The money is in my account and all I need to do is get out of this building."

"There's nowhere to go. It's a dead end. Haha, get it?" I waved a hand around the morgue, feeling slightly hysterical. "The police will be here any minute now."

"Yes, I think they will, but you, dear heart, are my ticket out. You're my hostage, and they can't harm me when I have a knife at your throat. Now stand up."

He didn't wait for me to obey, but dragged me to my feet. Now I felt pain where he'd stabbed me, cold and sharp. My blood-soaked jeans stuck to the wound and dragged on my skin.

Bending my arm behind my back, he shoved me forwards across the morgue to a steel door secured with another keypad. Punching in numbers, he eased open the door, which led outside to a small parking area. "This is where the hearses are loaded," he said. "So very appropriate."

The door closed behind us as he lifted an arm to summon a car waiting on the road. When the vehicle swung into the car park, I saw that it was the black Audi, with Lizardman at the wheel. So who had been in the autopsy room with Grace and Anita? I had to get back there to find out what had happened.

With my free hand, I dug into my coat pocket, held firmly on to the scarab paperweight and pulled backwards, planting my heels on the asphalt. For a second, Macintyre was just in front of me, the back of his head in reach. I slammed the heavy glass into his skull. He wavered, releasing my arm to clutch at the wound, which began pouring blood. Almost at once his collar was soaked with it. I took two steps back, bumped into the closed door behind me and raised the paperweight for another blow. Macintyre was fast though. He turned towards me, swinging the scalpel. It caught my arm, cleaving a red gash across my wrist. An astonishing quantity of blood bubbled out. I watched it swell and drip, forming a dark puddle on the ground.

I felt dizzy. I had to stay on my feet. If I fainted, they'd drag me into that car and I'd be dead in no time. Macintyre's expression sent my pulse racing. He looked smug, as though he knew he'd won. In desperation, I threw the paperweight at his head. It struck him on the forehead before crashing to the ground, splintering into a thousand golden shards.

Blood dripped down Macintyre's head into his eyes, crimson smearing his face. But still, like the villain in a horror movie, he stayed on his feet and swung his scalpel in my direction, slicing through my coat and slashing my upper arm. I pressed on the new wound, trying to stop the pain and the bleeding. My vision blurred.

Lizardman revved the Audi. It sounded like a hungry animal, crouching just a few feet away from where I stood. Where were the damn police?

Macintyre grabbed my injured arm, which burned and throbbed with pain. "You're coming with us," he said. "Move."

I felt sure I was going to pass out. Macintyre didn't look much better though. He was moving slowly, with blood still dripping from his head wound. Out on the road, in the distance, sirens sounded.

"Get in the car," Lizardman yelled. "Leave her."

I allowed myself to hope, for a second, that Macintyre would make a run for the car and leave me behind. Instead, he stopped, pulling me to a halt.

"Goodbye, Kate," he said, raising the scalpel towards my neck. The sudden and real fear of dying was like a jolt of electricity. I no longer felt any pain. The dizziness subsided. Drawing on some primal survival instinct, I jammed my fist into his throat. He coughed and gagged, giving me time to grab his hand and force it backwards, putting precious inches between the scalpel and my skin. He shifted on his feet, regained his balance, and thrust the blade back towards my neck.

The sirens grew louder, almost deafening, pulsating in sync with the thump of blood in my temples. Lizardman leaned on the horn, yelling at Macintyre to move. With one last look at me, Macintyre ran towards the car and wrested the passenger door open. At that moment, two police cars screamed into the parking area, blocking the exit.

Officers jumped out of both vehicles, rushing to surround the Audi. Two of them ran towards me.

"You have to find Anita and Grace," I said. "In the autopsy room."

The ground started to heave below me, rolling and pitching like a rough sea. I sank into the depths.

41

I woke up in a hospital bed with Anita and Detective Clarke sitting beside me.

"God, Kate. You gave me a scare." Anita said, looking haggard under the bright lights. I took in the beeping monitors, the faint smell of antiseptic. An IV ran into the back of my hand. My left arm was bandaged from shoulder to elbow and my right wrist was wrapped in gauze and tape. A white blanket covered my aching thigh.

"Glad to see you're doing all right," Clarke said.

Slowly it started to come back. I'd been in the morgue with Macintyre. He'd stabbed me with that scalpel. Anita and Grace had been yelling in the autopsy room.

"What happened?" I asked Anita. "How did you get out? Where's Macintyre?"

"In answer to the last question, Macintyre's in custody, with a monstrous headache, thanks to you," Clarke said. "We've got his accomplice, Phil Simmons, as well."

"Is Grace all right?" I tried to sit up.

"She's fine." Anita patted my hand soothingly. "Don't worry. In fact, she's coming to see you in a few minutes."

The woozy feeling I'd had when I first woke up began to dissipate. I looked more closely at Anita. The bruise on her cheek was turning purple and yellow and she still looked tired, with dark circles under her eyes. But I felt my dry lips crack into a wide smile.

"What's making you so happy all of a sudden?" she asked.

"Your aura's gone."

Clarke looked at Anita, who was running her hand over her hair. "It doesn't feel any different," she said.

"You'll have to take my word for it. What happened to you and Grace once I left the autopsy room?"

She and Clarke exchanged glances before Anita answered. "Dr. Marks showed up. I think Macintyre had paged him. He came armed with a surgical knife, but we overpowered him."

"Dr. Marks?" I asked.

"He worked with Dr. Schwartz on those three renal transplant patients. Remember Pauline said he'd called in sick at the same time as Schwartz did?"

"From what I can ascertain," Clarke said, "Anita went on the offensive. Marks commented in his statement that she was like a wild woman, screaming and throwing herself at him." He grinned. "I wish I could have seen it."

"I was mad," Anita agreed. "I'd had more than enough of these reps and doctors using drugs and scalpels to do harm. Fortunately, I'd already freed Grace so we took him on together. Believe me, Marks is a wimp. Nothing like Macintyre or Lizardman. It wasn't much of a challenge."

"And Dr. Schwartz?" I looked at Clarke.

He sighed. "We're working on it. Our good doctor appears to have left the country."

I glanced around the hospital room, which was mostly taken up by my bed and a couple of visitor chairs. A small window showed just a square of gray sky, almost the same color as the walls. My mind continued to clear. I remembered being at the Wentworth Hotel. I sat up suddenly on my pillows, feeling the drag of the IV in the back of my hand. The monitor began to beep faster. "What happened to Chris? Is Simon Scott all right?"

A nurse bustled in, ignoring Anita and Clarke. She fussed with my IV drip and checked the monitor. "You should be resting," she told me.

"She's fine," Anita said.

"Really?" demanded the nurse, swinging around to look at her. Anita wasn't wearing her white coat, so maybe the nurse didn't realize she was a doctor at the hospital. They eyed each other for a few seconds before the nurse turned and left.

"Chris is safe and so is Scott. But Kevin Lewis died," said Clarke.

"Dammit." I leaned back, feeling the weight of failure like a hand on my shoulder.

"Don't be so hard on yourself," Anita said. "You saved Scott. With some help from Chris, apparently?" She looked at Clarke.

"It appears that Chris rushed Scott and knocked the coffee cup from his hand," he said. "He hadn't even taken a sip. Unfortunately, Lewis had already drunk half of his. Enough to be fatal. He died within minutes."

"No one shot Chris?" I asked. "I heard several gunshots."

"They were warning shots. Because there were so many people in the room, the security guards played it safe and fired at the ceiling to scare him, not kill him. When Lewis fell unconscious, Scott took charge and ordered the guards to stop shooting. They handcuffed Chris and pushed him around a bit, but he was safe." He shook his head. "He took quite a risk, the idiot."

"I think he was very brave," Anita said, a faint flush of pink washing her cheeks.

"I need to see Scott," I said. "To make sure his aura has gone."

Clarke grinned. "That shouldn't be a problem. He's already asked to see you, to thank you in person for saving his life."

"And I'm thanking you for saving mine." Anita squeezed my good arm. "And apologizing for doubting you."

"That's okay." I flicked a glance at Clarke. "Some people doubt even when they've seen hard evidence. Maybe they'll come round eventually."

"I'll take your wild theories more seriously from now on," Clarke said, which I counted as a sign of progress. "Oh, and talking of wild theories, we charged your binoculars man, David Lowe, yesterday. There's no link between him and Macintyre. His bomb attack was, as you initially suspected, an attempt to avenge the death of his wife on the operating table, for which he held Scott responsible. Sad, really. He'll be tried for the murder of Scott's driver."

Clarke stood up, walked to the window and back, reminding me of a caged animal. I'd always thought he must hate the part of his job where he had to sit at a desk. He harbored so much pent-up energy.

"There's a lot I still don't understand," I said. "Lowe and Macintyre were targeting Scott for different reasons. Lowe's motives, I can understand. But how would Macintyre have known that Scott was aware of the LitImmune side effect issues?"

"Dr. Marks is being very helpful." Clarke had reached the window again. He turned and leaned on the sill. "We've only had him in custody for a couple of hours but, from what we've put together so far, it seems that Dr. Reid told Schwartz that he knew about the altered records. It's not clear whether he accused Schwartz of being involved or just shared his concerns with him. They were apparently very close friends at one point. Anyway, it seems that Dr. Reid knew Scott."

"Scott did his residency under Dr. Reid," Anita interrupted. "Dr. Reid mentioned it months ago, but I never made any connection between the two of them until now."

I recalled Anita commenting that a doctor in her department had supervised Scott's residency. I wish I'd remembered that earlier, although it wouldn't have made any difference.

Clarke nodded. "We believe that Reid told Scott of his concerns. And that is probably why Scott had a meeting set up with the Managing Director of Litton Bernhoff. We can check all that with Scott himself, of course."

I closed my eyes for a few seconds, waiting for a wave of vertigo to subside. Hundreds of questions filled my head, but my mouth didn't seem to be working very well. "What about PC Wilson?" I asked finally.

"Macintyre injected him with a sedative, stabbed him and left him in a janitor's closet," said Anita.

My stomach lurched, remembering how young he was. "Is he dead?"

"No," she replied. "One of the cleaners found him and, of course, he was in the right place to get immediate medical attention. He'll be all right."

Clarke set off on another perambulation around the cramped room. My thoughts skittered around like kittens chasing sunbeams. I realized I was furious with Clarke, although he wasn't, to be fair, the right person to yell at.

"The police should have been on site much faster than they were," I said, sitting upright. When the monitor began to ping loudly, Anita gently pushed my shoulders back against the pillows. "Stay calm or Nurse Ratched will be back."

"Parry did everything as fast as he could," said Clarke. "He got a team up to the Pediatric Unit pretty quickly, but it took a while to work out how to access the morgue." His tone of voice was even, but his eyes flashed with anger. "It took longer than it should have."

He ran his hand over his fair, closely cut hair. "Seems like you did okay without us, though."

Knowing that my very low expectations of Detective Parry were justified didn't make me feel any better. Macintyre had nearly escaped. He and Dr. Marks had come much closer to killing Anita, Grace and myself than they should have. I supposed I should just be grateful that the police had arrived in time to prevent Macintyre from killing me.

There was something else I wanted to know, but it was hard to concentrate until an image of a disheveled woman in a beige cardigan passed through my brain.

"Eliza!" I said. "You got my call? Did you arrest her at the hotel?"

"Well, we didn't arrest her at the hotel. You saw all the mayhem upstairs, but missed the excitement on the ground floor. A backpack was left unattended in the men's room. It was reported to security, who called Bomb Disposal. They cleared the building, and destroyed the bag. It wasn't a bomb, just someone's dirty clothes. Everyone was evacuated, and the crowds dispersed once they heard that Scott wouldn't be giving his speech after all."

That had to be Chris's backpack. What had he been thinking?

"However." Clarke picked at a loose thread in the white blanket on the bed. "She was the one who phoned in the Central London bomb threat. I only heard hours after the fact that it was a woman who'd made the hoax call. Based on what you'd told me, I thought it was worth bringing her in for questioning. She confessed immediately. I think she actually wanted to be caught."

"What will happen to her?" I asked.

"She's been charged with a crime under Section 127 of the 2003 Communications Act," he said.

Smiling, I looked at Anita, who gave an exaggerated shrug, which Clarke noticed. "Oh, sorry, well that means she'll probably get six months or less, or maybe appeal for community service."

"Why did she do it?" I wondered out loud.

"There are all sorts of motivations for making a bomb threat," said Clarke. "The desire for attention, however negative, or wanting to scare people. Some people do it to tie up police resources or disrupt a community." He rotated his shoulders, as if the weight of human folly was resting on them.

"There was a kid in Massachusetts who called in a bomb threat, just so he wouldn't have to sit an exam that day," said Anita.

"There's no end to the craziness," Clarke said, getting to his feet. "I'll let you rest. We'll need to talk in a day or two, to go over your statements."

"Of course. I want to make sure Macintyre is put away for a very long time."

Anita and I watched Clarke go. The room felt empty without him.

"I talked with the emergency room doctors," Anita said, when the sounds of his footsteps had faded. "You'll have three pretty little scars as mementos, but no lasting damage." She picked up a cup of water from the table next to the bed and held the drinking straw to my lips.

"I was terrified for you, Kate. When Dr. Marks turned up, I realized they intended to kill all three of us. Marks was no match for two very angry women, but you had to deal with Macintyre, that psycho. Thank God he's behind bars now. Clarke says there's absolutely no chance of him being granted bail."

She put the cup down, leaned over and gave me a hug, careful not to disturb the IV drip. When she sat up again, her eyes were wet with tears.

"Oh, and Josh is worried sick about you. He's on his way back from Bristol and he should be here very soon."

I closed my eyes, thinking about Josh. I was still mad with him for emailing Helena.

"Look at me," Anita said. "What's going on? You looked pained when I told you Josh was on his way. I thought you'd be happy. God knows I would be if some tall, hunky boyfriend was rushing to my bedside."

I told her all about Helena, the postcard, and the emails. "I didn't read them," I hurried to clarify. "I just saw how many there were."

"You love Josh, right?"

I nodded, finding it impossible to speak for a moment because of the lump in my throat.

"And we know that he is madly in love with you. So, my advice is to forget about it. He's a sensitive fellow, not the type to ignore a message from someone he cared about once. But did he rush off to Munich? No. Has he been calling me every five minutes to make sure you're all right? Yes. Let it go, Kate. In the overall scheme of the universe, an email is a tiny, irrelevant atom. Don't make it into something it's not."

"All right." I agreed, mostly to stop her talking. I was feeling dizzy.

Grace poked her head around the door. "Is this the right room?" She came in, dressed in jeans and a t-shirt, with one arm bandaged from wrist to elbow. There was no sign of her aura.

After she and Anita had hugged each other, she plunked a paper bag down on the bed.

"Chocolate," she said. "Better than any drugs they can give you."

She sat down on the chair that Clarke had vacated, looking at me with an expression of deep concern. I assured her that I was fine.

"How about you?" I asked. "What on earth happened when Macintyre turned up at the morgue?"

"I was scared," she admitted. "He wanted the notes and, after what you'd told me, I wasn't about to give them to him. Honestly, he could have just done a search and eventually found them by himself, but I think he enjoyed tying me down to that autopsy table and threatening me with the scalpel. If I had told him straightaway, he probably would have killed me before you two got there."

She leaned over and tore the wrapper off a bar of Dairy Milk. A faint smell of chocolate filled the room, making me realize I was hungry.

"He's a bloody madman," she continued. "But I had to deal with far worse back in the Twentieth Dynasty. Some of those characters would make our friend Macintyre look like Santa Claus."

"That reminds me," I said. "I broke that scarab beetle paperweight that was on your desk. I'm sorry if it was, you know, an authentic artifact."

For a second, Grace looked stricken. "I loved that beetle, but it's all right. I'll get another one when I go back."

"To Ancient Egypt?"

She laughed. "No, to the British Museum gift shop."

42

"Blue or lavender?" I held out two silk blouses for Josh to look at. We'd resolved our quarrel. Taking Anita's advice to let it go, I'd told him I didn't mind if he emailed Helena. I could tell he felt I'd overreacted in the first place, but he'd apologized and promised he had no intention of staying in touch. It was time for her to move on too. It was way past time, I thought, but I kept that opinion to myself.

"Blue," he said. "It matches your eyes perfectly."

I slipped on the shirt and buttoned it up, aware of Josh watching me from the bed. He was planning to work from home for the morning and was getting off to a slow start. I brushed my hair, tied it up in a chignon, then let it down again.

"Tie it up. It looks more polished." Josh offered an opinion. "You look great, so stop worrying."

After a final check in the mirror, I bent over to kiss him goodbye.

"You sure you have to go?" he asked patting the bed beside him. "You could be a few minutes late."

"Funny," I said. "Now get up and do some work. I'll see you at the office this afternoon. I've already told Alan I'll be coming in late."

Outside on the street, a black Mercedes waited for me. The driver hurried round to open the back door, making me feel like a celebrity as I slid on to the soft leather seat. Twenty minutes later, the car glided past a security checkpoint before pulling to a halt right outside the iconic black door with the number 10 on it. The driver gestured to me to wait. He got out and talked with a policeman for a few seconds before opening the car door to help me out. I was glad that I'd opted for linen trousers, so I didn't have to worry about any wardrobe malfunctions with a short skirt. The sun shone, warm on my shoulders. I smoothed my silk shirt with the palms of my hands, wishing I didn't feel so nervous.

At the front door, I was greeted by a tall, blonde woman in a navy blue suit. "Welcome, Miss Benedict," she said. "I'm Martha. Follow me please."

The chequered black and white floor of the entry hall was partially covered with red runners to protect the tile; they cushioned the sound of our high-heeled shoes so that all I could hear was the loud beat of my heart. Pitt and Disraeli, David Lloyd George and Winston Churchill had walked through this hall. I moved slowly, feeling their ghostly presence, absorbing the history of the building. I wanted to linger, to look at every detail, but Martha was obviously on a schedule.

"You'll be meeting the Prime Minister in the White Drawing Room," she said, route-marching us along a hallway lined with portraits. She stopped suddenly to open a door to a spacious room with high ceilings, elaborate moldings and a fireplace set in a white marble surround. Creamy white walls served as the backdrop for several gilt-framed landscapes, which looked like Turners and Constables, originals of course.

"Please take a seat," Martha said. "The Prime Minister won't be long."

She turned on her elegant heels and left me alone. Perched on the edge of a silk-clad sofa, I admired the pattern of the Persian rug under my feet.

"Hello Kate!"

I stood up when I saw Chris crossing the room towards me, arms outstretched. He enveloped me in a tight embrace. "I'm so happy you could come. Dad can't wait to meet you."

"I'm glad that things turned out well between the two of you," I said, when we were both seated. "That was one wild way to introduce yourself to your father."

I still trembled when I thought back to the day at the Wentworth hotel. Chris was lucky he hadn't been shot. Of course, I should have known he'd be safe. He'd had no aura. But in the panic of the moment I hadn't been able to think that clearly.

Chris laughed. "I have you to thank for everything. If you hadn't pursued Macintyre to the suite, I wouldn't have been there in time to stop Dad drinking that coffee." The smile faded. "And maybe he'd be dead now."

"So you've forgiven your father for his past transgressions? For leaving your mother and not responding to your letter?"

He leaned forward towards me. "He never got it. His assistant at the time opened all his letters and threw mine away because she thought it was a scam or a hoax or something. And Dad has told me he had no idea that my mother had kept their baby, or that she was back in England. I think I believe him. Mum…" He paused. His eyes darkened. "She had a tough life, but she was stubborn. She never reached out to him, never told him he had a son."

He stood up and walked around the room, pausing to look out of the window. All I could see from where I sat was blue sky. It was a welcome view after the long, long winter.

Chris turned and came back to his chair. "I know my father was wrong to leave Mum when he found out she was pregnant. He admits that. But he's changed. He's his own man now, away from the influence of his parents. And things were different back then. Nowadays it wouldn't be such a big deal."

I decided not to share my real opinion. I was just happy that Scott had openly welcomed Chris into his life. The papers had been full of the story, which had broken the day after the poisoning attempt. There were pictures of the two of them together under headlines that trumpeted news of an emotional reunion between father and son. It wasn't really a reunion, of course, as they'd never met each other before, but accuracy wasn't the goal of the stories.

My favorite article, the most thoughtful, had been written by Colin Butler, commenting not just on the sensational aspects of the affair, but on the pain and complications of unwanted pregnancies and broken families. Privately to me, Butler had remarked that the endearing images of Chris and Scott together had probably won Scott quite a few votes.

I'd wondered what Eliza Chapman thought of it all. Her malicious attempt to go public with the story about the pregnant girlfriend had completely backfired.

"What about your stepmother?" I asked. "How's she dealing with it?"

"I'm sure she has reservations. But she's a politician's wife, and she's putting a good face on it. Once she got over the shock of learning that Dad had got my mother pregnant at university, she seemed to accept me. The two of us have a good laugh together when my father's taking himself too seriously."

Chris reached out to turn my wrist so he could see the scar that ran across it. It was still red and sometimes sore, but was healing well, as were my other wounds.

"Are you doing okay?"

"Absolutely fine."

"That's good to hear." It was Simon Scott, striding across the room towards us. He was wearing a beautifully-tailored gray suit with a red tie. There was no sign of an aura.

"Sit down, sit down," he admonished as I jumped to my feet. He patted Chris on the shoulder as he walked past him, and then shook hands with me. A butler in a white shirt and black trousers followed Scott, bearing a tray of china cups and saucers, a silver teapot and a plate of Bourbon biscuits.

"It's all right, Bill, I'll do the honors," Scott said. The butler nodded and withdrew.

"I don't really know how to express my thanks," Scott said to me while he poured tea. "If it weren't for you, Chris wouldn't have been there to stop me drinking that coffee."

"Well, Chris was the brave one," I said, "Crazy, but brave."

When the two men laughed, it was easy to see the similarity between them. Chris had darker hair, but their skin tone and eyes were identical. Their mouths tilted up the same way when they smiled.

The Prime Minister passed a cup to me. "I only drink tea now," he said. "Coffee brings back bad memories."

"I can understand that," I said. "I'm so sorry about Mr. Lewis."

Scott's expression was somber. "He was a good friend and a first-class financial expert. Still, I'm happy with Robertson. He's popular and moderate. He'll do well."

Ever the politician, I thought. James Robertson was the new Chancellor of the Exchequer, taking the position that Lewis would have held had he lived.

We chatted for a few minutes about the events at the hotel. In my mind, that day was still a blur of gunshots and scalpels. "No more bomb scares since then, I hope?" I teased Chris. When he'd come to visit me in hospital, he'd confessed that he'd accidentally left his backpack in the men's room. Hoping to have the chance to introduce himself to his father, he'd changed into clean clothes, shaved, and then hurried back to find me. In his rush, he'd left the bag on the floor, where someone had found it and reported it to security.

Scott shook his head, but he was smiling. "Let's hope that's the last time you cause a full-scale evacuation, Chris. That wouldn't go down too well around here."

I finally relaxed enough to pick up my cup. "I heard from Detective Clarke this week that they found Dr. Schwartz in France. He's in custody back in England now. Anita's notes are with a special investigator, together with the electronic patient files, and LBP has already agreed to withdraw LitImmune, pending further trials."

"LitImmune is potentially an industry-changer," Scott said, echoing what Eric had told me. "But no drug is going to make it to market without scrupulous oversight. Not during my tenure, anyway."

"Good," I said. "Drugs are supposed to save lives, not kill people."

I sipped my Earl Grey, which was delicious.

"Prime Minister, may I ask how you knew about problems with the LitImmune side effects? You were due to meet with the Managing Director of Litton in the afternoon following your speech at the Wentworth. I haven't been able to work out the connection."

He nodded. "Dr. Reid and I had remained in touch, off and on, ever since my residency. He was a true mentor to me, and I admired him immensely."

He poured himself some more tea, looking thoughtful. "Dan, Dr. Reid that is, contacted me several weeks before this all blew up. He was sure that someone in his department was concealing information about the side effects of LitImmune by altering the records. He knew of my friendship with the head of the drug regulatory agency, so he asked if we could conduct a discreet investigation to check whether his concerns were valid. He didn't want to go public himself because he'd come to believe that his good friend Dr. Schwartz was the one faking the results. If you ask me, that's taking loyalty too far. But I agreed, of course. I arranged to talk first with Harry Ward, Litton's Managing Director, someone I also know from my university days. But that meeting never took place because of everything that happened at the hotel. I don't believe that Harry had any idea of what was going on, though."

The old boys' network still alive and thriving, I thought. Heads of state and heads of corporations, all in it together. I remembered what Macintyre had said about power and wealth. It seemed to me that he'd aspired to be part of that inner circle of the elite and influential. Or maybe he just wanted the money. And he'd nearly got it. Gerald Hunter had wired him a million pounds on receipt of the photos of Anita's notes. The police had since seized the funds of course.

Chris picked up the plate of biscuits and took one before offering it to me. I said no. Drinking tea was one thing, but spilling chocolatey crumbs on the PM's silk couch was going too far.

"I hope that answers your question, Kate," Scott said. "I have one for you too. Who's your source?"

"My source?"

"Yes, whoever told you about the threat to me. It must be someone well-informed. How do you know him or her?"

"I don't have a source, Prime Minister," I said.

Scott frowned and Chris shifted in his armchair. "It's okay," Chris said. "You can tell us. It won't go any further than this room."

I pressed my lips together, unsure what to say.

"You told me you knew someone," Chris went on. "Remember when I asked you how you knew about a threat to my father? You said you had an inside track."

"Ah, that inside track." Darn, he had a good memory. "It's not a source, it's more of an instinct. A feeling."

Scott stirred a sugar cube into his tea. "A feeling," he repeated.

"Er, yes."

"I'm sorry you don't feel you can be more candid," he said. "But that doesn't detract from the debt we owe you." His tone had gone from friendly to formal.

"C'mon, Kate. Really?" Chris crossed his arms, looking miffed.

I contemplated my options. Say nothing and be judged for keeping a secret about a source I didn't have, or tell the truth, and live with the consequences of coming out about my bizarre gift. Neither felt particularly comfortable. I risked losing Chris's friendship either way. My hand had begun to shake again, so I put my cup down on the table.

"All right," I said, bracing myself for the inevitable shock and skepticism. "I can see things. Auras that predict death. They appear as circles of moving air over the head of the person who is going to die. You had one, Prime Minister, and so did Mr. Lewis."

Scott set his cup down on the tray. "Do I still have it?"

"No. When Chris saved you from drinking that coffee, the danger passed."

"That's brilliant," Chris said, slapping his hand on the arm of his chair. "My grandmother can see that kind of thing too, although she sees a dark shape like a bird perched on one shoulder. You two should get together. She's never met anyone else who can see like she does."

The Prime Minister looked at Chris in astonishment. "Your grandmother Ariadne? So you think that what Kate just told us is normal?"

"Of course," Chris said. "It's unusual, I agree. But I believe Kate."

In the ensuing silence, the ornate gilt clock on the mantelpiece ticked loudly.

"And so do I," Scott said eventually, gazing at me. "I can't think of any other reason why you'd make such a determined effort to warn me." He smiled. "Yes, I remember meeting you in Hyde Park, and your little stunt with the faked injury. And it explains why you'd risk your life, which you did, by coming up to the hotel suite and facing off against my security team. You've been very courageous. You both have."

Chris beamed. I felt my cheeks grow warm.

There was a tap on the door, followed by the appearance of the punctilious Martha. "I'm sorry to interrupt, Prime Minister, but it's time for your meeting with the Italian President."

Scott stood, held out his hand to shake mine. "You two stay as long as you like. Come again soon, Kate. It's nice to have young people around here. And I want to hear more about your aura experiences." With that, he was gone, the door closing quietly behind him.

"Wow," I said to Chris. "Your dad really is the PM. Or should that be the PM really is your dad?"

He grinned. "And you can see auras. I can't wait to tell Grandma. You have to come to Greece with me sometime so you can meet her. Maybe Anita could come too."

Just then, my mobile buzzed and I grabbed it, feeling embarrassed that I'd forgotten to turn it off. There was a text from Alan Bradley. "When can we expect the honor of your presence?" Even tea with the Prime Minister didn't impress Alan. Work always came first with him.

"I should go," I said, standing up.

Chris stood. "Me too. I have a meeting with my chemistry professor."

We dawdled our way to the front door, pausing often so that Chris could point out pieces of art he thought I'd like. We peeked into offices and meeting rooms, small cogs in the grand machine of English government.

"Anita would love to see all this," I said.

Chris's face lit up. "Do you think so? I'll invite her over."

When we reached the front door, he took my hand in his. "I don't really know how to say thank you. You're responsible for bringing me and my father together. It wouldn't have happened without you."

"You'd have found a way," I said. "Remember what your grandma told you about achieving the impossible?"

"Maybe." He opened the door and nodded to the policeman outside.

"Let's all go out for dinner soon," he said, turning back to me. "You, me and Anita. Bring Josh as well."

"A double date?" I asked, raising my eyebrows. His cheeks reddened, but he didn't deny it. I wondered what Anita's father would say about her going out with the Prime Minister's son. Maybe that would put an end to the endless string of unsuitable suitors.

"I'll call you with some dates and restaurant suggestions," Chris said.

"I know a good teashop we could go to," I teased.

"No more teashops for me. We're going out for real food and good wine," he said. "My treat. See you soon, aura girl."

THE END

Praise for DOUBLE BLIND, the sequel to THE AURA

"*Double Blind* is a cozy mystery with intense characters who struggle in a world of pharmaceutical intrigue with political twists. Author Carrie Bedford writes with a high suspenseful flair and creates an engaging protagonist, Kate Benedict. Paranormal elements mix with murders, kidnappings, and a dash of romance, all racing through an unusual and satisfying plot. A fast read, well-written, and thoroughly enjoyable."
—Paula Cappa, author of *The Dazzling Darkness*

If you're looking for a likeable protagonist you can relate to, then Kate is the one for you. Carrie Bedford has done an exceptional job in creating a character with doubts and quirks just like the rest of us, which makes the supernatural spin all the more believable. This book draws you in and once it takes hold, doesn't let go. Carrie has set the bar even higher with Double Blind, which is great for readers, and keeps us authors on our toes. A cracking read.
—Andrea Drew, author of the Gypsy Medium Series

Praise for THE AURA, the first Kate Benedict Paranormal Mystery by Carrie Bedford

"Carrie Bedford is a real find… *The Aura* is an engaging paranormal suspense story whose heroine is smart, strong, and almost overwhelmed when she is suddenly able to see that someone— friend, family or stranger— is about to die. Bedford is a fine writer, an accomplished novelist, and a terrific storyteller whose characters ring true and pull us deep into the mystery."
—Shelley Singer, author of the Jake Samson-Rosie Vicente mystery series and *Torch Song*, first in the Blackjack near-future thriller series

"A terrific book with a likable protagonist, skilled plotting, and a supernatural spin. This gripping mystery had me hooked from the first chapter. "
— Janet Dawson, author of the Jeri Howard series

Also by Carrie Bedford:

NOBILISSIMA, A Novel of Imperial Rome

THE AURA, A Kate Benedict Paranormal Mystery

AUGUSTA, A Novel of Imperial Rome, the continuing story of Galla Placidia (*Coming Soon*)

A Respectful Request

We hope you enjoyed *Double Blind* and wonder if you'd consider reviewing it on Goodreads, Amazon or wherever you purchased it. The author would be most grateful. Thank you!